**Available from Nina Berry
and Harlequin TEEN**

**The Notorious Pagan Jones series
(in reading order):**

*The Notorious Pagan Jones
City of Spies*

CITY
OF
SPIES

NINA BERRY

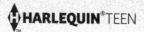
HARLEQUIN®TEEN

Recycling programs
for this product may
not exist in your area.

ISBN-13: 978-0-373-21189-0

City of Spies

For Paul "Doc" Berry.
Father, writer, teacher.

Hollywood is wonderful. Anyone who doesn't like it is either crazy or sober.

—Raymond Chandler

We dance tango because we have secrets.

—Marilyn Cole Lownes

MILONGA

A tango party

Going to Frank Sinatra's after-party was a mistake. But it wasn't the raucous laughter coming from darkened dens, the half dozen nearly naked women splashing in the fifty-foot swimming pool or Frank and Dean Martin fighting over Angie Dickinson that bothered Pagan Jones.

No, the trouble for Pagan came from the gentle clink of ice in a tumbler and the quiet sloshing of Scotch, vodka and rum. It came from the overstocked bar in every room, dozens of tiny paper umbrellas discarded on tables and the bright scent of cut limes.

Pagan clung to Thomas Kruger's muscular forearm with one hand, a bottle of Coke in the other, as they wound their way into the half-lit, high-ceilinged house with its glass walls and low-slung black leather sofas.

Thomas had been a big star back in his home country of East Germany before he and his family escaped to the West. Here in Hollywood he wasn't a star yet, but he was tall, blond and ridiculously handsome, with comedic timing that made casting directors swoon. He and Pagan had bonded as friends

for life during a movie shoot and a secret, breathless escape
from East Berlin back in August.

"My first big Hollywood party," he whispered to her, trying not to stare at the sparkling company lurking in every
corner of the house. "That's Jack Lemmon!" He stared at
the dapper, Oscar-winning actor, who, pool cue in hand,
was playfully holding it up to his eye like a telescope, pointing it at a petite blonde actress with the world's tiniest waist.
She aimed her own cue back at him like a rifle, sticking out
her tongue. "He's playing billiards with Janet Leigh! From
Psycho!"

"If you get too overwhelmed, imagine them naked,"
Pagan said, an in-joke they'd shared many times whenever
actor nerves overwhelmed them. She caught a powerful whiff
of Scotch as two men tottered past, drinks in hand. Suddenly
she needed to breathe anything other than alcohol-soaked
air. "Let me show you the rest of the estate."

They stepped out onto the long, roofed arcade beside the
pool. The cool night air banished the scent of liquor, but
not her longing for it. Above, the quarter moon was a silver
barrette clipped into the clouds.

"Sorry," she said, knowing Thomas would understand.
"It's *my* first big party since the night we danced on top of
the Hilton in West Berlin. Don't let me get too close to the
booze."

He put a hand over hers. "Of course."

She didn't say it, but the real problem with parties like
this was how fun they were. Here everyone was an adult,
and anything was permitted so long as you did it with style.

Sinatra's parties were secret and exclusive, and once you were in, nobody but Frank himself could question you.

Pagan hadn't attended a Hollywood party since the car accident where she'd driven drunk off Mulholland Drive, killing her father and little sister, and this was her first party of any kind since her last drink, back in August. She'd forgotten how much she craved the rampant creative juices fueled by a gathering of talented people, ramped up by alcohol, music and laughter. Random couples danced entwined in dark corners; heated debates became sudden duets.

Before she stopped drinking Pagan had attended many get-togethers like this one, some in this house, and she'd danced on top of a piano or two. She and her now ex-boyfriend Nicky Raven had been buddies with Nancy Sinatra and her husband, singer Tommy Sands, and Nancy's father, Frank, had taken Nicky under his wing, tried to win him away from his record contract to record with Sinatra's label.

But that was a lifetime ago. Nicky was married, for crying out loud. His wife was due to have their baby in a few months.

Pagan watched Thomas tug on his beer, eyes wide as he took in the sleek modern marvel of Farralone, Sinatra's current digs hidden high on a hill where no one ever complained about the noise, and all the beautiful, famous faces inside it.

"Was that Marilyn Monroe?" Thomas asked, glancing over his shoulder to watch a platinum-blond head disappear into the darkness at the edge of the grassy lawn.

"She's staying in Frank's guesthouse," said Pagan.

Thomas squinted at the distant white building gleaming next to its own pool. "That's a guesthouse?"

"It's a bit different from East Berlin, isn't it?" She shot him a half smile.

"A little." He tilted his head toward the splashing limbs in the pool. "It's December. Why aren't they freezing?"

Pagan contemplated the women in bikinis pulling on the arms of grinning men in suits at the water's edge. "Frank's money generates a lot of warmth."

Thomas shot her a look.

"And the water's heated."

"There you are! Looking marvelous." Nancy Sinatra emerged from the house, smiling. Her dark hair was piled high; the scooped neck of her black dress was cut low. Waving from the doorway was her husband, Tommy Sands, sucking on a cigarette, his thick dark hair swept back in an Elvis pompadour. "We so enjoyed the movie tonight. I hope it makes a million dollars."

"Oh, Nancy, a million's a lot!" Pagan released Thomas's arm to take Nancy's hand and leaned in for a cheek kiss, catching a whiff of hair spray and Chanel No. 5. "You look fantastic. And the honor of attending your party after his first Hollywood movie premiere has gone straight to Thomas's head."

Nancy's long-lidded eyes, heavily lined in black, slid over the tall, tan hunk of man that was Thomas Kruger. She pursed her lips and extended her hand. "You were even more gorgeous and hilarious than Pagan in the movie tonight."

Thomas lifted her hand to his lips, bowing as he did so. "A delight to meet you, Mrs. Sands. Thank you so much for your kind hospitality."

One corner of Nancy's wide mouth deepened in approval.

"We like 'em fancy, don't we, Pagan? To hell with Nicky Raven. Don't worry, we didn't invite him." To Thomas: "Please. Call me Nancy."

Thomas didn't bother to correct her, and neither did Pagan. But she and Thomas weren't dating, not in the way Nancy meant. Their bond of friendship and trust went far deeper than that. But no one could ever know why. Just as no one could know that Thomas preferred the romantic company of men.

"You okay?" Thomas murmured to Pagan as Nancy turned to say something to Tommy. Nancy's cavalier mention of Nicky might once have upset Pagan. But now her thoughts drifted off to an annoyingly charming dark-haired, blue-eyed Scot with a gift for accents and intrigue. Devin Black may have blackmailed and lied to get her out of reform school and back in the Hollywood game after her family tragedy, but he'd done it so MI6 could track down a double agent in Berlin, not to help her. Well, not at first. He'd posed as a publicity exec from the movie studio to recruit Thomas Kruger as a spy for the West and then used Pagan's desire to learn more about her mother's past to lure her to act in a movie shooting in Berlin. He'd gotten a judge to temporarily declare him Pagan's legal guardian, even though he was barely two years older than she was. All to use Pagan's fame to get Thomas to a garden party thrown by the leader of East Germany so he could search the place. Thomas had been caught, and it had taken every ounce of Pagan's determination and cunning to help get him and his family to safety.

Pagan could still remember the relief as she collapsed into Devin's arms. How safe she'd felt, how tenderly he'd cared for her. But even after all that, after all those nights sharing a hotel suite, after all their flirtations, deceptions and secret investigations of each other, when you got right down to it, one amazing kiss was all they'd shared.

"Damn Devin Black, anyway," Pagan whispered back. "I know I'm single. Why don't I feel that way?"

"Have you heard from him since Berlin?"

"Not a peep."

She'd been kissed before. And more. So why couldn't she stop thinking about him?

"I said, thanks!"

Pagan focused. Nancy was waving a 45 at her, the record Pagan had brought her as a hostess gift. Thomas had kindly carried the 45 in from their car, tucked under his arm, and she must've daydreamed about Devin Black right through him handing it over to Nancy. They were all now in the crowded living room with its white baby grand and Mark Rothko paintings.

"You're going to love it," Pagan said, gesturing at the record. "It hit the R & B charts earlier this year, but it should've been a huge crossover hit. She sings like nobody you've heard before."

"Aretha Franklin, 'Won't Be Long,'" Nancy read off the label. "Let's play this hot plate."

She pushed through the crowd toward a huge console where they kept the record player. "Hang on, Sammy," Nancy said to the slender man noodling on the piano. "Pagan says we need to check this out."

Pagan shrank back a little. She hadn't planned on her record taking over the party or interrupting Sammy Davis, Jr., at the piano. She was already infamous thanks to her drunken exploits. The last thing she needed was to upstage anyone.

But Sammy shrugged, took his hands off the keys and flashed her a grin. "Hey, Pagan, baby," he said. "Looking good."

"Same, Sammy," she said, smiling back. "Sounding good, too."

Nancy dropped the needle and stepped back. A jazzy piano riff and some cymbals ruffled over the conversational murmur in the room. Sammy nodded his head in time with the beat. Nancy followed suit.

"Baby, here I am…" A woman's voice cut through the air like a preacher's, lit with heavenly inspiration, except she was singing about how she couldn't wait for her lover to return.

Nancy's eyes widened. She elbowed her husband, and he nodded, his foot tapping. Three tipsy women sprawled on the couch stopped talking and sat up.

The beat was good, if conventional. The piano riff was catchy, and the woman's longing for lovemaking was a tad scandalous. But that voice. It lifted everything higher and then tore it all apart, igniting a desire to move.

"Dig it!" Sammy said, and grabbed Pagan's hand to spin her around. He had a light touch and lighter feet. Others watched as they danced in a low-key, exploratory way. The beat became familiar, and they picked up speed.

Nancy tapped her feet as she sidled up to Thomas, holding out her hand. He bowed and expertly swung her out. Her skirt fanned like a cape.

The piano rumbled with anticipatory joy as Aretha sang, "My daddy told me…"

Frank wandered in with Juliet Prowse and watched as the girls on the couch jumped up to jive. Juliet pirouetted, and Frank took her hand out of midair to do the Lindy Hop.

"Her voice—it's like a lightning strike," Thomas shouted to Pagan. "Or no, maybe my English isn't good."

"Sounds cool to me!" Sammy said, twirling Pagan as he brought her back in. They circled Nancy and Thomas, then crossed, changing partners in one smooth move on the beat. Nancy was laughing, waving at her husband, who grabbed a girl from the couch and jumped in to join the fray.

A few men in casual suits watched by the sliding glass doors, until the bikini girls from the pool noticed the crowd moving in time and stormed the living room to dance in their own wet footprints. The room filled with hoots and shimmying bodies. They were one now, connected by that clear, dangerous voice.

It reached a crescendo, crying out to her lover to hurry, hurry! The urgency convulsed inside Pagan's heart. It became her voice, calling out to Devin Black.

The song ended and the girls in bikinis, Frank, Thomas—everyone was laughing, raising their glasses in salute, yelling at Nancy to play it again. *Who was that?*

But Pagan's head was spinning. Her self-control was diffusing like cherry syrup in a Shirley Temple. She took a deep breath of the ever-present cloud of cigarette smoke. The pungent scent pushed a pang of longing through her. When she drank, cigarettes and alcohol had been twin siblings in her hands. She had a vivid memory of Devin Black handing her a pack of Winstons, and the longing for the old days before she'd become a killer, for a drink, for Devin, all tangled up into a huge knot under her breastbone.

But Devin wasn't here. She might never see his sardonic smile again, and the martini in Sammy Davis, Jr.'s hand would go very nicely with a cigarette instead.

Who do you want to be, Pagan? After four months of daily AA meetings, weekly therapy and gratitude for every sober breath. She could be the girl who didn't drink. Or she could be the messed-up loser who did.

"Going to get some air," she said to Thomas, and wound her way through the bodies, out into the clear air of the arcade. The swimmers and couples drinking and talking out there pushed her farther past the lounge chairs out onto the lawn.

Peace at last. She took a deep breath, removed her heels and sank her stocking feet into the damp grass. Above, the stars were startlingly clear, and the noise from the glowing glass mansion sank away into the night.

A shadow moved to her left. She startled, spinning.

"Well, if it isn't the notorious Pagan Jones."

Out of the darkness beside the arcade stepped a familiar form, tall, knife-thin, with dark hair and eyes like the ocean during a storm.

Her whole body wanted to open itself, to stretch out to him. Her pulse thrummed through her veins all the way down to her fingertips.

Devin Black was back.

BAILAMOS

More of a statement than a question the man asks a woman: Shall we dance?

"Devin." She breathed it more than said it. Had she conjured him with her thoughts? She took two steps toward him, on her tiptoes. "Are you real?"

"That's a matter for debate." He smiled at her with a delicious fondness that sent blood rushing to her cheeks. "You, however, look very real."

The impulse to obliterate the distance between them, to throw her arms around him, was almost irresistible. The fierce way he'd kissed her the last time they met was imprinted on her body like a brand. But something made her pull herself up short.

His gaze may have been more than friendly, but he hadn't walked up to her or taken her in his arms. He stood at a distance, all coiled grace in his custom-made suit, keeping a good six feet between them.

It had been four months and two days since they last saw each other. Anything could've happened. She needed to reverse the overeager impression she'd given him, and fast.

"Delighted to see you haven't been slaughtered in the line

of duty," she said, keeping her tone light. Years of actor training came in handy at times like this. "Last thing I needed was to be haunted by your ghost."

He took a step toward her. "It's good to see you."

His natural Scottish accent, which he could turn off or on, depending on which persona he needed to be, warmed as he spoke more personally. It fanned the tiny flames dancing inside her heart.

"Took you long enough, laddie," she said, using her own deadly accurate Scottish accent. "I was in your neighborhood a little over a month ago."

"Shooting *Daughter of Silence* in London." His voice flattened into a flawless American accent, as if answering an unspoken challenge. "Becoming an emancipated minor, and turning seventeen. Happy belated birthday."

"Thanks," she said, dropping the accent. "I got the flowers you didn't send."

He winced. "I'm sorry. I was rather busy. I promise."

It sounded like the truth, but with Devin you could never tell. "Oh, that whole 'I was away serving my country doing unspeakable things' excuse. Very handy." She smiled.

"I hear that the director is so happy with the movie, and with your performance, that he's submitting it to the Cannes Film Festival."

"So you're still pretending to be in the movie business?" she asked.

"I've stepped back in actually. That's why I'm here."

"And you're keeping tabs on me," she said. "Should I be scared?"

"*Could* you be scared?" His smile was knowing.

"Don't ask me to drive a red convertible." The only way to deal with the paralyzing anxiety brought on by memories of the accident was to puncture it with jokes. "Or wear something off the rack."

"How's your Spanish?" he asked.

It sounded like a non sequitur, but all at once she knew why he was here. It felt so good that it scared her. She took a moment before replying to steady her voice. "Why don't you ask the real question you came all this way to ask me?"

Admiration shone in his eyes. "No more facade between us, is that it?"

Of course he'd understood her immediately. But she hadn't been prepared for him to look at her like that. She clasped her hands to stop them from trembling. "We've pretended with each other enough for one lifetime."

He dipped his head in acknowledgment. "I've come to ask you to help us out, one more time."

"Us?" she asked. "Are you an American now? The last time I saw you…"

"I work for MI6, the British secret service," he said. "The CIA has asked to borrow me for this particular mission. I'm on loan."

"Because they think you have some kind of power over me." It was half question, half assertion.

"To be fair," he said with a smirk, "that's only one of my many valuable skills."

Her eyes fell to his lips. "I remember."

It was hard to tell in the dark, but she could've sworn he flushed. "It would be better if you didn't."

Her throat tightened. He was pushing her away, all right.

But she'd gotten a reaction, however much he might try to deny it. "Who is she?"

He glanced away from her briefly. His expression didn't change, but it was enough to make her feel like someone had stabbed her in the gut.

Carefully, he said, "What matters is that I never should have…done what I did the last time we met. I truly thought I'd never see you again. I thought…" He broke off and tilted his head back, eyes heavenward, inhaling a deep breath. "I'm not here to renew our acquaintance."

So after all they'd been through together in Berlin, after they'd shared a kiss that nearly burned down a hospital, he wasn't here to be with her. It shouldn't have surprised her, or hurt her. She should've been over him by now, on to some new sweetheart who didn't come and go like a thief. But it hurt so bad she had to shore up her face with a sarcastic look she'd overused in *Beach Bound Beverly*.

"You mean the CIA didn't send you all the way to Los Angeles to make out with me?" She raised her eyebrows. "But what better way to spend our tax dollars?"

He exhaled a small laugh. "If you're interested in helping us out, then you should accept a starring part in a movie shooting in Buenos Aires, which will be offered to you very soon."

"Argentina?" She knew very little about the country. Something about grasslands and cattle and Eva Perón. "I do all right in Spanish, but there's no way I could pass for a native speaker, even with all of Mercedes's coaching." Her best friend, Mercedes Duran, had grown up in a Spanish-speaking house and was fluent. Pagan, who had learned some French and Italian during her lessons on set and grew up speaking German and English, had picked Spanish up from her fast.

"You won't need to be anyone but yourself," Devin said.

Argentina. Something in her memory was stirring about that country. "Why send Pagan Jones to South America?"

He shook his head, regretful. "I'll tell you after you say yes."

"So I'm going to say yes?"

He paused, lips twisting sardonically. "Yes."

She eyed him. If he was that annoyingly certain about it, he was probably right. "Why?"

"Because you want to," he said.

He was right about that. Even her disappointment at him keeping his distance hadn't dulled the buzz in her fingertips, the lift to her ego at the thought that they wanted her back, that they needed her. No one before had ever thought she could make the world a better place, even in the smallest way.

"I *am* a glutton for punishment," she said. *Or maybe she was addicted to it.*

He took a step toward her now, his eyes intent. "But mostly you'll say yes because it has to do with the man from Germany who stayed with your family back when you were eight."

A chill ran down the back of her neck. That man, her mother's so-called "friend," had come to stay with the Jones family for a few weeks and then vanished. She couldn't re-member his name, but he'd been some kind of doctor, a sci-entist, and this past August she'd discovered that he'd written letters to her mother in a code based on Adolf Hitler's birth-day. "You mean Dr. Someone?"

Devin nodded. "The same man who gave your mother that painting by Renoir. You told me you remembered what he looked like, what he sounded like."

"Oh, yes, I remember." She did easily recall the man's angular height, shiny balding head, arrogant nose and sharp brown eyes draped with dark circles. His voice had been the most distinctive thing about him—high-pitched, nasal, commanding, speaking to her mother in rapid German behind closed doors.

Devin was watching her closely. "The Americans think they've found him in Buenos Aires. But photographs and living witnesses are scarce. They need someone to identify him. You may be the only one left alive and willing to help."

"*May be* willing to help," she said, but it was an automatic response. Her thoughts were a cyclone of questions and confusion. She hadn't told Devin about the coded letters. They'd been signed by Rolf Von Albrecht, who had to be the same person as Dr. Someone.

"Why would they want to track him down?" She had her suspicions, but they were too horrible, too unproven. So she let them stay unexamined in the darkest recesses of her mind. She'd recently discovered that her own mother hated Jews, and that she'd helped this German Dr. Someone quietly leave the United States nine years ago. There were only so many reasons the CIA would bother to find such a man.

The thought of Mama, the bedrock of the family, hiding her bigotry and helping Germans illegally kept Pagan up late many nights, trying to untie the knot that was her mother. She'd kept it all from her family and then unexpectedly hanged herself in the family garage one afternoon while everyone else was out. Pagan still didn't know why Mama had decided to die, and more than anything—well, looking at Devin she realized more than *almost* anything— she longed to find out.

"I'll tell you why," he said. "After you accept the job."

She glared at him. "We said no more lies between us."

"An omission," he said. "Which I'm telling the truth about."

Damn him. She was going to do it—because it made her feel good to be trusted, it was the right thing to do and because it involved Mama. It was Mama's death that triggered Pagan's alcoholic spiral, and it was Pagan's decision to keep drinking for years after that which led to the accident that killed her father and sister.

Mama hadn't left a note; she'd shown no sign of distress or depression. Pagan still had no idea why she'd taken her own life, why she'd left her two daughters without their fierce, controlling, adoring mother. A mother with her own dark secrets.

Thinking about it made it hard to breathe. But more than anything else, Pagan wanted the answer to that question. All the other terrible events had been her own damned fault. She couldn't help feeling responsible for Mama leaving, as well. But maybe, if she found an explanation, one corner of the smothering blanket of guilt and self-recrimination would lift.

"By taking the job," Devin said, "you'll help persuade the CIA to let you see that file they have on your mother. It may be the thing that does the trick."

"'Help persuade'?" she quoted, voice arching with skepticism. "It 'may' do the trick? You're the one who told me to be cautious if they asked me to help them again."

"Glad to see my warning sunk in," he said. "And I stand by it. But I know how badly you want to know more. And I'll be going with you, so I can be a buffer."

She lifted her head to stare up at him, her heart leaping into her throat. "You…"

"I will act as your liaison to the agency while you're in Buenos Aires," he said.

So that was why… "And there'll be no fraternizing because you'll technically be my supervisor," she said.

"It's not technical," he said. "I will be your boss while we're down there, and it's important that nothing get in the way of that. Your life might depend upon it."

"You're such a rule-follower," she said. "What if the rules are wrong?"

"You're such a rule-breaker," he retorted. "What if you're too blind to see why the rules exist?"

"That's what rule-makers always say," she said. "Rules are made to be broken."

"Rules are made for the obedience of fools and the guidance of wise men," he said in an exasperated tone that secretly delighted her. "Guess which one you are?"

She paused. "Was that Shakespeare?"

"Douglas Bader, fighter pilot," he said abruptly. "Those are the terms of the deal. If you say yes, a script for the movie will be sent to you tomorrow. All you have to do is call your agent and tell him you want the part. The movie starts shooting after New Year's. When you get to Buenos Aires, I'll contact you."

"Hmm." Two could play at being distant. And it might help keep her sane while she was working with him.

With her heels still dangling from one hand, she stepped carefully around him in her stocking feet, making it clear she was keeping at least an arm's length between them as she headed back toward the mansion. "I can't make decisions when my toes are wet and cold," she said. "Send me the script."

She paused, turning to look over her shoulder at him. "Maybe I'll say yes."

"Very well." He nodded curtly. The English accent was back, and a veil of formality fell between them. "Say hello to Thomas for me. I look forward to seeing you again soon."

She shrugged. "Maybe."

"There you are!" a voice called through the moist night air.

Pagan whirled to see Thomas's golden blond head bright under the low lights of the poolside arcade, moving toward her. "I've been wondering where you went," he said, striding over the grass now. "Are you all right?"

"Remember this old friend?" Pagan gestured toward Devin.

But Devin Black was gone.

Again.

"Typical Devin," said Thomas as they sat in the back of their limousine on the way back into town. "How did he look?"

"Amazing." Pagan shot Thomas a knowing glance. He'd developed a crush on Devin back when Devin was recruiting him to be an agent for the West in Berlin, a crush Devin hadn't discouraged until the hook was set. "You know how it is when he's wearing one of those perfect dark suits…"

"His hair gelled back except for that one lock of black hair that falls just so over his eyebrows. Ugh!" Thomas threw himself back into the deep leather seat. "Good thing I'm seeing Diego or I'd be jealous."

"You're seeing him tonight?" Pagan had known about Thomas's preference for men since Berlin, but few others did. He was a handsome young actor trying to make it in Hollywood as a leading man. Pagan thought he was good-looking and talented enough to get to the big leagues, if no one discovered his secret. It was horrible, him having to live like that. But it was a fact of life. Even Thomas's mother and sister, with whom he shared a small bungalow in West Hollywood, didn't know.

Thomas nodded. "I'm going to his place after we drop you off. Mother doesn't expect me until late because of the party."

"You are…over Devin after what happened in Berlin, aren't you?" she asked.

Pagan harbored hopes, which she shouldn't still be harboring. But she tended to do things she shouldn't.

"Occasional flare-ups of resentment and memories of lust past," he said. "Don't worry. I won't mind if you fly off to paradise with him. You deserve it."

"Well, it's better to date a man who's actually, you know, *around*. I probably won't see Devin again unless I take the job," Pagan said.

Thomas shook his head. "He is the worst tease. But I bet he still likes you."

Pagan frowned. "He did look very happy to see me. But he made it very clear there won't be any of *that* on this trip."

"The two of you, working together, facing danger in a beautiful city far from home?" Thomas grinned. "There's absolutely no chance he'll change his mind."

Pagan smiled over at him. "I can be persuasive."

"And you said he knew all about your movie shoot in London, knew you'd been legally declared an adult, had a birthday... None of those things are connected to this new mission of his. He's probably following us right now." Thomas turned to look out the back window of their big-finned limousine, half in jest, and froze. "I was joking, but I think the same white Plymouth Valiant was behind us on our way to the party, as well."

"Very funny," Pagan said, frowning out the back window. It was hard to tell in the dark, but the 1960 Valiant behind them did look familiar. "There must be a million cars like that in LA."

"There's a million of every kind of car in LA," Thomas said. He'd frequently remarked on the ridiculous number of vehicles populating the city's roads, but of course anywhere would appear jammed with cars compared to East Berlin. "But how did he know where you'd be tonight?"

"It wasn't exactly a state secret," Pagan said without conviction. Devin had posed as a studio publicity executive when they first met, and he'd exercised some kind of power, probably blackmail, over Pagan's agent, Jerry. He'd also somehow persuaded the judge who convicted her of manslaughter to let her out of reform school more than a year early. "He is a man with a lot of powerful connections."

"So it's probably not him following you personally," Thomas said, turning back to settle into his seat again. "It's someone working for him."

"Or it's just another car heading home on a Friday night."

She changed the subject to the party—Thomas was still agog at having met Frank Sinatra and Dean Martin—and the white Plymouth Valiant stayed behind them all the way through the Valley and up Laurel Canyon. But when they turned up the tiny side road leading to Pagan's house in the Hollywood Hills, the Valiant kept going down the hill toward the city. Pagan saw Thomas eye its red back lights with relief before it vanished around a curve.

"Don't worry, no one would be following you," she said. "No offense, but you're not famous enough yet."

"I'm sorry," Thomas said. "I shouldn't be so paranoid. But if anyone ever found out about me…"

"No, I'm sorry," she said. "Sorry that you have to worry about that."

The limo had stopped in front of the house. The porch light illuminated the big wooden front door and part of the slightly ramshackle two-story building that climbed up the hill behind it.

"Say hi to Mercedes for me," Thomas said as the driver opened the door, and Pagan gathered up her stole and her handbag.

"She's probably up studying," Pagan said, glancing out at the house. The front porch light was off. That was odd. Maybe Mercedes had gone to bed after all, and turned it off automatically. "You and your family are still coming over for Christmas Eve, right? I'm determined to start some new traditions. Mercedes is going to make tamales. They're delicious."

"I'll call to see what we can bring," he said, and leaned in to kiss her cheek. "You're going to take the job with Devin, aren't you?"

She kissed him back and then wiped the lipstick trace from his tan skin with her thumb. "See the world by spying on it!" she said. "That's my plan."

She was fumbling with her keys in the dark, waving at the limo driver to go on and leave, when the porch light flicked on, blinding her. The front door swooshed open.

"Mercedes?" She blinked into the dark doorway.

"Yeah, sorry. It's been a weird night." Mercedes took her arm in an unnervingly tight grip and tugged her inside.

"What's wrong?" Inside, the house was dark, and Mercedes didn't let go of her gloved wrist. They'd been best friends since they met in reform school, but Pagan could count on one hand the number of times they'd touched. "You okay?"

"Someone's watching the house. Or they were." Mercedes released Pagan to give the limo driver a quick wave, and shut and locked the door. "I haven't seen anything in the last two hours."

Pagan glanced around the quiet house, instantly focused. Until recently, Mercedes had been an enforcer for one of the toughest gangs in Los Angeles, and her nose for danger was not to be trifled with. She must have turned the house's interior lights off to see outside better. Pagan said, "Thomas and I think a car might have followed us here from the party."

Mercedes nodded. "Your people, then."

"Probably." Pagan's past experience with the CIA, MI6 and the East German Stasi wasn't extensive, but if anyone was following her and watching the house, it was most likely connected to that. "Where were they?"

"I was doing homework at the kitchen table, when I saw someone moving down the hill in the backyard."

"Did they notice that you saw them?" Pagan got up and padded over the wood floors down the hall and into the kitchen, a large room at the back of the house with big windows and its own door opening onto the backyard. The upward slope was nothing but darkness and moonlight shifting through the trees.

"Not at first. He had binoculars. I was just thinking about calling the police when he left." Mercedes came to stand next to her. "I've been keeping a lookout, but no sign of anyone else."

"If they come back, they'll have an exciting night watching us sleep." Pagan flipped on the lights and opened the back door. Cold night air rushed in, infused with the sweet medicinal tinge of eucalyptus.

She stepped out onto the back patio. The backyard was a short stretch of lawn followed by a series of grassy terraces cut into the hill rising behind the house. Pagan's mother had insisted on orange, lemon and avocado trees on some of the terraces, and a small pond with a waterfall. The pond had once contained Asian carp, but the raccoons had made short work of them.

"Maybe it was someone come looking for me," Mercedes said. "The gang was not happy when I decided not to go back after reform school."

"We're quite a pair, aren't we?" Pagan shivered. "Let's go inside."

She clicked the lights off, locked the door, and followed her roommate into the living room. Mercedes sat down heavily on the couch. "I'm sorry," she said, "I should have called the cops right away, but given my past history with them…" She shrugged. "I never should have moved in with you."

Pagan went over to sit next to her and couldn't resist tugging slightly on her thick black ponytail. "Stop it. Having you as my roommate is the best idea I've ever had," she said.

"Are you okay?" Mercedes nodded, turning to look Pagan in the eye. "What if my old gang has followed me here and they want revenge? They could break in, steal something."

"I couldn't care less if anything got stolen," Pagan said. "They could burn our house down—they'd probably be doing me a favor—so as long as you got out safe, it wouldn't matter. Don't you see?" Her throat tightened, aching, as she stared at her friend. "After everything that's happened, you think I give a damn about things? About *stuff*?"

Mercedes's cheeks were red. Her eyes glittered in the dim light. Pagan had never seen her cry, but she looked darn close.

"No," she said shortly. "I know you don't. But you say 'our house,' and you welcome me here. And what do I do? I study, and I can barely pay a few bucks toward the bills."

"You don't need to work. My parents left me enough money for us to live for ages. But still you work harder than I do sweeping floors at that comics store while getting your high school diploma at the same time," Pagan said.

Mercedes frowned at her. "I'm not going to sponge off you or anyone."

Pagan smiled. "Well, you're contributing the brains to this sorry partnership of ours, sweetheart, because I sure as heck don't have them. And I know you want to try for college. If that happens, this crazy world might stand a chance."

"College." Mercedes swallowed, her dark-lashed eyes flicking wide to stare into the distance. Pagan almost didn't recognize her for a second. Was *that* what M looked like when she was scared? "I have to pass my exams first."

"As if that's in any doubt."

Going to high school without distractions had given Mercedes an appetite for learning that left Pagan in awe. It was like her brain had been starved, and now she couldn't wait to eat up every piece of knowledge the teachers and librarians cooked up for her. The principal hadn't wanted to let her into the physics class. He'd said girls didn't belong in science except for cooking class. But Mercedes had promised him she'd get an A, and he'd finally given in.

It made her the weird girl at school, but she didn't care. Her affinity for formulas coupled with her access to comics thanks to her part-time job at a comic book store had made her one of the most popular kids in her physics class.

"All that time I wasted, fighting people." Mercedes gave her head a small shake, as if she couldn't quite believe it. "Violence is so stupid. I'm never going to fight again."

Pagan peeled off her gloves, easing her feet out of their punishing heels. The bottoms of her stockings were black from walking around the yard at Farralone. She leaned her head back and gazed up at the beautiful swirl of gemlike color that was the Renoir above them. The figure of a woman with a blue parasol was just visible through the press of lilacs and sun-dappled leaves. It was, literally, a master-piece, and a grateful Dr. Someone had given it to Mama back when Pagan was eight years old.

Pagan had always loved the painting, and had moved it from above her parents' bed to the living room so she could see it every day. The move had marked the beginning of a new era. The house and the painting belonged to her now, not to her parents, and she'd gotten legally emancipated last month so that she no longer had to answer to a legal guard-ian.

But if Dr. Someone was who Pagan thought he was, the painting might not have been his to give. It would always be glorious, but maybe it no longer belonged in her living room. Its home was a mystery, a secret probably lost forever in the midst of the looting, murder and deceit of the Sec-ond World War. Seeing it now only made her throat tighten. Was there any part of Mama's life that wasn't tainted by her lies and secrets?

Never mind the dang painting. The night had been full of its own drama.

Pagan slapped her gloves onto the side table. "You totally should have come with us to the party. You would've en-joyed it."

"And I told you I have to study."

"I know, I know. I'm still getting used to this whole 'tak-ing school seriously' thing. And guess what? Devin Black came to see me at the party tonight," Pagan said.

"He's like the Shadow," Mercedes said, referring to her favorite crime fighter with psychic powers who posed around town as a wealthy playboy. She had never met Devin, but Pagan had told her everything that had happened in Berlin back in August. "You think he came here afterward to loiter in your bushes?"

Pagan snorted. "Can you imagine him in his thousand-dollar suit, crouched behind a cactus with binoculars? It wouldn't be him personally, but it could've been someone from the CIA. They've been keeping tabs on me because they want me to do them a favor."

Mercedes smiled one of her rare smiles. "What if a government spook staking out your house ran into one of my old friends casing the joint?"

"A convention of ne'er-do-wells that would put Frank Sinatra's party to shame. All in our backyard."

She started to tell Mercedes everything that happened that night, so they broke out the Oreos and milk. "Tell me everything about the party," Mercedes said, dunking her cookie. "What was Nancy Sinatra wearing?"

Pagan gave her the details, dwelling on the things she knew Mercedes would like most—the tension between Frank and Dean Martin over Angie Dickinson, Tony Curtis trying hard not to stare at Juliet Prowse's legs, Jack Lemmon's gentlemanly manners.

Mercedes watched Pagan's face as she talked about Devin and sometimes frowned down at her own strong fingers, the nails clean, unpolished, short but not too short, lying relaxed on the polished wood of the table.

"They could dangle your mother's file in front of you for

years to keep you on their string," she said. "The file might not exist. Devin himself told you not to trust them."

"I don't trust them. But I know Mama was up to no good," Pagan said. "She was helping this Dr. Someone, or Rolf Von Albrecht, or whatever his name was. Mama's gone, but he might be down in Argentina, doing more bad things. If the CIA doesn't give me what I want, at least maybe I can help stop him, bring him to justice."

Mercedes said nothing, her eyelids at half-mast as she stared at Pagan.

"What?" said Pagan.

"You were eight years old when this German man visited your house," she said. "You were twelve when your mama took her life. A little girl."

"I know," said Pagan. "But I'm not little anymore, and if I can make a difference now…"

"If you can right your mama's wrong, you mean."

"She was my mother!" Anger at her friend surged through her. How could she try to take away Pagan's strong connection to her mother, good or bad? "Everything she did had a big effect on me! And if she was a bad person…" She stopped, not knowing where that sentence was going.

Mercedes leaned forward, dark eyes ferociously intent. She tapped her index finger on the table with every word as she said, "What she did is not your responsibility."

A surge of emotion flooded up from Pagan's chest. Her eyes filled with tears. "But what if Mama died because of me?"

Mercedes did not relent. She shook her head. "That woman had all kinds of things going on, way over your head. You could be risking your life here—again. Why are you doing that?"

Pagan got up and grabbed a kitchen towel, wiping her eyes. The cloth came away streaked black with mascara and eyeliner. "I don't know, M. But even if I never find out why Mama killed herself, I want to help them get this guy. My mother aided in a Nazi escape. Isn't that reason enough? Right now I'm the only one left alive who might be able to identify him."

"Okay," Mercedes said. "Let's call it patriotism and justice for now and see what happens. But I'm going with you."

Pagan's mouth dropped open. "But school—that's really important to you. I wouldn't want you to miss…"

Mercedes considered this. "Okay, I'll go for the first week, as long as I can get the reading assignments in advance."

The corners of Pagan's mouth turned up into a huge grin and she darted across the room to throw her arms around Mercedes's neck.

For once, Mercedes didn't grumble and pull away. She patted Pagan's arm awkwardly. "Guess that's okay with you."

Pagan laughed and stepped back. "It's great with me! I promise I won't suck you into it too much. No violence."

"We should review the self-defense moves I taught you back in reform school. And when we get back here, we should get a dog."

"A big dog." Pagan looked out the kitchen window at the backyard and switched off the lights. "And maybe some electric fencing, snares and booby traps."

Thump!

Pagan jumped two feet in the air as something slammed

into the front door of the house. Mercedes frowned. "They wouldn't be stupid enough to come back."

They walked side by side down the hallway to the foyer. Mercedes sidled up to the side window and peered through the curtains. "A man's walking back down the driveway. Nobody I know. And there's nobody else."

"Well, then, what...?" Pagan unlocked the door and tugged it open a few inches.

A large brown envelope flopped down from where it had been leaning against the door. In black marker someone had printed *Pagan Jones* on it.

Pagan stooped to pick it up, pulling up the flap.

About a hundred pages of three-hole paper slid out, bound together with metal fasteners in the top and bottom holes.

The print on the front page said Two to Tango. A Universal Pictures Production.

Pagan laughed. "It's the script for the Buenos Aires movie."

"It better be good," said Mercedes, and locked the door.

CHAPTER THREE

DECEMBER 16, 1961

HOLLYWOOD, CALIFORNIA

SEGUIDILLAS

Tiny, quick steps, usually seen in *orillero* style tango.

The script had been written by monkeys pulling random phrases out of a hat full of Hollywood clichés. After reading a few pages, Pagan had trouble forcing her eyes over the hammy dialogue and overwrought scene direction.

The plot was something she'd seen a thousand times—a girl on the cusp of womanhood from the US goes to exotic Buenos Aires on vacation, where she can't decide between the two men vying for her affections. One was a tall handsome blond American—kind, but a little boring. The other was a darkly handsome Argentinean gaucho, their version of a cowboy, whose seductive tangos and moonlit serenades on his Spanish guitar were too much for the naive girl to resist.

Ten pages in, Pagan knew her character ended up with the American boy. It was too obvious that the "exotic" man was up to no good, and that his dangerous foreign ways and wandering hands would send the silly American girl scurrying back to the safety and security of the American boy.

Mercedes threw it down after five pages. "You're going to have to tango and sing and say these terrible lines. You're going to have to—" she grabbed the script and read from it out loud "'—fall under the gaucho's tropical spell.'"

"Is Buenos Aires tropical?" Pagan frowned.

Mercedes snorted. "Don't you know? All dark-skinned people live in jungles."

"I wouldn't count on his skin being all that dark. They've cast a Broadway actor named Tony Perry as Juan, the seductive Latin man who—" Pagan grabbed the script from Mercedes "'—tangos with the dangerous stealth of an enormous black panther.'"

Mercedes let out a scornful laugh. "And plays the guitar while riding a horse."

"Excuse me, but don't you mean—" Pagan read from the script again "'—caresses the neck of his smooth wooden instrument with the consummate skill of a virtuoso'?"

Mercedes shook her head. "His instrument's wood? Don't let him get anywhere near you with *that*."

Pagan gasped with mock horror. "Dirty jokes before breakfast! I better make us some eggs."

After breakfast, Mercedes went back to studying for her exams, nose in her astronomy textbook, while Pagan called her agent, Jerry Allenberg. "Tell them I'll do this *Two to Tango* movie," she told him.

"I'm sorry, what?" Jerry said, speaking as if to an idiot or small child. "Have you lost your mind?"

"Maybe, but I'm doing it, Jerry. I'll need to brush up on my tango before it starts shooting in January."

"And dance your way right out of a career? No way, Pagan. I'm not letting you do it."

Pagan took a deep breath. Jerry's concern over her career

went straight past paternal to pathological now that she was on the wagon and doing better. "You don't get to decide what I do, Jerry," she said.

"But you're in the middle of a comeback!" Something in the background thumped, as if he'd dropped his feet off the desk to stand up and yell at her. "I never thought I'd say this after your disasters last year, but Bennie Wexler thinks you're gold and Tony Richardson loved working with you so much on *Daughter of Silence* he's talking awards at Cannes. Not for the movie, but for *you*. Did you hear me? You could be nominated for Best Actress at Cannes, Pagan! Somehow you're moving away from movies like *Beach Bound Beverly* into A-list material with the best writers and directors. It's a miracle! Don't do this turd of a script and mess it all up. I'm begging you."

"Most people don't yell when they beg," Pagan said. What he said made her uneasy. "You really think one mediocre movie could cancel out the good ones?"

"This could cost you the award at Cannes," he said. "And, I didn't want to say anything, but they're talking about a possible Oscar campaign, too."

Once upon a time, getting an Oscar had been Pagan's biggest dream. But now, when she weighed that against the chance to find out more about her mother, to help her country, to catch a Nazi who probably escaped from justice? The awards seemed like Tinkertoys.

Time for the trump card. "Do you remember our friend Devin Black?"

Silence. Then a thump and a squeak of chair springs as Jerry sat back down. Jerry had caved in to Devin before, when he'd negotiated Pagan's contract for *Neither Here Nor There* in Berlin in August. Pagan had never learned exactly what hold Devin had over Jerry, but it seemed to involve blackmail. Jerry probably didn't know who Devin worked for, but he was no fool. "Devin Black's involved in this tango turd?"

"He asked me to do it. And I want to do it," Pagan said. And waited.

Another silence. "Okay. So. You're doing it," Jerry finally said. "But if at any point you or Mr. Black wish to extricate yourself from this awful picture, you let me know. It'll be worth the penalties to your contract."

"Thanks, Jerry," Pagan said.

"Yeah, yeah." He paused. "The studio's going to owe you big for this one. Anything special you want during the shoot I can demand? Caviar every day, maybe? A personal masseuse?"

Pagan glanced over at Mercedes, who was underlining something in her book. "I want to bring my best friend along with me for a week. They could pay for a nice hotel suite for the two of us, and her airfare as well as mine. If you think you can manage that."

"Best friend, airfare, hotel suite," he pronounced, as if writing it down. Sharply, he added, "Is Devin Black okay with her being there?"

Pagan hadn't thought of that. The CIA might not want her to have someone living in her suite with her, for secrecy's sake. Well, that was too bad. "If anyone kicks back over her being there, you tell them she comes or I'm out."

"If we're lucky, they'll kick back," Jerry muttered. "When

producers ask me about this horrible movie later, can I tell them you were back on the bottle when you agreed to do it?"

"Jerry!" Pagan scolded.

"Yeah, yeah, that would be even worse for your rep. I know." He sighed heavily. "You really okay with this, kid?"

Which was as close as Jerry Allenberg would ever come to making sure Devin Black wasn't blackmailing her into doing this movie.

"I'm great, Jerry. Really. If we're lucky maybe the movie will be so bad they won't release it."

"Your lips to God's ears," he said.

"Have the studio's dancing instructor call me so I can brush up on the tango, okay?"

"Sure, sure." And he hung up.

"Jerry doesn't think it's a good idea," Pagan said, setting the handset back in the cradle of the phone on the kitchen wall.

Mercedes didn't look up from her astronomy book. "Too late. You've crossed the event horizon."

"Is that a tango step?" Pagan grinned.

"It's a boundary that surrounds a black hole." Mercedes looked up from the book. "Do you know what a black hole is?"

"What Jerry Allenberg has instead of a soul?" Pagan shrugged off Mercedes's look, "Oh, come on, you know I was either drunk or distracted between the ages of thirteen and sixteen. My high school diploma's strictly ceremonial, thanks to Universal Pictures and all those lovely tutors fudging my scores."

"A black hole is this area in space with gravity so strong it sucks everything, even time, into itself. Nothing, even light, can escape." Mercedes wasn't reading from her book as she spoke, and her eyes lit up as she went on. "This physicist, Finkelstein, discovered the event horizon, which is like a boundary around the black hole. Once you cross the event horizon, you can't go back. You're trapped forever."

"So you're saying I've been sucked into a one-way pit of darkness?" Pagan nodded. "Wouldn't be the first time."

Mercedes went back to reading. "The constellations are different in the southern hemisphere," she said. "Maybe I can find a telescope while we're there so I can see them."

CHAPTER FOUR

PATADA

A kick between the legs, usually executed by the follower.

The Warner Bros. studio lot lay shrouded in morning fog at the foot of the January-green Hollywood Hills. Pagan rolled down the window of the limousine as the guard waved them through the gate to inhale the crisp air and get a better view of the famous water tower perched like a long-legged heron over the blank-faced soundstages and trees still leafy for the California winter.

Pagan had always loved the bustle of the Warner lot, but she hadn't been there since they'd shot exteriors on its Western street for *Little Annie Oakley*, when she was ten. It was 7:00 a.m., and the studio was abuzz, an uncanny small town all its own, but one populated by time travelers and circus folk.

Transferred from the limo to a golf cart driven by an assistant in a Yankee hat, Pagan watched an eight-seat electric vehicle hum past, carrying a flock of flappers in feathered headbands and spit curls.

Her cart zoomed by the commissary, turned left and nearly smacked into a clutch of cowboys, guns at the hip. Nearby, three ten-year-old girls practiced a soft-shoe in an empty parking space. Their mothers sat in folding chairs nearby, knitting or watching critically. "One and two and ba-da *bam*!" one woman shouted, smacking her hand hard on her thigh. "Do it again."

Hang in there, kid, Pagan thought. She'd been that girl. Mama had been that woman. No tap dance had ever been good enough. No line reading was ever exactly right. That was how excellence was earned, Mama had said. She may have been right, but it was so very exhausting.

The cart purred onward. The soundstages loomed like windowless mausoleums on either side as grips and wardrobe assistants ambled along, paper coffee cups steaming.

"What are you shooting?" Pagan's driver asked.

"Not shooting yet," she replied. "We've been rehearsing at a dance studio since Christmas, but now we need a soundstage big enough to choreograph this big number before we head to Buenos Aires to shoot."

"All the stages at Universal taken?" He shook his head. "Didn't know they had such a busy slate."

"Maybe yours are just better," Pagan said. "But don't tell anyone over there I said so."

He laughed as they pulled to a stop in front of Stage 16 and she alighted from the cart. "But I'll be sure to tell everyone here you said it."

Smiling, she sailed through the door cut into the side of the soundstage with its Authorized Personnel Only sign, and stepped into the echoing dark of the stage. She stopped to let her eyes adjust to the spot of light along the back wall. A dusty piano crouched there. A wizened woman with a face like a walnut, her hair pulled severely back in a bun, sat on the bench smoking and flipping through sheet music.

"She's here!" More lights flickered and came to life, illuminating the empty cavern of the space and a tall, graceful man she knew, the movie's choreographer, gliding toward her. He wore flowing black trousers and a black turtleneck over his long, sinewy limbs, and he paused to extend one leg in front of himself, bowing with hands to his chest to her as if he were a courtier paying homage to the queen.

"Jared!" Pagan leaned in as he rose and gave him a kiss on the cheek. "You look marvelous. How was your New Year's?"

"Busy, my beautiful. Busy and scandalous and everything New Year's should be!" Jared said, taking her arm as they walked toward the piano together. "And yours?"

"Sober and boring and everything my New Year's should be," she said.

He laughed. "Which means you won't have forgotten everything we practiced last week."

"I better not," Pagan said. She'd spent the week between Christmas and New Year's with Jared at his dance studio, learning the steps to the dances for *Two to Tango*, with him standing in as whatever partner she had in the dance. Today was the first time she'd be dancing with one of her costars. That must be him in the T-shirt, trousers and scuffed dance shoes, stretching out his calf muscles by the back wall.

"Do you know Tony Perry?" Jared left her to take the man by the elbow and tug him toward her. "Tony, you've heard of Pagan Jones, of course! Your delightful and delicious dancing partner."

"Miss Jones," Tony said, taking her hand in a grip that was a shade too tight. "I'm a big fan."

Tony Perry was a hair under six feet, with thick hair dyed so black the bright stage lights didn't reflect off it. His dark tan, overlaid with a new painful pink burn, had been so recently acquired she could still smell the coconut oil. His lips disappeared when he smiled. It was a tight, fake, assessing kind of smile. His eyes did the elevator, riding up and down her body in a way that made her want to throw off her trench coat and yell, "How's this?"

She'd heard of him vaguely: he'd recently starred in some semipopular Broadway musical. *Two to Tango* was his first movie, and his overly curious, voracious energy announced that he was on a mission. He was going to be a big star if it killed him. Or her.

She hoped he'd relax a bit so they could dance together, but she didn't tell him to call her by her first name. "Miss Jones" was fine with this guy for now. "Hope I haven't kept you waiting."

"Not at all, not at all!" Jared lifted a finger at the piano player, who carefully rested her half-finished cigarette on the edge of the piano before hitting a chord. "But shall we warm up a little? I have such plans for you, my lovelies."

"Can't wait." Tony lifted an eyebrow at Pagan and smirked. "Shall we?"

Pagan removed the trench coat and threw it and her purse into the corner. "Let's."

Jared led them through a quick series of ballet warm-ups—pliés, ports de bra, coupés and posés, while the wizened one pounded out stately chords. Tony looked limber enough.

But then the tango didn't require great kicks, leaps or lifts. It involved close, complex footwork between the two partners and perfect timing, but you didn't have to be a complete athlete to look good doing it.

Until Tony started pointing out how Pagan's turnout could be wider, how her extension was limited, how, when he'd danced with Gwen Verdon, *she* hadn't done it that way. He did it with long, lingering touches on her knee and thigh and in a patronizing "I'm here to help" tone low enough that Jared didn't overhear him as he paced in front of them, declaiming over the chords from the piano.

Pagan stopped herself from swatting Tony's hand and edged away from him. It was tempting to wonder out loud whether his bony arms were strong enough to lift her when required, but at this early stage of rehearsal, creating more conflict would only backfire. She was the one with the bad reputation. She was the drunk, the killer. So she had to continually earn everyone's trust and respect. She found a half-hearted smile somewhere and produced it.

"And now, the tango," Jared said. "A labyrinth of emotion, as it is a labyrinth for your feet. To truly dance the tango, you must have experienced great sorrow, yet still be open to joy. You must surrender to the music, yet remain alert. The tango is relationship as movement. It is the most demanding of dances, the most intricate. Yet at bottom it is very basic— listen to the music, pay attention to your partner, and love. That's what the tango is—love. And we will use it to show how our characters may—or may not—be falling in love."

He finished with his hands clasped in front of him, his head bent over them, as if in prayer.

Oh, the drama. Jared never failed to milk it for all it was worth, but that was part of a choreographer's job. She didn't mind it in small doses, but she couldn't help hoping the director would be a little more no-nonsense during the shoot.

The scene they were rehearsing involved Tony's seductive gaucho character, Juan, following Pagan's lonely character, Daisy, as she walks down a deserted street in Buenos Aires after she's left a party where no one would dance with her.

Pagan had been followed down empty streets before, but by men who wanted to kill her, so the idea struck her as the opposite of romantic. Nonetheless it was in the street that Juan would lure the reluctant Daisy into a passionate tango after a convenient accordion player shows up.

Jared used chalk on the floor to map out the lines of the "street" Pagan and Tony would walk and tango down, with the back wall of the studio serving as the line of buildings. Pagan had done this a hundred times with Jared in his cramped studio, but here in the soundstage she could take the longer steps he wanted up and down this pretend street in Buenos Aires.

Pagan began it seemingly all alone. The accordion would start (cue the wizened one at the piano hitting some mournful chords) and Daisy would do a few little dance steps sadly to herself, dreaming of doing them with a partner.

Jared put himself in front of Pagan and had her follow him as he reminded both of them how it went. Slow, slow, step forward, side. Then back, back, quick, quick, slow— and cross. The pace picked up as he did it again, moving into a forward ocho.

Pagan followed him easily. These were the basic steps of

the tango, the first thing beginners learned, moving into slightly more complicated flourishes. She mimicked Jared's sad little slump in the shoulders and the dreamy tilt to his head, so that he clapped once, loudly, in approval. People always thought you were doing it right if you did it exactly like them.

"And that is when you—" he gestured to Tony "—take her hand and begin the dance for real. All right? Now, together at last!"

Tony stepped into Jared's spot and took Pagan by the waist with one hand, taking her other hand in his. His grip, like his handshake, was a little too firm. But she stepped backward in a surprised back ocho, as she'd rehearsed it, and Tony did a good job of keeping up.

Pagan's character went through a predictable series of emotions as her solo dance became a duet. Taken aback at first, she then tried to run away from Tony, only to have him interpose and show her a few more beguiling steps. Pulled in for a few seconds, she would reject him again, and again, as he pursued and persuaded, until at last she was swept up in the dance.

The more she thought about it, the more obnoxious Tony's character became. *If a girl doesn't want to dance with you, leave her alone!* The more she thought about the script, the worse it seemed. But she'd said yes to it. She was as much to blame for the darn thing as Jared, Tony and Universal Pictures. Might as well give it her all.

Clearly Tony had been rehearsing in New York with someone, as Pagan had been practicing with Jared here in

LA. They promenaded smoothly through the first part of the dance three times.

However, Tony's eyes kept dipping down to her cleavage. His hands pushed and pulled her roughly. Whenever he could, his hot hands pulled her hips in so close his hip bones poked her waist, which was both nauseating and wrong, tango-wise. Jared had to keep correcting him.

But Tony seemed to think that because Pagan's character was playing hard to get, Pagan must be doing the same. He dug his thumbs into her waist and stroked her palm with a finger at odd little moments, and when she startled or pulled away, he treated it as part of the dance.

You didn't have to like your costar to act with them. But the more Tony Perry manhandled Pagan and flashed leering smiles at her neckline, the tenser and more resentful she became. Her shoulders tightened, her arms stiffened to keep him at bay.

Maybe it was good for the dance because the fifth time they did it, Jared clapped twice, nodding. "We are getting there. Your resistance is excellent, Daisy, but you need to melt more when we get to the sentada. Again, but with more feeling, please. Remember, Daisy—" he'd taken to calling them by their character names "—Juan here is the center of gravity, and you circle around him, like a planet around the sun."

Or like a girl around a black hole, Pagan thought. She really did not want to cross Tony's event horizon.

Tony grinned, his lips vanishing against his teeth, which gleamed unnaturally against his newly tan skin. "I'll make sure she stays in my orbit."

Men. Always the center of everything.

She did her damnedest to set aside her percolating dislike as they ran through it again. Pagan was a better actress than a dancer, but years of lessons and hard work enabled her to keep up with anyone and give it a bit of flair. She tried to make up for anything lacking in her dancing with her acting, lending her reluctance a subtext of longing and desire. Rex Harrison couldn't sing for beans, but he'd acted up a storm while he sang in *My Fair Lady* and it turned out wonderfully. Maybe she could do the same for dancing.

It finally started to flow. She was feeling confident, graceful, sexy, until Tony threw her backward into a deep, romantic dip, brought his cheek to hers and whispered, "We're gonna do it after this, right?"

Pagan's head reared back, and she shoved at him with her free hand, trying to get her feet back under her. His grip on her right hand tightened painfully, and they struggled, with Pagan still dipped over backward.

"Let me go!" Pagan snapped, and he dropped her. She thumped to the floor, flat on her butt.

"What is this?" Jared spread his arms wide. "It was going so well."

Pagan got to her feet, roping a leash around her mounting rage to keep herself from striking Tony. "That," she said to her costar between clenched teeth, "was not appropriate."

"Oh, come on," Tony said, pushing greasy hair out of his narrowed eyes. "You put out for Nicky Raven, and I'm better looking than him. No reason you won't put out for me."

Pagan's stomach contracted; her throat closed. For once

she had no smart remark. She was shrinking inside, getting smaller and smaller. Soon there'd be nothing of her left.

How had he known? Or was it only a guess?

She was accustomed to the hatred that came her way for killing Daddy and Ava in the car crash. But most of the world didn't know the intimate details of the ten months she'd dated Nicky. Pagan's image until the crash had been sweet and spotless. Good girls didn't sleep with their boyfriends. Good girls waited for marriage, and she'd seemed like a good girl till it all came falling down.

After the crash, few people ever learned she'd started drinking at age twelve. The studio's publicity team had made sure any previous, smaller incidents were never brought to light.

Fewer still knew that she'd gone further with Nicky than good girls allowed.

Jared took Tony by the shoulder and pulled him aside to speak with him alone on the other side of the room. Tony looked over at her, his nose wrinkled with contempt, and she had to look away.

Pagan had started dating Nicky when she was fifteen and deep into the bottle to numb herself after Mama's suicide. Having Nicky's delighted attention, knowing he desired her above all else, had been almost as intoxicating as the martinis. He'd nearly filled the dark hole in her heart. For that reason alone she would've done anything he asked, as long as he loved her.

And Nicky had truly loved her. He still might, even though he'd impregnated and married another girl, a girl who looked an awful lot like Pagan.

Whether or not she'd truly loved Nicky, Pagan wasn't so sure now. The alcohol had clouded her judgment, to say the least. She'd done a lot of things she might not have, if she'd been sober. She regretted so much, but before the accident there had also been good times. That period in her life could be smeared with either a gritty or a rosy haze, depending on the day.

She realized she was leaning against the bare wall, shoulders hunched, so she forced herself to stand up tall. Good posture was the key to faking self-assurance, Mama had said. And once you fooled everyone else into thinking you were confident, somehow you fooled yourself. Right now she needed to fake it, hard.

Jared left Tony and came to stand in front of her, a watchful look in his eye. "How are we doing?" he asked.

"I'm fine." She kept her tone cool, distant. At least she wasn't trembling.

"I've asked Tony to change his attitude, and he has agreed. We need to make this work. How do you feel about that?"

Pagan glanced over at Tony. He was staring fixedly at a chalk mark on the floor.

"I think we should take a break for the rest of the day and try again tomorrow."

Jared shook his head. "We need to get you both back on the horse immediately, to mend this. Then I'll let you go." He paused, trying to get a read on her face. "You're still not up to speed, my dear. You need the practice."

Pagan kept her face very still. She could do this. "Then let's practice."

Jared smiled and leaned in to speak in a lower tone. "You

know he's an insecure little bitch and you're going to dance him off the screen, right?"

It was a transparent attempt to bolster her, but she couldn't help a tiny smile. Underneath her humiliation, a little spark ignited and began to burn it away.

People said ugly things because they were ugly inside. Or at least that would be her theory until she got through the rest of this rehearsal.

"Excellent. Tony, let's do it a few more times, please. Nadia?" Jared cued the wizened one at the piano as Tony got into position and Pagan began her lonely initial steps.

Tony stepped in and grabbed her hand vigorously. Stiff, Pagan turned toward him and did her back ocho in surprise. As he pulled her in again, she couldn't help it; her resistance was real, and his grip on her hand tightened until her finger bones cracked.

Only a few more steps. She forced herself to melt, to yield as they went through the dance. She twirled around him, resentful planet to his glowing, annoying sun, yielding to his pull.

The last flurry of intricate moves involved hooking her leg around his, then withdrawing, followed by a series of little flicks of her heel as she pivoted within his embrace. As they began, Tony shoved her this way and that.

"Angle, angle your hips!" Jared shouted at Tony. That was how you guided your partner, not by force.

But Tony wasn't listening. The angry glitter in his eyes, the power in his grip, was frightening, as if he might throw her instead of dip. He pushed her hip too hard and squeezed her hand cruelly. Pain shot down her arm.

She managed the first two kicks perfectly, anyway, but on the third she pivoted too far. The pointed heel of her dance shoe jabbed right into Tony's groin. He let out a sickened grunt of agony and released her.

She hadn't meant to do it.

Had she?

Either way, his anguished grimace was very satisfying. She stepped back as he doubled over, hands clutched between his legs.

"Sorry," she said, her voice calm, as if she'd stepped on his toe. "My fault."

Tony fell to his knees, sucking in air. "You bitch," he said with a groan.

Oh, yes, she was feeling better now. Amazing what a little accidental violence could do for your spirits.

"Your face is purple," she said. "You might want to change your tanning oil."

Jared rushed to Tony's side, eyes wide. "Are you going to be able to keep dancing?"

Tony shook his head. His lips completely disappeared as he pressed them together.

Pagan gathered up her trench coat and purse. "Same time tomorrow?"

Tony's burning glare as he struggled to sit up was a balm to her soul.

"I think tomorrow maybe we'll go through your little rumba number with David instead," said Jared.

David was Pagan's other costar, a dim, sweet boy she could wrap around her finger with one flutter of her eyelashes.

"If you think that's best," she said, and sauntered out the

door, even as her spirits sank. Tony Perry and the terrible script were only the first challenges this movie was going to throw at her.

CÓDIGO

The code of behavior which governs the dance.

Eight days of rehearsal and several grueling flights later, Pagan and Mercedes landed at Ezeiza Airport in Buenos Aires, rumpled and grouchy.

Devin Black was not waiting for them.

It was at a sunny eighty-five degrees as they made their way down the rickety metal stair onto the tarmac. A strong humid wind nearly snatched Pagan's pillbox hat off her head and whooshed the skirt of Mercedes's Zuckerman pink cotton piqué sheath dress so high her garters showed. The Pan Am stewardess in her chic blue uniform ran easily down the stairs after them to ask for an autograph for the captain, smiled her regulation Revlon Persian Melon lipstick smile and trotted back up the stairs.

"How does she look so unwrinkled?" Mercedes asked as they straggled into the terminal.

"I know," Pagan said. "My garters have found a new home, embedded in my thighs."

Inside they found a short, square man in a neatly pressed black uniform and cap holding a sign that said Señorita Jones.

"My name is like a terrible alias," Pagan said to Mercedes. *"Buenos días, señor. Soy Pagan Jones."*

He blinked at her and Mercedes, then looked down at his sign and back up at them. *"Buenos días, señoritas,"* he said. Under his formidable black mustache, his uneven teeth flashed in a smile. "I'm sorry. They didn't tell me you spoke such beautiful Spanish."

Pagan laughed and continued in Spanish. "Mercedes is the real expert. What's your name?"

"Yo me llamo Carlos Cavellini," he said, except he pronounced *yo* and *llamo* with a *zsh* sound at the beginning of the word instead of a *y*. He gestured for them to follow him and they fell in as he led them through the airless, bustling airport. "Pleased to make your acquaintance."

Pagan said, "Cavellini. That's a beautiful name. Is it Italian?"

Carlos's smiled widened. "There is an old saying. A Porteño—that is what we who live in Buenos Aires call ourselves—a Porteño is an Italian who speaks Spanish, lives like a Frenchman and wants to be English."

They tucked themselves into the backseat of his big black car as Carlos and a porter loaded their luggage. Beyond the airport were green fields, but as they drove, the gray smudge of a city lurked on the horizon.

"They weren't kidding when they said it's summer here," Pagan said, rolling her window down to feel the wind in her hair.

Half an hour later they pulled up in front of a ten-story building that looked like something from a movie about Paris in the 1920s, with flags from a dozen countries waving over the grand entrance. The entire neighborhood reminded Pagan of Europe, with grand boulevards, green parks and many-storied gracious buildings dotted with window boxes and fancy decoration over the doorways.

"The Alvear Palace Hotel," Carlos said. "Finest in the city."

"Which barrio is this?" Mercedes asked, folding up a map she'd been studying. She'd read two books on Argentina before the trip, and had agreed to do a report for her social studies class at school when she got back. Pagan, as usual, was going in blind.

"We're in Recoleta," Carlos said. "North of the city center, where there are many colleges, museums, churches and fine homes."

Devin wasn't waiting for them inside the ornate hotel lobby, either. The place had a sort of between the wars grandness and Pagan half expected to find Devin there chatting with girls dressed in sparkly flapper dresses, like something out of *The Great Gatsby*. But no matter how hard Pagan scrutinized the gold-bedecked marble columns, the red brocade benches or the high-ceilinged archways, he did not appear.

"Where the hell is he?" she muttered to Mercedes as Carlos ordered the bellboys to take their luggage and walked soundlessly along the thick Persian carpet to hand their passports to the hotel clerk.

Mercedes shrugged. "Maybe his flight was delayed."

Pagan shook her head, irritated. "His flights are only late if he wants them late."

"Will you require the car this afternoon, *señoritas*?" Carlos asked.

Pagan exchanged a look with Mercedes. They were both exhausted from the trip. "Thanks, Carlos. I'll see you down here tomorrow morning to go to wardrobe fittings."

As he touched his cap and walked off, the hotel clerk, a thin woman with ash blond hair and sharp blue eyes, was writing their information down on some cards. She looked up, pushing an official smile onto her lips. "*Buenos tardes*, Señorita Jones. We're so delighted to have you staying here for the next few weeks. We have the suite ready for you and your maid." Her eyes flicked to Mercedes briefly, dismissively, then back to Pagan.

Heat rose up from Pagan's heart. Beside her, Mercedes got very still.

"My maid?" she asked, as if not quite understanding, although she understood all too well.

The woman nodded. "Did you not want her in the same suite?"

"Do you mean my sister?" Pagan blinked innocently and linked her arm through Mercedes's, leaning into her warmly. Mercedes's whole body was rigid, but she didn't push Pagan away. "Did you hear that, sis? She thinks you're my maid. What would Daddy have thought of that?"

The clerk's eyes got wide, first with surprise, then with disbelief. Pagan and Mercedes were close in height, one skinny, the other strong, one pale and perfectly platinum blonde, the other darker with a strictly controlled mass of black curls. But they both had brown eyes, and they were both staring right at the hotel clerk.

"Daddy would've checked us into a different hotel," Mercedes said in a low tone. "One with better service." Mercedes wasn't half as good a liar as Pagan, so she kept her voice low on the rare occasion when she did it. The louder your voice, the more likely the strain of lying would show.

"And he would've told the studio and everyone he knew what a horrible mistake they made," Pagan said to her. "Do you think other people from my movie are staying here? We'll have to tell them all about this."

The clerk's eyes bounced back and forth between them, a nervous sweat dotting her upper lip. But Pagan could see that she still didn't believe them. "I'm so sorry, ladies. You have different last names on your passports, so naturally I assumed…"

"Mercedes Duran equals maid?" Pagan said, smiling prettily. "Sure. There's no possible way I could have been born a Duran, changed my last name to Jones and dyed my hair. No one in Hollywood ever changes their name. Just ask Rock Hudson."

The woman paled. "My mistake, *señoritas.* I do beg your pardon. Sisters. Sharing a suite. How nice…"

"We'd like to speak to the manager, please." Pagan's voice was still sweet, but edged with iron. "And we'd like anyone other than you to serve us for the duration of our stay."

An apologetic manager showed them to their lush suite, ushering in a bellboy with a complimentary bottle of champagne to earn their goodwill, only to have Mercedes tell him to take it away. The rooms were opulent, shiny with gold-patterned wallpaper, fresh flowers on the marble tables and two large bedrooms with giant satiny beds. The heavily draped windows featured a view out over the rooftops and the busy boulevard below.

As the door shut behind the last bellboy, Pagan took off her white gloves and threw them on the gold brocade sofa. "What the hell? We're in Latin America. You'd think the name Duran would be a badge of honor down here instead of Jones!"

Mercedes shook her head with resignation, which somehow made Pagan angrier. "From what I read, most people in Buenos Aires are of some kind of European descent. The indigenous people were driven out and mostly disappeared."

"Disappeared?" Pagan put her hands on her hips. "You mean killed."

"Probably. But that woman who checked us in, her family probably came from Germany originally, or maybe England or Sweden. Anyone who doesn't look European here is considered lower class and referred to as *indio*, or *negra*."

Pagan shook her head. "I'm sorry, M. I wanted to smack her."

"You can't smack them all." Mercedes slumped onto the sofa. "But you did confuse her. You're good at that."

"Everyone needs a specialty." Pagan came over and flopped next to her on the couch, leaning her head back against the carved gilded wood lining the back. "Does that happen to you a lot back home, too?"

"Not in my old neighborhood," Mercedes said, using her right toes to tug her left shoe off her heel, then switched to do it with the other foot. "But where we're living now? They all think I'm your live-in maid."

"What!" Pagan swung up to her feet again in agitation. "What do we do with these people? It's not like we can put a big sign over your head saying I'm Your Equal, You Sons of Bitches." She paused, thinking. "Can we?"

"Stop trying to save me," Mercedes said. "I'm fine."

Pagan stopped pacing and looked at her friend. Mercedes had leaned sideways onto the fat pillows on the sofa and closed her eyes, feet tucked under her. Pagan kicked off her own shoes and flung them into her bedroom. They thumped satisfyingly against the wall. "Okay. I'm ordering us some sandwiches and putting up the Do Not Disturb sign. I need to rest up before wardrobe tests tomorrow."

"But what if Devin Black comes knocking?" Mercedes said with a sly, sleepy smile.

"Damn you," Pagan said. Without even opening her eyes, Mercedes knew exactly why Pagan was so agitated.

Mercedes started giggling, burying her face in the pillows as her shoulders shook. She must be tired indeed to descend into such girlishness.

"While I'm at it, damn him, too," Pagan said. "Devin Black can sit on it. And rotate."

Devin did not appear that night, and he still hadn't called by the time Pagan left for costume fittings the next morning. She'd awoken at 2:00 a.m., unable to fall back asleep while her mind raced, wondering whether she'd made the right decision to come all this way to shoot a terrible film.

She was risking her career, a career that had recently been revived on the brink of death due the accident and her conviction for manslaughter. The comedy she'd shot in Berlin had started to warm the public to her once again because it was actually funny. And *Daughter of Silence* was likely to win over the critics. But one truly terrible picture and not only might the audiences turn away, but the studio might rethink using her in anything else of quality. She was still a box office risk. Taking this part in *Two to Tango* might turn her into something worse—box office poison.

And what if Devin never showed up? What if he'd been hurt or killed? Okay, so that was a farfetched late-night fear whispering in her ear. But he could've been pulled into another assignment, in which case they'd stick her with some idiot who didn't understand her, someone who wouldn't allow her to get what she needed out of this whole patriotic mission thing.

And now, fittings. Given how much she hated the character she was playing in the movie, Pagan was not looking forward to seeing the clothes Daisy would wear.

"If there are too many frilly dresses, I'm rioting," she said, finishing her second cup of coffee.

Mercedes didn't look up from the morning paper. "Trying on hand-tailored clothes is such a chore."

Great. She couldn't even be grumpy with justification. Because Mercedes was right. It was one of the most irritating things about her.

"Girdles are torture devices," she muttered, and put her cup down with a click.

"Bras are worse," Mercedes said. "But on the plus side, they make your chest look like it's about to launch two rocket ships. And rockets are cool."

Pagan laughed, threw a long trench coat over her jeans and wrinkled white shirt and left to find Carlos waiting for her in the hotel lobby.

The day was already slightly breathless with heat as she walked out of the hotel. Overhead, the flags flapped in a strong summer breeze. Sunshine blared off the windshields of passing cars. Carlos drove her by the gates of what he said was a famous cemetery and north to an area called Palermo.

Through her open car window, Pagan watched stylish women in pencil skirts walking small dogs on the sidewalks and men in summer suits eating outside at cafés or gazing at shop windows. Large leafy trees lined many of the streets, and between the tufts of greenery she caught glimpses of multistoried blocks of gracious stone buildings and open parks with splashing fountains.

What a contrast to the divided city of Berlin. When she'd been there in August, Berlin had been visibly recovering from the huge destruction wreaked by the Allies during the war. Buenos Aires had avoided the war altogether, like all of mainland United States, but with these magnificent mansions and wide, well-kept avenues, this city was more like a dream of Paris than New York.

The wardrobe department was lodged on the second floor of another genteel stone building with decorative flower finials over the windows. The door at the end of the dark hallway led to a huge open room with sunlight cutting yellow squares on the hardwood floors and racks of clothing. A sewing machine whirred invisibly nearby. Between the headless mannequins and shelving with metal bins for accessories, Pagan could see that the opposite wall was covered in mirrors.

"Hello?" she called out, brushing past a rack of black jackets. Tony Perry's name was scrawled on big yellow tags attached to each one. "Madge?"

"Pagan, honey!" a woman's scratchy voice called from somewhere to her right. "Over here!"

Pagan spotted a column of smoke trailing up near the ceiling and wound her way between ball gowns, shelves of hats and rows of linen trousers toward it. "They've buried you alive, Madge. I'm here to save you."

She rounded a trestle of frilly yellow skirts to find Madge Popandreau, wardrobe mistress for *Two to Tango*, seated at a huge black sewing machine. She had her eternal cigarette clutched between narrow, red-lipstick-smeared lips, her sharp black eyes following the line of white tulle as she threaded it under the bobbing needle. Madge had frizzy unnaturally black hair pulled back in a giant bun, square, deft hands and an eagle gaze that could spot the head of a pin on a sequin-covered dress.

"I'm just finishing up your petticoat for the big rumba number. Throw on that black suit for me in the meantime, will you, sweetie? Mind the pins." She jerked her head toward a rack of clothes with tags that bore Pagan's name. "Rada!"

"Coming." The voice was gloomy and Russian. A lanky young woman with a leonine mane of dark blond hair emerged between racks of fur coats. "Hello," she said to Pagan in the same sad tone. "I will help you with the clothes."

"You wearing a girdle, honey?" Madge asked, still sewing, and didn't wait for a reply. "If she's not, get her one, will you, Rada?"

Rada nodded and scanned Pagan's hips as she took off her trench coat. "No girdle today?"

"I'd rather jiggle like Jell-O," said Pagan.

Rada nodded mournfully, as if Pagan had announced a sudden death, slid the tape measure from around her neck and whipped it around Pagan's hips. "A full-body one is required for this suit." She shook her head. "It is very tight."

"I don't need to breathe," Pagan said as she slipped off her sneakers and unbuttoned her jeans. Near-nudity was the norm in wardrobe. Rada turned, and pulled a black sheath of elastane and straps off its hanger attached to the suit.

Pagan wiggled and wrestled her way into it, adjusting the bra straps, as Rada slipped the silky wool suit off its hanger. The pencil skirt was tight as hell at the waist—Rada hadn't been kidding—and it clenched tighter still as it slid down her hips.

"I know you're all about the A-line Dior these days, honey," Madge said. "You like to be able to move, maybe have a snack, like a real-life person. But this director, Victor, he didn't want you looking human and told me to make it as close-fitting as possible. I said okay, since you don't have to dance in it."

Victor sounded like a treat. Pagan hadn't met him yet, and was dreading it more each day. "I might need to walk," she said, squeezing her feet into the four-inch black heels that went with the suit. "I don't think I could sit down in this."

"We'll get you a slant board," Rada said.

The dreaded slant board, a simple contraption that allowed actresses to recline on a wooden board that could be leaned back at an angle to take the weight off your feet.

"Those things make me feel like I'm about to be buried at sea," she said.

"Before you die, this director wants to see every twitch of your derriere. It's a part of his 'vision,'" Madge said tartly.

"Twitching, but not jiggling," Pagan said, eyeing her clearly outlined rear end in the mirror. "So he likes 'em fake."

"We are here to create illusion," Rada said, her sorrowful voice lending the sentence an unexpected profundity. "Reality is of no importance."

"Film's an illusion, honey," Madge said tartly. "Might as well make it pretty."

"It's not how we feel that's important," said Pagan, reciting the old, sarcastic Hollywood line. Madge joined her in saying the next part of it: "It's how we look."

Madge moved expertly from sewing tulle to repinning the black suit, pegging the skirt hem a shade narrower to emphasize the curve of Pagan's hips. She had to take mincing little steps in it. Good thing she hadn't had to run around in this boa constrictor the night the wall went up in East Berlin.

But then good girls didn't *do* things. They liked being hobbled in tight skirts and heels so they could have things done for them, and to them. But heaven forbid they climb scaffolding or crash through a barricade manned by armed members of East Germany's most feared soldiers.

Or damned well walk normally.

Not that she, Pagan, would ever do such things. Bless you, no. She was nothing but a silly teenage girl, and the most you could expect out of her was to make faces at a camera.

Before her adventure in Berlin she'd thought that way about herself, too, if she thought about herself at all. But then she'd ended up on the wrong side of the Berlin Wall the night it went up, with people she cared about in danger. Desperation had forced her to realize that people's condescending expectations could be used against them. She'd pretended to be exactly what the leaders of East Germany thought she was so she could escape and get Thomas and his family to safety.

Give most people exactly what they expected and they never bothered to look deeper.

She'd thought she could pretend to be the sort of girl who wore a suit she could barely move in, for the sake of this sad little movie. But it was challenging these days to act like a shallow little dimwit.

On screen, sure. But in real life? Now that she knew a bit better who she was, the facade was becoming difficult to maintain.

Madge and Rada wrestled her out of the mummifying black suit and replaced it with the foofiest big-skirted ball gown Pagan had ever worn.

"I knew it," she said, flicking the ruched trimming that wound around her torso. She was a fish caught in a very fancy net. "I know Daisy's a small-town girl, but…"

"The director wanted frills," Madge said flatly. "So he gets frills."

"And I get chills," Pagan said, swaying the hooped skirt to and fro. "Fit's great, but I'm going to knock over every piece of furniture I walk past."

"Can you waltz in it?" Madge asked, her lips moving around the cigarette lodged in her mouth.

"If Scarlett O'Hara can do it, so can I." Pagan did a tentative one-two-three around the sewing machine. The skirt swung like a large white gauzy bell. "I could signal ships at sea with this thing."

"Pearls," ordered Madge.

Rada draped a multistrand pearl necklace with a large rhinestone clasp around Pagan's bare shoulders.

"It's like *Breakfast at Tiffany's* set in the Civil War," Pagan said.

Madge snorted. "Exactly what Victor requested. I told him it was derivative, that we should set the style, not follow it. He said, 'It's not that kind of movie.' Of course it isn't if you think of it that way! Ach." She made a helpless gesture with both hands, exhaling smoke through her nose. "I'm going home tomorrow, and you'll get to deal with him. Rada will be here for the shoot."

"The suit will tear," Rada said gloomily. "The netting will rip. It is inevitable."

"Is he that bad?" Pagan lowered her voice, even though they were the only ones in the large cluttered room. "Victor?"

"You haven't met him?" Madge lifted her painted eyebrows and paused to remove the burned nub of her cigarette from her mouth. "You won't like him."

"Tony likes him," Rada said, and raised a melancholy eyebrow that said it all.

Pagan's heart sank. Why couldn't things ever be easy? The thought of a man who was anything like Tony Perry in charge of an important movie in her career made her want to dive straight into a martini glass. But then a nice, sunny day sometimes did the same thing.

"There should be a word for men who prefer the company of other men—not to sleep with, mind," Madge said, stubbing out her cigarette in an overflowing ashtray by the sewing machine. "But who cannot abide to speak to women unless it is to condescend or seduce."

"I believe the word for men like that is *jerk*, Madge," Pagan said.

Madge snorted and lit another smoke. "Sorry to be so blunt, honey. But you should be prepared."

"I'm always ready for men like that," said Pagan. "My whole dang life has prepared me."

CHAPTER SIX

AMAGUE

From amago, meaning threat.
An embellishment done on one's own
before taking a step.

"I hate this movie," Pagan said.

She and Mercedes had changed into cotton frocks and were walking down the grand avenue to end all grand avenues in Buenos Aires. Pagan had returned from the wardrobe fittings in a baleful mood, and at Mercedes's request, Carlos had dropped them off in front of the Casa Rosada, or "Pink House," where the presidents of Argentina lived and worked. The casa was indeed as pink as the desert hills outside Los Angeles, squatting like a sun-baked birthday cake at the eastern end of the plaza. This was where Eva Perón and many others had spoken to assembled crowds from the balcony. Now, beside the yellowing grass and weary jets of the water fountains, tourists wandered, and women in sensible shoes supervised tours of shuffling schoolchildren.

Mercedes kept consulting her guidebook, telling Pagan the history of each statue and plaque in an eager voice that was cute for the first fifteen minutes. After that Pagan tuned her out and tried to enjoy the sunshine until Mercedes finally asked how the wardrobe tests had gone. The whole story about her first rehearsal with Tony and what she learned about Victor the director at the fitting today came pouring out.

"I almost feel guilty about kicking that snake Tony that first day," Pagan said. "I was so angry, but at least he's behaved since then. What is it?"

Mercedes had stopped by the ubiquitous statue of some guy on a horse in front of the Casa Rosada and was staring up at the huge baby-pink arch over the entrance. "There's a museum inside," she said, and smiled at Pagan.

Oh, God, Mercedes and her eternal thirst for knowledge. It made Pagan feel positively stupid sometimes. She should go to more museums probably, to fill up all the empty places in her brain. But right now she was too restless and discontented to stand in front of display cases listening to M drone on about political movements and population growth.

"Maybe some other time, if that's okay." Pagan took a few steps away from Casa Rosada, trying to pull Mercedes away from it. "I'm starving. Where's that café you wanted to go to?"

"Down the street that way." Mercedes pointed toward a tall white, elongated, pyramid-type monument with a small Statue of Liberty on top. "We *could* eat soon, but I might not get a chance to come back here…"

"You can come back while I'm on set. Time to eat." Pagan turned decisively and walked toward the pyramid thing.

Education and history were important and all, but…you know what? No. To hell with them. To hell with books and museums and, most of all, to hell with Devin Black. What was she doing here, ruining her career in a terrible film, putting up with handsy jackass costars and rendered immobile in ugly outfits for a guy who didn't bother to show up?

Through the heat of the day, a tantalizing mirage of a glass filled with ice, rum and lime swam into her view. She was more of a vodka-martini girl normally, but when the weather was warm, her thoughts turned to rum.

Mercedes caught up to her silently, a line between her brows, and they moved in silence through the plaza, keeping to the shade of the leafy green trees. The strain between them tightened like a guitar string being tuned too high.

The huge, open square narrowed to a broad, busy avenue lined with tall, European-style buildings and bustling with sharply dressed pedestrians. The warm summer air was filled with dust, and the scent of grilled meat wafted out of the restaurants and cafés as they passed.

Pagan's stomach growled. She really was hungry. And cranky.

A cranky, hungry alcoholic. That pretty much made her the worst person in the world.

"God, I want a drink," she said. "I just… Holy hell, M. I'm ready to jump that street vendor for a beer."

Mercedes's face cleared. "Yeah," she said. "Sorry."

"No, I'm sorry," Pagan said. "I do think food will help, though. Just don't let me order a rum and Coke."

"We'll eat soon," Mercedes said. "It's not far. And don't feel guilty. About Tony."

Dang, M was savvy, changing the subject from drinking to the crap underlying her need to drink. Pagan's shrink had told her that while she was out of town and unable to go to an AA meeting or contact her sponsor, she should to talk to her friend. She'd almost forgotten that advice.

"Tony thinks I'll put out because that's what everybody thinks about a girl who isn't pure," Pagan said, head down staring at the sidewalk moving slowly under her feet. "No one's ever going to want to date me properly if they know my history. I'm ruined."

"Pure?" Mercedes looked her over from her brown oxfords to her pink flowered sundress to the ribbon holding her ponytail. "It's strange that I hadn't noticed you were 'ruined.'"

"Mama would be ashamed of me if she knew," Pagan said, her voice small.

"Your mother—the Nazi sympathizer?"

Pagan swiveled her head to stare at her.

Mercedes shook her head, not backing down. "Your mother had plenty to be ashamed of herself. You remember the Nazis—people who thought those with blood that didn't fit their definition of *pure* should be wiped out."

Mercedes had an irritating way of making sense that clashed with Pagan's self-pity.

"Okay, so much for *pure*," Pagan said. "And maybe Mama's opinion would be questionable. But everyone thinks girls who don't wait for marriage are dirty."

"Well, *everyone* can get bent," Mercedes said.

She talked tough, but she had to know as well as Pagan that the mixed messages were everywhere. Society loved it when you were sexy, like Marilyn Monroe, but they thought you were morally bankrupt if you fooled around, like Marilyn Monroe. So you had to keep the fooling around very quiet.

They walked in silence for a few moments. "Do you think Devin knows?" Pagan asked. "About me and Nicky?"

"Ah," Mercedes said in a tone that said, *So that's what this is about.* "What does it matter? He said no monkey business during this trip."

"He knows everything else. Why wouldn't he know that?" Pagan's heart was made of lead. "Maybe that's really why he said no monkey business."

"You think Devin's the same kind of guy as Tango Tony?"

A small laugh escaped Pagan in spite of herself. "Yeah, no. They're nothing alike."

"Your past is nobody's business but yours," Mercedes said.

"What about your past?" Pagan glanced over at her friend. "Is that none of my business?"

Mercedes wrinkled her nose, suddenly a little shy. "What do you want to know?"

"Have you ever…?" Pagan didn't know how to say it. She and Mercedes had shared their worst deeds and fears during their months as roommates in reform school. But M had never talked about a boyfriend, or dating, or any kind of romantic interest. "Did you ever get really serious with a boy?"

Mercedes took her time, the way she did, pondering the question, as Pagan's heart beat hard and fast, hoping she hadn't offended her. "I thought about it," Mercedes said, her eyes screwed up tight, like she was wincing. "I had a few chances. Cute boys, too."

"But you had more self-control than I did." Pagan tried not to feel disappointed that she was the only one with a stained reputation. "Figures. You weren't a drunk."

"No, I just didn't want to." She looked over at Pagan as if she'd said something dirty or wrong.

Pagan bumped her shoulder into her friend's. "Very funny."

"No, it's true. So…" She swallowed hard and seemed to force herself to keep talking. "I went to a bar where women go to meet women. To see if that's what I wanted."

Pagan stopped in her tracks. Mercedes glanced back, but she kept walking. Her cheeks were pink. Was she actually blushing? Pagan hustled to catch up. "Was it?"

Mercedes shook her head, staring down at her feet as she walked. "Nope. Girls are nice and pretty and all, but I didn't feel a thing."

"But then…" Pagan didn't know where to go from here. "You probably haven't found the right person."

"Maybe." Mercedes frowned. She actually looked worried. "So far no one's tempted me. All I want to do is read the next issue of *Fantastic Four* and study astrophysics."

"So—you don't want to get married? Have children?" Pagan was trying to wrap her head around this.

"It just never occurred to me. Do you?" Mercedes asked.

"Of course!" Pagan said automatically, then thought more. "But I'm not sure why."

"Everybody says that's what makes women happy," Mercedes said. Her voice was unusually uncertain for her. "So if I don't want it, what does that make me?"

Pagan frowned. "You're still a girl! You're still a woman. What else would you be?"

Mercedes said nothing, staring fixedly off into the distance. A couple of young men lounging in a doorway pursed their lips and made kissing noises at them as they walked past. Pagan resisted the urge to throw them a rude gesture.

"Well, nobody's going to want to marry me, so we can be spinster old ladies together," she said.

Mercedes thought that over as they passed a shop filled with colorful glass bottles, and another selling shiny leather goods.

Mercedes glanced over her shoulder, then back at Pagan, her expression softening. "As long as I do the cooking."

Pagan laughed. "Deal."

Mercedes squinted at her thoughtfully. "Except, you like kids."

Kids. *Ava*. Her little sister, dead for more than a year now.

How Pagan missed pressing her cheek against that soft head of blond hair, missed making crazy faces to turn that that serious, frowning expression into a laugh. Pagan's and Ava's fingers had warred over the piano keys in furious duets. Their voices had meshed and clashed as they read *The Lion, the Witch and the Wardrobe* out loud in tandem. They were so different yet so close.

What would Ava be like now if she had survived the accident Pagan had caused? What would Ava say about Pagan's quest to find the mysterious Dr. Someone who had visited them so many years ago?

"I wouldn't mind having kids if they were like Ava," Pagan said. It was getting easier to say her sister's name, but still it made her throat close, her fists clench.

"You'd be a fun mom," Mercedes said.

"I'm still figuring out how to go a day without drinking," Pagan said. "One thing at a time, please. Mostly I wish I didn't have to go back to the movie shoot tomorrow. I used to think the tango was wonderful, but now…"

"Maybe you haven't found the right partner," Mercedes said tartly. She glanced over her shoulder again and a frown had creased the smooth skin between her eyebrows. Her almond eyes flicked briefly over her shoulder again. But she kept walking.

"What?" Pagan said.

"Don't look. But the same man that's behind us now was behind us before, in front of the Casa Rosada."

It took all of Pagan's self-control not to look over her shoulder. Her stomach tightened, but inwardly she told herself to remain calm. "He's probably a tourist, like us. You said this is a popular street."

Mercedes shook her head. "He's not acting like a tourist. The café's a block up on the other side. Let's cross here."

Pagan didn't want to question M's instincts. In reform school, she could look at someone once and know if they were an actual threat or bluffing. But the real world was more complicated, and Mercedes wasn't running with a gang now.

They crossed to the southern side of the street, and Pagan took a casual glance back the way they'd come. Two men talked and smoked as they walked together, a young woman pushed a stroller and a bent old woman all in black crossed the street behind them.

Mercedes scanned the same people as they reached the other side. "He's not there now. He was wearing a gray suit and hat. He must've seen that I noticed him."

They reached the dark-wood-and-glass doors of the Café Tortoni with its flamboyant art nouveau sign above in red.

Pagan opened the door as Mercedes said sharply, "There he is again."

"The man in gray?" Pagan stepped back out and looked down the street, but saw no man in gray.

"Gone again," Mercedes said. "I took my eyes off him for one second, and poof!"

"Maybe he thinks you're cute," Pagan said, and hauled open the heavy door again.

M gave her the side eye and walked in. Past the curtained-covered glass door, the Café Tortoni became a glorious high-ceilinged fin de siècle restaurant, its glittering chandeliers shrouded in cigarette smoke. Greek columns with curlicues on top held up a ceiling with a stained-glass skylight in the center. The murmuring voices of the patrons bounced off the glowing wood walls covered with Cubist paintings and autographed photos of patrons. Pagan recognized the shock of white hair belonging to Albert Einstein in one of them. The warm smell of steak make her stomach grumble.

"My guidebook called it one of the ten most beautiful café's in the world," Mercedes said.

It was indeed *trés elegant*. They could have been in the chicest café in Paris. A waiter in a white shirt and black pants ushered them over to a table under the gold-and-black stained-glass skylight. The chairs were red leather and dark wood, the table plain but polished. They ordered iced tea and a cheese plate to share to start, followed by steaks and French fries, please and thank you and as soon as possible would be nice.

The drinks and hors d'oeuvres arrived, and Pagan began

devouring the slices of apple and brie. Mercedes sipped her tea and glanced around uneasily.

"You're worried," Pagan said, wiping crumbs off the corner of her mouth. "About that guy in gray."

"I'm telling you, he was up to no good." Mercedes tapped her fingernails on the tabletop. "Do you mind if I go outside for a minute to make sure he's not still there?"

"'Course not," Pagan said. "As long as I eat a large steak soon, I'll be the happiest girl in the world. The beef in Argentina's supposed to be the best."

"Great." Mercedes, distracted, was already standing up. She didn't carry a purse and never wore gloves, so she set the guidebook down on her seat. "Back in a moment."

Then she was gone, moving quietly with her determined stride toward the front door. Pagan finished off the brie and speared a few olives from their tiny bowl with a toothpick. Olives made her think of martinis, which made her miss the icy bite of vodka moving down her throat, but she was too hungry not to eat them, and the sharp need for alcohol was dulled as her hunger abated. The waiter came by and she ordered more iced tea.

As the waiter moved off, the weird dizzy feeling in Pagan's head and its accompanying depression brought on by the confrontation with Tony, hours of dancing and lack of food faded.

What had she been so worried about? She could handle this whole silly movie situation. She'd made some choices she regretted in the past, but she wasn't going to let Tango Tony, as M called him, get on her nerves about it. Maybe now that he had some reason to fear her, he'd behave. And she'd find a way to charm the director, even if she did have to pretend to be the silliest clown in the circus.

"Alone at last." A familiar voice floated over her shoulder.

Pagan's heart beat once, very loudly. She turned to find Devin Black lounging at the table behind hers, a coffee and folded newspaper before him, his dark hair, gelled back, curled slightly around his temples in the summer humidity. His dark, turbulent eyes, like the ocean at twilight, took their time looking her over.

Pagan swallowed her last bite, her pulse accelerating, and dusted the crumbs off her hands. "Just you, me and the cheese. I think I'm in love." She paused. "With the brie."

One corner of Devin's mouth turned down in amusement. It had been weeks since she'd seen that characteristic smirk of his, and it was as annoyingly beguiling as ever.

"Wait till you try the steak," he said.

Why, oh, why did that remark make her flush? Or was it the way he was looking at her? Either way, her cheeks were hot, damn him.

She shook her ponytail, rallying. "Mercedes is going to laugh. She thought someone was following us with evil intent, but it turns out it was you. Or wait..." She surveyed his long, slender form again in its freshly ironed white shirt and crisp khaki pants, slightly scuffed brown leather oxfords on his feet. He was the picture of effortless summer sophistication, but he was not wearing a gray suit and hat. "That couldn't have been you."

He frowned, leaning toward her subtly, eyes scanning the room. "Mercedes saw someone following you *here*?"

"Yeah, but..." She was about to say Mercedes was being

paranoid, but the look on Devin's face stopped her. He dropped his paper on the table and signaled the waiter. "You think it's true?" she asked.

He was reaching for his wallet, pulling out paper Argentine pesos. "Buenos Aires is a hotbed for espionage, especially since the Israelis kidnapped Eichmann in '60."

Pagan had a vague memory of hearing about Eichmann in the news—an infamous Nazi war criminal in hiding who'd been captured in Buenos Aires by Israeli intelligence agents and whisked away to be put on trial in Jerusalem. He'd recently been convicted of orchestrating the Nazi efforts to exterminate the Jews and sentenced to death. His capture had been daring and illegal. Because of it the little-known Israeli secret service, the Mossad, had emerged as bold and utterly ruthless. She had a vague memory of that caper causing a lot of tension between Jews and non-Jews in Buenos Aires when it was discovered.

Devin was saying, "You know Mercedes's background. She of all people would recognize a threat when she saw one. This man in gray must've realized she'd spotted him and may be gone by now. More likely, he got a follow-up man to take his place. I'll meet you back at your hotel room. They'll have finished sweeping it by now."

He was settling his bill with the waiter, so Pagan canceled the order for steaks and asked for her bill, as well.

"Sweeping?" she said when the waiter had gone. "For dust bunnies?"

"Every afternoon while you're out, some friends of mine will sweep your suite for listening devices." He took a linen jacket off the back of his chair and slid his wallet into the breast pocket. "That way we'll always have a safe place to talk. So you might want to keep your unmentionables put away."

"What!" She managed to keep the exclamation low in volume and not to stare at him dramatically. The angle of his body and his gaze told her they were supposed to be acting as if they were in casual "we just met" conversational mode for anyone watching. "Every day? Is it really that dangerous here?"

"Having fun yet?" He grinned, sliding his gaze back to her.

There was an impact as their eyes met, like a meteor striking the earth. She was flushing again. "Yes," she said. "Yes, I am."

"I'll meet you back at your suite." He started to get out of his chair.

"Wait!" She resisted putting her hand on his arm. They were still faking casual chitchat, acting as if they were strangers. "Shouldn't you be staying to protect us from this guy?"

"Fear not, fair lady. He's got to be tailing you in these public places for information, not assassination," Devin said. "And I don't want him tailing me. So act as if you're leaving because you changed your mind, and don't let him know for sure you've made him."

"So we shouldn't try to lose him?" she asked. "If we see him again."

"No. He probably knows where you're staying by now. See you soon. Give my best to Mercedes." And with that he was gone, weaving toward the back of the restaurant, no doubt to slip through the kitchen and out a back door the rest of the world had no idea existed.

Pagan was finishing paying the bill when Mercedes came back, looking frustrated. Her eyebrows drew together as she saw the table being cleared and Pagan sliding her purse strap over her shoulder.

"Devin sends you his best," Pagan said. "I told him you thought someone was following us. He's got a full file on you, so he figured you knew what you were talking about, but he says we're not in any danger. I need to meet him back at the suite to talk."

"That explains the look on your face," Mercedes said. "I couldn't find the man in the gray suit again."

So her excitement at seeing Devin did show on her face. How aggravating. "Devin said he probably noticed you noticing him and left, or got replaced with a follow-up man. I wonder if that's a technical term. Oh, and they're sweeping our suite every day for bugs." She put down a few pesos for the tip. "You're probably hungry. Stay if you like."

Mercedes snorted and shook her head. "And miss a chance to finally meet Devin Black?"

They caught a cab back to the hotel. Pagan tried not to keep glancing out the back window to see if anyone was following them, but she caught Mercedes looking in the driver's side-view mirror more than once.

"Anything?" she asked.

M shook her head. "Hard to tell."

Devin was waiting in their suite. It was a little unsettling to walk into their private space and see him lounging in the side chair, reading the paper. He stood and held out his hand to Mercedes, smiling while she shook it. "I was going to introduce myself," he said. "But I'm thinking that might be unnecessary."

"I might have heard a thing or two about you," Mercedes said, taking her hand back. "But apparently nothing like the research you've done on me."

Devin gave a one-shouldered shrug. "It's research like that which makes my job so interesting."

Mercedes's lips pursed in an appreciative little smile. "A compliment that doesn't sound like a compliment. Pretty smooth for an art thief."

"Former art thief," Devin said. Pagan could see he was tickled by Mercedes tweaking him. "I never stole cars, but compared to taking a Picasso out of a guarded museum, it doesn't sound that hard."

Pagan opened her mouth to shush him, and then shut it. As Devin well knew, Mercedes had stolen her share of cars, and other things. She was in reform school for armed robbery and extortion because she'd been one of the top enforcers for the Avenidas, one of the most powerful Mexican gangs in Los Angeles, a gang headed by her brother, who'd been shot and killed. A gang that still wanted her back.

Mercedes's eyelids dropped to half mast as she reassessed Devin. "It's not hard," she said, "unless Clanton 14 has six guys chasing you from both ends of Rampart Avenue and the only car you can get to has two more of them inside it."

Clanton 14 was the rival gang to the Avenidas. Reform school had taught Pagan a lot of things Hollywood could not.

Devin lifted an impressed eyebrow. "I retract my statement."

"Look at us, three little criminals," Pagan said.

Mercedes and Devin turned as one to look at her, faces wearing identical looks of skepticism.

"You think she qualifies?" Mercedes asked Devin, as if Pagan wasn't standing right there.

"As a criminal?" Devin shook his head. "She lacks the killer instinct."

Pagan blinked at them. "But I…"

"She's got a thing for the criminal type, though," Mercedes said.

"Obviously," said Devin, turning back to her. "Now this man in gray you saw following you. Can you describe him?" He ushered Mercedes to take the gold brocade chair behind him. "I ordered steaks for you both, by the way. The hotel cook's pretty good."

"Hooray," Pagan said, still trying to deal with the two most important people in her life bonding without her. "I'm starving."

She took the sofa while Mercedes lowered herself into the chair and said, "He was young, maybe early or midtwenties, over six feet, white, reasonably handsome with reddish brown hair under a light gray fedora. Gray suit, white shirt, narrow gray tie."

"Thorough," said Devin. "And what made you think he wasn't a fellow tourist?"

Mercedes squinted, thinking. "He wasn't looking around. He had no curiosity about the things or people around him. No guidebook. He kept staring at Pagan."

Pagan straightened. Devin said, "He wasn't some fan of her movies, maybe?"

Mercedes shook her head. "I thought of that. But he didn't want an autograph, and not because he's shy. He was intent, focused, and he didn't want her, or me, to see him."

Pagan was impressed, and convinced, and Devin was taking everything Mercedes said very seriously. "Will you let me know if you see him again?" he asked.

"Sure. Do you know who it is?"

It was like being at a tennis match, her eyes bouncing back and forth between them.

"No," Devin said. "But we'll find out."

Mercedes nodded. "He'll be back."

"I knew Berlin was a garrison of spies," Pagan said, turning to Mercedes. "But Devin says Buenos Aires is, too, even more so since the Israelis kidnapped that war criminal Eichmann back in '60."

"I did some research for my school report that said there's a large Jewish population here," Mercedes said. "But also a large German ex-patriot population."

"Exactly," said Devin. "And those are only two of the factions that come into conflict. Many of the old aristocracy resent elements within the German community and the former Perónist government, which harbored Nazis like Eichmann and Mengele. Then there are local gangs who follow various brands of fascism and Perónism, who agitate against the current government and target Jews. Not to mention that the Israelis and other foreign agencies are still active, all with their own agendas."

"Why would any of them want to tail Pagan?" Mercedes asked. "For all they know she's a harebrained movie star. Sorry." She shot an apologetic look at Pagan.

Pagan grinned. "I drank a lot of martinis to give that impression. Glad they didn't all go to waste."

"Much as I'd like to discuss this with you in more detail, and much as I appreciate your sharp eye," Devin said to Mercedes, "I can't officially talk to Pagan about her job for us with you here." He turned to Pagan. "Shall we adjourn to my room, perhaps? It's down the hall."

Pagan was on her feet. "You're staying down the hall?" It was silly how that news made her pulse race.

"Don't leave," Mercedes said, getting up. "Pagan needs her steak, and it's coming here. Send mine in when it comes." And she sailed into her adjoining bedroom and shut the door.

Pagan was alone again with Devin Black.

CORTINA

Curtain. A brief musical interlude between dance sets.

"Alone at last," said Pagan, echoing Devin's words back to him as she sat back down with a thump. Devin took the chair beside the sofa with his usual careless grace, an arm's length away.

Now that Mercedes was gone Pagan was free to notice how the long, powerful muscles in his shoulders pressed against the fine cotton lawn of his white shirt, and how narrow his waist was where the shirt was tucked neatly into his pants. She pulled her eyes away so he wouldn't see her staring.

"Sorry it took me a little while to get in touch," he said. "I had some background research to do before I talked to you and…"

He broke off, staring at her. His eyes, normally layered sapphire and indigo, caught sunlight coming through the hotel window and glowed nearly royal blue. His high cheekbones and long straight nose had tanned since she'd seen him at Sinatra's house in December. He looked fit and coiled for action.

"Are you all right?" he asked. "You seem agitated."

She relaxed slightly. "I'm fine, but this morning wasn't fun. The wardrobe is derivative, dated and way too tight, which is exactly how this whole movie's going to be. The script is terrible. I keep hearing the director's a jerk, and my costar thought dance rehearsals back in California were the right time to proposition me."

He didn't move, but something behind his eyes tightened. "Which costar?"

The protective note in his voice was strong, immediate. She looked down so he wouldn't see how happy it made her. "Tony Perry. He's…" She wanted to tell him how Tony's assumptions about how "easy" she was had made her feel awful, to hear Devin's reassurance that he didn't see her that way, but instead she trailed off and finished, lamely, "He's just a jerk."

"I'll have a word with him," Devin said. "For all he knows, I'm still a studio executive."

"Oh, I think I fixed that particular situation," Pagan said. "But thanks. He's finally able to walk around now without help."

His eyebrows quirked together. "Ouch?"

She nodded. "You look like you've been lounging at a resort since I saw you back in Los Angeles."

"Not unless you call staking out the home of a possible war criminal resort living," he said. "The summer sun down here is relentless."

"Where does Von Albrecht live?"

The astonishment in his face was gratifying. "How did you know his name? I never told you he goes by that name. Did I?"

"No, but in a way, my mother did." She got up and went to the fancy mirrored desk in the suite's living room, where she'd laid one of her smaller suitcases and pulled out an accordion file. She tossed it to Devin, who caught it easily. "Rolf Von Albrecht wrote to my mother in coded letters in the summer of '52, a few months before Dr. Someone came to visit us. I assume they're one and the same person. I found the letters in my father's safe last August. I broke the code in Berlin."

He looked up at her from the file. "In Berlin? When?"

"The night before I went to Walter Ulbricht's little garden party, the night I saw Nicky with his wife and had a couple of drinks. You remember." She paused, recalling it well herself. As Nicky had started playing on Pagan's sympathy, trying to win her back, Devin had literally shoved him away and told him to go back to his wife.

Devin's mouth curled at the memory, too. She continued. "It was something you'd said about Hitler's birthday before that which helped me break the code. Take a look at the letter on top."

Devin pulled Von Albrecht's letters out of the file and untied the string holding them together. His eyes swept over the first letter, taking in all its innocuous phrases, until he came upon a notation in different handwriting. "Twenty, four, eighteen eighty-nine," he read. "April 20, 1889. Hitler's birthday."

"That's the code, in my father's handwriting. I don't know how he figured it out, but it worked. I used those numbers—twenty, four and the numbers in eighteen eighty-nine—and found the real message. In them, Von Albrecht says Mama was a 'sympathizer.' He asks her to help him—specifically to give him a place to stay and arrange to get him on a ship leaving the country."

"Did he say anything about coming to Argentina?"

Pagan shook her head. "No destination is mentioned, and nothing concrete about exactly who he is, why he needs to leave or what my mother was a 'sympathizer' to, but given that the code is Hitler's birthday..."

She trailed off. Director Bennie Wexler had made it clear Eva Jones was anti-Semitic. He'd experienced her bigotry personally. That was bad enough. But if this Dr. Someone aka Von Albrecht was the type of person Pagan feared him to be, her mother was something worse.

"Who is this man you want me to identify?" she asked, coming back to sit on the sofa. "What did he do?"

Devin set the letters and file aside. "Early in 1952, a Nazi war criminal named Rudolf Von Alt escaped detention in the United States and fled the country. We believe that he changed his name to Rolf Von Albrecht, keeping the two names similar to make it easier to respond to, and that he found help from sympathizers all over the country. A sort of evil Underground Railroad. They housed him, kept him safe, funded his journey across the country. The evidence indicates that he stayed at your house in the summer of '52."

Pagan inhaled sharply and nodded as Devin threw her a look. It was exactly what she'd feared after decoding the letters. Her mother wasn't only a woman who hated Jews. She'd helped a Nazi war criminal escape justice.

"It's okay," she said, although it was far from okay. "But I feel a little sick."

He got up and poured her a glass of water. "After his stay with your family, Von Alt left on a ship from the port of Long Beach. We don't know his exact route from there, but we think we've tracked him down here, to Buenos Aires."

"Tracked him—how?" She took the glass from him. Although none of this was a surprise, it was unsettling to hear the story coming from Devin, who was as close to an official government source as she could get.

"I don't know all the details, but during the war, the FBI knew that your mother was a Nazi sympathizer and kept a file on her. They didn't think she was dangerous and weren't actively watching her in '52, so Von Alt was able to get away. Later, I don't know how, they learned that she had helped a man who resembled Von Alt. Meanwhile, I learned that Walter Ulbricht's daughter was a fan of yours."

She sipped her water. How could the FBI have known about Mama during the war when Pagan herself had just found out? Mama had been an excellent actress in her own right. "And you got me to Berlin, using my desire to learn more about Mama to get me there," she said. "You knew by then she had helped the Nazis."

He nodded, eyes on her as if braced for a bad reaction. "I'm sorry I couldn't tell you."

She raised her hand briefly, waving off his apology. She'd forgiven him long ago. He'd been doing his job, and they'd had no connection then, no relationship, if that was the right word for whatever lay between them now. But could she trust him?

"Do you know anything else about my mother or father

now that I don't know?" she asked. She held her breath, not knowing if she would believe the answer, whatever it was.

"No."

He looked right at her, brows steepled sadly, his eyes concerned, and warmth spread through her chest, like hot tears, melting away her uncertainty.

"All right," she said. "I had to ask."

He gave her a small smile. "Keep in mind, the CIA does know more. I can tell that the file they gave me on your mother was only part of the story they have on her. I knew she was the daughter of your grandmother Ursula, and that Ursula claimed to have married Emil Murnau and said he was the father of her baby."

"But Emil Murnau wasn't my grandfather," she said. "He probably never knew Grandmama. He's someone who died at the right time so she could cover up the fact she had a baby out of wedlock."

"I wonder if your mother knew."

Pagan considered this. "Grandmama would never have told her. She was too proud. And Mama was so sure of herself, of her place in the world…" She trailed off.

"Until the end." Devin's eyes were fixed on her, steadying her as the bleak, heavy thoughts about Mama's death came over her. It was always like this, a smothering weight pressing the breath out of her. She'd started drinking to erase that weight, and it still made her long for the icy bite of vodka sliding over her tongue. She concentrated on breathing and pushed through it all.

"That's not enough," Pagan said, thinking out loud. "Mama wouldn't have been happy if she learned that she was born out of wedlock, but it wouldn't be enough to make her leave us. I know she wasn't the best person in the world, that she helped this Nazi escape, that she pushed us hard. But she loved us. She loved me and Ava more than anything in the world. She wouldn't have left us for that."

She still couldn't quite bring herself to say that Eva Jones had been a bad person. But maybe she had been. Loving your children didn't absolve you of everything.

Devin was nodding, accepting her verdict. "So, if the Rolf Von Albrecht living and working here is the man you knew as Dr. Someone when you were a child, the same man who wrote those letters, then we can confirm we've found Rudolf Von Alt, Nazi war criminal, in Buenos Aires."

"And I'm the only person who can connect the man living here to the one who wrote these letters?" she asked.

"We think so. I hope it won't be too dangerous or difficult for you. Seeing him may not be enough to identify him because he may have had plastic surgery. And he will have aged since you saw him last."

"I remember his voice better than his face," Pagan said. "If you get me close enough to overhear him, I'll know."

"We're hoping that won't take very long. Once that's done, you can wrap up your movie and go home."

"But the US can't prosecute him here in Argentina. If it's the right man, do they plan to kidnap him like the Israelis did with Eichmann? Take him back to the US and put him on trial?"

Devin shook his head very slightly. "They haven't told me what the long-term plan is, and they have to be careful. After the Israelis took Eichmann, there was a wave of anti-

Semitic violence. The fascist gangs haven't forgotten and are always looking for an excuse to lash out at the local Jewish population. But if this man is indeed Rudolf Von Alt, then he deserves whatever they have planned for him."

"What did he do?" Pagan said, her voice quavering ever so slightly.

Devin hesitated. "He's a doctor. A medical doctor with a second degree in physics. He started off working on the German version of the atomic bomb, but when that program collapsed, he started...experimenting. On the prisoners in the camps."

Pagan pressed the palms of her hands against her closed eyes, trying to keep the images those words conjured from appearing in her mind. It didn't help. She swallowed hard against her rising nausea. "He experimented on people."

"With doses and implants of radiation, used without anesthetic, often combined with other typical Nazi experiments like limb transplants, using twins and pregnant women and anyone else he could get his hands on. Hundreds of them," Devin said.

She swallowed the bile that rose in her throat. "A doctor," she said stupidly. "Dr. Someone. My mother's friend."

"Your mother may not have known his crimes," Devin said.

"Maybe," Pagan said, remembering how her strong, stylish mother had laughed over dinner with the angular, balding Dr. Someone while her father sat stony-faced. Ava had been there, too, only four years old, piling her peas into the center of her mashed potatoes, seated on a booster next to a man who had done the unspeakable.

Pagan's skin was going to shudder right off her body. She jumped to her feet, pacing over to the suite's bar. It hadn't been stocked with the usual welcoming bottles of Scotch, vodka and rum, and she was grateful. Nothing like Nazi atrocities involving your mother to make you want a good stiff drink.

"I'm sorry," Devin said, getting to his feet. "I almost didn't tell you."

She leaned on the bar with shaking hands. "I don't want to know, but I need to."

Two sharp knocks on the front door made her pivot.

"Probably your steak," Devin said. "You still up to eating?"

"Maybe in a bit," she said, starting to move to the door.

"I'll get it," he said, and was at the door in one swift move, tipping the server right at the doorway and wheeling in the cart himself, pausing to knock on Mercedes's door. "Steak's here."

Mercedes poked her head out. "Thanks." She grabbed her plate and utensils off the tray. "Hey, do you know if they sell American comics here? I'm missing the second issue of *Fantastic Four* because Pagan's a spy."

Devin let out a surprised laugh.

Pagan smiled in spite of herself. "You can get it when you go home next week!"

"Might be sold out," Mercedes said, raising her eyebrows. "It's a whole new thing for Marvel, you know."

"So you keep saying," Pagan said.

"I'll see what I can do," Devin said. "No promises."

"Thank you," Mercedes said with a sly grin, and vanished once more into her room with her food.

"You do not have to get her a comic book," Pagan said. "You're not her butler."

"I don't mind asking," he said, picking up a covered dish and a cold bottle of Coke off the tray.

Pagan walked up, hands out to take the food from him. "She is obsessed! Thanks."

"Sit down," he said, his lips softening. "I'll serve."

She bit down a smile and sat down in the chair by the suite's desk as Devin set the plate down and opened the Coke bottle. He handed it to her. Her fingers slipped on the outside condensation and touched his. A brief touch, then his hand was gone.

"They don't call it Her Majesty's Secret Service for nothing," he said, and lifted the cover off her plate with a flourish.

A cloud of fragrant steam rose from the large, beautiful steak lying there. Pagan leaned in to inhale, as Devin unfurled her napkin and laid it on her lap.

He leaned over her as he did it, and her shoulder brushed his chest. For a moment the heat from his skin enveloped her reassuringly. A whisper of his breath touched her temple.

She turned to him and looked up. He was looking down at her. Their lips were inches apart. Any moment now he'd close the gap to kiss her, pull her close.

Then he stepped back.

"You don't have to do this for us." Devin walked over to stare out the window, his back to her. "I know you want to, but maybe it's best."

So they weren't going to make out. Fine.

"I'm going to do this," she said, and took a fizzy sip of Coke to settle her nerves.

"You're not responsible for what your mother did," he said. "You don't have anything to prove."

"Mercedes said that, too, but neither of you grew up loving your mother only to find out later she hobnobbed with war criminals. She *helped* them." Pagan took another sip of Coke. The saturated sweetness coated her tongue, a memory of hot summer days playing tag with Ava in their terraced backyard while Mama yelled at them not to get too dirty before dinner. How could that woman be the same one who welcomed Dr. Someone into their home, who helped him escape?

"Do you think she regretted it?" Pagan asked suddenly.

"Your mother?" Devin turned from the window, puzzled, until realization eased the line between his brows. "You're thinking that's maybe why she committed suicide."

"Is it strange that's the answer I'm hoping for?" she said.

"No." Devin's voice was gentle. "But whatever else she did doesn't cancel out the fact that she really did love you. And Ava."

"Why do people have to be so complicated?" She didn't expect an answer. "I want to understand why she did it, but if I do figure that out, what good does it do me?"

"You're the only one who can figure that out," he said. "Identifying Von Albrecht might not get you the information about your mother that you're looking for. It might get you her file, and it might not. You could go through all of this and still not have any answers."

Pagan picked up her fork and knife. "All the stuff with

Mama is secondary. If the man you've found here is the one who did those experiments on people, he needs to be brought to justice." She cut a tiny piece off the steak. Slightly pink inside, the way she liked it. "Tell me more about him."

Devin took a seat, watching her eat. "The man we found here named Rolf Von Albrecht is the right age to be Von Alt, the right height, we think, and he has the right sort of knowledge. He's a professor of physics at the University of Buenos Aires, not far from here. He also lives nearby. He moved to Buenos Aires in March of 1953, which jibes with him leaving your house in November of 1952.

"He was later joined by his two children, Dieter and Emma, and his wife, Gerte. We know Von Alt had a family back in Germany during the war, but the records of their names and ages were destroyed. So we can't trace him that way. Gerte died in 1960 of cancer. Dieter goes to a high school right next to where his father teaches and has been accepted into the university. He's also part of a dangerous gang of teenagers that split off from a larger fascist gang recently. We think he may even be their leader."

"He sounds delightful," Pagan said.

"It makes all kinds of sense if he's the son of a Nazi war criminal," Devin said. "That's another reason we think Von Albrecht's our man. The fight between the gangs seems to have been over how 'pure' bloodlines were. Dieter and his friends are children of recent German immigrants, too new to Argentina for the leader of the other gangs."

"So even the purest Aryan son of a Nazi wasn't pure enough for this other gang?" Pagan shook her head. "If the fascists are fighting among themselves, they should do us all a favor and kill one another off."

"Unfortunately, they haven't forgotten that they hate the Jews more than anyone. The barrio where Dieter's school is, and where Von Albrecht teaches, has a large Jewish population and a history of anti-Semitic violence. So it's very lucky for us that you'll be shooting a scene of your movie on the grounds of that school tomorrow."

"The big dancing-in-the-courtyard scene?" Pagan had memorized the entire horrible script in spite of its awfulness, as well as the shooting schedule. "How'd you manage that?"

Devin raised his eyebrows in an exaggeratedly innocent way. "Who says I had anything to do with it? To round out the report, Von Albrecht has a daughter, Emma, two years younger than Dieter, sixteen."

"Von Albrecht's a professor, so maybe I can wander into one of his classes tomorrow—a lecture," Pagan said through a mouthful of steak. It was tender and succulent. "As soon as I hear him speak, I should be able to tell you if it's the man I knew."

"We thought of that. But he took a sabbatical, a full year, and won't lecture again until the fall."

"Why have the movie shoot near his workplace, then?" Pagan asked. "And don't keep pretending you had nothing to do with that."

"Dieter and Emma will be there," Devin said. "And it might be useful to have you near them, perhaps to meet them."

"Maybe I could join Dieter's gang," Pagan said, waving a forkful of steak airily. "I could establish my bona fides by telling them how I foiled the Communist East German army in Berlin."

"A gang of fascists might elect you their leader if they learned how you humiliated those Communist leaders," Devin said in the same light tone. "Let's hope gang membership won't be necessary. But you do have a connection to their family via your mother. Emma and Dieter likely don't know about her at all, but Von Albrecht will remember."

Pagan nodded, chewing. Perhaps she could use Von Albrecht's sense of obligation to her mother to her advantage somehow. But first she needed a way to meet the man. "The more we know about him, the better, right?" she said. "Even though he's not there, this is where he works and where his kids go to school. I could potentially learn a lot."

Devin stood up to pace over to the window, look down onto the tree-lined road and then pace back. "We've been following Von Albrecht for the past two months, hoping to find a pattern so we could set you up to run into him. But for the past three weeks he hasn't left his house at all. Not once. He's always spent the bulk of his nonworking time at home, but not to poke his head out of his own front door once in three weeks is very odd."

"Maybe he's dead."

"Doubtful. Nothing else has changed. His children come and go in the same pattern—to school, errands, to parties with their friends and so on, with no sign of mourning or visits from mortuary personnel. The daughter, Emma, buys the same amount of food every week. So we're pretty sure he's still alive. No doctor visits, so he's probably not ill, at least not seriously."

"Personnel," Pagan said. "Never heard you use that word before. Sounds…military."

"I'm officially a lieutenant in Her Majesty's Navy." He pronounced it *leftenant*. "Unofficially, the men who face real combat wouldn't consider me very military."

"So how do I get to see and hear this guy if he's locked up in his house?" she asked. "I'm way too messy to be convincing as his new maid."

"I told you that you wouldn't need to pretend to be anyone but yourself. I've got an idea." He stopped pacing. She detected a challenge in his stormy gaze. "You're a movie star of German descent, after all. And a lonely girl in a strange city."

Pagan, who didn't feel the least bit lonely, met his eyes with a small, pleased smile. "So empty inside and in need of rescue. How well you know me."

CONFITERIA BAILABLE

A café–like establishment where one can purchase refreshments and dance tango.

The tires rumbled over cobblestones. Dim light from streetlamps flashed through the dark interior of the car, over the back of Carlos's head, flashing bronze on Mercedes's dress as she stared out the car window.

Pagan was headed out to a bar. She, an alcoholic. The things she did for Devin and for her country...well, they were dangerous in all kinds of ways and she enjoyed them. That probably meant something was wrong with her, but that fault could get in line behind all the others.

She glanced over at Mercedes, calm and glowing in that knee-length burnished dress, her thick, curly black hair teased at the crown. The winged black eyeliner Pagan had drawn on gave her dark brown eyes a newly mysterious look.

"Cobblestones on the streets, and the buildings are shorter here," Pagan said, watching the two-story edifices fly past, their window boxes overflowing with flowers, closed up for the night.

"The guidebook said San Telmo's the oldest barrio in Buenos Aires." Mercedes glanced over at Pagan. "You may be a little overdressed for it."

Pagan glanced down at her Dior ivory silk dress, covered in tiny silver beads that glinted as she moved. It was a thing of beauty, tailored perfectly to hug her waist and flow like a waterfall down her hips. And it was a good dress for dancing. She'd brought a dark coat in case she needed suddenly not to glow like a sky full of stars.

"Overdressed? It's not even floor-length," she said half-sarcastically. Her silver heels weren't exactly casual, either. "I need to be noticed tonight. Devin said the bar was casual. So I figured I wouldn't be."

"You'll be noticed," M said. "If you're sure that's what you want."

Mercedes not only didn't approve of Devin's plan; she hated it. At first she'd refused to go with Pagan that night, hoping to keep Pagan home that way. But Pagan was not easily deterred, and M's need to help her out had trumped her resistance. She'd put on her own casual dress and black heels, and only fought Pagan for five minutes when Pagan offered to do her hair and eyeliner.

"It's what I need," Pagan said. "Don't look at me like that. It's a public place. Nothing's going to happen. Well. Nothing bad's going to happen. To us."

They pulled up in front of a graffiti-covered wall, two doors down from the bright windows of a café. The light spilled onto the sidewalk and the cobblestones, revealing the entwined silhouettes of several dancing couples swaying right outside. Laughter filtered through the warm night air, peppered with beats from an unseen band and the clink of bottles being cleared from a table.

"We've reached Gläubigen, *señoritas*," Carlos said, turning in the driver's seat. "Are you sure you don't want me to wait?"

Pagan reached over to hand him a fistful of paper pesos. "For all your help today, Carlos. Thanks. But you should go home. We'll catch a cab back."

Mercedes looked around the quiet street. The bar was the only sign of movement and life. "If we can find a cab."

"Walk one block that way," Carlos said, pointing to the right. "You'll be sure to find one near Plaza Dorrego."

"*Gracias,*" Mercedes said. "Wish us luck, my friend."

Carlos looked her up and down. "*You* are going to need it in there."

Pagan froze, about to open the car door. "Why her in particular?"

"Look at them." Carlos jutted his chin at the young people crowded in the doorway of the bar. "None of them look like her, like me."

The people spilling into the street and hanging out in the doorway were all fair skinned with a high percentage of blondes. The name of the bar was German for "Believers," and Devin had said it was a mostly ex-patriot crowd, but not always.

After what they'd encountered at the hotel reception desk, Pagan hesitated. "Maybe you should go home, M."

"Am I a liability to you?" Mercedes asked, her voice level, reasonable.

"No, just the opposite. But I don't want to push you into anything dangerous," Pagan said.

"I didn't like it before," Mercedes said. "This doesn't change anything. But are you sure?"

Pagan caught her friend's eye and gave her a sly smile. "I want to be noticed, don't I? Let's go."

Carlos got the door for Mercedes while Pagan let herself out and raised her bare arms to the sky, stretching luxuriously. Over at the bar, a few heads turned.

"*Gracias*, Carlos," she said, and clicked over to the sidewalk with as confident a stride as the cobblestones allowed to join Mercedes. *"Que tengas buenos noches."*

"Ustedes tambien, señoritas," he said, touching his hat.

Pagan looped her arm through Mercedes's and they walked in sync toward Gläubigen. "How are we supposed to know which one is your guy?" Mercedes asked in a low tone.

"Tall, dirty blond hair, blue eyes, mole on his right cheek," Pagan muttered. "Let me know if you spot him first."

The music got louder as they approached. It sounded like a local band's version of "Blue Hawaii," sung in a pretty good imitation of Elvis with a slight German accent.

It was time to turn the movie-star wattage up to supernova level. Channeling all she'd learned during many walks down the red carpet, Pagan breathed deep and imagined herself as the center of the universe, filled with light and power. She wasn't just a movie star; she was an actual star, brighter than the sun. Everyone would revolve around her tonight.

If she could pretend to believe it long enough. The thoughts were ridiculous, but they had never failed.

The swaying couples turned their heads. Chatter near the

doorway died slowly as they sauntered up. Well, Pagan was sauntering. Mercedes kept to her usual neutral tread.

"It's not as cute as they said," Pagan said in English to Mercedes, loud enough to be heard.

Mercedes shrugged. "The band sounds pretty good."

"We shall see," Pagan said skeptically, and favored those near the doorway with a dazzling smile as she sashayed inside.

There was no bouncer, no cover charge, no maître d'. The place was more café than club, but as Pagan and Mercedes paused on the threshold, several young men turned to stare. The place was packed with teenagers and college-age kids, and after hearing what Carlos had said, Pagan noticed that all of them were fair-skinned. The girls were mostly wearing stretchy skirts with their button-down shirt tied at the waist and ponytails, while the boys favored linen short-sleeved shirts left untucked over khakis and pompadours. Pagan stood out like a princess at a barbecue.

The bartender was older, over forty, and the two waitresses looked experienced, and one was darker-skinned. Against the far wall, the band—six men also older than the crowd—earnestly and expertly plied their instruments. Pagan let her eyes sweep over the nearest knot of boys. None of them had a mole on his right cheek, but two were moving to intercept.

"There's a table," she said, taking Mercedes by the hand and walking right past the boys with the confidence of someone who always gets the table she wants.

One of the boys muttered, *"Indio,"* as Mercedes passed him. But nobody stopped them. Heads turned as they wove between tables toward one where a blonde girl in a red-checked dress was sitting alone, sipping on something frothy through a straw. The table was one row back from the band, a prime seat.

"Do you mind if we join you?" Pagan asked in English, leaning down to speak in the girl's ear. She had a sweetly pretty heart-shaped face and thick honey-blond hair reined in with a headband. Pagan straightened and gave her a bright smile. "We're new here."

The girl's eyes widened. Recognition fluttered over her face. "Sure!" Her English was accented with an odd mix of German and Argentine Spanish. "Aren't you…?" She trailed off as her gaze came to rest on Mercedes.

"Thanks!" Pagan took a chair and Mercedes followed suit. "Everyone told me how nice people in Buenos Aires are, and now I believe it! What's your name?"

"Emma," the girl said. She was still eyeing Mercedes uneasily. "Those seats might be taken."

"I'm Pagan!" Pagan said, as if she hadn't said anything about the seats. "This is my friend Mercedes."

"I know who you are," Emma said, ignoring Mercedes. She blushed and looked away from Pagan shyly. "I saw *Beach Bound Beverly* twice."

"Oh, that old thing!" Pagan waved her hand in an "aw, shucks" gesture. Her eyes were sweeping the crowd, trying to find her target. "You're sweet. And what are you drinking?"

"It's a *submarino*," Emma said, stirring the ivory liquid in the tall glass in front of her. She picked up a square of chocolate that was sitting on the saucer and dropped it in. "The milk is hot, and you drop the chocolate in and let it melt."

"Mmm, I like the sound of that. Want one, M?" She

glanced over at Mercedes, whose eyes were fixed on some activity at the bar.

"Sure," Mercedes said, catching Pagan's eye, then slinging her gaze back over to a group of boys at the bar. "The waitress looks busy. Maybe you should order at the bar."

"Good idea." Pagan didn't see any boys with a mole on their right cheek at the bar. But it was crowded over there, and not every right cheek was visible from here. Mercedes must've seen something she hadn't. "Can I get you anything, Emma?"

"Oh, no!" Emma seemed startled by this offer, and blushed again. "Thanks."

Pagan turned away from her and mouthed, "Good luck," to Mercedes before heading for the bar.

Head up, shoulders back, dress glinting. It worked. The crowd parted before her. She was Charlton Heston. They were the Red Sea.

People were staring. She kept a Mona Lisa smile on her lips, searching for a boy with blond hair with a mole on his cheek.

A tall dark-haired young man at the bar with eyes like a turbulent twilight sky was gazing at her, one corner of his mouth deepening in admiration.

Devin. Before she could think, she beamed a smile straight from her soul at him. He brightened, grinning back at her for one blinding second, his pleasure at seeing her clear as the stars in his eyes.

She nearly forgot everything and ran across the room to him. It took every ounce of self-control to keep up her steady progress, to pretend she cared about anything else.

Then Devin's face shut down, the expression vanished. Pagan, too, had to bite her smile down fast, hoping no one important had seen. But she couldn't help it. Her heart was still hammering inside her so hard she worried everyone would hear it. Everyone would know.

Know what? What was there to know about her and Devin? Nothing. Right?

She was at the bar. Devin was to her left at the far end, maybe fifteen feet away, sipping a beer labeled Quilmes and avoiding her gaze. The slump in his shoulders, the tilt of his head away from her, told her not to greet him.

The bartender came bustling up to her the moment he was free, eyes big, lips tight with recognition. He dipped his head in a sort of bow and said in English, "Señorita Jones. An honor."

"You are too kind," she said. "Two of those *submarinos, por favor.*" Then added in excited English, "They look delicious!"

He smiled. "Coming right up," and he walked down the bar to her right to heat up the milk.

Pagan smiled at a girl gawking at her and scanned the crowd. She was here to find Dieter Von Albrecht, son of Rolf Von Albrecht. He needed to notice her. But so far it was all a choppy sea of slightly sunburned pale-skinned guys with gelled-back hair trying not to let their gazes linger too long on her cleavage or her legs.

Devin had said Dieter would be here. He hadn't said he himself would be here. He really should've warned her. The sight of him had nearly undone her.

She risked a casual glance in Devin's direction. She

couldn't help it. He must be here for a reason. He was looking right at her, and it sent goose bumps down her bare arms.

Devin's eyes flicked to her right, then back to her, then
back to the right.

She turned her head casually. In that area ranged a group
of boys that looked the right age. She couldn't see how many
were all talking to one another in loud German because three
broad backs were blocking her view.

"It's all set," a boy next to her was saying. Pagan was nearly
fluent in German, thanks to long afternoons spent with her
grandmother as a child, but she had to listen carefully here.
The words were familiar, but inflected differently. "While
all the mongrels are distracted at the race, we'll get to the
docks."

Calling people mongrels. She turned her nose-wrinkle of
distaste into a smile and sidled along the bar. She was moving toward the bartender and keeping her eyes on him, as
if fascinated by how he was heating up the milk for their
drinks. The boy next to her gave way, turning, and she was
able to see more of the group he was talking to.

"Tomorrow," another boy was saying in German, "we tell
the *judios* the time and place."

Judio. It took Pagan a moment to sort through the German
words in the sentence to realize that was Spanish for Jew.

"And we parlay with the Tacs to get more manpower," a
deeper voice spoke. The boys around her looked at one another, uneasy.

What were Tacs? She didn't recognize that word in any
language. Some gang term, probably.

"We don't need those snobs!" the boy next to her said too loudly.

Trust those who called people mongrels to get on their high horse about snobs. But she couldn't think that way. She had to be one of them, for a little while at least.

"If I say we need more manpower, then we need it," the deeper voice said in a tone that brooked no disagreement. "You don't like it, you're out."

"*Nein, nein*, Dieter," the boy said, shuffling his feet in apology, his voice rising in appeasement. "Whatever you say, of course. I'm sorry."

Dieter?

"Excuse me," she said in English as flat and American as she could make it. "Those *submarinos* looks so yummy!"

The group of boys, maybe ten of them, opened up enough for her to see they were circled around a tall young man with bright blond hair in a crew cut. He was handsome in a square-jawed, sturdy sort of way, with flat blue eyes, thick, stubborn lips and a dark mole highlighting his right cheek.

Pagan suppressed a smile of victory. Dieter Von Albrecht, son of the man she was hoping to identify. Perfect. From the looks of it he was surrounded by the gang Devin had told her about. So these were the kids who harassed Jews, defaced synagogues and the Israeli embassy with anti-Semitic slogans, and agitated against the current government in whatever way they could.

This jostling, ogling, slightly sweaty group of teenage boys in their bowling shirts and slicked-back Elvis hair looked like any other group of boys you might see at the malt shop or soda parlor in America. Except for the edgy energy of their movements, and the tall blond boy at their center.

Dieter overlooked them all with a wary, watchful eye, listening, judiciously granting one lucky boy or another his attention. From the way the other boys competed for it, it was clear Dieter was the leader. Unlike the others he exuded an impatient confidence that wasn't about posturing or masking insecurity. Here was a boy who knew he was right.

She turned to face him, and put her elbows on the bar behind her, leaning back and smiling, a pose guaranteed to get any man to eyeball your décolletage. But Dieter's expression didn't change as his gaze slid over her. The other boys were easier to read. They liked the view.

"Glad to see this place has a good band," she said, directing her words at Dieter. "But I heard sometimes there's dancing. Is that right?"

He gave her a condescending smile and replied in excellent English, "Real men don't dance."

"We've got better things to do," another boy chimed in. He and a couple of others had obviously recognized her and were elbowing one another, bumping around the way restless teenage boys do when they meet someone famous who happens to be a pretty girl. It had happened to Pagan a lot in her life, and it was normally kind of cute. Here it all had a fierce edge to it that raised the hair on the back of her neck.

"Oh, yeah?" Pagan raised an eyebrow challengingly, again right at Dieter. "Like what?"

"We're going to…" began the other boy.

"You brought in that *indio* girl," Dieter said, his mouth lingering on the word *indio*. He cast a glance around and the other boys snapped to attention. "I don't care what movies you starred in if you're hanging out with trash like that."

So he knew who she was, and he didn't care. This was not going the way she and Devin had hoped. She opened her mouth to reply, to lie and say Mercedes was nothing but a servant, but Dieter's gaze wasn't on Pagan anymore. It was burning a path across the café, aimed right at Mercedes.

Damn it, he was supposed to be interested in Pagan, to be mesmerized by her fame and her pretty face. Not that Pagan gave a fig for any of that, but if he liked her enough he might invite her over to the house where his father was holed up. All she needed was to set one foot in that house, somehow. Dieter Von Albrecht was her way in. But he wasn't playing along.

"I just…" Pagan reached out a placating hand and touched his arm.

Touching young men usually got their attention. But Dieter walked away without looking at her, heading for the table where Mercedes was seated, an empty chair between her and the uneasy Emma.

The group of young men by the bar followed Dieter like sweaty ducklings, weaving between the tables. Such a large group moving with determination turned heads, and brought some to their feet. Pagan ran after, trying to catch up to Dieter, but he had stopped beside Mercedes already.

"What are you doing here?" Dieter said, towering over Mercedes. He spoke in Spanish, inflected with the Argentinean lilt.

Mercedes did not appear surprised, shaken or curious at his hostile, unprovoked question. She swung up to stand in front of him, her hands loose in front of her, and met his gaze without hesitation.

"We haven't been introduced," she said in English.

Dieter's eyes flicked up and down her body, his lips curled back in a predatory smile. "I know your dirty kind," he said, also in English. "And I don't allow them to sit next to my sister."

So Emma was Emma Von Albrecht, Dieter's younger sister. Devin hadn't said anything about her being here, too. Maybe he hadn't known. Pagan was still twenty feet away from the scene. The press of bodies between her and her friend was impeding progress. Not that there was much she could do against Dieter and ten other boys if she got there.

"Dieter, she didn't know," Emma was saying. "It's okay…"

"Shut up," Dieter said casually. His eyes were still fixed on Mercedes. "How are you going to make it up to me, *negra*?"

Dear God, was he somehow interested in Mercedes? That's what it looked like. But how could that be when he insulted her so?

Mercedes didn't bother surveying the young men ranged around her. She looked right into Dieter's eyes and her face went blank and cold.

That same look had terrified Pagan the first time she'd seen it. It was a look that made armed adults clear their throats and change the subject. It had intimidated rival gang members into giving up their drugs and their money and sent hardened reform-school girls scurrying. Pagan had tried practicing that look herself when she was alone, in case she ever needed it.

Now Mercedes became so still, so ready, like a cobra

about to strike, that the boys beside Dieter drew back. They threw questioning glances at their leader, whose own version of the look was fading under Mercedes's glacial stare. Dieter Von Albrecht wasn't used to people with more confidence than him.

The café had gone mostly quiet. Cigarettes burned, disregarded, between fingers as people stared, waiting.

Only Pagan continued to winnow her way toward her friend. Almost there.

Dieter didn't break eye contact, but he shifted his weight uneasily, sticking his chin out, and tapped the back of a chair with his fingers.

Pagan slowed, relaxing. If what Mercedes had taught her was right, Dieter wasn't going to hit Mercedes, at least not right now. He was trying to figure out how to back down without looking like a chump.

"Come on, Emma," he said, and held a hand out to his sister.

Emma exhaled, in relief or exasperation, and stood up. "Fine," she said, and stomped off to the bar without taking her brother's hand.

That was it. Surrender without the white flag. The other boys meandered away from the table. Dieter grabbed the back of the chair Mercedes had been sitting in and lifted it a few inches to slam it hard on the floor.

Mercedes didn't blink.

"Stay away from my sister," he said, and stalked back to the bar.

Pagan got there as Mercedes slid back into her chair, face

impassive. "Cripes," Pagan said, keeping her voice low. "Are you okay?"

"Is every evening out with you this much fun?" Mercedes asked with unusual sarcasm.

"What if he'd hit you?" Pagan asked. "You swore off violence, but no one would blame you if you smacked him."

Mercedes shook her head. "I knew as soon as he saw I wasn't scared of him that he'd fold like a card table."

"So you don't think he's dangerous?"

"Oh, no, he's dangerous." Her matter-of-fact tone made the words all the more unsettling. "And he's angry now. We should get out of here. And you should stay away from him."

"Well, don't worry. He couldn't care less about me. So much for Devin's grand plan. I think Dieter actually liked you, except maybe *like* isn't exactly the right word for it."

"He wants what he hates." Mercedes's nose wrinkled. "It's disgusting."

"Do you mind if we stay a little longer?" Pagan looked over toward the bar and found Devin's dark head, exactly where it had been before. "The bartender just finished our *submarinos*."

"And Devin's here." Mercedes cracked a smile. "I saw. Don't worry. No one's going to bother me now."

Pagan patted her arm. "Be right back."

Devin was paying for the *submarinos* as she walked over. "My treat for two brave ladies," he said in the flirtatious tone of a man buying drinks for women he didn't know. "My name's Devin."

"Pagan," she said, and they shook hands, hanging on to each other for a second longer than strangers would. It was like some weird game. "We're lucky my friend Mercedes knows how to handle herself."

"She sure does." Devin picked up one of the *submarinos*. "Let me take this to her."

His eyes shot to the empty bar stool behind her and back to her face. He was trying to tell her something. "Wait for me here, if you don't mind," he added in a quieter tone.

She looked at the empty bar stool again and realized that seated next to it was Emma Von Albrecht, all alone again while her brother and his crew talked loudly at the other end of the bar.

Pagan leaned in to Devin and said quietly, "Plan B?"

"And C," he said, and he headed over toward Mercedes.

Wrapping her hand around the hot glass of the *submarino*, Pagan settled onto the bar stool and plopped a chunk of chocolate into the milk.

"Do I stir?" she asked Emma, who had glanced shyly over at her as she settled in.

"You can," Emma said. "Sometimes I like to put my straw up against the chocolate at the bottom and drink it. It's more chocolate than milk at first that way."

"Let's try it." Pagan dropped another square of chocolate into the steaming milk, followed it with her straw, leaned in and drew on it. "Mmm!" Her eyes got wide. "Scrumptious! You're a genius."

Emma laughed, blushing, and ducked her head, her eyes sparkling, almost like she was flirting.

Maybe she was.

Pagan's heart gave an off-beat thump. Flirting with a girl had never occurred to her. There was no reason why it should feel weirder than flirting with a man. But it did. So much of flirting was deception and withholding. She was used to being herself with girls.

But maybe flirting with a girl involved being yourself? Or maybe there was some secret code or something... *Oh, don't be silly*, she told herself. *If you can try to beguile a boy like Dieter, you can sure as hell give the much nicer Emma a smile.*

Still at sea, Pagan gave Emma that smile. "It's strange being alone in a foreign city," she said. "It's easier to meet people, but when you go back 'home' it's still a hotel room, and you're all alone in it, you know?"

"Are you alone?" Emma glanced back at Mercedes, who was chatting with Devin over at her table. "Isn't that your friend?"

"Just a girl I met on set." Pagan internally apologized to her friendship with Mercedes as she gave a dismissive little wave of her hand. "She's okay, but we really don't have anything in common."

"Does that mean you're shooting a movie here in BA?" Emma asked, eyes wide. "Who else is in it?"

"Nobody big." Pagan made a note. "BA" must be how locals referred to Buenos Aires. "I have to shoot a scene with a blockhead named Tony Perry tomorrow, and I hate him more than stiletto heels that are one size too small. I was hoping to make friends I could go out with and do fun things with, you know? Like this, here, now."

Emma gave her another shy smile that made Pagan flush a little with shame. Why was she feeling like more of a jerk for cozying up to this girl than she ever would with a guy?

"I'm having fun now, too," Emma said. "Hey, I got some

new 45s yesterday—the Marvelettes and that new Dion song. Would you like to come over to my house tomorrow after school, maybe, and listen?" Then, as if overcome at her own temerity, she shrank back and added, "You're probably busy at rehearsal or something. That's okay. Never mind."

"No, no, I'd love to come over!" Pagan's heart was singing. To hell with Dieter Von Albrecht and his ugly soul. With a little help from Devin and the downtrodden Emma, a way into the house had been found. "I have my first day on set tomorrow, but I could come over by, say, six o'clock. Would that work?"

Emma sat up straight, eyes bright, her mouth falling slightly open in such surprise and delight that Pagan was more ashamed. "Six o'clock is perfect! We live on Vicente Lopez, near Montevideo. Here…" She turned to the bartender. "Have you got a pen?"

Pagan didn't really need the address. Devin would know it. But she patiently sipped her delicious hot chocolate as Emma scribbled it down. In the meantime, the band had left the stage and another had taken its place. This one had eight members, but instead of guitars and drums, these men had a violin, a viola, a piano, a double bass and three small concertinas called bandoneóns, which they took, groaning, out of their cases.

The crowd had also grown larger, and more diverse. Among all the light-haired people with paler skin were scattered now more people with hair and skin of darker tones. Dieter's group had tightened into a defensive circle. They were talking in lower tones, glancing around nervously.

Emma lifted her head at the sound and glanced over at her

brother's group. "Uh-oh. An *orquesta tipica*. Tango music. Dieter's not going to be happy."

"Terrible dancer?" Pagan couldn't help a smirk. "He won't mind me coming over tomorrow, will he?"

"Oh, he won't care," Emma said, and hesitated. "You're not bringing your friend, though, right? Sorry."

"Her? No." Pagan sucked down the last of her *submarino* with a noisy burble. "I don't want any trouble."

"Sorry," Emma said again. Pagan had the feeling she was often apologizing for her brother. "Dieter's not into making friends outside his usual circle."

"But his sister is already an expert diplomat," Pagan said, taking the address on the cocktail napkin from her with a smile. "Don't worry about it, and thanks. I'm really looking forward to hanging out tomorrow."

"Me, too." Emma was blushing again. Pagan fought another twinge of sympathy for her.

The band had launched into an insistent, fleet, old-fashioned tango, and some of the patrons were pushing the tables back from the bandstand to clear a dance floor. Two couples already had their cheeks pressed together, shoulders close, hips angled slightly away from each other so that their feet could stalk and kick and intertwine. They looked so much more comfortable together than Pagan had been with Tony Perry. The man was leading, but they looked like they were moving as one.

A slim male form sliced through the press of bodies, heading toward the back of the café. Devin paused and glanced over his shoulder, and their eyes met. He tilted his head toward the door to the kitchen and kept going.

"I need the little girls' room," Pagan said to Emma. "But see you tomorrow!"

"Goody!" said Emma, sounding like an eager kid. It was sweet.

Too bad that she, Pagan, was evil.

She wound past the dancers and around the bandstand. She was on her way to see Devin, and with every step toward him, her senses heightened. She became acutely aware of how the heavy beaded silk of her dress brushed against her thighs. Cigarette smoke burned the back of her chocolate-milk-coated throat. The concertinas groaned like lovers entwined as the dancers' bodies coiled and twisted on the dance floor.

She placed one hand on the dark wood of the swinging door to the kitchen and pushed it open slowly, casting a glance back. Had anyone seen?

The violins slashed through a haze of pizzicato notes as she crossed the threshold. They merged with the crash of plates being thrown in a sink. A sweating man in an apron behind a screen of hanging pots yelled at another in Spanish to hurry, hurry!

A hand slipped into hers, and snaked her sideways, like the opening steps of a tango. She knew his touch, and followed without hesitation into a tiny alcove, spinning so that her back was to the towering wall of wooden barrels, facing Devin, her fingers still tangled with his.

"How'd it go?" he said, voice low.

His scent enveloped her: clean cotton and leather. She looked up into those restless blue eyes, now only two feet away, and had to lean against the casks behind her to stay steady.

"Victory," she whispered, so that he leaned in closer. "Six o'clock tomorrow night at the Von Albrecht house."

His gaze lowered to her lips as she spoke, then traveled down her neck. She rested her free hand on his chest for a bare second before lifting it to adjust his collar. Her fingertips brushed his collarbone.

The collar wasn't crooked. But he didn't know that.

"Well done." He pulled his stare back up to her face, one corner of his mouth turning down. She lifted her right hand up and slid her free hand smoothly onto his shoulder. The warmth of his body was tantalizingly close. The violins were reaching a furious crescendo outside.

"Do Scots tango?" she asked.

"Tangle?" he said back.

She gasped as he twisted his torso slightly and thrust his knee behind her, brushing his leg against the backs of her thighs. He lifted her off the floor for a heady second, seated on top of his thigh.

He set her down lightly and withdrew to a self-contained space three feet away.

"Sentada," she said breathlessly. That was the name of the tango lift. "And *soltada*." That was the break away. She wished he'd take her in that closed embrace again, but the violins and concertinas outside had come to the end of the song. "Maybe I don't dislike the tango as much as I thought."

"A good leader follows his partner," he said. "The great paradox of the tango. I'm sorry about Dieter harassing Mercedes. He's quite the scaffbag."

She smiled. "I do love the Scottish sweet talk. Fortunately, Mercedes can handle herself, and, lucky us, Emma's got a crush on me instead."

"Someone was bound to fall for you." He said it casually, but then his eyes stopped, as if snared, on her lips. A small, knowing smile played around his mouth.

She slung him a look from under her eyelids. "Someone?"

The affection in his expression froze, replaced with a more distant, professional smile. "That's why we recruited a movie star."

Stung, she glared at him. "What's Scottish for jackass?"

He squinted with amusement, which only irritated her more. "We've so many words for that, *mo gràdh*, it could take all night to name them. So we'd best be getting you home instead."

She frowned. *"Mo gràdh?"* She couldn't quite pronounce it with the same lilt.

"It doesn't mean jackass," he said, and swept his hand toward the swinging door back out to the café.

She passed him, but stopped with one hand on the door. "Mercedes didn't see anyone following us here," she said. "But we can't be sure. We're going to walk over a block and catch a cab, which should give us a chance to find out."

"Don't worry about that," he said. "I'm dealing with it. Go home and get a good night's sleep."

Which sounded suspiciously like, *Don't you worry your pretty head about it*, to Pagan. "It's me they're following, not you."

He held up a hand, as if to acknowledge the truth of her statement. "It's that you're still jet-lagged and you've a big scene to shoot in the morning," he said. "If we ask too much of you your cover could be blown."

Which was a little less patronizing but didn't assuage her. No point in discussing it with him further, apparently. She'd have to take things into her own hands, as usual. "How do I reach you after I visit Von Albrecht's house tomorrow?"

"I'll be in touch," he said, and smiled.

"Can't wait." She stalked out.

A sighing violin scraped out a screech, and the music died. Over a general hubbub, the loudest voices were shouting at the far end of the bar. No one was dancing anymore. Pagan craned her neck, burrowing through the jostling press of bodies, to finally see Dieter Von Albrecht, his gang backing him up like a phalanx of troops, shouting right into the face of a young man holding a bandoneón. Behind him, a different group of young men was gathering. They tended to have darker skin and hair in a variety of tones.

All around Pagan, the throng was dividing up into those who looked more like Dieter and those who more closely resembled the members of the *orquestra tipica*.

"Apologize!" Dieter shouted in Spanish, thrusting an empty glass into the musician's face. The front of Dieter's striped shirt was damp, and the other man's concertina was dripping. Pagan could smell the spilled beer from twenty feet away.

"You bumped into me—it's your own fault," the musician said, thrusting a finger into Dieter's chest. "You looking to start something?"

Dieter threw the empty tumbler to the floor. It shattered, littering the floor with glass. "What if I am?"

Dieter's gang surged forward a few inches, like a school of angry fish. They outnumbered the group behind the musician at more than two to one.

"Hey, now!" the bartender said from behind the bar. "Everyone remain calm."

"This is our place," Dieter was saying to the musician. "Take your degenerate trash somewhere else."

"You don't own this café!" the concertina player shouted at him. The crowd behind him muttered approval as the crowd behind Dieter roared in protest.

Mercedes had been right about Dieter being dangerous. His encounter with her had left him full of anger. He was a time bomb. They should have left when M said so.

Pagan headed for their table. Best to get the hell out of here now. Where had Emma gone? Pagan saw no sign of Dieter's sister, but Mercedes was ready with Pagan's coat and purse.

Pagan grabbed them, throwing the coat over her shimmering dress. "Let's get out of here!" More than a few people were already exiting, fast. By the bar, most of the crowd had gathered around Dieter, while a small but determined group around the musicians faced them down.

The bartender had the phone receiver to his ear, probably calling the cops. Any second now someone would punch someone else and the whole place would erupt. Pagan headed for the door, but Mercedes didn't. She was staring as the groups jostled and shoved at each other.

"What?" Pagan halted in her tracks.

"Someone's got to stop him," she said. "A lot of people could get hurt."

Pagan looked at Dieter, jabbing his meaty index finger into

the bandoneón player's chest. Spit flecked from his mouth as he shouted. He really wanted a fight, and so did his gang.

And Mercedes—Pagan had never seen her look so torn.

"I'll help," Pagan said. "If I can."

The anger in Mercedes's face eased. She shot Pagan a look and they were united. Pagan put her purse down.

"After I distract Dieter," Mercedes said. "You get the other guys out of here."

Pagan had no idea how she was going to do that, but she nodded. "Be careful."

Mercedes strode right toward Dieter and the concertina player, inserting herself between them in one fluid move.

Pagan took two steps forward and made herself stop, hand to her throat. From farther down the bar, Devin was watching. She caught his worried gaze, and he tilted his head toward the kitchen door. It was only a few feet behind the bandoneón player and his crew. A possible route out.

Dieter was blinking down at Mercedes as she stood not two feet from him, her arms crossed. As Dieter hesitated, the press of people behind him suspended their forward push. Behind Mercedes, the band players were exchanging puzzled glances. The momentum of their anger was being diverted.

"Get out of the way," Dieter said. His tone was dismissive, but confused.

Mercedes said nothing, only lifted both her eyebrows deliberately and tilted her head. The whole effect was one of mild amusement and adamantine resolve. In the jostling, testosterone-fueled crowd, she was a short, still point, the center around which they all revolved.

"What…?" the bandoneón player behind Mercedes started to say.

"What do you want?" Dieter asked Mercedes, at the same time and in the same vein.

Good. Mercedes had both sides off balance.

There were only eight band members, pressed in on all sides except the very back by Dieter's larger crowd. Pagan edged up to the man nearest the back, an older man with a bristling mustache holding his double bass beside him like a dance partner, and took his other hand.

He whipped his hand away and turned, surprised and defensive. She gave him a flirtatious smile and said in Spanish, "My friend over there thinks you should go with him."

Mustache Man frowned at her, following her subtle point to the kitchen door. Devin stood there, holding it slightly open, and gave him a half bow.

The frown deepened. "I can't leave my…"

"Your friends will follow," Pagan said, keeping her voice low, and nodded toward the man beside him, who had his viola in his arms like a baby. "Take him now. I'll get the rest. Save your instruments."

The bass player nudged the viola player and showed him the kitchen door. The viola player gave him an "are you crazy?" look.

Meanwhile, Mercedes had the full attention of Dieter and his crowd. As Pagan watched, the German gang members pressing on either side of the musicians pulled back to get a better look at their leader angrily questioning this strangely confident young woman.

As the press of angry men around them withdrew, the

musicians glanced around, reassessing. Pagan tugged on the piano player's arm and flashed him a conspiratorial grin. "The kitchen is open."

The piano player gave several of his fellow band members a questioning look, and in reply the bass player lifted his instrument off the ground and quietly backed up toward the kitchen door. The viola player followed suit as the piano man tapped one of the other men on the shoulder.

Up at the center of things, Mercedes had taken two steps to her right, pulling the attention of Dieter and his boys that way. Dieter was leaning down, right in her face, his eyes devouring her smooth neck, her bare arms, as he spoke. "Your kind always sticks together. You don't know these men, but here you are, risking your life for them?"

Mercedes's lips twitched in amusement. She still hadn't spoken. "Are you laughing at me?" Dieter roared.

In reply, Mercedes turned her shoulder to Dieter and took two more steps away from him and to the right, leading him away from the musicians, who, one by one, were vanishing into the kitchen. She walked casually but solidly, as if the mass of dumbfounded young men was bound to give way before her.

And they did.

Dieter didn't know what to do with her. *"Say something!"*

Mercedes paused, and, taking her time, gave him the once-over, her eyes cold, clinical. "This grows dull," she said in English. "I've got bigger cats to chase."

She slipped between two of Dieter's guys, and was swallowed in the crowd.

"Come on!" Devin said to Pagan. The last of the musi-cians had vanished into the kitchen. "She'll be fine."

As Dieter craned his neck and tried to follow Mercedes, Pagan darted through the door and into the kitchen once more. Devin had her by the elbow, and they hustled past several men in aprons, who gave them a nod, and out a nar-row door to an alley and the cool evening air.

The musicians went one way, merging into the dark, and Devin steered Pagan the other way, back toward the front of the café.

Mercedes was waiting for them in a dark niche. Just around the corner, by the front door, Dieter was yelling at his friends. Something about *indios* and invasion and revenge.

Pagan went right to Mercedes's side. "You were amazing."

Mercedes shrank into her. She was trembling. "Get me out of here," she said. "Before I kill him."

PLANEO

Pivot, glide. May occur when the man stops the woman in midstride.

Men and women tangoed in tight circles through the golden squares of light shining through the windows of the Plaza Dorrego Café, while others leaned forward over tiny tables, holding hands. Trails of cigarette smoke wafted up through the lamplight to evanesce in the faint glow of the waxing crescent moon.

Pagan hustled Mercedes quickly over the red-brown bricks of the wide-open plaza toward the taxis waiting on the other side. The brisk block-long walk had begun to alleviate Mercedes's shivering rage.

"How did you know what to do?" Pagan asked Mercedes. "Somehow you did exactly the right thing."

"It's like a dance, fighting," Mercedes said. "You have to get to know your partner. I knew him the moment I saw him, but he had no idea what to make of me."

"Those musicians would've gotten a bad beating if you hadn't stepped in," Pagan said. "That was kind of heroic."

Mercedes looked over at the dancing couples moving sinuously to the music, at the men and women laughing together over drinks. "No, it was necessary," she said.

Pagan knew exactly what she meant.

She glanced over her shoulder. A number of people were leaving the café at the same time, and the plaza itself had more than one café open into the wee hours. But she saw no one in particular tailing them. Devin had followed them out of the café for half a block before he cast them one last glance and got into a black car with a rounded white top.

But that didn't mean the man in gray wasn't following her tonight.

Mercedes let herself into the backseat of a cab and said, "Alvear Palace Hotel," as Pagan got in and slammed the door.

"Can we go south a few blocks first, though?" Pagan asked. Off Mercedes's weary look, she added in a low voice, "I want to see if anyone's following me. It won't take long."

Mercedes took a deep breath. "Okay." She leaned forward and said in Spanish, "A brief tour of La Boca, please. Perhaps some of the most colorful buildings?"

The driver, a lanky older man with a floppy mustache and a drowsy air, cast a puzzled glance at her via the rearview mirror. "At night?"

Pagan threw some pesos onto the seat next to him. "Yes, please. And I might ask you to suddenly speed up, or turn, or stop. Is that all right?"

The man's drooping eyelids flew open at the money. He scooped up the pesos with one hand and stuffed them in his pockets. "Of course, *señoritas*. Whatever you want." He turned left, then right down a narrow street, and they rattled down tiny streets between darkened houses for a few blocks. Pagan kept glancing behind them.

A pair of headlights appeared, thirty yards back. They passed a park on their right. Their own headlights splashed up against the buildings, revealing bright walls of banana yellow, leafy green, royal purple.

"Turn left when you can, please," Pagan said.

The driver shrugged. *"Sí, senorita."* He turned left down a narrower street.

"You're squeezing too hard," Mercedes said in a low tone.

Pagan realized she'd grabbed her friend by the arm in a death grip. "Sorry," she said, letting go.

The headlights behind them reappeared.

Pagan squinted. "Is that car black with a white roof?"

Mercedes swiveled around to look. "No. It's blue."

Pagan shot her a look. "It's not Devin, then." To the driver: "Turn left again. Let's go back north."

"Sure," he said, glancing nervously in his rearview mirror, and slowed down to turn left into a street that was little more than an alley.

By the time they'd traveled two blocks, the same headlights were behind them again. For Pagan that confirmed it—they were still being followed.

She rested her chin on the back of the seat, staring out the back window, studying the car. "Who is it? And why?"

"Do you think it's the man in gray?" asked Mercedes.

Pagan shrugged. "And if so, who is he? I need to see his face, so I'll recognize him again if you're not around." She turned to the driver. "Speed up a bit—let's get closer to the hotel first."

"How are you going to see his face?" Mercedes asked as the cab picked up speed. "With the car headlights shining in our eyes, he's nothing but a silhouette."

"I'll have to get another angle on him." Leaning over the front seat, Pagan said to the driver, "Let me know when we're maybe seven or eight blocks from the hotel, please."

"You're going to hop out once we're close to the hotel?" Mercedes asked.

Pagan grinned at her, skin prickling with excitement. "Exactly."

"You still might not get a good look at him."

"Or I might," Pagan said.

It was after midnight. The broader avenues were dotted with occasional taxis picking up late-night revelers, but the smaller streets were deserted. That made it easy to tell when their shadow caught up with them again, which he did within a few seconds.

"We're about eight blocks from the hotel now, *señorita*," the cab driver said. "Maybe seven."

"Great. After I finish speaking, I want you to turn right and stop quickly after the turn. I'll get out, and then you gun it and keep going, as if I'd never left the car. Take Mercedes to the hotel." She turned to Mercedes. "I'll meet you there."

Mercedes was regarding her with a bemused look. "You're going to walk seven blocks to the hotel—in those shoes?"

"It'll be more like five blocks by the time we turn."

"Lista, señorita?" the driver said, motioning toward an upcoming intersection.

"Ready," Pagan said, feet primed underneath her, fingers clutching the door handle.

The driver had gotten into the spirit of the evening. He didn't angle the taxi as if it was going to turn, but waited until the last possible minute before yanking the wheel over hard without braking. Pagan and Mercedes slid across the backseat from the force of it, then jerked forward as he turned the corner and slammed on the brakes.

Dislodged from her ready position, Pagan scrambled out of the cab much less gracefully than she'd planned, turned her ankle and hobbled across the sidewalk to a dark doorway, panting.

She had time to see Mercedes shut the door and wave to her before the taxi took off again, tires squealing like sneakers on a clean floor.

Pagan held her breath and waited, willing the blue car to zip around the corner and hover long enough in a slant of dim streetlight so she could see the man inside.

The waiting went on, the seconds dragging out. Had they somehow lost him? Or had time slowed down because she was waiting?

She heard the rumble of a car's engine before she saw it. The sound confused her, then she saw the submarine shape of the vehicle outlined against the glowing windows across the street.

He'd turned the headlights off.

She'd been sure the car was following her, but this confirmation sent goose bumps down her arms. He wanted to remain hidden and had suspected something when the taxi turned so suddenly, so he'd slowed down and turned off his lights, coasting down the street.

Was he scanning the street? Had he spotted her? What did he *want*?

The car floated down the street. Without the lights from the dashboard, she could get no sense of his coloring or any real detail of his face or clothing. Still, as the car came even with her, the cut of his profile was delineated before her like a cameo. A high forehead, long nose, firm mouth, strong chin.

A proud profile.

A familiar face.

She knew him. Somehow. She'd seen him before. But where?

Pagan almost cried out in frustration as his car kept going. If she had a few more moments more to stare at him, maybe she'd figure out who he was. But she didn't have those moments. As it turned left, the blue car accelerated, and the strangely memorable but nameless profile vanished from sight.

She didn't know how long she stood there, staring after him before the breeze made her shiver. She needed to get back to the hotel before Mercedes started worrying. She was so deep in thought that she barely noticed how her ankle smarted as she limped down the dark, deserted sidewalk. She was riffling through her memory, going through every person she'd seen recently, trying to place that face.

She turned left, pretty sure that was the correct direction, and took no note of the deserted courtyard to her left until a tall, slender form stepped out of it and said, "I told you I had this situation covered."

Pagan leaped nearly three feet in the air and came down

with her heart in her throat. "Damn you!" she said. "How the hell did you find me?"

It was Devin Black, of course, looking far too calm and debonair to be hanging out in the shadows of Buenos Aires after midnight.

"But no," Devin continued as if she hadn't cursed him. "You had to pull an amateur's stunt to see who was following you. What if he'd spotted you?"

"But he didn't," Pagan said, and kept walking doggedly toward the hotel, trying not to let him see her limp. "Instead, I saw him."

Devin glided over to walk by her side, on the outside of the sidewalk, like a gentleman. "So you must also have noticed the type of car he was driving."

Pagan thought hard. "Blue, a sedan. No one else inside it. Makes and models aren't my specialty."

"And the license plate?"

She tried not to glower at him and said nothing.

"No? Then you must've noticed it was a rental car, registered to a local business not far off the Avenida de Mayo."

"What I noticed," she said, "is that he looked familiar."

That jolted Devin out of his smug "I'm a better spy than you" lecture. He took her by the elbow and pulled her into a tiny shadowed alley, scaring off a couple of warring cats. There was no one else in sight.

"Who was it?" His dark eyes glittered in the faint light from the street.

She shook her head. "I can't put a name to the face. All I saw was the profile, but I know him. From somewhere, not

that long ago. It'll come to me. If I hadn't pulled my amateur stunt, we never would've known that."

Her caustic tone slid right off him as he pondered what
she'd said. "Where could you possibly know him from? Did
you spot him following you back in Los Angeles, perhaps?"

She hadn't actually seen the face of anyone following her
in Los Angeles. "There was that Plymouth that might have
been following me and Thomas after the party at Frank's,"
she said. "But I couldn't see who was in it. We thought it
might've been you."

"Not me," he said, dead serious. "Did they follow you all
the way home?"

"Almost. To Laurel Canyon, but not up my street from
there," she said. "When we got home, Mercedes said someone had been lurking in our backyard, keeping an eye on
the house."

"So it's possible the same person or people have been following you since that night. Or even earlier."

His words sent a chill through her. "So it wasn't one of
your men?"

He shook his head. "I'll have to look into it. Now." His
gaze traveled down her body, stopping at her ankle. "How
badly does it hurt?"

"Does what hurt?" she asked, not wanting to admit she'd
messed up her exit from the cab. "I'm fine."

"You're an excellent liar," he said, hunkering down in
front of her, and put one warm firm hand on her calf, lifting her foot from the ground. "But you're limping."

His fingers probed the bones above her heel. "Ow!" she

said when he hit a tender spot. "It'll be fine if you don't make it worse."

"A sprain," he said, standing up. "Not a bad one, but still a sprain. And you have a dance scene to shoot tomorrow."

"I could outdance Tony Perry with both legs broken," Pagan said. "Don't worry about it."

"We need you to keep shooting the movie to maintain your cover story," he said. "So we can't risk further injury." And before she could stop him, he swept her up in his arms.

"What…?" She automatically put both arms around his neck. The strong arms firmly supporting her beneath her shoulders and knees brought back the physical memory of the only other time he'd held her like this, before she fainted at the end of her adventure in East Berlin.

Which automatically led to the memory of waking up next to him, fully dressed, in bed. Her body temperature rose a few degrees. "I'm okay, really."

"I'd like to keep you that way," he said. Their faces were very close. His warm strength enveloped her and the world spun.

She put her head on his shoulder, closing her eyes to stop the vertigo. "I'm sorry. Just dizzy." She couldn't tell him that it was his fault for making her that way.

His arms tightened around her, pressing her closer. She could feel the slightly sped-up beat of his heart, smell his smooth clean skin. "It's been a long day for you. And you've done so well," he said.

"Have I?" She lifted her head to find his mouth inches from hers.

His lips parted. She slid one hand up the back of his strong neck, wanting to bury her fingers in his hair, unable to think of anything but pressing her mouth to his, of his hands moving over her.

As if snapping out of a dream, he pulled his head back and stepped out of the alley still carrying her, moving down the street. "My car's very close," he said. "I'll drive you the rest of the way."

She settled her head on his shoulder again, pressing her forehead into his neck so she could breathe him in. "My hero."

A laugh rumbled out of his chest. "Mercedes was the hero tonight."

Pagan popped her head up, thinking. "Do you know any astronomers here in BA?"

They had reached his car, but he stood there holding her for a moment longer, giving her a puzzled look. "I could make some calls," he said.

Pagan kicked her feet in their sparkling heels in the air, bouncing in his arms a bit from the excitement of her idea. "Mercedes got As on her latest high school exams, and an A-plus in astronomy. I think it really interests her. I'm trying to convince her to go to college, so how great would it be if she could look through one of those really big telescopes while she's here? Or talk to a real scientist? She said something about the stars looking different in the southern hemisphere."

Devin eyed her fluttering feet, a little smile on his face. "They do. And I might be able to arrange something. Putting you down now."

As he lowered her carefully to the sidewalk, she made a

show of standing only on her good leg, the other bent at the knee, shoe in the air behind her like a dance move. He still had his arm around her shoulders. And she kept her arms around his neck.

She leaned against him, her chest against his, her hip bone digging into his upper thigh. "Nobody would know if we tangoed right here for a moment."

His hand tightened on her shoulder. "Pagan…" he said warningly.

"It's only a dance, silly," she said. "Didn't you see? Back at the café they did it like this." And she slid her powdered cheek along his, her lips near his ear. She resisted the urge to sink her teeth into his earlobe.

His chest rose as he inhaled slowly. His warm breath tickled her own ear as he exhaled. Carefully, he placed his free hand on the bare skin of her neck. His thumb stroked the line of her jaw.

"If you only knew how much I wanted to," he said.

Her bones were made of liquid. The boundaries between her body and his were disappearing. Any second now she would melt into him.

"But we can't." He released her, and she had to put her bad foot down or she would have fallen. His dark hair was mussed from her hands, black locks falling over his eyes, which glittered at her with a look so intense it might scald her. "I'm sorry."

"You care about me," she said. "I know you do."

The fervor in his eyes altered. For the barest moment he looked much younger, like the boy he was, a boy who had lost something that meant everything to him.

"My feelings don't matter," he said.

Tears pricked at her eyes, but she refused to let herself cry. "They matter to me," she said.

"They're testing me," he said. "They're probably watching me, too. I can't…" He broke off and leaned down to open the passenger's side door of the car for her. "This assignment is important to me, too. I don't want to fail them, or take advantage of you."

"Take advantage!" She took a limping step toward him. He automatically put out a hand to steady her, and she grabbed it. "I'm the one trying to take advantage of *you*."

His brows came together in an unhappy frown. "No, you don't understand. You're younger. You've been hurt. I could…" He ducked his head, stopping himself. When he continued, his voice was cooler, sterner. "I'm your boss. Now please get in the car."

His touch was impersonal as he helped her in, and he slammed her door a little harder than was necessary.

He drove the few remaining blocks to the hotel in silence. Pagan stared straight ahead, in turmoil. As he pulled over to the curb, she said, "I'm sorry."

He put the car into neutral. "It's not your fault. I shouldn't mislead you."

"No," she said. "You're worried about your job and you want to do what's right. You always try to do the right thing. It's one of the reasons I love you. Like you!" She sucked in air. *What had she said?* "I mean…"

Devin's eyes looked hollow, as if the wind had been knocked out of him. He leaned toward her. "Pagan…"

She refused to look at him. "Good night!" She hauled open her own door and sprinted into the hotel as fast as her ankle allowed.

CHAPTER TEN

DISOCIAR

Disassociation. A position in which there is disassociation between torso and hips.

The moment Mercedes glimpsed Pagan's face, she stopped yawning and said, "What's wrong?"

Pagan threw her coat into the closet. "Nothing. It's late. Go to bed." And she stomped into her room and shut the door. She stood there, breathing hard, staring at her empty bed with its gold brocade cover and its huge pile of useless pillows. She wanted something now, more than she wanted to take back what she'd accidentally said to Devin. The need drove every beat of her heart.

She opened her bedroom door again gently. Mercedes was still standing there, arms crossed, eyebrows raised.

"I'm sorry." Pagan took a deep breath. It was still hard to say the words to her best friend in the world. "I really want a drink."

Mercedes dropped her hands and walked over to the sideboard, where she clinked ice into a glass and splashed water into it. "Rough night," she said, handing Pagan the glass.

"For all of us." Pagan gulped it all down. Not as satisfying as a vodka martini. Nothing was. But it was a ritual she

and M had now. She wanted a drink? Then have a drink.
Of anything except alcohol.

"I saw the profile of the man following us, and I feel like
I know him, but I can't remember how." She set the glass
down. Her throat hurt. "And then I ran into Devin."

"Ah." Mercedes paced, thinking. "Maybe it's not good for
you to be around him," she said. "Since you can't have him."

Pagan dropped to sit on the couch, her head drooping.
God, she was tired. And, by God, she was an idiot.

"Too late," she said. "Too late. It's happened."

It had happened. She'd said those stupid words to Devin
because they were true. A thousand angry butterflies fluttered against her skin. She was vibrating like the steering
wheel of her damned Corvette when she'd revved the motor
before sending it over the cliff. She was falling over a different kind of cliff now, with no idea when she'd hit bottom.

Mercedes sat down next to her, their shoulders touching.
Her warm strength steadied Pagan. It wasn't like Mercedes
to get so physically close. Which meant that she knew. She
had to. She knew what Pagan was saying. Which was good,
because no way was she saying it again.

"It happened a while ago. You just didn't realize it," Mercedes said carefully.

"Back in Berlin." Pagan swallowed hard, but the lump in
her throat wasn't going away.

"Maybe," Mercedes said. "Tomorrow you'll probably see
this man they want you to identify. After that, this whole
mission thing will be over. It might be best if you ditched
the movie and we went home."

Pagan lifted her head and looked at her friend. Mercedes

knew: there was no way it could work with Devin. Maybe that was why Pagan hadn't wanted to admit to herself that she had any feelings for him. He was a spy. He lived in another country. However much she amused him, he was probably using her to get the mission done. All of her longing and confusion was for nothing.

"Either way," she said. "When this is done, he'll be gone."

Mercedes nodded and stood up. "You're limping. Let me get you some ice for that ankle."

Pagan's ankle was only slightly swollen the next day, with no tenderness, so she wrapped it up tight and stumbled out into the foggy street at 5:00 a.m. to find Carlos and the car waiting. Fallout from the emotional storm last night and lack of sleep cramped the edges of her brain. She took deep breaths and tried not to think about a Bloody Mary. Oh, what a happy breakfast that would make. Until she found herself at the end of a three-day bender in Chang's Bar in San Francisco at midnight with Nicky Raven asleep in the red leather booth beside her.

She gulped the cup of coffee she'd brought with her instead and scalded the roof of her mouth.

Clearly this was going to be the best day in the history of the world.

By 7:00 a.m., Pagan's hair and makeup were stiff perfection, and her tulle-bedecked gown frothed around her like the foam left after a giant wave. Rada had fitted her with a bra that lifted her breasts so far up it hurt to cross her arms. They'd taped the fabric into place, but still she'd have to be careful during the dips in her upcoming dance number or something untoward might pop out. Her tight, pointy heels squashed her toes mercilessly as she stood under a colonnade looking out at the large courtyard of the Colegio San José, where the first shot of the day, and of the movie, would take place.

The wide square space, surrounded on all sides by three stories of vine-covered nineteenth century columns and doorways, was paved in beautiful alternating squares of black and white marble, a vast chessboard for the dancers and film technicians. As the best boy ordered his techs to turn on the huge lamps required for shooting in Technicolor, the polished stone gleamed, and the dark archways where grips, extras and wardrobe assistants lurked lit up as if it was noon, everywhere.

This was where Rolf Von Albrecht taught physics. Within this same complex, his son and daughter went to high school. A few blocks away, Devin Black was keeping an eye on the Von Albrecht house, and if any members of that family headed this way, he would come tell her to be ready.

Pagan was one of the stars of this wretched movie, and she would be dancing and flirting through most of the upcoming scenes with her costars. But making a movie also involved a lot of waiting while the technical details were worked out, problems were solved or other actors got their close-ups. She might learn a lot about Von Albrecht or bond more closely with Emma in between shots.

Later, during lunch break, thanks to Devin's mysterious connections, Mercedes would be visiting. She'd stop by to say hello, of course, but she was primarily there to check out the college's observatory, housed in a pretty cupola down a few hallways and up a lot of stairs from here.

M had babbled on about the history of the observatory and the quality of the telescope inside, but frankly, Pagan hadn't paid much attention. If Mercedes had her way, she'd get permission from some dusty professor to come back tonight and actually look through that telescope at the Southern Cross. And if that made her happy, Pagan was happy.

If you could be happy and anxious at the same time. Even as she waited for word from Devin that a Von Albrecht, any Von Albrecht, was in the vicinity, she was also waiting to start a new movie and to meet *Two to Tango*'s director, Victor Anderson. She'd heard him shouting something at the director of photography earlier, and outbursts of loud male laughter, but he hadn't bothered to come introduce himself during her long sit in the makeup chair, as was customary.

This movie didn't have the luxury of a table read or weeks of rehearsal at the filming location. They'd rehearsed the dance numbers on the soundstages at Warner Bros. for weeks, but Victor Anderson hadn't visited once. Perhaps he'd been busy.

Or perhaps he was as much of a self-absorbed jerk as the wardrobe mistress had implied.

Pagan had glimpsed him this morning, a tall man with distinguished wings of gray decorating his dark hair, striding around, shouting orders all over the courtyard. But she knew better than to walk up and introduce herself. That would be seen as arrogance on her part, thinking she was important enough to interrupt his work. Directors were the dictators of their movie sets, and this one clearly enjoyed that role.

Rada fluffed a section of tulle near the hem of the dress, pursing her lips sadly. "I told them white would get dirty too fast. Already there is some dust. By the end of the day, the hem will be black."

"Looks like they polished the floor," Pagan said. "It's pretty clean."

Rada gave her head a doleful nod. "Wax. I hope it's not so slippery that you slip and fall. You could break something and the whole movie would be canceled."

Rada was not the best kind of person to have around when you were apprehensive. Pagan looked around for a chair, a bench, preferably far away from Queen Gloom.

"It's okay if I sit down in this dress, isn't it?" she asked.

"Only if I put a towel down first, very carefully," Rada said. "I'll fetch one."

"Miss Jones!"

The loud voice she'd been unconsciously following around the courtyard boomed through the archway at her. Boot heels clicked, and something smacked against fabric as Victor Anderson strode into view. "About time I came to say hello, isn't it, little lady?"

He showed his teeth under a narrow Clark Gable mustache in what passed for a smile. He was a vigorous man with an athletic build in his late forties, but Pagan had a hard time tearing her eyes from his jodhpurs and riding crop. Famous movie-maker Cecil B. DeMille had worn that type of outfit, back in the thirties, but now it was a movie director cliché. No other director Pagan had ever worked with had worn such things. Instead of lending him authority, the outfit made him look oddly out of place, as if he was about to hop on a horse with a braided mane to go foxhunting, rather than stand around a movie set all day.

"You look better than I thought you would," he said, and smacked his crop a few more times against the leather of one shiny black knee-high boot, as if eager to whip her into action.

She felt sorry for anything he did ride.

Pagan blinked hard to keep herself from saying exactly that to him and instead issued her most vacuous smile. "Thank you so much, Mr. Anderson. It's a pleasure to finally meet you."

She managed to keep the edge out of the word *finally*, but it hadn't been easy.

His eyes ran up and down her body. "Have you put on weight? Come here."

She forced herself to take two steps toward him. *Make nice with the awful man, Pagan. He can make or break how the next few weeks of your life go, on set.*

Victor took her chin between his fingers firmly, and turned her face to the right and left as he scrutinized it. "Left side's a bit better. We'll have to light carefully around that nose. Eddie!"

He released her so suddenly she tottered on her heels, and he strode back out into the courtyard as if forgetting her existence. He beckoned the director of photography, no doubt to discuss the problems posed by her nose and her possible weight gain.

Pagan had heard critical things about her figure and her features all her life. That was part of being an actress. But according to Mama, Pagan was beautiful, no matter what others said. Eva Jones had been a tough taskmistress, pushing her daughter every day to work harder on her dancing, her singing, her line reading, but thank goodness for her pragmatic German views on eating and exercise. Eat well to stay strong, keep your body flexible and fit and pay attention only to your mother's criticism. No one else's opinion mattered.

Not even your own.

And Mama had been very critical. But in this, at least, she'd served Pagan well. So many of the actresses Pagan knew were always on some strange diet of watercress or celery, or taking uppers or laxatives to shed pounds they didn't really need to lose. Mama had made Pagan promise never to take those "terrible pills" or starve herself. She'd needed Pagan hearty enough to keep earning money to pay the mortgage.

All of which meant that nasty men like Victor Anderson, who saw Pagan as an object that wasn't pretty or thin enough, could get bent. Mama would have gone over Victor Anderson's head and spoken firmly with the head of the studio if she'd heard him say that kind of thing to Pagan. And the studio head would have privately warned Victor to tone it down or else Eva Jones would make their lives a living hell.

Now Pagan had to navigate this nonsense without her bulldog mother to shield her. The words didn't hurt, but they were just the beginning. Days, weeks, of this would wear her down. Victor Anderson was the last thing she needed while working an important, anxiety-producing case with Devin.

"Places!" shouted the second assistant director. "Extras—places, please! Pagan, David, places, please!"

Already? No one had warned her. Usually a production assistant came to give you a heads-up before they called places for the first shot of the day. And before that, the director or the AD showed you where your place was and walked you through the scene as it would be shot. Apparently there was no such courtesy on Victor Anderson's set.

Pagan walked out into the courtyard as dozens of extras emerged from the other archways. The black-and-white floor was covered with men in tuxedoes and women in long, big-skirted dresses, each a slightly less fluffy version of her own, although no one else was in white. She'd stand out among a sea of red and blue dresses, during this fictional ball thrown by the American embassy in Buenos Aires. It was clever if you liked things obvious.

She smiled at several of her fellow dancers as they took their places. But no one had told her where to stand. So she headed toward the camera, lodged for now in one corner of the courtyard. She spotted the choreographer, Jared, talking to some of the dancers nearby, and her other costar, hand-some sandy-haired Dave McKinney, was standing there in a tuxedo tight enough to show every bulge in his biceps. A makeup lady was giving his tan cheeks one last pat-down of powder.

"Tell me you're not going to make a habit of being this late," Victor Anderson demanded as Pagan clicked over the marble toward them in her heels. He was slapping his riding crop impatiently against his calf. "It's gonna be a tough shoot if this keeps up, won't it, Dave?"

Dave shot him a frowning look and did not reply as Pagan's stomach dropped. She took a deep breath and hoped her breasts wouldn't pop out of her neckline. Ever since she'd stopped drinking she'd made doubly sure she was never late, to always know her lines and her blocking backward and forward. An accusation of lack of professionalism when it wasn't her fault was much tougher for her to take than random jabs at her looks.

"But nobody told me…" Pagan began. Then she closed her mouth and gave him a sickly sweet smile instead. Weeks of working with this man lay ahead. Sugar drew more flies than vinegar and all that crap. Although vinegar was getting more tempting all the time.

"Hi, Dave," Pagan began again, favoring her costar with a genuine smile, and then beamed that smile like a spotlight at the director. "Mr. Anderson. Your powers of telepathy don't appear to be working, so if you'll kindly speak aloud the place you'd like me to be when the shot begins, I'll be delighted to oblige."

She draped the words in so much honey, and swept her lashes down over her cheeks so demurely, that he read her tone instead of listening carefully to her words and puffed out his chest.

"Movie's like a marriage, sweetheart," he said. "As long as you promise to honor and obey, we'll get along great. Come on over here."

He walked her to her position in the line of dancers, and pointed to the camera, which sat on a metal track that had been laid over the black-and-white marble floor.

"The camera's over there, getting your left profile when the shot begins," he said in a tone so condescending she couldn't help a look of surprise. "See it?" he added, mistaking her look for confusion. "We'll dolly—that means move the camera—around this way. See where the metal track goes? As you and Dave speak your lines. We'll rehearse it a few times before we roll, so don't worry. You've got a few tries before it has to be perfect. Makeup!" He bellowed for the makeup lady so loud Pagan flinched. The woman who'd been dusting Dave hustled over to dab at Pagan's cheeks with a powder puff.

Victor turned on her. "Where the hell have you been?"

The woman frowned, puzzled. "I'm sorry, Mr. Anderson. I was finishing up with Mr. McKinney…"

"If I see her nose shine like this again before a shot I'm going to fire you, okay?" Victor gave her a tight smile. "Okay, then. Do we all understand what's going on here, girls?" He favored them both with raised eyebrows and widespread hands of an exasperated man. The makeup woman didn't look at him, but kept pressing powder carefully onto Pagan's face. Pagan made her eyes round and innocent, and nodded.

"Good," he said, nodding. "Don't make me have to explain it again." As he stalked away, he muttered, "Women!" loud enough for everyone nearby to hear.

"What an ass," Pagan said under her breath as he strode away. "I won't let him fire you. What's your name?"

"Janet," the woman replied. "Thanks, but don't worry about me. Save yourself."

Lips pressed together tight, eyes lit with warning, Janet threw Pagan a look and jogged off.

Dave walked up, smiling at Pagan. "Sorry about that. What is his problem?"

"Nobody told me where to go, or that the shot was coming up." Pagan couldn't help defending herself. Thank God

Dave was funny and sane. They'd gotten along swimmingly during rehearsals.

Dave made a face. "That's weird. A nice PA came and got me ten minutes ago."

"Well, I'll be making best friends with that PA today, that's for sure!" Pagan said.

"Don't worry about it. You're the biggest star on the movie and you look gorgeous."

Good old Dave. His wife was a lucky woman. "Thanks, Dave. Gotta say, that's a hell of a tux they put you in."

"Tell me about it." Dave put his weight on his left foot and shook out his right leg. "They made the crotch too high to give me a bigger bulge, so if you see me wincing while we dance, it's not your fault."

Pagan's eyes couldn't help traveling down Dave's lean torso to the area in question, which did indeed show a clear outline of his anatomy.

"I mean, look at this!" With a lifelong actor's complete lack of modesty, Dave shook his hips like a go-go dancer. The bulge at his crotch didn't budge. "It's really jammed in there. I don't care, but my character is kind of a decent guy, so you'd think he'd tell his tailor to be more subtle, you know?"

Pagan laughed, some tension in her shoulders easing. The dancers around them were tittering. "I think the same tailor made my bra."

"Romance!" Victor shouted from behind the camera. "This isn't comedy, it's romance. Hand me that." He twitched a megaphone from the hand of an assistant and put it up to his mouth, although they were only about twenty feet away from him. "This is a ball thrown by the American embassy, and it's the greatest night of your lives! Romance! Happiness! Sex! That's what this scene's about, so let me see it. Actors—you know when to say your lines as the dance progresses. Let's rehearse. Sound!"

The soundman switched on the Nagra recorder and watched the tape wind into the plastic spools. The boom man hoisted the pole holding the microphone that would pick up their dialogue, although, because the music was playing, that would also be rerecorded later and dubbed back in. "Speed."

"Roll camera," Victor shouted. He seemed to grow taller and more pleased with himself with every command.

"Rolling," said the cameraman.

"Begin playback!"

"Playback!" shouted the assistant director.

Someone switched on a second recording device attached to a speaker behind the camera. A slow Southern reel swam blearily up to speed. Its very American strains sounded out of place here in an Argentine courtyard.

"Action!" Victor announced.

"Five, six, seven, eight!" Jared's voice shouted the count from somewhere beyond the fluffy dresses of the dancers.

In perfect unison, the line of female dancers, with Pagan near one end, walked forward in time to the music toward the line of male dancers. Dave lifted his hand at the right moment, and Pagan took it. They swayed, circled and swayed again.

"Why, Daisy," Dave said to Pagan in character, his voice half an octave lower than his normal tones. "You dance divinely. I had no idea."

"Don't sound so surprised, Billy," Pagan replied in Daisy's playful tone. "You're not the first man I've ever danced with."

A cloud settled on Dave's handsome brow as the lines of dancers parted and then came back together. He wrapped his arm around her waist and they spun, looking into each other's eyes. "You dance quite...expertly, in fact. How many others have there been?"

Pagan fought off a feeling of revulsion at that line. Why did men care so much if a girl had been with other men? Daisy was a caricature of virginity, but if she had fooled around—so what?

She wished her character could throw the accusation back into Dave's character's face. "How many others have *you* been with?" Let's see how boys liked being judged that way, too.

Instead, as Daisy, Pagan pushed his arm off her waist and glared. "What are you implying?"

Dave kept circling her, even though they were no longer touching. "You just seemed so sweet, so innocent, when I saw you at the races yesterday. Tonight... You're different tonight."

Again with the sweet and innocent. No wonder she hated the script. "Dancing's not illegal, last time I checked," Pagan said, a fond smile taking over her face as her character remembered the tango she'd danced the night before with that seductive Argentine man named Juan. "Are you afraid of a little competition?"

"Cut!"

The music and dancers kept swaying for two awkward beats, and then came to an uneven halt.

Dresses and tuxedoes parted as Victor strode toward Pagan

and Dave. "You were terribly offbeat during that last line, sweetheart," he said.

My favorite thing in the world is to have a ridiculous egotistical jackass erroneously criticize me while calling me sweetheart.

That's what she wanted to say. Or better yet, she wanted to kick him. In the shin. Or the crotch.

It hurt to rein in her natural reaction, but she was a decent actress, damn it, and she would get through this day without killing Victor Anderson even if it gave her an ulcer. He was a minor distraction in the dance she was dancing right now. She would have more difficult steps to get through today.

Victor went on. "You bobbled the steps when you said 'little competition,' and that's when you should be the most confident, the most on beat. Do you understand what I'm saying?"

Oh, she understood. But she hadn't been off beat. She'd bet a hundred dollars she'd been precisely on beat. But if she told Victor that…

Choreographer Jared had walked up to consult, and began, diplomatically, "I'm not so sure she was offbeat there, Victor…"

He said it in the softest, most conciliatory tone possible, but Victor rounded on him.

"No fairy's going to tell *me* when someone's off the beat."

Jared went pale, eyes wide. But Victor had no time for that. He turned on Pagan again. "Stay. On. Beat. Get me?"

"I will," she said, her throat tight, hand itching to smack him, just once, for Jared.

"Again!" Victor shouted, and stomped back to the camera, smacking his whip against his boot.

And so it went for hours as the temperature rose under the blazing lights and the humidity forced the makeup assistants to run around dabbing at foreheads and cheeks between every shot.

Victor had nothing to say when Dave stepped on Pagan's foot during the seventh take, or when the camera operator forgot to change out the mag and they ran out of film midshot. But Rada received sneering remarks as she sewed up a rip in Pagan's hem, and Pagan endured a steady stream of condescending eye rolls, angry corrections and one very loud declaration that teenage actresses would one day be the death of them all.

She took it all without screaming back or punching him in the throat, but she stopped smiling. By lunch break the set simmered with tension, silent except for the blare of the music playback and Victor's braying voice.

But lunch at least brought a chance for Pagan to sit, on a towel, and take off her evil shoes. A kind set nurse dabbed her two fresh blisters with ointment and was just finishing bandaging them as Mercedes walked up.

"M! Sorry I can't stand up," Pagan said. "Thanks, Sandy," she added to the nurse, who was getting up to go. "That's a huge help."

"Bleeding for your work, I see," Mercedes said, raising her eyebrows at the mound of white frills that surrounded Pagan like a frothy sea. "Who says movie stars have it easy?"

"At least I get to dress up as a wedding cake on a warm summer day," Pagan said, taking a plate with a sandwich and potato chips on it from an assistant as Rada wrapped a huge napkin around her neck to protect the dress. "Thanks, Brian.

Can I get a Coke, too? You're a doll." To Mercedes she said, "There's lots of food, but let me guess. You already ate."

"Can't be late to meet with the astronomy professor." Mercedes bounced on her toes in anticipation. She never got this excited about anything. Pagan almost didn't recognize her nervous smile. "Is Devin around? I want to thank him for setting this up."

"Not yet, but I'll tell him if I see him."

Mercedes sat down next to her, careful to avoid stray flounces. "How's it going?"

"Well, so far the director's insulted my nose, my weight, my dancing, my enunciation, my fingernails—he wants to use a hand double for the close-ups where Dave holds my character's hand—and my upbringing." Pagan kept her voice low. "So—great!"

"He's thorough," Mercedes said, her voice dry, looking around. "Which one is he?"

Pagan slung her eyes over to a table set up in the shade where Victor had corralled Dave and men from the crew to sit with him for lunch. She had not been invited, which suited her just fine, thanks. "He's the *pendejo* holding court over there, with the gray streaks in his hair. He's lucky my mother's not here. She'd make short work of him."

Mercedes regarded Victor Anderson with her flat, assessing gaze. "Anyone wearing those pants has no right to insult anyone."

Pagan laughed as Mercedes got to her feet. "Do you have to go already? You were just helping me back to sanity."

"Can't be late." Mercedes's small smile of happiness returned. "Good luck with…whatever it is that happens today."

"Same to you!" Pagan said to her friend's back as she strode down the colonnaded hallway toward the stairs up to the observatory. At the very least, this trip was turning out to be a success for Mercedes. Even if Pagan had to endure weeks of Victor Anderson and never got into Von Albrecht's house or saw him or any of that, at least her best friend was getting to fulfill some of her dreams.

Loud, angry voices echoed off the stone columns and the marble floor from across the courtyard. Pagan craned her neck and bit into her sandwich. A security guard was waving at a group of people on the opposite side of the courtyard and yelling in Spanish. They were yelling back.

She could just catch the words: *"Esta es nuestra escuela,"* meaning, "This is our school," and something about *"tenemos el derecho"*—"we have the right." It sounded like some students were angry they couldn't cross the courtyard, which was currently being repolished by a team of people with cloth mops.

The security guard responded with canned phrases like, "We have the permission of the school president," and "Signs were posted," as another guard walked over to back him up.

Quick arguments followed, until a more reasonable female voice interrupted with words Pagan couldn't overhear. She could see, however, that a pretty dark-haired girl in a chic white shift dress was making the students' case.

She must have been convincing, because a few minutes later, Pagan was done with her sandwich and the group of students had been allowed to go around the outside edges of the courtyard to get across it. Their path brought them within twenty yards of Pagan, as they headed off the same way Mercedes had gone.

The girl in the white dress had her dark hair up in the latest beehive style, her big dark eyes perfectly lined in black. She held hands with a tall, lanky young man with his long hair slicked back wearing a trendy bowling shirt, cuffed jeans and boat shoes. The dozen or so teens following them looked a lot like the crew that had gathered around Dieter last night at the café, but Pagan didn't recognize any of them.

"Of course Dieter picked this place to meet," the girl was saying in Spanish. "His father probably pays off the security guards to harass us."

Dieter? His father? She had to be referring to Dieter Von Albrecht. But from her scornful tone, it sounded like these kids weren't part of Dieter's gang. Maybe a rival group. Devin had said he'd try to let her know if Dieter or Emma, or even Von Albrecht himself, were headed her way. But there'd been no sign of him.

There wasn't time to call or wait for Devin. As the girl in the white shift and her friends headed away from the courtyard, Pagan put her Coke down and took off after them, giant skirt swaying.

BOLEO

Whip. When the woman's *ocho* suddenly changes direction, producing a whip-like action with her leg.

The kids Pagan was following had disappeared into the cool dark of the hallways, but their footsteps echoed against the stone walls. She skittered, light-footed in her slippers, as quickly and quietly as she could to just out of sight as they turned first down one hallway, then another, voices bouncing off the Colegio's carved ceiling.

The damn dress, though, was going to be a problem. Its hem was tailored for her to wear heels of a certain height, so in these slippers several inches of it dragged heavily on the ground, which meant she had to grab it with both hands and hold it up, very Scarlett O'Hara–like, to keep it out of the dust and keep herself from falling on her face. It may have looked fluffy as a cloud, but all that fabric and wiring weighed enough to make her wrists ache.

Her heart was bumping with exhilaration, and her skin thrummed with anticipation. Even more than alcohol, the risks of spying gave Pagan a thrill. Victor Anderson was fading below the horizon of her awareness like a sunset dying into twilight. Bring on the night; she was doing what she was meant to do. She was going to make a difference.

The hallways narrowed away from the courtyard and the movie shoot, and the floor here was plain stone instead of black-and-white marble. She passed wooden doors set into alcoves, doors that probably led to classrooms.

Ahead, around a corner, two voices were speaking low. Pagan slowed and caught the scuffling of moving feet, of dozens of people breathing, of some maybe holding their breath. It was the sound of tension, of conflict waiting under the surface for the right moment to erupt.

Two young male voices argued, speaking in Spanish inflected with that strange German/English tinge that marked them as being from Buenos Aires.

One sounded more German than the other. Dieter.

"Los muelles," he was saying. Pagan was pretty sure that meant *the docks*.

"I know where," the other boy said in less German-tinged Spanish. "Just don't forget to bring that garbage you call a car, and I'll be happy to leave you in my dust."

Dieter let out one scornful "Ha!" and followed with a stream of invective Pagan had a hard time following except for "in your dreams" and "Christ-killers."

Hand it to Dieter to give her such an unpleasant way to discover that the rival group must consist of Jewish kids.

The other boy shouted a word Pagan didn't know, and feet skidded on the stone floor. Something—a fist?—thudded against flesh. Grunts, scuffling, and voices rose in alarm.

"Para, para!" A girl's voice cut through the confusion. *Stop it!* "Not here!"

Pagan recognized the voice of the girl in the white shift who had convinced the security guard to let them edge around the courtyard.

The sounds of violence stopped. The boys threw a few more angry words at each other, but the chance for an all-out rumble eased.

"Fine," the rival gang boy's voice spoke. "The docks, tomorrow night. We'll learn who's boss then."

Dieter uttered a low, satisfied chuckle that made the hair on the back of Pagan's neck stand up.

"That we will," he said.

Footsteps clattered, getting closer. The Jewish gang of kids was heading back their way, and it was better she not be seen.

Hoisting her skirt high, she lunged heavily into an alcove just as the girl in the shift and her boyfriend in the bowling shirt rounded the corner. Damn this dress for being so big and so white. If the kids looked slightly to their right, they'd see her for sure.

"Don't let him draw you in like that, Hector *querido*," the girl was saying. She was strikingly beautiful up close, with thick dark hair and brown eyes like velvet. "I couldn't bear to see you in jail."

"You're right," her boyfriend, Hector, said as the couple passed the alcove. He had his arm around her shoulders, their heads together. "Can you get away tomorrow night?"

"What Papa doesn't know won't hurt him," she said with a laugh, and they were out of sight, the dozen or so other boys trailing after them, muttering to one another.

Something big was set for tomorrow night for these kids.

And if Dieter's tone was any indication, that something was bad. Scary bad.

Dieter. As quietly and quickly as she could, she padded out of the alcove to peer around the corner where the meeting between gangs had just taken place.

This hall was wider and longer than the rest, and completely enclosed. The last of Dieter's crew was disappearing behind two large doors at the far end. The doors swung closed, and the hallway lay empty.

Pagan ran down it, skirt skimming the floor so it must have looked like she was floating along instead of galumphing, which is how she felt. The midday heat was stifling in the airless hallway, and sweat dripped down between her shoulder blades.

Okay, so the dress was the opposite of ideal espionage attire. She couldn't follow Dieter's crew into any tightly enclosed spaces. But maybe, if she was lucky, she could overhear some of their plans.

She put an ear to the door and heard their heavy treads, getting farther away. She eased one door open and peered inside.

A winding staircase ascended and descended inside a wood-paneled vestibule. She could hear the deep voices of Dieter's boys booming up from its lower depths. Otherwise, the place was empty. Dusty photographs of swirling galaxies and a drawing of the solar system hung in plain frames on the walls.

This had to be the entrance to the observatory that Mercedes was visiting. Pagan moved to the foot of the stairs and stared up. Her best friend was up there somewhere while

Dieter Von Albrecht and his fascist buddies tramped into the basement below.

"Nein!" Dieter's voice bellowed from down below in German. "Not from here, *Idioten.* From my house."

Interesting that he'd switched to German while with his gang; maybe because it was less likely for local students to understand them. The stairs were wide enough for two people to use side by side, albeit awkwardly, which meant it was big enough for Pagan and the cursed dress. She heaved it up yet again and glided as soundlessly as she could down the curving staircase.

It was easier to catch their conversations here. The wooden walls sent sounds echoing up and down. Like their Spanish, the German these boys spoke was spiked with words, slang and intonations from other languages that made it a challenge to follow.

"Today we'll deal with some of the animals," Dieter was saying. "But most will have to wait for the big move tomorrow night."

"Who do you think built the tunnels, anyway?" another boy asked. "They look so old."

Tunnels. Is that where they were going? And what was this about animals and a big move tomorrow? It was horribly possible that by "animals" they meant people. And they'd just set up a meeting with the Jewish kids for tomorrow. Did they have some terrible "move" planned against the other gang then?

"Whoever it was, they had no idea of the glory they'd be used for," Dieter said. "Our names will ring in history after my father's done. You'll see."

"That girl Naomi's pretty," another boy said. "For a Jew. She either hates you or loves you, Dieter. Did you see the looks she gave you?"

The boys all laughed, low and suggestive, in a way that made Pagan's skin crawl.

"I'll give her something to love and hate," Dieter said. "Just you wait."

More laughter, bouncing off the close walls, bounding up the steps at her.

Pagan's hem chose that moment to slip out of her weary grip. The heavy skirt thumped onto the wooden stair with an audible thud.

She froze, sweat breaking out over her forehead.

The footsteps below slowed.

"What was that?" said a voice, closer than Dieter's had been.

"Sounded like someone dropped something," replied another, farther below.

"But I'm the last one, which means…"

Pagan's heart was beating so hard she could barely hear what they said next. She turned awkwardly on the narrow stair, grabbed her blasted skirt hard with both hands and ran back up.

Damn it, damn it! She had no idea how far below her the nearest boy was, but she had no doubt he could outrun her.

Steps were pounding up the stairs toward her now. More than one set. Maybe all of them were coming after her.

She swerved around another corner, the banister slipping under her perspiring hands. Once out of the vestibule, the only place to run was down that long hallway, with no turns for at least twenty yards. If they didn't catch her in the stairs, they'd see her there for sure.

They were nearly close enough to see the white of her dress turning up the staircase ahead of them now. She forced herself to run faster, ignoring how her girdle jabbed into her ribs, how her sweaty feet flapped inside her slippers and nearly tripped her.

When they saw her, her cover would be blown. Devin's entire operation, her chance to help catch a possible war criminal, to learn more about her mother's mysterious past— all of it would vanish.

All because she'd been stupid or arrogant enough to follow a group of fascist thugs in a ball gown with a hoop skirt. Whatever horrible thing happened now, she'd brought it on herself.

Breath coming in ragged gasps, she made it to the vestibule. She reached for the double doors as footsteps descended the stairs from above as well as below her.

Were there members of Dieter's gang above her, too?

She didn't wait to see. She shoved one of the swinging doors and yanked her big skirt through. The door swung shut with a thump as two voices, one male and one female, exclaimed aloud in surprise.

The female voice. It was familiar. Pagan turned, slippers skidding.

"Why were you following us?" the male voice was saying in Spanish.

"I wasn't," the girl said with flat certainty in Mexican-tinged Spanish that was all too familiar. "Who the hell are you?"

Mercedes.

"Here's who was following us, Dieter," the boy called. "I've got her."

"No, you don't," Mercedes said with the confidence that would brook no denial.

The boy cried out, more in astonishment than pain, and something large thumped to the floor.

Pagan came to a full halt, her heart in her throat, unable to call out her friend's name.

"If you get up, I'll just have to put you down again," Mercedes explained.

Oh, thank God. She must have thrown the boy to the floor. Pagan never should have doubted her. Gang life and violence were old hat for Mercedes, something she'd wanted to leave behind forever. And here Pagan had brought it right up the observatory stairs to harass her again.

"You!" Dieter's voice cut clearly through the thick wood of the doors. "What are you doing following us?"

Pagan, gasping for air, moved back toward the doors. She had to go in there, tell them it wasn't M who'd been following them. She hesitated, her hand on the wood. She should be rushing in there to her friend's defense. But here she was, waiting instead.

"I was up in the observatory, arranging a time to come back to see the Southern Cross actually," Mercedes said in a voice of supreme calm. "Why would I give a damn about any of you?"

Mercedes could be quite persuasive. Maybe she could handle this on her own without further danger, and without blowing Pagan's cover. Pagan hated that she wasn't rushing to her friend's defense, but if she did, she might never get inside the Von Albrecht house.

"You were at the café last night," Dieter said. "Protecting those *indios* in the band. I think maybe you should come with us now, so we can find out what the real story is. Come on…"

Pagan couldn't see him lay a hand on her friend, but through the door came a pained male grunt, and the other boys called out in astonishment.

For the second time in a few seconds, something fell heavily to the floor, and Dieter let out a long groan of anguish.

"If any of you take one step toward me, I'll break his arm," Mercedes said in a voice that made Pagan shiver. "Two steps, and he's dead."

The vestibule went quiet except for Dieter's moans.

"She hasn't got a gun or a knife," one of the boys finally said, his voice quavering. "How's she going to kill him?"

"Shut up!" Dieter screamed. "Aaaah, you bitch! Let me go!"

"Hey! What's going on down there?" a deep male voice echoed down the stairwell. "I'm calling the security guards."

About time. Adults were never around when you needed them.

"All of you will go back down the stairs now," Mercedes said in the same dead voice. "Your friend will join you in a minute."

"Just do it!" Dieter's voice was ragged, but still commanding.

"Come on," one of the boys said, low. "Get him up."

He must have been referring to the first boy Mercedes

had knocked down. Feet began treading slowly down the stairs. Their voices grew more distant, until there was only Dieter's jagged breathing.

"You can follow them now," Mercedes said.

"Ah!" Dieter shouted in pain. A slow dragging sound signaled he was getting to his feet. "You'll regret this."

"If I do see you again," Mercedes said, "I won't be so gentle."

"Oh, you won't see me," Dieter said in a hissing, quiet voice. "Not at first."

His footsteps thumped down the stairs, and Pagan leaned against the wall in relief.

The double doors swung open with a smack, and Mercedes stalked through, a small, square thundercloud.

She snapped her head to look at Pagan. "I should have known," she said, and kept going.

"Are you okay?" Pagan cast one last look at the double doors and then scurried after Mercedes. "I'm so sorry. They heard me following them, and as I ran out, you ran right into them."

Mercedes did not look at her. She was walking too fast for Pagan to catch up. "I came here to see a telescope," she said. "Not to participate in a rumble."

"I know. I'm sorry." Pagan held her hands out helplessly. "It was an accident, but I promise it won't happen again."

"No." Mercedes stopped dead and stared at her. Her normally rosy brown skin looked ashen. "It won't. I told you— no more violence, and I meant it. You will never involve me in your nonsense again. I was stupid enough to go with you last night. That was my fault. Today was an accident, you say. All right. But no more accidents, Pagan. I can't bear it."

Mercedes, she of the ironclad nerves and deadly fists, looked like she was ready to faint. It made Pagan queasy.

"I…" Pagan gulped to get ahold of herself. The ground was dropping away beneath her feet. If she didn't have her friendship with Mercedes, she was lost. She had no other family. "I didn't realize how important it was to you, M. I'm sorry."

"I feel sick," Mercedes said. "I hate this, don't you see?" She swallowed hard and sucked in a breath. "I hate myself when I'm like this."

"But you were defending yourself!" Pagan said. "You had every right…"

"I didn't use to," Mercedes said, interrupting. "This… It takes me back to the way life was for me. Back when I had no right to do what I did. To so many people."

Then Pagan understood. She hadn't been a gang enforcer the way Mercedes had. But she'd been a drunk, and she'd messed up a lot of days of shooting movies for hardworking people, and killed her father and her sister because of it. She never wanted to be that again. Never.

"Okay," she said. "Maybe after you see the stars and planets, you should get on a plane and go home. Hold down the fort and read the *Fabulous Four* or whatever. What do you think?"

Mercedes managed a small laugh and nodded. "*Fantastic Four.* Yeah. I think you're right."

She turned and started walking again, but this time she let Pagan walk next to her all the way back to the movie set.

AFICIONADO

An enthusiastic follower or fan, in this case,
of the tango.

Somehow Pagan made it through her remaining scenes after lunch. Victor switched to a side scene where Dave's character has a heart-to-heart with his best friend, and Pagan was done for the day. When Carlos got her back to the hotel by 4:00 p.m., she stripped off everything and crawled into bed.

A few minutes later, Mercedes breezed in, back from sightseeing, as the phone started ringing. She picked up the receiver. Pagan listened drowsily from her bed.

"Oh, hello," Mercedes said, her tone cool. "One moment and I'll get her…oh, you want me? Why?"

Pagan sat up as Mercedes set a bag down on the sideboard.

"The observatory said yes?" Mercedes's tone warmed. "Tonight at 10:00 p.m.? I guess the sun sets pretty late here in the summer. That would be wonderful. Thank you."

A brief pause as Pagan smiled to herself. It had to be Devin on the phone. He'd made sure the professor Mercedes had met with earlier had said yes to her coming back to look through the telescope.

"I think she's napping," Mercedes said, and her voice froze up again. "She had a very late night on top of jet lag and a busy day of shooting, among other things."

She paused again. Her tone wouldn't have given away today's adventure to anyone who didn't know her, but the implication was there. Pagan sat very still.

"The ankle wasn't painful for her this morning, but I haven't spoken to her since she got back from the set." Another pause. "Ask her yourself."

A longer pause. "What do *you* think she'll do? You know her plans for the evening better than I do," Mercedes said, and added, a little scornfully, "You know this isn't high school, and that I'm not going to give you any dirt, if in fact there was dirt to give. Did you go see her on set today? Maybe you should have."

Another pause.

"I have only one thing to tell you—take better care of her."

Pagan's hands were clasped together, fingertips white, as she listened hard.

Mercedes voice was soft when she spoke again. "Don't make promises you can't keep, Devin Black."

And she hung up the phone.

By 6:00 p.m., Pagan had taken a shower, put thoughts of Devin Black in a cordoned-off corner of her brain and donned her most comfortable slim-leg black trousers, a crisp white collared shirt and white sneakers. Time to head out to Emma Von Albrecht's house. Time to meet the man she'd come all this way to see. She couldn't help wondering whether Dieter would be there, too.

It took no more than five minutes for Carlos to reach the Von Albrechts' brick building on Adolfo Alsina Street, older and shorter than its surrounding neoclassical edifices, across the street from a pretty park. Pagan told Carlos not to wait. She had no idea how long she'd be, and Mercedes might need him later to get to the observatory.

Von Albrecht's name was nowhere to be seen on the entrance, and when Pagan lifted the brass door-knocker, Emma herself answered the door, beaming, her cheeks flushed pink.

She'd dressed up in a pretty but slightly dated navy skirt and jacket over a silk shell. An elaborate bouffant hairstyle rose above her heart-shaped face, giving her more height, and her eyeliner had changed to mimic exactly how Pagan had drawn hers last night.

Pagan gave the outfit an appreciative smile that made Emma flush, then completed her delight by leaning in to kiss her on the right cheek. She'd heard that kind of kiss was typical when greeting friends in Buenos Aires. And Emma seemed to enjoy it. Was it flirting? Probably, but might as well keep the girl happy.

"I brought us some candy necklaces!" She pulled on the stretch cord that held the brightly colored candy "jewels" together to put it around Emma's wrist. She spoke English, since that was the language they expected her to know best. Pagan's German was excellent, but it had been to her advantage in the past to conceal that she knew the language, so she was keeping the information secret for now. "We should invent candy earrings or something and make a fortune!"

"Thank you! Come in!" Emma said in her German-Argentine-accented English, and backed up to let Pagan into the foyer of their apartment. "Please excuse the mess. I try to keep it clean since Papa fired the maid, but Dieter keeps messing it all up again."

A long hallway funneled back into the building, with stairs both up and down to Pagan's right. A dusty hall table held trays for keys and piles of mail, with shoes shoved underneath it. The Persian rugs on the creaking wooden floor were thin and threadbare. The air smelled like unwashed men.

And Von Albrecht had fired the maid. If he were a Nazi war criminal, he might not want people coming in very often to scrub things, replace carpets or snoop.

"Anyone else at home?" Pagan said, following Emma down the hall. To the left, two closed wooden doors. Ahead, a dining room with a dusty dark wood dining table and four unpolished chairs. They passed through it into a large, echoing kitchen.

"Dieter had something to do after school, but Papa's here. He's always here these days." She opened up the door of a mint-green refrigerator that had been new ten years ago. "Want a Nehi? We've got grape and orange."

"Grape, thanks." Pagan scanned the scantily stocked pantry and peered out the window on the back door, which overlooked a small alley. "I'd love to meet your dad if he's home."

Emma gave her two bottles of grape soda and the bottle opener. "Papa works in the afternoons. And the mornings and the evenings. He does *not* allow interruptions."

Nothing was ever easy. Pagan popped the caps off the bottles. She handed one to Emma. "Cheers."

Emma clinked hers against Pagan's. *"Salut."*

"What does your father do?" Pagan asked, oh so casually.

"He teaches physics at the Colegio San José, close by." Emma opened a cupboard and pulled out a box of crackers called Tostos. "But he's on sabbatical this semester, researching something. We barely see him. You might meet him at dinner. We eat around eight. He does need to eat, after all! Dinner will be good. I made pot roast last night, and it's even better the next day."

"That sounds delicious," Pagan said, inwardly singing with relief. If his own children barely saw Von Albrecht these days, she needed every chance to meet him.

"Let's go up to my room," Emma was saying, grabbing two plates, the crackers and some cheese. "I forgot I also have that new song by the Tokens on 45. Have you heard it yet?"

"'The Lion Sleeps Tonight'?" Pagan trailed after Emma back down the hall. "Just on the radio. What's down there?" She pointed at the descending march of stairs.

Emma wrinkled her nose. "The basement. Papa has a laboratory down there. Dieter helps him sometimes. I'm not allowed, and it's probably for the best." She leaned in and whispered, "Sometimes the worst smells come out of there!"

"Ew!" Pagan made a face. Dieter and his pals had been going down to a basement earlier, a few blocks away at the Colegio. They had spoken about animals, and tunnels, and tomorrow night. She stared down the unlit staircase, but the darkness there was not forthcoming. She inhaled deeply, but no terrible scent hit her nose. How disappointing. Nothing but dust and carpet layered with old sweat.

She needed to snoop down there, alone if possible. If Dieter's tone of voice earlier was anything to go by, something bad was in the works, down in basements and tunnels.

"And that's Papa's office." Emma kept her voice low as she pointed to the second door in the hallway as they passed it. "We try to keep the noise down on this floor while he's working."

Pagan wondered if the door was locked. "But we can blast the music upstairs, right?" she asked in a whisper.

Emma grinned. "Right!"

Emma had the room upstairs in the back, the smallest of the three bedrooms on that floor, overlooking the alley. She'd cleverly covered up the peeling paint on the walls with posters of Elvis and Pagan's own film *Beach Bound Beverly*.

"Sorry," Emma said, glancing at the poster of a smiling fifteen-year-old Pagan in a gleaming white one-piece bathing suit seated on the shoulders of her two hunky shirtless costars. "But you knew I was a fan of yours when you agreed to come here."

"Oh, my God!" Pagan set the bottles of soda down on the floor and flung herself melodramatically onto the neatly made twin bed, the back of one hand to her forehead. "I shall never forgive you!"

Emma laughed, and flopped down next to Pagan on the bed, her hands in prayer position. "Oh, please—you must forgive me!"

Emma's calf was pressed against Pagan's. It didn't feel accidental, and it didn't exactly bother Pagan, but it wouldn't have been her choice under the usual circumstances. If she continued to allow it, she would be misleading Emma pretty horribly.

But then she'd been misleading Emma about everything from the start. This was just one more lie.

You've played plenty of love scenes with costars you liked but didn't want to see naked. Pretend this is one more.

Teasing. That would do for starters. Pagan steepled her hands thoughtfully. "You must make amends."

Emma frowned, caught for a moment outside of their playacting. "Amends?"

Not exactly good movie dialogue.

Oh, she didn't know the word. "Amends. It means you have to make it up to me, compensate me." She lowered her voice suggestively. "You owe me."

"Oh!" Emma's face cleared. Her eyes were searching Pagan's. Pagan did her best to reflect that eagerness right back.

"I like your lipstick," Emma said.

Pagan pursed her lips. "Lournay. Coral Fire, I think."

Emma was staring at Pagan's mouth the same way Nicky used to just before he kissed her. Pagan considered Emma's lips and planting a kiss there. They were thin, slick with pink lipstick and slightly parted. She'd never kissed a girl before. How bad could it be? But with two people each wearing lipstick, did it get kind of waxy?

"I like the color you're wearing." Pagan leaned toward Emma, her own mouth slightly open, and rubbed her thumb lightly across the other girl's lips. "Max Factor?"

Emma's cheeks flushed pinker than her lipstick. "Yes." Her voice was husky; her eyelids fluttered. She leaned in closer to Pagan, their noses almost touching. "How did you know?"

Pagan smiled, waited a heartbeat, then ducked her head

away and got to her feet. "Hours in the makeup chair, re-member? Hollywood nonsense."

Emma actually gulped. She was breathing fast. Poor kid. It was weird to have this kind of power over another girl. Although why it should be any different from toying with a boy, Pagan really couldn't say. Maybe it was harder to de-ceive someone so like herself.

Emma was having trouble forming a coherent thought, so Pagan babbled for her. "I've worn every brand and every shade of lipstick on the face of the earth, I bet you. And I remember that photo shoot." She pointed at the *Beach Bound Beverly* poster. "I was horribly tipsy, and Scotty James had this painful sunburn on his shoulders, and I had to sit on it. What a nightmare!"

Emma's eyes were traveling up and down Pagan's body. Pagan was used to that, from boys, but God, it was so much safer with a girl like Emma than it ever would have been with the evil Dieter, or any other boy, really.

"Did he hate you sitting on his sunburn?" Emma asked. She was able to form complete sentences. Good.

"Scotty was a trooper. They kept oiling us up, you know, to make us look good." Pagan pointed at the bare chests of Scotty James and Robert Torkelson, gleaming above their bathing trunks. Pagan's legs were also as shiny as cellophane.

"We were all slick as seals. And then Scotty and Bob would lean down so I could sit on their shoulders and Scotty would groan in agony as they stood up with me. As soon as we got it almost perfect, I'd slip and fall over backward, and Scotty would scream! That happened, like, eight times.

I think they dropped me on my head once." She rubbed the spot where she'd landed.

"Sounds like fun!" Now that Pagan was keeping a little distance between them, Emma got ahold of herself, sat up and pulled a pack of Winston cigarettes out of her dresser. "And the movie is so fun. How long did it take you to learn how to surf?"

Pagan waved her hand dismissively. "Oh, they weren't going to waste time teaching us to surf. All that footage of us hanging ten is done with Hollywood magic."

Emma moved to the open window, tapping the pack of Winstons against the sill. Winston had been Pagan's brand when she drank and smoked. Had Emma bought that brand because she knew Pagan was coming over? "But there were waves all around you, and water splashing."

Pagan reached into her purse, fishing for her trusty Zippo lighter. "They filmed each of us on a surfboard in the studio and added the waves in later using optical effects," she said. "We were up on a platform, so a guy could crouch below us and throw buckets of water up into our faces on cue. It was freezing cold."

Emma drew a cigarette out of the pack and tapped it on the sill. "Want one?"

"No, thanks. For me, smoking goes with a cold martini like Hope goes with Crosby, bacon with eggs. And I can't have the eggs, so I don't eat the bacon." Pagan offered the lighter to Emma, flicking on the flame. It was a romantic gesture, used in thousands of films to get the hero and heroine in close proximity. She was hoping Emma would take it that way.

Emma smiled coyly and placed the cigarette between her lips. "Thanks. This is perfect. Lighters don't make as much smoke as a match, and I don't want Papa to sniff us out." She put her hand, shaking slightly, around Pagan's and leaned in to touch the tip of the cigarette to the flame, sucking in her cheeks.

The tip of the cigarette glowed orange, and Emma exhaled a plume of smoke, aiming it out the window, but keeping her hand on Pagan's. Her skin was clammy. She cleared her throat nervously. She was so sweet, so scared. Pagan felt a hundred years old in comparison. But then she'd been taught to flirt with everyone since she was a child.

Pagan clicked the lighter closed, briefly enclosed Emma's fingers in her own and then slid her hand from under the other girl's with a little smile. *How's that for flirting?*

But Emma was staring at the lighter. "Is that the symbol for East Germany on your Zippo?"

"Oh, yes." Pagan glanced at the red-and-gold symbol engraved on the lighter. Of course. Emma had been born in Germany and would recognize the hammer and compass ringed by two ears of wheat.

Emma recoiled from Pagan slightly, as if she might carry germs. "You're not a Communist, are you?"

Pagan laughed. "Heck, no. I got this because…"

She hesitated. The moment she'd taken the lighter had been one of the most memorable in her life, but it was also top secret. "I shot a movie in West Germany back in August, and one day I went over to East Berlin to have lunch with my costar Thomas Kruger's family."

So far so true. There had been tabloid shots of Pagan visiting tourist attractions in West Berlin, if Emma or anyone was interested in checking up on her. When lying, it was always best to stick as closely as possible to the truth. You had less to remember that way, and so were less likely to be caught.

"I still can't believe those horrible Communists divided the country and now the city itself," Emma said, flicking ash out of the window. "When Germany was once the most powerful country on earth."

Pagan schooled her face not to react to the nostalgic tone in Emma's voice. Many Germans probably said the same sort of thing. And maybe Emma's father was just a physicist.

"Do they sell the lighters as souvenirs?" Emma asked.

"No," Pagan said, then wished she'd said yes and turned the whole thing into something completely innocuous. "We ran into a couple of the military police there, and they recognized my costar, Thomas," she lied.

The truth was that she'd been running for her life through East Berlin the night the Berlin Wall went up, pursued by a very determined member of the East German *volkspolizei*. He'd been intent on killing her and nearly succeeded. But she'd knocked him unconscious, thrown his gun in a water barrel and taken his lighter as a souvenir. She had been sorry for him as he lay there, his head bleeding. What had happened to him?

Alaric Vogel. That had been the name she found in his wallet. Something about it itched at her brain, but Emma was looking at her expectantly.

"Thomas is quite famous over there," she continued. That part was true. Thomas had been a big teen star in East Germany, but he hadn't been there when she took Alaric Vogel's lighter off his unconscious body. He'd been fleeing across the new border between East and West Berlin, saving his family while Pagan provided a distraction. "One of the officers flirted with me. I didn't like him, but when he pulled his Zippo out to light Thomas's cigarette, I asked for it as a souvenir."

"And he gave it to you?" Emma shook her head, puffing smoke out the window. "Must be nice to be a Hollywood star."

"It comes in handy. Sometimes." Pagan didn't look at Emma. The girl clearly hadn't made the connection that Pagan was using her stardom right this very second, to seduce Emma, if *seduce* was the right word.

"But sometimes not?" Emma sounded doubtful.

"Sometimes not." Pagan rubbed her thumb over the raised emblem of the *volkspolizei* on the Zippo. Stardom had gotten her and Thomas into a high-level East German party that night, but they'd both nearly died. The lighter was a token of how she'd overcome that and so many other obstacles, through luck and sheer, cussed unwillingness to give up. The lighter tapped her back into a time when she'd been useful, worthy of being alive.

And here she was, trying to do it again. If only she could catch a glimpse of the elusive Rolf Von Albrecht. She'd rather not have to kiss Emma to keep that chance alive, but she realized that she was quite willing to do it if she had to. It was dishonest and wrong, but it was for a good cause.

She put the lighter away. "You said you had the latest 45 from the Tokens?"

Emma nodded, smiling.

Pagan gave her a taunting look. "You owe me, remember? Play it for me!"

Moments later they were blasting "The Lions Sleeps Tonight." It was so catchy they played it five times in a row. After they segued to "Please Mister Postman," which Emma insisted was undanceable until Pagan grabbed her hand to show her how. Emma kept a hold of her hand as long as she could, until Pagan twirled away. They acted out the lyrics and then played it again so they could go over the choreography together.

It was fun, dancing with a girl. You could be sexy or silly, sweaty or alluring, without worrying that a man would get the wrong idea and come on too strong. Well, Emma was definitely getting the wrong idea, but that was manageable. Emma was probably too shy to make a real move unless Pagan made a move first. And if she did, one cross glance would send her scurrying away again.

Pagan leafed through all of Emma's 45s, throwing the danceable ones onto the turntable. "Peppermint Twist," "Tossin' and Turnin'"…that made her smile. She and Thomas had danced their hearts out to that one on the rooftop of the Hilton Hotel one fateful night in West Berlin. She kept leafing through 45s until she saw "The Fairest Stars" (N. Randazzo) Nicky Raven.

Nicky, her ex. The boy she'd given everything to until the accident with Daddy and Ava had taken everything. Nicky was a big name in music these days.

"The Fairest Stars" had hit number two on the Billboard charts, so it really shouldn't surprise her to find a copy of it here, in the bedroom of a teen girl in Argentina. But seeing Nicky's name never failed to give her a jolt of pain. He'd loved Pagan so very much, but when she needed him most, after the accident, he'd abandoned her. Now he was married, about to be a father. He hadn't called since the night he'd tried to get her back, on that Hilton rooftop in West Berlin. She'd probably never speak to him again, and that was the right thing, of course.

Why, then, did it make her feel so sad to see his name like this?

Under "The Fairest Stars," Pagan spotted "Sticks and Stones," and she put that on first, shoving Nicky's record away. Emma got red-faced and out of breath dancing to that and begged off to have another cigarette while Pagan put on Del Shannon's "Runaway."

"Hey, *Verlierer*!" a male voice called from outside. Pagan recognized the German term for *loser*. *"Erhalten hier unten!"*
Get down here.

Emma spurted out smoke and peered down at the alley through her open window. Whatever she saw there made her shoulders slump. "Why?" she called back in German. To Pagan, she said in English, "Dieter. Sometimes he can be a pain. Most of the time."

"I'm hungry," Dieter yelled up, still in German. "Come down and make me a sandwich."

"We're having dinner in thirty minutes," Emma said, and Pagan noticed that it was getting dark outside. Time flew when you were dancing. "Just wait."

"Now!" Dieter barked. "Or I'll tell Papa you're smoking."

Emma exhaled hard and smashed her cigarette out on the windowsill. "Can you believe this?" she muttered low to Pagan in English. "I have to do whatever he tells me or else he tells Papa I'm smoking. Now he wants a sandwich—

right before dinner! Mama spoiled him so, before she died. He thinks I should do the same."

"There must be something you know about him you can counter with," Pagan said, turning the music down. "He almost started a fight in the café last night. Tell him you'll tell your father that and then tell him to go to hell."

Emma held her arm out. The wrist was ringed with yellowing bruises. "That's what he did to me last time I tried something like that. He's a beast."

Pagan stared at the marks, anger pulling on her like a tide. "I can show you where to hit him when he tries that," she said. "I promise you, he'll never try it again."

Emma shook her head, looking defeated. "You don't understand. I have to live with him. He could come into my room while I was asleep... Anyway!" She forced a smile on her face. "Sorry to be pulled away. Listen to whatever you like. I won't be long."

Pagan watched Emma thump unhappily down the stairs. Dieter's selfishness made him a terrible brother, but it also meant Pagan wouldn't have to make out with Emma for now. She couldn't help feeling a rush of relief. The girl deserved to make out with someone who really liked her.

A boy like Dieter could very well be the son of a Nazi war criminal. Pagan had her story ready if she ran into Rolf Von Albrecht and he recognized her. But first she had to run into him. And then there was that basement, waiting for her to explore. With Emma busy for a few moments, now might be the time.

She set the record player up to drop six of Emma's 45s in a row, turned the volume up and padded down the stairs in her silent sneakers, in search of Dr. Someone.

ARREPENTIDA

A quick evasive movement for avoiding collisions.

As Pagan's toes hit the ground floor of the Von Albrecht house, a clash of falling plates rolled down the long hallway toward her from the kitchen.

"Careful!" Emma admonished Dieter distantly in German. "You'll disturb Papa."

"You can clean it up, smoker," Dieter replied. His feet thumped hard on the floor as he moved around the kitchen.

Pagan could remember tormenting her little sister in the way siblings did. But Dieter was in a class by himself. The urge to run down the hall and kick him where she'd kicked Tony Perry was strong, but Pagan made herself pad noiselessly over to the office door and press her ear against it instead.

Nothing. She laid a hand on the doorknob, tempted to turn it. If it wasn't locked she could stumble inside, meet Herr Von Albrecht, apologize for her idiocy and stumble out. At that point it wouldn't matter what he thought of her. He could throw her out of the house if he wanted, as long as she got to see his face and hear his voice.

"Cool your jets!" Emma said in English to her brother.

He laughed and replied in German. "Talking like you're the movie star. Shut up and hurry up. I'm hungry."

What would happen to Emma if Pagan stumbled "accidentally" into her papa's office? Pagan was Emma's guest, so Emma was the one most likely to be punished if Pagan trespassed.

Fine. Pagan could wait half an hour until dinner to meet Rolf Von Albrecht. Not long now.

She turned to go back up to Emma's room and caught a glimpse of the stairwell heading down to the basement.

The basement, which was Rolf Von Albrecht's laboratory, where Emma wasn't allowed. If there were tunnels, as Dieter had said, that would be the place to find them.

She might never get back into this house after tonight. The dark stairs beckoned her, like a half-opened envelope.

Pulling two hairpins from her ponytail, Pagan zipped lightly down the stairs, slowing as she neared the bottom to allow her eyes to adjust to the deepening gloom.

The wooden door had two locks, but she concentrated on picking the newer bolt-type lock above the doorknob first. When they were in reform school, Mercedes had taught her how to break into almost anywhere, and it had come in handy getting into lockers full of forbidden food or finding tools to help them with their escape. They'd been caught as they went over the fence, but Pagan retained the image of a typical locking mechanism in her head. It was simple to pick one when you knew how. But it took time.

She bent one hairpin and slid it into the bottom of the keyhole, testing the cylinder inside to see which way it turned. From there it was a matter of raking the pins, finding the "stubborn" pin and getting it and the other pins pushed up far enough to turn the cylinder all the way.

It went faster than she dreamed. The bolt slid out of place. Now for the lower lock…

She put her hand on the doorknob, and it turned. The lower lock wasn't engaged! Thanking the gods of alcoholic movie stars, Pagan eased the door open, happy to find the hinges well oiled and silent. Maybe that meant Von Albrecht came down here frequently. She sent up a second prayer asking that he not come down here again, at least not for another ten minutes or so.

Damp air whooshed over her, smelling faintly of burned hair and something worse. Something dead.

Dread prickled over her skin and settled into her bones. Something terrible waited in the basement. She nearly shut and relocked the door then. She didn't need to see the lab. That wasn't her job. Her job was simply to identify Von Albrecht, or not, and get the hell out.

Devin wouldn't want her to go in. If she was found in there, it might jeopardize his mission.

But beneath the fear and the worry, a spark of something else made her push the door open wider. She didn't know quite what that spark was, but it told her that she had to know what lay in Von Albrecht's basement laboratory. It was always better to know, somehow. Ignorance was bliss until the secret things turned around like sea monsters and swallowed you whole.

More steps down. It was very dark. She fumbled for a light switch, found it and clicked on a single dangling bulb as she shut the door silently behind her.

The stairs descended and turned. She couldn't see the bottom. But the smell was worse, a combination of stomach-turning decay, hair that had sat too long under the dryer and sharp pine cleanser.

Down the stairs, wooden now, splotched with nameless black and red stains. Down into a thickening, invisible cloud of hot metal and dead things.

She sensed but could not see that the space opened up around her at the bottom of the stairs. Another light switch. She touched it, hesitating, then flicked it on.

A large room with a cement floor and high ceilings covered with rusty pipes and greenish lights that cast complicated shadows down on the metal tables, tubes, equipment and cages arranged in a rough square.

Nothing stirred. Pagan heard no sound but her own pulse hammering in the veins of her neck.

On the other side of the room, another set of stairs sloped down. On the central metal table, amid test tubes and burners, lay a stack of paper piled neatly on top of some notebooks.

Pagan flitted noiselessly past a large metal cage filled with putrefying trash, and a series of empty smaller cages with filthy floors, not looking at them too closely, and made a beeline for the papers. Now she could see, stacked along the other walls, large sacks, barrels and crates. The equipment on the table, unlike the cages, was clean and well kept. She didn't recognize half of what she was looking at.

The piece of paper on top of the stack was covered in jagged black handwriting and looked like gibberish until she found some plus signs and parentheses. Mathematical formulas of some kind.

Well, that was no help. Even if Pagan had studied hard in school, she was pretty sure formulas several lines long each would be way over her head. She lifted the page and squinted under it. The language was German. She couldn't decipher it well, though not because it was code, but because the handwriting was so terrible. Something about shipments, Berlin and 30 January, 1962, with a side note that said, *Twenty-nine years to the day*, followed by an exclamation mark.

January 30, 1962. That was more than two weeks away. Twenty-nine years ago it had been 1933.

Goose bumps rose on Pagan's skin. She was no history expert, but she and everyone in the world knew that 1933 was the year the Nazis consolidated their power in Germany. She didn't know what particular event happened that year on January 30, but *twenty-nine years to the day*, the note said. Who but a Nazi physicist would want to commemorate any date in 1933 with weird experiments in a secret lab?

And how, exactly, was Rolf Von Albrecht planning to commemorate it? What did this basement full of nauseating vapors have to do with it?

She didn't have time to go through the notebooks, and she couldn't take anything away with her, or it might be missed. She needed to get the hell out of here before anyone came looking.

She set the paper down and tiptoed over to the other stairs, the ones descending to another level. The old, crumbling brick steps looked like they would take her back in time as well as deeper into the earth. At the bottom she could see the outline of another door.

She walked down a step, then stopped herself. The mystery of what lay down there, the possibility of unlocking more secrets, crooked its finger at her. But it would be stupid to go farther. Every second that ticked by put her in greater danger.

She didn't have time to learn more about all the strange things in this room. Barrels and crates lined the wall near the stairs. Sacks of what looked like dry dog food lay on top of a heavy metal trunk with some sort of emblem on it. She took two steps toward it, frowning at the black-and-yellow symbol. It was circular with three trefoil shapes radiating out from the black circle at the center.

Radiation. That was the warning sign for nuclear radiation.

The trunk bearing the symbol was made of thick black, heavy metal. She couldn't be sure, but it might be lead.

Pagan backed up two, three steps. That large metal trunk contained radioactive material. Or it had contained it in the past.

Or it would in the future.

In the horrified jumble of her mind, she picked out a relevant memory. Devin had said something about the war criminal they were after, Rudolf Von Alt, having worked on the Nazi version of the nuclear bomb. When that program hadn't panned out, he'd gone on to experiment on people in the concentration camps, using radiation.

Bam! Bam! Bam!

Pagan whirled, scanning the room wildly. The metallic

thumping was loud as cannon fire in the utter silence of the laboratory.

Something rustled, and then barked. Over by the wall to her right.

Barked?

More rustling, and that rhythmic thud.

Pagan sucked in air, hoping it wasn't too horribly radio-active. There was no one in the room. No people, that is.

The banging sound came from inside the large cage. The other sounds—from other, smaller cages lining the wall.

Whatever was in those cages…was alive.

One hand pressed to her heart, Pagan forced herself to walk toward the large cage. Around some kind of cabinet, past the central metal table covered with paraphernalia, she turned that corner and saw that the large cage didn't contain a pile of rancid garbage, after all.

Two eyes stared up at her. A large gray-and-red body now up on all fours swayed as its tail waved.

She almost didn't recognize what it was at first. The furless skin was covered with terrible, oozing sores. A large patch of pinkish flesh seemed to have been stitched onto its shoulder. One ear was gone, and one eye was white as a blind man's, the other brown. The paws were scaly when they should have been furry, the nails ripped, gone or bloody. The tall body was emaciated to the point where it resembled a skel-eton more than a creature.

But the tail was wagging, banging against the metal back of the cage. The one good eye gleamed up hopefully at Pagan. A small whine escaped the scarred throat.

A dog.

A small, disbelieving sob rose up Pagan's throat. She gulped, kneeling by the cage, and put her hand up to the mesh.

The dog licked her hand.

"No," she breathed. "Please, no."

She stood up slowly, turning toward the other cages. More than a dozen of them lined up against the wall, filled with smaller animals. Dogs, cats, rats. All ravaged as sunken ships, their eyes shining at her in the dark.

Pagan now knew without a doubt who Rolf Von Albrecht was. He had to be the man once known as Rudolf Von Alt, Nazi war criminal. And he was continuing his odious experiments here in Buenos Aires, on animals.

Dieter had said something about moving the animals. These poor creatures must be the ones he'd been talking about. Was Von Albrecht done with his horrific trials? And if so, what came next?

She put her hand on the lock of the dog's cage, reaching for her hairpins, but the cold metal on her skin shocked her out of her fugue.

She couldn't save them.

Something in her chest was cracking, breaking apart. More than anything in her life since the accident she wanted this—to open the cages and take these animals home, all of them.

Von Albrecht had once done the same thing to human beings.

Don't! Don't think about that now. The nausea from seeing the dog's condition alone was making her dizzy.

People would've been… She couldn't think about that or she'd scream. She'd give herself away. She'd march upstairs and kill Von Albrecht here and now with her own bare hands.

And more likely get killed.

Think, think, Pagan. You can't let the animals go or he'll know you were here. If she tried to get out with them, he'd hurt her, or kill her, and the animals. There could be no doubt now of what he was capable.

She had to get out of here.

Praying that Dieter had kept Emma occupied all this time, Pagan ran over to a half-open bag of dog food. She grabbed it at the bottom and tipped it over the open tops of the cages lining the wall, jogging up and down so that the kibbles sprinkled down into the cages. She had no time to differentiate between cat, rat and dog now. And they needed water more than food. But they gobbled down the bits of food so fast she knew there'd be no trace of her visit for Von Albrecht to find.

She knelt by the large cage with a handful of food and shoved it through the mesh. The dog licked at her hand as she did it, gulping the dried chunks down, tail wagging like mad.

"I won't forget you," she whispered.

Her hair was sticking to the back of her neck. Her mouth was dry. She tore herself away from the dog and returned the nearly empty bag of dog food to its spot in a dark corner. It almost slipped from her shaking hands, but she hoisted it up on top of its stack of crates and ran back up the stairs, not looking back at the animals.

If she did, she'd never leave without them. Her feet kept going, but the compulsion to turn back, to somehow gather them in her arms forever, nearly overcame her.

She couldn't. Not now. But she or someone else would come back.

And Von Albrecht would pay.

Icy certainty stiffened her spine and pushed her farther up the stairs. She would tell Devin, and he'd tell his contacts. They would swiftly deal with Von Albrecht. The US government had brought her here to find him, and she'd done that. Now they could punish him.

"I promise," she whispered. The words cloaked her with the calming weight of a solemn vow.

She slowed as she neared the door, taking the hairpins down with fingers that no longer trembled. The promise of vengeance was powerful indeed.

She saw now that the back of the door was covered in some kind of black foam, the same kind she'd seen in sound studios when she recorded extra dialogue for her movies. Soundproofing.

The acting job of her life now lay ahead of her. She needed to seem not only calm, but frivolous. Happy. As if she'd never seen what she had seen. For a little while, she could not know what she knew.

So Pagan took everything she'd seen in the basement and locked it all up in the little box in the back of her brain. She kept her memories of the night of the car accident, when Daddy and Ava had been killed, in the same place. Sometimes traumatic moments escaped. But if she didn't keep them prisoner most of the time, they would run riot and take over everything.

She turned off the light and stepped through the door, turning swiftly to use the hairpins to relock it behind her.

Her hands were shockingly steady. In less than half the time it had taken her to unlock, she'd turned it back with a quiet *thunk*.

Up the stairs again, cautiously, taking deep, tranquilizing breaths. She made sure her collar was straight, dusted the crumbs of dog food from her hands and pressed her lips together to smooth out whatever was left of her lipstick. As far as she knew, the Von Albrecht basement did not exist. Right now, she was a silly, privileged girl with nothing more on her mind than which song to play next on the record player.

Emma's voice said something sharply from the kitchen, which meant she was still occupied with Dieter. Hallelujah. It couldn't have been more than fifteen minutes since she left Emma's bedroom, but it weighed on her like a lifetime.

She made it to the top of the basement stairs safely.

"I'm out of milk," Dieter was saying.

"Get it yourself," Emma replied.

How sweet the sound of their discord was now. It meant she was safe. She could go back up to Emma's room as if none of this had ever happened.

A door clicked behind her. The office door.

A man's voice spoke in German: "Who are you?"

AMAGUE

Fake, or feint. A move that begins in one direction that suddenly changes direction at the last moment.

That voice.

Nasal. High-pitched with a whine to it, even when speaking the harsh consonants of German. Pagan hadn't heard that voice since she was eight, but she would have known it anywhere.

She turned to face him in one smooth move, one hand lightly on the railing. And she made herself smile, wide, right at Dr. Someone, aka Rolf Von Albrecht, aka Rudolf Von Alt, Nazi war criminal.

As soon as she saw him, she remembered. His pointed, crafty face could take on the look of a rat, or a wolf, depending on his mood. He stood an inch under six feet, skinny through the chest, with a shoulder stoop that was new to Pagan. His belly pooched out farther, too, but he wore the same glasses with heavy black frames perched over his long, disdainful nose. The thick lenses made his squinting eyes seem smaller. His thinning brown hair receded farther than she recalled, emphasizing his high, lined forehead. Deep creases on either side of his nose curved down to the flat line of his mouth.

For a man who had created so much evil, he looked harmless, almost pathetic. To anyone else, in his burgundy cardigan and stained baggy pants, he would seem like nothing more than a cranky old college professor. Only his hands, large, veined and habitually clenched, spoke of his strong will.

Dr. Someone. He'd had no plastic surgery, only eight years of aging. She was taller now than she had been when she last saw him, so he seemed smaller, shrunken in on himself. But the glare from his pale blue eyes was as sharp as ever.

"Is that…Pagan Jones?" he said, eyes flaring open in astonishment, and switched to English. "What are you doing here?"

That was the question. Fortunately, she'd prepared herself for it.

"Dr. Von Albrecht." Pagan stepped forward, hand extended. "Didn't Emma tell you I was coming? How nice to see you again."

The "again" was the key. He'd recognized her, so if she claimed not to know his connection to her family, her presence in his house would be too ridiculous of a coincidence. His suspicions would be triggered. Better to admit the connection up front, and then show herself to be his ally.

He didn't take her hand. He wasn't buying it. Yet. "I asked—what are you doing here?"

"Visiting." Pagan stretched her smile to its most blinding, and empty-headed, proportions. "I'm in town shooting a movie and ran into Emma last night. She invited me over and I had to say yes. I had to know if she was related to the same Von Albrecht I remembered from when I was little."

Von Albrecht cast a glance down the hall toward his children's voices. "You remember me?" It came out flat, disbelieving.

"Of course!" Pagan lowered her voice to a conspiratorial level. "Mama and I had many talks about you. I know how important it was for her to help you."

"Really." He drew his head back like a turtle, creating a triple chin wattle. "Tell me, then, why was it so important?"

It was like doing the tango, this question and answer. But ten times more dangerous. He was the leader, the man in the dance, asking her the questions. She was the follower, trying to keep up. Except he didn't realize how her answers were quietly impelling him to dance in the direction she desired, as the woman's ability to follow the man in tango could drive him to lead a certain way.

She shrugged. "All Mama said was that the dream of our Fatherland would never die as long as men like you were around."

She must've answered correctly, because his shoulders slumped farther, relaxing. "Your mother is a remarkable woman. How is she?"

Pagan had to stomp down on her astonishment so that she could manifest the requisite look of sadness.

Von Albrecht had no idea her mother was dead. But really, why would he? It's not like they would've stayed in touch. That would endanger them both. And a professor and physicist living in Buenos Aires with a penchant for torture had other matters to concentrate on. He wasn't the type to go see *Beach Bound Beverly* with his daughter or read the tab-loid stories about the daughter of the woman who saved him. There was nuclear material to fuss with down in the base-ment, after all.

If he didn't know about her mother's death, he probably had no idea about her alcoholism, or the car crash where she'd killed Daddy and Ava. If she wanted him to trust her, to like her, that was just as well.

It wasn't hard to look sad. Her feeling about Mama's death were right beneath the surface. "You didn't know? She passed away when I was twelve." No need for gory details.

His graying eyebrows drew together, more in surprise than sorrow. "That's too bad. A strong, intelligent woman, your mother. A true believer."

"She taught me everything I know," Pagan said, and didn't like how close to reality that statement was. Only her father's distracted kindness kept it from being completely true. She could only hope Daddy had rubbed off on her, too. "I still have the painting you gave her. Such a beautiful gift."

"She deserved all that and more after what she did for me," he said. "And the others."

Pagan forced herself to remain very still.

The others?

"But what are you doing here, in the hallway?" His small eyes shot a sidelong glance down the stairs toward the base-ment door and then narrowed at her, suspicious. "Didn't Emma tell you I don't like to be disturbed?"

Gather your wits, Pagan. You're still in the spotlight, and it exposes every flaw. "I was coming down from her room to tell her that I think I need to go back to the hotel."

Yes, that was it. She needed to get out of here, before the fury she'd locked away came raging forth and got her killed. She continued. "I can feel one of my migraines coming on, so I should go lie down somewhere dark before it gets too bad. I'm sorry that I won't be joining you for dinner, after all." She fluttered her eyelids against imaginary pain. "Perhaps another time."

"Perhaps." His lips quirked up slightly at the corners. "I'm heartened to meet a girl of good German stock who values her Fatherland. Have you met my son, Dieter?"

Dear God, he had a glint in his eye. She knew all too well what it meant. She was "good German stock" he could breed with his son. Yuck.

"Yes," she said, adding a happy lilt to her voice as best she could. "I've met Dieter. He's very….tall." She couldn't quite manage a blush, but she lowered her eyes as if suddenly shy. Imagine his expression if she told him that Dieter preferred anything but "good German stock," and that it was Von Albrecht's daughter who'd taken a liking to her.

"If I want a second sandwich, you'll damned well make me a second sandwich, you stupid bitch!" Dieter's voice echoed down the hall.

"Leave me alone!" Emma sounded as if she was crying from anger. "That's all I want—just leave me alone!"

"Dieter!"

Von Albrecht had only to raise his voice slightly for silence to fall in the kitchen. It was the voice of a man used to being obeyed.

"*Komm her,*" Von Albrecht said. "Both of you." To Pagan, he said, "I apologize for my children."

Pagan shook her head, but said nothing as slow foot-steps clomped through the dining room toward them. Dieter came first, his tan cheeks spotted with red, then Emma, her shoulders slumped. Dieter glanced up at his father, then over at Pagan, and down at the floor. His shoulders were hunched, his hands balled into fists. He could not look his father in the eye.

"Papa?" Emma said, wiping wetness from her cheeks. "I'm so sorry if we disturbed you."

"I will speak to you shortly, daughter," Von Albrecht said, and Emma shut down, withdrawing a step, her lips trembling. "My son. What was that name you called your sister?"

"Name?" Dieter cleared his throat, shot a look at Pagan, then stared at his boots again. "Her name is Emma, Papa. I am sorry if I raised my voice and disturbed you."

"Are you?" Von Albrecht raised one gray eyebrow over the top of his thick black-rimmed glasses. "To me you seem angry, at your sister, at me. Is this how a real man conducts himself?"

Dieter swallowed hard, as if trying to gulp his feelings down, and straightened. "No, Papa. I just..."

"You offer me excuses?" His father cut him off. "Is there any excuse for so much unseemly emotion, or for calling your sister, a good Aryan woman, such a terrible name?"

Pagan couldn't help noticing: it was only good Aryan women who didn't get called names. Everyone else was probably fair game.

"No," Dieter mumbled.

"No, what?" Von Albrecht said, his voice growing harsh. A muscle in Dieter's jaw twitched. The ever-present violence that simmered beneath his skin was still there. But for this man, he controlled it. "No, Papa, there is no excuse for such emotion or for calling a good Aryan woman like Emma such a name. Emma, I apologize."

He didn't look at his sister when he said it. He looked only at his father.

Von Albrecht nodded slowly, pleased.

Emma shook her head and wiped angrily at her eyes. When she spoke, the words were flat, as if she'd said them many meaningless times before. "Thank you, Dieter."

"Well done, my boy." Von Albrecht moved forward and formally shook his son's hand. To Pagan, who had been hugged by her father every day until he died, it looked stiff and odd.

But at his father's touch, Dieter visibly relaxed. He smiled for the first time since Pagan had met him, and his square-jawed, wary face lit up. "I'm sorry, Papa. You know I want to make you proud, to be a good representative of the Fatherland."

"And so you are, my boy." Von Albrecht's washed-out eyes narrowed in his own closemouthed version of a smile. "You know that to me you are indispensable."

Dieter's eyes were shining with a fanatical gleam. "Thank you, Papa. I'll go get the pot roast out of the oven for dinner."

As Dieter clomped down the hall, Von Albrecht narrowed his squinty eyes at his daughter. "Emma, my dear, you must understand that your brother is under considerable strain. He is the man of the house while I am busy with my research. And I ask a lot of him."

"Yes, Papa," Emma said dully.

Emma made dinner, and cleaned the house, and shopped for groceries, while Dieter started fights with people he didn't like. Emma was more of the adult in the house than either of these men, as far as Pagan was concerned. She wanted to blurt that out to this disgusting creature beside her, wanted to grab Emma's hand and take her far from this terrible house.

But none of that could happen. Not yet, anyway. She had to get out of there, and soon, before she blew her cover and started screaming.

"Dinnertime, is it not?" Von Albrecht's narrow jowls shook as he gave Pagan a tight smile. "Shall we?"

"I'm so sorry," Pagan said, squinting up at Emma as if through a haze of pain. "But as I told your father, I feel a migraine coming on, so I'd better head back to the hotel."

"Oh, no, I'm so sorry!" Emma walked up to take Pagan's hands and peer with concern into her face.

"No, it's I who am sorry to miss your pot roast. But when these things come over me, I don't much feel like eating." Pagan gave Emma a quick kiss on the cheek. "I'll go up and get my purse."

"No, no, you stay here. I'll get it." Emma gave her hands a squeeze and ran up the stairs.

Pagan was alone once more with Rolf Von Albrecht. He was eyeing her with much more approval now. "Emma knows nothing of our previous acquaintance, I take it," he said. His English, aside from his accent, was perfect.

"Of course not," Pagan said, rubbing her temple, but giving him a faint smile. "Nobody knows that now but you and me."

"You've inherited your mother's discretion as well as her

beauty," he said. "Good." He lifted his voice. "Dieter, come say goodbye to Fräulein Jones."

Pagan lifted her hand, about to ask him not to bother, but stopped herself. She might as well stay in Von Albrecht's good graces, in case she ever needed to enter the house again. But she never wanted to cross this threshold again. The desire to get out of this house was growing inside her like a balloon inflating with air. Any minute now it would pop.

Dieter clomped down the hallway as his sister ran back down the stairs and handed Pagan her purse.

Emma looked with concern at Pagan's furrowed face. "Are you all right? Should we have Dieter drive you home, perhaps?"

"We can call her a cab," Dieter interposed. Such a gentleman.

A drive with Dieter was the last thing she needed. "No, thank you. It's not far, and I find a brisk walk can sometimes stop the pain in its tracks."

"Gets more blood to the head," Von Albrecht said with a nauseating approximation of what a doctor would say to a patient. "Which may ease the tension."

"Exactly." Pagan gave them all a pained smile and faded toward the door, her escape hatch. "Thank you so much, all of you. This has been a wonderful evening."

Emma walked with her to the door. Leaving Von Albrecht behind was like dropping a fifty-pound weight. Not much farther now and she'd be free. She couldn't wait to walk, to run, to leave the stench of this place.

"*Auf Wiedersehen*, Fräulein Jones," Von Albrecht said. "Hope to see you again soon."

"Yes, goodbye," Dieter added abruptly.

Thank God, they were at the front door. Only a few steps now.

"Are you sure you don't want me to call you a cab?" Emma asked as she opened the door, her voice low. "I can understand not wanting to be around Dieter, but it's getting dark, and you're new to the city."

"I'm quite sure," Pagan said. Out, out, out. She needed out. "But you're so kind, and I had such a lovely time."

Emma blushed, smiling, and gave her a shy kiss on the cheek. "It was wonderful. Would it be all right if I called you at the hotel tomorrow?" She backed away, the red in her cheeks going scarlet. "To see how you're feeling."

"That would be nice." Pagan set foot outside the house and took a deep breath. Almost there. "Sorry to cut it short. Goodbye."

Emma's expression was wistful. *"Auf Wiedersehen."*

Pagan made her way carefully down the front steps, as if in pain, until the door shut behind her. She took it slow, turning right up the street, back toward her hotel. Emma would likely watch her go for as long as she was in sight, or until one of her nasty relatives barked at her to serve them dinner.

She turned right at the corner and made it a few more steps before she had to lean against the gray stone of the building beside her.

She didn't have a migraine. That had been a lie. But her head had decided it now weighed eight hundred pounds.

Breathe. She'd faced worse. No one had shot at her or slapped her tonight the way the Communists had in East

Berlin. The Von Albrechts liked her, except for Dieter, and he wasn't hostile. Just apathetic.

She'd drunk their grape Nehi and smiled and lied—to become friends with a Nazi war criminal. Thank the gods of movie stars and liars that he hadn't shaken her hand. She felt slimy enough.

She'd gone so far as to tell Von Albrecht he was an important remnant of the godforsaken Fatherland.

As her mother probably had done.

Mama had helped that man. How was Pagan supposed to feel about her now that she knew it for sure?

Was it possible to love your mother and to hate her at the same time? And how could Pagan be a good person if she loved a woman like her mother?

The others, Von Albrecht had said. Others like him, maybe. How many others had there been? The more she dug into her mother's secret life, the deeper the pit became. The walls might cave in and bury her there.

Maybe Mama hadn't known what Von Albrecht's crimes were when she housed him in secret and got him on a boat to South America. Maybe she'd found the truth out later and that's why she'd hanged herself. Pagan could almost imagine it. Her own revulsion penetrated her flesh like an X-ray.

She gradually became aware of cold bleeding through the thin cotton of her shirt from the stone wall she was leaning against. Her shoulder prickled with goose bumps. She looked around.

Twilight was deepening into night, and the air was chilly and thick with purplish gray fog. A woman in a fur stole clicked past on high heels, one gloved hand floofing her carefully curled hair.

Fur. Pagan had never thought about it before, but that was some animal's skin. An animal not that different from the nearly furless dog she'd seen in Von Albrecht's basement. How could Pagan ever wear fur now? She'd better stop doing jobs like this for Devin or she'd have nothing left to wear. Nothing left to believe in.

Don't think about that dog now. Concentrate on getting back to the hotel. Devin was probably there, waiting for her report. And she had something to tell him.

Something other than those three awkward words she'd blurted out to him last night. Maybe if she pretended it had never happened, so would he.

The woman in the fur stole slowed down. Her walk changed. Her hips swayed further, and her shoulders straightened, head high.

And coming from the other direction, Devin Black. He nodded at the woman, but sailed past her, his eyes lighting on Pagan with that appreciative smile.

The woman in the fur stole turned to watch him go, her red lips slightly parted.

Pagan didn't blame her. The sight of him lifted Pagan away from the wall and sent a flush of warmth through her chilled frame. All she wanted was right here, walking toward her.

Too bad she couldn't have him. Nice as it was to see him, she made herself settle back onto her heels, pushing the bangs from her eyes.

"Hi," she said.

His face altered as he took her in. She knew him so well

now. The faint crease of worry between his eyebrows told her that he knew something was wrong.

"Come with me," he said, putting his hands on her shoulders to turn her around and sweep her across the street. "And tell me everything."

She couldn't help leaning toward his warmth. He lifted his arm, as if about to put it around her, but he shoved that hand into his pocket instead.

Damn him and his self-control.

"It's him," Pagan said, keeping her voice low. The vapor twisting around them deadened every noise and gave the impression they were alone in a damp pillowed world of gray. "Von Albrecht. I remember his face, his voice. Everything."

He slowed as they reached the sidewalk, took her upper arms in his hands and turned her to face him. His eyes were shining with triumph. "You're sure."

It wasn't a question, but she nodded.

"You did it," he said, his fingers tightening around her arms. "You can relax now. And thank you."

She squelched down the desire to lean into him, to feel his strength wrapped around her. But she couldn't relax yet. She said, "There's more."

He peered into her face. "Are you all right?"

"He's got a secret laboratory in his basement, and I broke into it."

"You—what?" He glared at her. "Is your own safety not a priority? Did he see you?"

She shook her head. Her throat was almost too tight to speak.

"Tell me," he said. "Everything."

She schooled her voice to stay level. "He's conducting experiments. On animals. There are cats and dogs in terrible shape down there. Awful. Horrible." She swallowed down more words like that. They were all she could think about.

His face was carefully blank, his eyes focused on hers to help her get through this. "Go on."

"I saw a big metal box with the radiation symbol on it," she said. "It looked like it was made from lead. And I tried to read his notes. It was mostly math formulas way beyond me, but I did read a thing that said in German *30 January, 1962. Twenty-nine years to the day.* With an exclamation mark."

He let go of her, his eyes shifting in calculation. "January 30, 1933. What's he commemorating?"

"And is he marking the occasion with radiation?"

Their eyes met. Neither of them said the words *nuclear war*, or *atomic bomb*, but during the war Rudolf Von Alt had worked on the Nazi attempt to build the bomb. They hadn't succeeded, but he'd had nearly twenty years to continue his research.

"Okay," Devin said, and looping her arm through his, he began to walk her steadily down the sidewalk. "You did a bang-up job, my bonny."

Her hand tightened on his arm at the Scottish endearment. Maybe it would be all right between them in spite of the three little words she'd said to him last night. If she couldn't have him the way she wanted, at least she could have this collaboration, this friendship, of equals.

Devin flicked his eyes back behind them and altered the rhythm of his steps briefly.

"What is it?" she said. Some instinct told her to keep her voice down.

He leaned his head down to her, like a lover whispering to his paramour. "We're being followed."

CHAPTER FIFTEEN

JANUARY 11 , 1962

RECOLETA, BUENOS AIRES

CONTACT TANGO

A version of the dance in which dancing partners may change roles, from leader to follower, and back again.

"How can you tell?" Pagan forced herself not to look over her shoulder. She probably wouldn't be able to see the man following them, anyway, given the fat puffs of fog clotting up the streets. "It has to be the same guy who's been after me all this time."

"Never a dull moment with you, is there?" Devin grinned down at her. "I was going to take you out to a celebratory dinner, but now..." He cut across the street between cars with her still on his arm.

"Now we have to find out who it is," Pagan said, matching him stride for stride. "I'll be damned how you spotted him."

"Heard him," Devin said as they sprang onto the side-walk. "Listen."

Pagan lowered her eyes to stare at her own sneakers and pushed her hearing past Devin's steady breathing and their footsteps.

A car engine rumbled off down the street as the high whine of a motorbike whizzed in the opposite direction. A door slammed, a song on a radio cut to a commercial and two female voices argued, their words tumbling down from a window above.

Beyond that, softened by the fog, came a faint echo of their own footsteps, as if the light tap from Devin's boot heels had bounced off a building. It was so exactly in time with his rhythm that she threw Devin a quizzical look.

"Watch," he whispered, and abruptly slowed his walk, pulling her up short beside him.

The echo kept going for two clicks, then it, too, decelerated.

"And he's listening to us!" Pagan whispered.

"Which will make it hard to lose him. Not that we want to."

"We could turn around and, you know, confront him," Pagan said.

"He'd run," Devin said, steering to the right down a smaller street strewn with the tiny purple jacaranda blossoms. The street must have been lined with jacaranda trees, but the fog was so thick you couldn't see the branches overhead. "So we turn the tables."

Pagan's pulse accelerated with excitement. The Von Albrechts, the radiation, the horrible lab, all vanished into the fog at the prospect of an adventure with Devin. "We follow him?"

He looked down at her, one eyebrow raised. "Only if you're up to it. You've had a long day, and…"

"Shut up and show me," she said.

A sly smile spread across his face. He slid his hand down her arm to clasp her hand. "Come, my bonny wee Pagan.

We'll turn this man around so fast he'll think he's died and gone to the great merry-go-round in the sky."

They ducked left, following a sleeve of fog that lingered in a narrow trough between buildings. Shoe-sized shapes scuttled away from their feet as they moved away from the streetlights.

But Pagan didn't care. Bring on the rats. She was running through the streets of a strange city with a Scottish spy who would use any excuse to hold her hand.

"Hope our friend doesn't mind rodents," she whispered.

Devin's shrug was barely visible. "Hope he's not a vampire, because we're going to church."

"We're going…where?" She peered ahead. Faint light signaled the end of the alley.

Devin slowed, and the echoing footsteps followed suit.

"Perhaps he'll think we're on a date," Devin said, flashing a grin back at her. "Since we just passed your hotel."

"We did?" She looked back down the alley. Was that a man-shaped form skulking after them?

Then the sense of Devin's words sank in. "Are we on a date?"

"A date only possible with the intrepid Pagan Jones," he said, and pulled her out of the mouth of the alley, and across a wide street to an expanse of greenery empty of all but a few dog walkers and couples, strolling very close together.

"Plaza San Martin." Devin pulled her nearer to him, slowing so they looked more like lovers enjoying the evening. If it hadn't been for their invisible companion twenty yards back, they might have been.

Something large reached toward them through the haze.

Pagan cringed closer to Devin until the shape resolved into a vast tree, seated on a staircase of roots like a king on his throne.

"Strange ghosts they have in Buenos Aires," she whispered, unnerved. "Are we sure our follower isn't one?"

"I don't mean to frighten you, but our ghost probably has friends." He shifted direction and they darted across the lawn, the grass damp and gray in the fog. "Let's find out."

They crossed a wide avenue and entered a more formal garden, heading for a brightly lit white church with a five-story bell tower and locked iron gates. It reminded Pagan of the missions she'd seen in Santa Barbara and San Juan Capistrano.

"*Buenos noches*, Nuestra Señora del Pilar," Devin said, walking right up to the gate, and pulling two narrow metal bars out of his jacket pocket. "Welcome to our lady of the pillars. Will you be my pillar tonight, Pagan? Here."

He put his hands firmly on her waist and pressed her back against the metal door of the gate, his body close. He then slid his hands around her and fumbled for only a moment before she heard a metal click behind her.

He was picking the lock to the front gate of the church, using her as cover. She put her arms up around his neck and looked over his shoulder, waiting for the form of their follower to coalesce out of the fog.

Devin fumbled for a moment, brushing his fingers against her lower back and even lower. Pagan never wore a girdle under pants and was all the more grateful for it now. She shimmied in closer to his hands.

"Pagan," he said in a warning tone.

"We need to make this look real," she said, putting her lips up to his ear. Her eyelashes brushed his cheekbone. "Don't mind me."

"Didn't say I minded." He leaned into her, his chin over her shoulder to see what he was doing. The rise and fall of his chest quickened.

"Out of curiosity," Pagan murmured, her lips against Devin's neck. "Why are we breaking into a church?"

"Because after hours it's the best way into the cemetery," he said, and the gate clicked open.

Whoever was following them must be lurking out of sight, watching their every move. It was unnerving. "Do you take all your dates to the cemetery?"

"It is one of the emptier spots on earth at this hour. If you don't count the ghosts." He disengaged and swept her through the gate, which he closed but did not lock, and over to a side door into the starkly white church. "There'll be no question that anyone else in there is our follower. And if we do it right, you'll get a good look at him."

"Right, then. I'll keep an eye out now, too," Pagan said, moving to cover Devin's back and hoping to catch a glimpse of their pursuer.

But Devin had the church door open in two seconds, ushering her inside to slightly warmer air. The near-total blackness eased as her eyes adjusted to a faint light coming down a set of steep stone stairs. They were at the base of the bell tower.

"How did you get in here so quickly?" Pagan whispered as Devin shut the outer door and led her to another one off to the side.

"My father and I stole some of our best art from churches," he said, teeth flashing in the dimness. His father had been a top art thief and had trained the youthful Devin to be his accomplice. "I got pretty good with their locks."

Pagan took Devin's fingers in hers again as they tiptoed through an empty, wood-paneled office, down a few steps and through an outer door.

The night air was chilly. Fog blurred the tall stone edifices, and for a moment Pagan thought they'd exited onto a narrow city street.

An angel's wing atop a dome came into focus, and a granite skull leered at her from a lintel. Swirls of vapor whorled past statues shrouded in marble veils. Light from the city bled through the fog enough to see perhaps thirty feet in any direction, but there were no spotlights or safety lights splashed up against the walls, embellished with gargoyles, bats and tearful babies. Crosses decorated plaques and lay clutched in stone hands laid peacefully over unmoving chests.

They were in a different kind of city now. The city of the dead.

Pagan edged closer to Devin as he squinted down a narrow lane between the tombs. "Fancy," she said, an unexpected tremor in her voice. "It's like Beverly Hills for the afterlife."

Devin turned his dark head toward her, smirking. "Are you actually scared?"

"Don't be silly," she said, and it came out perfectly insouciant, scornful. But his smile widened. She had a tough time fooling him.

"You've faced down armed troops, the head of the East

German secret police and gangs of reform school girls," he said. "I didn't think anything could scare you."

"The last time I was in a cemetery," she said, "was for Daddy and Ava's funeral."

His eyes were clear, understanding. "They're not here."

"But they are," she said. "They're with me. Always."

His smile softened. "That's why you don't need to be afraid."

She tried to smile back, but she could never do enough to make up for what she'd done to her father and sister. It wasn't possible. She wasn't sure what to think about heaven and all that, but if it existed, she sure wasn't headed there.

Devin moved in close and put his arm around her waist, warm and secure. "Well, I love cemeteries," he said. "They're a history lesson and a reminder to enjoy life now all in one. Come with me, Pagan Jones. I'll keep the ghosts at bay."

She hesitated. The door behind them vibrated with a whomping sound, as if a portal beyond it had closed.

Devin's arm tightened. Their pursuer was near.

That should have frightened her more than the cemetery. Instead, it and Devin's nearness jolted away her fear and replaced it with exhilaration. She wrapped her arm around him and they ran side by side deeper into the misty graveyard.

The vaults rose high on either side of them, engraved with every sort of sorrowful face and weeping figure. As they ran, four-legged forms with fluffy tails scattered before them, meowing.

She and Devin were like the cemetery cats. There was no place for them in the real world, so they found a dark place full of ghosts where they fit right in.

"We need him to know where we are, at least for the moment…" Devin said under his breath. "Run loudly!"

They hammered their heels on the flagstones, angling down a wide avenue lined with two-story mausoleums punctured by narrow gated doorways. They ran noisily past thoughtful Greek gods and vine-covered women clutching sleepy children.

Behind them ran their shadow.

As they came upon a nexus of wide thoroughfares, Devin slowed and softened his footfalls. Pagan did likewise. He drew her into a narrow doorway carved to look like sagging drapery.

They had entered a musty crypt. The darkness coated everything, thick as mud. It struck her that as old as many of the monuments looked, this was still a place where people buried their dead.

Devin put one finger to his lips and pressed her shoulders back into a niche beside the door before taking up a position on the other side of it. It was so dark in here, all she could see of him was the glint in his eyes.

Outside, the fog puffed past. The man following them should walk past them any second now. Pagan needed to get a good look at him, if she was ever to figure out how she knew him.

Deep inside the tomb, something scraped, like bones rasping over stone.

And something—the same thing?—was thrumming. A distant murmur, moving closer, coming at her from the sooty void of the sepulchre.

Pagan froze. There might be more than dusty bones inside this tomb. There might be a fresh body, with plenty of flesh on it, beginning to rot.

Something brushed her hand.

She shot two feet into the air and banged her head on the arch above. Her skull thunked loudly on the stone.

She somehow kept herself from crying out, eyes squinched in pain, rubbing the top of her head with one hand. She looked down to see a large gray tabby, white whiskers fanned wide, a loud purr humming in its throat.

The cat rubbed its cheek against her hand again, and she stroked the rough fur, pain morphing into silent laughter.

"You okay?"

Devin had abandoned his post on the other side of the doorway to check on her.

"The ghosts have found me," she whispered, pointing at the cat.

"So I see." Devin stroked the cat's head and moved in beside her. The cat gave one last trill and wandered back into the dusk of the tomb, which suddenly was a lot less scary.

Light as a pair of dice falling onto felt, footsteps padded on the walk outside.

Too loud to be a cat. Too quiet to be a caretaker.

Pagan edged her eye around the lintel of the tomb entrance, hoping no light would glint off her white-blond hair. The fog was opaque as a blanket, but after a moment it yielded a human figure.

He was tall and broad shouldered, wearing a gray trench coat and fedora. He wasn't walking toward them, but at an angle that showed only his back and the side of his head.

Pagan leaned out farther. Beside her, Devin did the same, arm around her shoulders.

A terrible, urgent feeling of déjà vu pitched in her gut. She'd seen this man before. They way he turned his head, the angle of his shoulders, the firm, light walk…she knew them all. Somehow.

He paused with his back still toward them, head down. He was listening. For them.

Pagan realized she was holding her breath and forced herself to exhale slowly, silently. The man in gray held still, listening for another moment, and then glided forward. The fog swallowed him.

Pagan shook her head at Devin. She still hadn't seen the man's face. Damn it! She stepped out of the tomb, padding on her sneakers. When Devin didn't move with her, she stopped, glaring at him.

"You sure?" he said in a noncarrying tone. "Your ankle…"

"Is fine," she said. "Come on!"

His smile lit up something inside her chest. "Listen," he said.

Faint footsteps clicked at an angle she hadn't expected. She held her hand out to Devin, and he took it. This time he followed. They ran on tiptoes, nearly blind in the fog, toward the sound.

Tomb upon tomb flitted past. Once Pagan glimpsed the man's fedora, but then the vapor eddied around him, and he vanished. Within moments, she was lost. She had a vague feeling they were going in circles, as if the man in gray were a shark, circling as he looked for his prey. He didn't yet seem to know that the roles had been reversed.

Until Pagan nearly cannoned into a small statue of a dog and inhaled a gasp loud enough to bounce off the nearby stone gazebo festooned with cherubs.

"Oh, hell," she whispered.

The footsteps had stopped.

Devin paused, seeming to hover in a murky batch of fog. "No, it's perfect actually," he said. "But which way..."

The footsteps took off at a run, away from them.

"That way!" Pagan said, and they sprinted after.

They dashed between crucifixes and urns. Cats scattered through the fog before them. They bumped into the outer wall, too high and smooth to be easily scaled, and pelted alongside it, heading back toward the church.

"It's the only way out," Devin said. "If the doors have been relocked, it might stop him long enough."

But the doors into and out of Nuestra Señora del Pilar stood open. Pagan and Devin left them that way as they snaked through the bell tower and back out the front gate. The mist had thinned enough to see the lone figure of a man dashing over the groomed lawns, heading north.

Pagan didn't hesitate. How much more fun it was to be the pursuer than the pursued. Together she and Devin negotiated the fog, dodging trees and hopping small fences set up around flower beds, swooping around strolling couples, startling squirrels.

It was a fine summer night for a late supper in Buenos Aires. A perfect time for a nice Malbec with dinner and perhaps some dancing. Several dozen couples were doing exactly that as Pagan and Devin streamed past them in a picturesque plaza while an *orquestra típica* ground out a sultry tango. It was exactly the sort of evening she'd had with Nicky back when she was drinking.

Now she was sober and tracking down a spy. Things had changed.

"We're dancing a different sort of dance," Devin said breathlessly.

Pagan gave a quick laugh. "With a much faster pace!"

The fog thickened again on the far side of the plaza, and they had to slow down as they approached a wide road. Pagan's chest heaved as she scanned up and down. Which way could he have gone?

"Hold your breath for two seconds when I say go," Devin said. "And listen."

"Over the cars?" Pagan said. There weren't many engines rumbling up and down the avenue, but there was at least one every few seconds.

"Worth a try," he said. "Ready?" Off her nod, he drew a very deep breath. "One, two, three—go."

Pagan sucked in a last bit of air and held it, straining to hear something, anything, over the accordion music in the distance and the crackle of tires on pavement. She wiped impatiently at a trickle of sweat running down her temple.

A faint breeze shook the leaves, twirling the fog around like nebulous ribbons. A taxi growled by. As it drew away, familiar, barely audible treads ricocheted over the pavement.

Devin's head turned toward it the same moment hers did.

She released all her breath in a whoosh. "Across the street!"

He grabbed her hand, hesitated to let a truck rattle past, and they galloped across, earning a blared horn from a speeding sedan as it swerved around them.

Pagan waved at the driver and leaped up onto the side-walk. More greenery here, lit with red, yellow and green lights bleeding through the murk from somewhere nearby. Muted carnival music floated over their heads.

"Italpark," Devin said. "He's gone into Italpark."

Before Pagan could ask what he meant, the mist parted to reveal the entrance to an amusement park lit by red and yellow arches of neon light with huge letters spelling out *Italpark* in loopy script above. Flying saucer–shaped bulbs of glowing red and blue decorated the gates, like friendly invaders from Mars. Beyond, towering loops of metal track and rumbling cars half full of screaming people announced a large roller coaster. Families with petulant children were exiting.

Only one person was entering. A tall man in a gray trench coat.

Devin was already at the ticket booth, shoving money at the weary woman inside, convincing her in excellent Spanish that they didn't mind if the park was closing in less than thirty minutes, and perhaps he could offer her a little something extra as a thank-you?

The woman perked up and seconds later they were pushing through the turnstile into the park against a tide of sticky, exhausted children and their sunburned parents.

"He's trying to lose us here," Devin said, craning his neck to see over the heads of the departing crowds. "Not a bad plan."

"Except he's the only one heading into the park instead of out," Pagan said, pointing at the lone gray figure moving against the tide of brightly dressed park-goers.

"Not the only one!"

They wove past strollers and jumped over dropped ice-cream cones. One girl's eyes lit up with recognition when she saw Pagan, and she began to say something, to point… but then Pagan had flown past her.

The man in gray looked over his shoulder at them. It was too foggy, and he was too far away, for Pagan to distinguish his features, but the turn of his head, the posture of his body, gave her another jolt of unnamed recognition.

"So close," she said, and darted forward.

"Pagan, wait!"

Devin ran to catch up as she zoomed around a ride featuring a large octopus, its arms spinning cups full of screaming kids. She was in time to see the man in gray leap the short line in front of the bumper cars. Pagan lost sight of him as he ran across the interior of the ride, ignoring the angry shouts of the operator.

"You go around," Devin said, pushing her to the right. "I'll go left."

Pagan pushed him back. "You go left. I'm going straight."

Before he could catch her, she wormed past two young men smoking in line, leaped over the low railing and was running across the hard cement of the ride's floor.

A bumper car screeched past her, showering sparks from the pole scraping along the ceiling above. A very confused girl stared and screamed, heading right for Pagan, her hands frozen on the wheel. Pagan dodged the collision and stepped up on the hood of a young boy's car jammed against two others so she could vault over the far railing.

A haunted house ride to her left. Dumbo flying cars to

her right, and a line of brightly colored gaming stalls straight ahead.

But the man in gray was nowhere to be seen.

A woman screamed, and the yelling of the bumper car operator increased markedly in volume as Devin leaped over the railing to land at her side. "With any luck, we'll all be arrested together," he said.

"I don't see him," she said. "Should we split up and look?"

His eyes narrowed with calculation. "All right. I'll find you again in two minutes. Where do you want to look?"

He was asking her instead of telling. He learned fast. "I'll go straight ahead, into the games. See you in a second."

She was off before he could say another word. The brief glimpses she'd already had of the man had galvanized her. She had to see his face, remember his name, know she wasn't crazy.

The game booths were like ones she'd seen at parks and carnivals at home: throw the ball in the basket, shoot the gun at the moving target, race your miniature camel and jockey. Only the cartoons painted on the walls and counters were unfamiliar; the signs in Spanish and the brightly colored stuffed animals hanging from the ceiling were different enough to let her know she wasn't at the LA County Fair.

There weren't many people left playing, which made it easier to see that the man in gray wasn't one of the boys firing water pistols at the clown's nose, and he wasn't near the mother helping her crying daughter get cotton candy out of her hair.

Things were pinging, dinging and buzzing at lazy intervals, and several booths were closing their shutters. Pagan slowed and began checking the narrow spaces between stalls, making sure her man wasn't using the park's back alleys. She hunkered down to pull up a muddy cloth skirt ringing the bottom of a cubicle to see if he was crouching under there. But she found only half a moldering sandwich and the still-smiling decapitated head of a pink teddy bear.

She stood up, wiping her hands on her pants, and found him, his back to her, of course, inside a telephone booth.

Using the line of stalls as partial cover, she treaded closer. *Don't get too excited now.* It could be some other man in a gray trench coat.

But it was him. She'd know the line of those shoulders anywhere now. He was on the phone, glancing around him. His jaw moved as he spoke, but that's all she could see. She needed a better angle.

There weren't many people left in this area. A man in khaki shorts was examining the rubber duckies across the way, and a family was arguing as they walked together with the painful slowness of people who have done nothing but amble in circles for hours.

Pagan darted across the dusty walk between the line of games and weaseled her way in behind the family. The mother was rather wide, and the father rather tall, with three teenagers slumping along beside them. So Pagan pushed in as close as she could, matching their drowsy pace as she got closer to the phone booth.

The man in gray was hanging up the phone. Pagan allowed the family to move away as she focused on his face. He wiped his hand across his upper lip and tipped his hat back, looking away from her, to the left.

Any second now...

Something overhead creaked ominously. She looked up. The metal-framed canvas awning above her swayed.

A winch creaked. Pagan spun to see the man in the khaki shorts releasing a cable holding up the awning. It swung at her head, hard.

She threw herself at the ground. The edge grazed the slightly teased top of her hair and slammed into the wooden frame of the stall beside her. She stared at it for a second, disbelieving. If it had hit her, she'd be out cold. Or dead.

She twisted around to stare at the man in khaki shorts. He was two steps away, a shovel in both hands raised to strike her.

She rolled. The shovel smacked into the dirt where her head had been.

"Hey!" she shouted. "Stop!" Maybe Devin or someone would hear her.

Khaki Shorts Man squinted tiny hamster eyes at her and lifted the shovel with both hands again.

Pagan was on her feet. He lunged, lashing out with the shovel. But at the last second, she moved toward him instead of away.

The shovel hit dirt as Pagan slammed into Khaki Shorts' shoulder. He staggered sideways, and she booked it down the line of game stalls.

Khaki Shorts was only a pace behind.

He was fast for a short-legged, rat-faced man. Pagan vaulted over a counter into a booth featuring balloons and darts.

Moments before, its keeper had finished tying up a giant net full of stuffed animals to one corner of the ceiling.

"Oye!" he barked. *"No mas!"*

"No mas!" Pagan agreed, ducking under his outstretched arm.

Khaki Shorts hurdled over the counter after her.

The gamekeeper stepped right into the man's face. "What the hell do you think you're doing!" he screamed in Spanish.

Khaki Shorts punched the gamekeeper in the solar plexus and stomped on his foot. The gamekeeper doubled over, hopping on his good foot, yelling in pain. Khaki Shorts shoved him to the ground and leaped for Pagan as she untied the net full of stuffed animals.

A fluffy rainbow avalanche bounced onto Khaki Shorts and the gamekeeper. The net appeared to be holding a year's supply of prizes or more, because they kept coming. The game guy, already injured, was knocked flat. But Khaki Shorts stayed up for several seconds, batting away purple kitty cats and blue turtles as he waded through the rising tide, until an orange carp the size of a Great Dane smacked him in the face. Down he went.

Pagan dashed out the other side of the stall before it filled up like a bowl of fuzzy water. Someone grabbed her arm.

She yelped, whipping it away.

"Pagan! Sorry—it's me!"

It was Devin, wonderfully familiar except for the blood trickling from a cut on his forehead.

"Are you all right?" he asked, staring at the sea of toys still pouring into the booth.

"Yes, are you?" She reached up. "You're bleeding."

"A woman tried to hit me with a pipe," he said. "Did someone..."

"Yes, and he's buried in there, so we better run before he digs out," Pagan said. "This way."

Devin jogged beside her toward the park's exit. "Our friend in gray has friends of his own. This must be their prearranged place to come when they're being followed."

"I saw him in a phone booth," Pagan said. "What happened to the one who attacked you?"

"Fast asleep under the roller coaster," he said. "You *saw* the man in gray?"

"Not his face. His friend made sure of that."

"Damn it," Devin said. "With that kind of help, he's got to be a professional. And now we've lost him."

"A professional—working for whom?" Pagan asked. "And how could I know him?"

They'd reached the turnstiles at the exit. Devin let her go out first, and they were immersed again in the fog. Their quarry was nowhere to be seen.

"Do you think they'll come after us again?" she asked. They crossed the street, moving once more across the shrouded plaza back toward the elegant apartment buildings of Recoleta.

"I don't think they wanted us dead, just to stop us from following their man," he said.

"Listen," she said, and abruptly slowed their pace.

The echoes of their footsteps were a half second behind in slowing along with them.

"You learn fast," Devin said.

"I'd bet a million dollars I don't have it's the man in gray again," Pagan said. "He's relentless."

Their eyes met. Devin raised his eyebrows in a question. She raised hers along with a slow smile in reply.

He took her hand. "You sure? I could take you back to the hotel and…"

"He's my tail," she said. "And I want to keep learning how this works."

He nodded shortly, his eyes traveling up and down her body, still clad in practical capri pants, white shirt tied at the waist and white Keds. "At least you're not in heels. Lesson one, always wear shoes you can run in."

"Oh, I can run in heels," she said.

They headed south instead of toward her hotel. Devin had something in mind. "Lesson two," he said as they crossed back in the general direction of Italpark, "try to go somewhere you find familiar that will be confusing for your followers."

She considered this. "Well, I'm very familiar with my hotel suite, and…that's about it."

"In lieu of that." He allowed a smile into his dark eyes and reached for her hand. "Find someone who knows the location better than you do, and have them help you out."

"You *are* useful," she said.

They rounded the south end of darkening Italpark. Not fifty yards ahead, a freight train rumbled down some tracks. Its front lights were the only illumination, save for a few safety lights along the tracks.

"Lesson three," he said, "stay in well-populated, crowded

places. Don't turn down empty alleys or run through deserted rail yards."

He pushed through an unchained gate onto the rockstrewn dirt of a railroad yard. To their right the tracks led to more lights and a large building that was probably the terminal station. Ahead and to the left lay nothing but blackness.

"Welcome to one of Buenos Aires' finest rail yards." Devin pointed to the first set of tracks as he stepped over them. Behind them, the footsteps were getting closer. "Shall we pick up some speed?"

He ran a step or two ahead of her in a gentlemanly fashion, making sure she knew when a track or other obstacle was about to appear ahead of her. This was handier than she liked to admit, because it was shockingly dark and the place was littered with large rocks.

The man behind them had no such arrangement. At first he was gaining on them. But halfway across he tripped and fell over something with a scrape.

That gave them an extra forty yards, enough to find a hole in the fence on the other side of the rail yard, get them down an embankment and into a warren of brick buildings.

Here the darkness was nearly complete. The brand-new moon hadn't shown up yet, and when it did, the clouds and fog would keep its light at bay.

"Welcome to Villa 31," Devin said, keeping his voice low. "Under no circumstances are you to leave my side while we are here."

Pagan was about to give him a smart retort, but they passed by three men whispering and exchanging something in the shadows she was glad she couldn't see. They cast narrow glances at Pagan and Devin until they flitted past.

They weren't in the Argentina of broad, tree-lined avenues and gracious Parisian-style apartments anymore. The hand-built ramshackle buildings had graffiti-covered brick walls and roofs of corrugated tin. Trash crawling with rats littered the dirt path between buildings, and a stomach-churning smell of stagnant sewage and fresh urine kept wafting up from disgusting holes in the ground or through irregular doorways.

Without any source of light but what spilled weakly through the occasional door frame, they slowed to a walk. There weren't a lot of windows here. Many of the doorways were shrouded by tarps, or reinforced with broken-off pipes and uneven strips of steel.

"Who lives here?" Pagan whispered.

"The poor, the marginalized. You could call it a shanty-town, but it's been here for over thirty years so it's become more permanent than that," Devin said. "It started when immigrants from Paraguay and Uruguay weren't welcomed in the nicer areas, or couldn't afford them. Now their children's children are growing up here."

Pagan shied away from a fat shape, then laughed when a trace of light revealed it to be a giant cardboard ice cream cone, advertising *helado* for sale. "So this place has ice-cream shops, but it's so dangerous, I can't leave your side."

"People outside Villa 31 think all the residents are criminals and thieves," Devin said. "But many are bus drivers and construction workers and owners of ice-cream shops. But after dark…"

"You're more prone to run into the criminals," Pagan finished for him.

"One writer called it a *villa miseria*, but the locals gave them all numbers. This is Villa 31, or sometimes the residents call it Villa Esperanza."

"Hopeville," said Pagan. "They haven't lost their sense of humor."

"No sanitation services, no electricity and no running water but what the residents fix up for themselves. Don't touch any wires you might come across. They hook themselves into the grid illegally where they can, but it's not exactly reliable."

Pagan caught a whiff of campfire smoke. That must be how some of the residents kept warm on cool nights like this, or how they cooked their meals. She jumped over a pile of garbage and risked a look back. Her eyes were adjusting to the lack of streetlights, but the darkness was too thick to allow her to see how close their pursuer was.

"We have bad neighborhoods in Los Angeles, too," she said. "But at least they get city services."

They passed an open door with firelight casting writhing shadows on the ground outside. Inside, two guitars competed in a sparkling, rigorous duel. Pagan risked a glance through the door and saw two seated, mustached men playing the instruments while another in a sort of cowboy hat, boots and puffy pants tucked in at the knee clicked his boot heels in a vigorous, demanding tap dance.

"Gauchos," Devin said. "Argentine cowboys."

Pagan watched them for another moment. "That dancer would make a better costar than Tony Perry."

The narrow passage between brick buildings had widened into a broader expanse with a few poles and odd-shaped structures planted in the middle. As they passed, she could see tall swings, an abandoned child's red wagon and a jungle gym constructed from sturdy pipe. Someone had put quite a lot of work into a homemade children's playground.

Behind them, footsteps clicked, perfectly in time with their own.

"He's there," Pagan said.

"Let's see if we can get him to show you his face," Devin said, letting go of her hand. "Grab that wagon for me, will you?"

They were on the other side of the playground now, approaching a lopsided three-story building with a white cross painted on the front door and a battered but recognizable wooden statue of the Virgin Mary holding a glowing oil lamp out front. She was nearly as tall as Pagan.

"You'll help us do a good deed, won't you, *Madre*?" Devin asked the statue as he grabbed it around the waist, dragging it toward another murky opening between buildings. Pagan wheeled the wagon after him as he shuffled into a courtyard darker than the cemetery crypts.

"In the corner," Devin said shortly, conserving breath. Pagan rattled the wagon over to the darkest corner of the courtyard. Devin followed, setting Mary down carefully onto the wagon. Her oil lamp swayed, sending their shadows crawling up the walls like monstrous spiders.

"Wait by the entrance to the courtyard," he said. "Keep your eyes peeled, and when I tell you to run…"

"I run!" she said. She galloped over to the eerily lit entrance to the courtyard and flattened against the wall beside it. She nearly knocked over a shovel, and sent a nest of cockroaches squirming in all directions. Pagan had never been one to squeal and bolt at the sight of a bug or a mouse, but that was enough to make her grunt and grab the shovel in case any of them came closer.

The wagon squeaked as Devin got it into position. The Virgin's silhouette was cast larger than life-size behind her by the lamp. Devin took off his jacket and draped it over her shoulders. Then he removed the lantern from her hand, and placed it at her feet.

The shadow loomed larger now, with more manly shoulders. Seized with an idea, Pagan bolted back over to him and handed him the shovel. "My prayers go out to Our Lady of the Spear," she said.

He took the shovel thoughtfully. The light from the oil lamp, striking his face from below, sent diabolical shadows up from his eyebrows. "Or perhaps Our Lady of the Spar," he said. "Good thinking. Now get back there!"

She hurried back to her hiding spot, watching as he laid the shovel horizontally across the Virgin's hands, yanked his fine leather belt from its loops and used it to secure the shovel athwart the Virgin's waist. The shadows from it swept outward, so that the Virgin appeared to be some knight of old, brandishing an antique weapon in each hand.

Devin crouched behind his creation. At the same moment footsteps approached the courtyard. They slowed and went silent. A cockroach crawled up the wall near her ear, and Pagan fought the urge to scream and smack it. She should have kept that damned shovel.

At first the man in gray was nothing but a moving spot in the blackness. Then he stepped into the weak light from the oil lamp. He was holding a gun.

His eyes were as gray as his trench coat, and steely. His nose was hawk-like, his chin strong, with what could have been a charming dimple between it and his full lower lip. He would've been handsome but for the coldness in his gaze.

And then she remembered.

The cute one. The relentless one.

Alaric Vogel.

The man in gray was the East German soldier who'd nearly killed her the night the Berlin Wall went up. He'd been a grunt then, unspooling wire along the border at 1:00 a.m., when she'd stolen his gun, made a fool of him, gotten her friends across the border and then run away. He'd chased her for miles.

The last time Pagan had seen him, five months ago, he'd been lying unconscious at her feet after she knocked him out using a bronze bust of Karl Marx. She'd looked at his identification card and memorized his name. Alaric Vogel.

The cool night air that had seemed refreshing after all her exertion was now clammy, cold. Why the hell was Alaric Vogel following her?

A terrifying rattle erupted from the looming shadow in the courtyard, and Mary trundled forward, brandishing her weapons. Devin was invisible behind her in shadow. Pagan was positioned perfectly to see Alaric Vogel's eyes widen in surprise.

He raised the gun. "Halt!" he shouted, exactly as he had once shouted at Pagan. "Halt!"

But the Virgin was picking up speed. Alaric Vogel shouted once more and fired. The bullet broke off a few wooden folds of her veil and put a hole in Devin's suit jacket.

But it didn't stop Mary. Propelled by Devin, she lurched forward, shovel ends scraping the side walls of the courtyard's opening.

Uncertain and unwilling to face a looming giant immune to bullets, Alaric Vogel turned to run.

Not fast enough. As the Virgin passed her, Pagan darted in behind the statue to join Devin and push it. The extra speed sent the blade end of the shovel into Alaric Vogel's shoulder.

He stumbled, but didn't go down. Shadows danced.

"One…" Devin said under his breath. "Two…three!"

They each gave the Virgin one last huge push. She teetered dangerously and hurtled forward. The shovel's shoulder smacked into Alaric Vogel's back. He went down in a heap.

"Run!" Devin said.

She ran. Past the moaning Alaric, and around the Virgin, now trundling to a stop.

"This way!" Devin guided her with a hand on her waist, and they angled to the right.

Pagan glanced back one last time at the East German who had followed her all the way from Berlin. Auburn hair, that's right. It was closely cropped. She'd thought he was attractive until she got close and saw that cruel look in his eye. Remembering it now made the hair on her arms stand on end.

The Virgin ground to a stop on her wagon. A breeze caught Devin's jacket and blew it around her like a cape.

Alaric Vogel was still lying facedown as they rounded a corner.

"Did you see his face?" Devin said, turning down another dirt alley, hopping some low-strung wires.

"Yes," she said, still not quite believing it. "It's Alaric Vogel."

It took a second for the name to register. "The soldier in East Berlin you brained? Are you sure?"

"Sure as shooting," she said. "Which is what he did at me."

"From soldier to spy," Devin said. "Not bad for five months."

"Or he's working for himself, stalking me," Pagan said.

"He's no amateur. He had professional help at the ready," Devin said. "That means he's part of some larger organization."

"And he's East German, so that means Stasi." Pagan didn't like how that made her stomach tighten. "They must've found out it was me who helped Thomas and his family escape."

"Vogel probably figured out the girl who cut him down to size was the famous Pagan Jones, so he used the knowledge to get an assignment working for the Stasi. He's ambitious."

"Why would they give a damn about me?" Pagan rubbed her upper arms. The cold was sinking into her bones.

"In case you were working for the CIA or MI6." Devin put his arm around her, now that he no longer had a suit jacket to give. "Which you weren't, technically, back in Berlin."

"But I am, technically, now." She huddled in close to him. "Do you think they know what's going on with Von Albrecht?"

"Not as much as you, and now I, know." Devin steered

her under a line of laundry hanging out to dry. "My friends did find two bugs in your suite when they swept it this afternoon."

"Bugs?" She envisioned cockroaches, then realized what he meant. Devin's nearness was distracting. "They're listening to our suite?"

"The devices weren't there when the place was swept yesterday afternoon," Devin said. "They must have been put in place after that. We don't know for certain it was the Stasi, but it's looking likely now."

Pagan thought back. "I don't think I said much about Von Albrecht, maybe that I was going to Emma's. And they might've heard Mercedes talk to you about the observatory thing you set up for her tonight. Which was wonderful of you, by the way. And..." She broke off. She'd said a lot more things, of a personal nature, last night. Things she wasn't going to tell Devin.

"And, what?" he asked.

"Last night," she said, editing it down in her head before she said it out loud. "I said I really wanted a drink."

He didn't need to know that she'd especially wanted a drink because she had feelings for him. It unnerved her, knowing that Alaric Vogel might've heard her say that. Her alcoholism was well known, but her feelings about Devin were the most private thing she could think of.

"Ah." Devin's arm around her tightened. He hadn't brought up the scene between them from the night before. She hoped he never did. Unless maybe she could hear exactly what she wanted, and that was too much to hope for.

"In a way it's reassuring that it's the Stasi," he said. "They have a reason to be following you, based on what happened in Berlin. If it was the Israelis or the Russians or anyone else, I'd think the whole investigation into Von Albrecht was blown. But the Stasi's probably tracking you both in Los Angeles and here as a sort of fishing expedition. They assume you're up to no good again."

"They know me well," she said.

Ahead, light spilled from a well-kempt cement building. As they approached, a roar of laughter rattled the plastic doorway. Tinny radio music swelled, and Devin took his arm away to open and hold the door for her.

It was a lot warmer in here, with real electric lights and a bar along one wall. The room was about thirty feet square and jammed with men and women dancing around the small round tables and wobbly wooden chairs. A small *orquestra tipica* played vigorously in the corner, while a plump woman in her midforties with absurdly black hair passed out bottles of beer and shots of some dark brown liquor along with bottles of Coke. The place smelled dark and rich, like charred steak and black licorice.

"*Che*, Beatriz!" Devin said, moving over to give the woman a kiss on the cheek. "You look spectacular as always." His Spanish was rapid and tilted with an accent Pagan was beginning to recognize as Argentine.

The woman's dark eyes lit up at the sight of him, and she kissed him on either cheek before stepping back to get a good look at him. "*Che! Mira vos*, Devin."

Devin moved in close to her dangling earrings and said something low. Beatriz's eyes took in Pagan, painted eyebrows slowly rising. When he lifted his head, she nodded, but said, "It's up to her, boy. Not me. She's upstairs."

Pagan hadn't noticed the narrow stairs made of cinder block at the back of the room. Devin gave Beatriz another kiss on the check, thanked her and gestured for Pagan to take a seat while he headed toward the steps.

Beatriz sent a glare out to a few men gawking at Pagan at a nearby table that made them shrink like turtles back into their shells. She gave a pleased nod as Pagan sat down in a three-legged chair. "Would you like something to drink, *señorita*?" she asked in Spanish.

"*Sólo un Coke, por favor, señora,*" Pagan said. "*Gracias.*"

The room was pulsing with the energy of the dancers and the band. A light sheen of sweat on everyone's skin gave it all a glow Pagan recognized from her days of drinking and partying.

But the little shot glasses of dark liquor and bottles of beer weren't half as interesting to her as Devin. He was about to ascend the stairs when two long brown legs picked their way gracefully down. One side of his mouth curved up appreciatively and he backed up to let the woman down. She was a tall, beautiful creature probably in her late twenties, with long honey-brown hair and dark eyes set in big spiky lashes. She was wearing a tight skirt and a sleeveless top, and the smooth tan skin on her bare arms and legs gleamed. More than one head turned to take in the view. In comparison, Pagan was sadly pale, underdressed and sweat-soaked.

The woman cocked an eyebrow at Devin and allowed him to take her hand and help her down the stairs. They began to talk, their heads very close.

"Who is that?" Pagan asked Beatriz in Spanish as the woman deposited a warm bottle of Coke on her table. "She's lovely."

"Julieta is the owner here," Beatriz said. "So she controls the entry."

"*La entrada?*" That was the word Beatriz had used, and Pagan didn't quite understand what she meant.

"*Sí,*" Beatriz said, and moved away before Pagan could say more.

Pagan thirstily drank every drop of her warm Coke as she watched Devin smirking and flirting with Julieta. They obviously knew each other, and the longer they talked, the more certain Pagan became of some kind of history between them.

The way Devin tilted his head, the sidelong glances... Pagan had no idea what he was saying to the girl, but Devin's manner was awfully familiar. He'd flirted with Pagan in exactly the same way. It would've been fascinating if it didn't feel as if every one of Devin's sly, admiring looks at Julieta was a stab in Pagan's gut.

Julieta gave Devin a small nod after he made one particular request and then pointed at two young men lounging with beers nearby and said something sharply to them. Both immediately put their beers aside, stood up and listened attentively as Devin spoke. The moment he was done, Julieta nodded again, and they sprinted through the crowd, past Pagan and out the door.

She turned to watch them go. Had Devin asked for help in dealing with Alaric Vogel? Those men were probably going to check on him, and perhaps detain him for longer.

At least, that's what Pagan would've asked for if it were she. But Devin hadn't seen fit to include her in the conversation. The whole evening had been a wonderful tango of sorts for the two of them. Until now.

Julieta cast a sidelong look over at Pagan, tilted her nose into the air and shrugged. Devin's demeanor altered slightly. He withdrew, became cool, remote. He shrugged in return and moved to go.

Oh, good, he was turning away. Julieta put a hand on his shoulder and didn't let go when he pivoted back to face her, his back to Pagan.

Julieta eyed Pagan again as she spoke, then moved in close. Nearly as tall as Devin in her heels, her lips were on level with his. They were full, and red and shiny, and as she tilted her head at him and said something challenging, Devin kissed her.

Pagan heard a gasp, and realized it had come from her. All the blood fled from her body as Julieta's glossy eyelids closed in bliss and her arms snaked around Devin's neck. Devin's arms were wrapped around her waist, their bodies pressed together.

Pagan's head swam. How well she remembered what it was like to be held by him like that, to happily drown in the scent of cotton and tobacco leaves he emanated, to have his kiss steal the breath from her body.

She forced her eyes open and made herself look at them. Dang it, she was not going to throw up in some shantytown bar because a stupid man kissed some woman who "controlled the entry" or whatever it was. Pagan had greeted her ex-boyfriend Nicky's pregnant wife with a big phony smile, and she could damned well fake her way through this, too.

The kiss was over. Julieta was wiping her lipstick playfully off Devin's lips and smiling as she spoke. Devin turned his head toward Pagan, also smiling, and beckoned her with one free hand. The other was still at Julieta's waist.

Pagan touched one hand to her collarbone, raising her eyebrows in a "who, me?" gesture.

But Devin had turned back to Julieta, holding her hand as she led him toward the concrete steps leading up.

Fine. Pagan got to her feet and found Beatriz at her side, picking up the empty bottle of Coke.

"What can I give you for your hospitality?" Pagan asked. The Spanish she'd learned from Mercedes during their long hours together in reform school was really paying off.

"Oh, nothing, my dear," Beatriz said. "Devin gave us far more than we deserve long ago."

Pagan slowly took her hand out of her pocket and nodded. There was some kind of history here that went deeper than a flirtation. How little she really knew of Devin.

"Thank you," she said. "You've been very kind."

"It was nothing," Beatriz said with a wide smile. "I'll wave at you next time I see you on the big screen."

Pagan put two fingers to her brow in a salute, and weaved her way through the tiny tables and tangoing couples over to the concrete steps. Devin's shoes were vanishing at the top.

She manhandled her feelings into a ball and shoved them into the dark little suitcase in the back of her brain so she could trip lightly up the steps, rounding the corner and farther up to find herself on the flat cement roof in the open air.

Faint light and noise drifted up from the cantina below. The view showed a dark, uneven jigsaw puzzle of rooftops laid around her. To one side, clouds scuttled over a sliver of moon rising over the water. To the other, across the rail yard, glittered the brighter radiance of the rest of Buenos Aires. Villa 31 was a bit like one of Mercedes's black holes. No light escaped.

Devin and Julieta waited a few steps away. "This is Pagan Jones," Devin said. "Pagan, this is our hostess, Julieta."

Pagan showed her teeth in a Cheshire cat smile and took Julieta's limp hand in a firm grip to shake it with an over-abundance of enthusiasm. "How lovely to meet you after such a difficult evening," she said in Spanish. "Thank you so much for your kindness."

Julieta let her grip drop away and nodded, as if satisfied. "Miss Jones. You are exactly as I imagined you to be," she said. "Mr. Black speaks very highly of you."

Devin was staring out over the rooftops, his expression carefully blank.

"He's a liar, of course," Pagan said with a touch of impatience. She'd had enough of Devin for the moment, and this was an opportune moment to let it show. Clearly Julieta wanted Devin for herself. Well. She could have him. "But I suppose he's a charming one when he puts some effort into it. As for me, I'll be glad to get back to my own little hotel suite and forget this night ever happened."

Julieta eyed her, smiling slightly. "That would be best," she said. "You will never speak of me or of this place to anyone. Please."

"I swear by my hairdresser's enormous stash of peroxide," Pagan said.

Julieta laughed, surprised, and Pagan squashed down a stab of fondness for the woman. It was a special gift to make people like you when you hated them. And clearly Julieta was someone they needed to make happy. So Pagan would do what was needed, even if it made her want to throw up.

Julieta had taken Devin by the hand and was leading him across the roof, picking her way over a rail-less wooden bridge to the roof of the building next door. Pagan followed, consigned to the back like the thirdest of third wheels. She wasn't surprised to see Julieta knock four times on a trap-door. After a moment, it lifted open, and a large man with a rifle emerged. At Julieta's nod, he walked all the way up onto the roof and allowed them all to descend into the other building while he waited above.

They trailed down a very closed-in set of steps, almost too tight to fit Devin's shoulders. Pagan decided it was a secret staircase, and indeed, they went down at least four flights of stairs by Pagan's calculation before they encountered a door.

The exited into a brick tunnel fifteen feet wide and arched high like an old Roman church. A tiny portion of it was lit by one bare bulb, snaked down on a cord from the building above. Beyond lay cavernous musty blackness. The air was cold. Somewhere in the distance, water dripped.

Tunnels. Dieter had mentioned tunnels. Were these the same underground passages, or was Buenos Aires riddled with them?

Julieta pulled a key off a necklace tucked into the neck of her dress, and unlocked a large metal strongbox at the bottom of the stairs. She pulled out a flashlight and handed it to Devin.

"Leave this on the bottom stair when you reach the other side," she said. "You will know it is the other side because you'll see stairs, made of brick like these walls, that go up. If you go past the stairs, you may get lost in the tunnels."

"And after we go up the stairs made of brick?" Devin asked, gently taking the flashlight from her.

"Knock three times on the door at the top and tell them your name is Romeo." Julieta's teeth gleamed very white in the darkness as she smiled. "A little joke they like to make on me."

As she spoke, Pagan grabbed the flashlight from Devin and flicked it on. The diffused yellow beam illuminated another fifty feet of tunnel. The masonry was covered in mold and dead tree roots. The floor was also brick, but covered in years of dirt and dust. She was like an archaeologist wandering into a very old tomb.

"What is this place?" she said. "Who built it?"

Julieta shrugged. "Some say it was the monks who built the first churches of the city, and wished to connect them all underground. Some say it was the smugglers or the slavers who wished to move their goods from the harbor secretly so they wouldn't have to pay the tax. Or maybe it was both. All I know for sure is that this tunnel goes under the train station and comes up inside the cellar of my friend's bar. As long as your name is Romeo, he will let you out."

"Thank you, beautiful Julieta," Devin said, and leaned in to kiss her cheek.

She did not move her head to kiss him on the lips, but

accepted it as if it were her due. "I will not be seeing you again, I think," she said.

Devin half smiled. "One of your visions again? Did you see my death?"

She laughed and shook her head. "Not yet. But I have seen, I think, a vision of your future." And she looked right at Pagan.

Pagan's eyes became perfectly round as Devin turned to stare at her, too. He looked a little pale.

"As long as his future involves taking me straight back to my hotel room and then going away forever so I can finally get some sleep, that's a vision I can get behind," she said.

"She is good," Julieta said, and turned her velvety gaze to Devin. "Better than you."

He nodded and smoothly kissed her hand. "Thank you."

"It is we who thank you," she said. "Forever. Good night."

And her gleaming brown legs trod lightly up the stairs.

ATRÁS

To dance backward.

"So your girlfriend has visions of your death?" Pagan said.

She'd kept the flashlight and was leading the way down the tunnel. Devin had made no objection, following close behind. But they weren't holding hands anymore. "That must put a damper on things."

"You know quite well she is not my girlfriend," he said. "But Julieta is known to see things that haven't happened yet. As far as I know, she's always right."

"Fate's a crock," Pagan said. "Which means prophecies are, too."

"You make your own fate," he said. "I know."

"And you make yours," she said. "By flirting outrageously with every girl or guy who might be useful."

"I do my job," he said, an edge in his voice.

"Kissing is your job?" She couldn't help the jealous arch in her voice. "Did you kiss Thomas when you were persuading him to spy for you? Is that why…?"

She broke off, unable to ask if that's why he'd kissed her back in Berlin. To keep her on his string.

A horrible thought struck her, a thought she hated herself for having the moment it came to her. But maybe Devin had thought she was perfect for the job in Berlin partly because she'd gone all the way with Nicky. Perhaps he thought that meant she could be easily swayed by a handsome face, that she'd be willing to give herself to other men if it helped the mission. Didn't spies often sleep around to get information? That hadn't happened yet, but they'd asked her to flirt with Dieter. Devin himself kissed and manipulated her using his charisma and wiles. Had he slept with people to get what he wanted from them? Had he assumed that now she was no longer a virgin, Pagan would be fine treating herself like a piece of meat?

No, Devin wasn't like that. He'd shown time and again that he valued her for herself.

But maybe at the beginning he'd seen her that way. Tony Perry had said men would only want her for one thing now. Tony was a jerk and a half, but he wasn't the only one to think that way.

Their footsteps echoed against the brick ceiling for a moment as he didn't speak. "Sometimes flirting and kissing are part of the job," he finally said.

"Flirting, kissing and sometimes more?" she said.

He kept walking but threw her a look. "That's not something a minor would be asked to do."

She let that sit. So he'd never expected her to sleep with anyone. Or so he said. "You're not a minor," she said.

He put a hand gently on her shoulder and pulled her around to face him. His blue eyes were stormier than usual in the dim yellow light. "Does it bother you—about Thomas?"

he asked. "I never kissed him, but I did give him the wrong idea."

"No," she said. "I mean, yes, it's not right to mislead people, but he's fine now and you did it for a good reason. I tried to do the same thing with Dieter and nearly kissed Emma tonight. So it's not like I can judge you."

"So why does it bother you that I did it with Julieta?" he said. "Yes, she's an old friend, but you know I only wanted her to keep Alaric Vogel at bay while you and I got away safely."

The words should've made her happy, but she couldn't quite believe them. "You looked like you were enjoying it," she said.

"I've had worse," he said with a half smile. "But I'm not a bad actor myself, you know."

"Oh, I know it all too well," she said.

His brows rose in realization. "So that's it. You think…" He broke off as some unnamed emotion nearly erupted out of him. She'd never seen him quite so disturbed before. "It's not as if I planned to get close to you, Pagan."

"Yet somehow you ended up sharing my suite," she said in her worst snide tone. "You practically killed me when you found me in your bathroom, and later you fell asleep in my bed."

"Only because you're a stubborn pain in the ass who won't do as she's told!" he erupted, and then checked himself. She could see him mentally counting to ten, and it was gratifying to know that she'd gotten under his skin. But he wasn't the type of man you could provoke into saying he loved you back. He wasn't the type you could normally provoke at all.

He went on. "In fact, my boss was hoping you'd fall for Thomas so we could be sure you'd accept his invitation to Ulbricht's little garden party."

"You wanted me to fall for a man who likes men," she said flatly, and quickened her pace down the tunnel away from him.

He followed. "No, that's what the higher-ups were hoping..." He broke off and swore something too Scottish for her to understand under his breath. "I'm not going to be drawn into a pointless argument with you."

"Yes, my feelings are pointless to you. I understand that," she said.

She heard his footsteps stop behind her. "This isn't the time or place to discuss it."

She slowed and turned the flashlight beam toward his feet. His shadow stretched back behind him like a dark ghost. "Did you pick me because I'd been with Nicky?"

His face lay in darkness, but she could distinguish a thunderous frown. "We picked you because the daughter of the leader of East Germany loved your movies, and we knew you'd want to find out more about your mother's past. That's all there is to it."

He stalked toward her, tweaked the flashlight from her hand and stomped on down the tunnel.

"You never want to talk about anything important," she said, following him. "It's never the right time or place."

"And it never occurs to you that there might be something more imperative than your emotions," he said.

"Yes, it does," she contradicted. "What about *your* emotions?"

He paced ahead of her, his boot heels echoing on the cold wet brick. "You may bend the world to your will, Pagan Jones," he said. "But you will not bend me."

For once she had no reply.

A few moments later, he said, "Here it is."

The flashlight's ray found a crumbling brick staircase along one wall, going up. As they clacked up it, the reality of all that had happened overshadowed her once more. They were in a secret tunnel beneath Buenos Aires, and she'd identified a Nazi war criminal with radioactive material and clandestine plans to use it in a couple of weeks.

"Promise me one thing." The words had a hard time leaving her lips, but it was too important to leave unsaid.

"Mercedes told me not to make promises I can't keep," he said without looking back at her.

"You have to save the animals in that basement," she said. "Please."

He exhaled and turned to look down on her, his face unreadable. "I'll do everything I can."

Three knocks and a "Romeo," and Pagan and Devin were walking out of a small café in Recoleta, unsmiling, hands stuffed into their pockets or under their arms against the cold.

Devin left her without another word in the lobby of the Alvear. Once back in her suite, Pagan nearly panicked when she found Mercedes gone, until she remembered that her friend would likely be at the observatory very late.

She went to wash her face only to stare at her sweaty, brick-dust-covered face in the living room mirror. Devin had said it never occurred to her that something might be more important than her emotions. What he didn't understand was that a constant monitoring of her thoughts and feelings had to be her first priority. One slip, and she'd be buying everyone in the Hotel Alvear's bar a drink, including herself.

It did occur to her that he had a lot of things other than Pagan Jones on his mind—the fate of his mission and now a possible nuclear attack for starters. He'd always made it clear that as long as he was her supervisor, nothing truly intimate would happen between them. He was scrupulous that way, and she loved and hated him for it.

Oh, God, she loved him.

Stupid Scotsman.

She walked straight to the suite's bar and drank a large glass of water instead of the martini she craved.

Showered and pajamaed, she was still too wired to sleep. So she practiced her tango steps around the suite's living room, flinging her imaginary partner more violently around the room than the choreography called for.

Mercedes came in after 2:00 a.m.

"You're up late, too. A successful evening?" she asked. She looked tired but happy.

"I guess you could call it that. I saw him. It's Dr. Some-one." She gave Mercedes a quick version of all of the events of the night. Mercedes changed into her own pin-striped flannel pajamas as she listened, and they ended up both under the covers in Mercedes's giant bed, talking.

"Well, I'm glad you're done with this thing," Mercedes said. "I know you enjoy it at some level, but that Von Albrecht guy is a nutcase. You and I and everyone else on earth are better off far away from him."

"I've seen what he does with my own eyes and still can't believe it," Pagan said. "He did that to *people*."

"Cruelty doesn't need a reason," Mercedes said.

"It needs to be stopped." Pagan hugged herself. "Oh, God, I wanted to take that poor dog home with me. But Devin said he'd ask his friends to make sure the animals don't suffer much longer. I just wish..." She turned her head on the pillow to look at her friend. "He said you told him not to make promises he can't keep. Maybe that's why he won't talk about anything with me."

Mercedes nodded once, lips pursed in thought. "Maybe. Even if he did feel something for you—what could happen? Where could it go?"

"I don't know." Pagan half sat up, propping pillows behind her against the headboard. She hadn't thought that far in advance. Even if Devin returned her feelings, the long-term prospects were not promising. "There have to be traitors and crazy plots going on in LA," she said, knowing it sounded weak.

"Maybe he could investigate how the Dodgers screwed over the home owners in Chavez Ravine when they bought up land for the new stadium," Mercedes said. Her eyelids were starting to close.

"And you had fun at the observatory," Pagan said. They'd discussed Mercedes adventure there, as well. "I'm so glad the fog didn't affect you."

"They built it up high for a reason," Mercedes said, and turned on her side, her back to Pagan. "And I got to see the Southern Cross, a double star system and an arm of the

Milky Way. Your Devin guy got me there, so don't be too hard on him, *hereje*."

Pagan threw her pillow on the floor and closed her eyes to sleep. "I'll be nice," she said. "Right up until the moment I kill him."

BIEN PARADO

Literally, well stood. Standing straight up.

Mercedes picked up the phone when Emma Von Albrecht called for Pagan the next morning. Pagan was already running late for the day's shooting, and took the phone impatiently. "Hey, Emma, sorry, but I can't talk long. How are you?"

Emma's voice came through filtered and tinny. "Oh! I'm so sorry! You can call me back later if you need to. I know you're busy…"

"It's okay. So sorry I missed dinner last night."

"Are you feeling better?"

Oh, right, the imaginary migraine. "Yes, much," Pagan said. "But I'm not looking forward to shooting a scene with evil Tony Perry today. Wish me luck."

"Good luck! And I might have something for you to look forward to afterward, if you're available after dinner tonight."

"Tonight?" Pagan's heart sank. She never wanted to enter that house of horrors again. But Dieter had said something big was going to happen, a lead box of nuclear something-or-other was down in his basement, and for the moment,

Pagan was the only outsider able to easily get inside. "I've got some things up in the air for tonight. Why? What do you have going on?"

"Something really fun." Emma did sound gleeful. "I know you'll enjoy it, but I can't say more unless you promise to come. It's a secret."

That could either be intriguing or incredibly lame. "Well, I don't think I could stay long…" Pagan said, hoping for more information.

"You can leave any time you like," Emma said. "But you won't want to, I promise."

She could always cancel on them later. And the vision of that poor tortured dog kept flashing in Pagan's brain. "I should be done by six or so. What time should I arrive?"

"Just before sunset, seven thirty," Emma said. "I'm so excited to see you!"

"Me, too," Pagan said, shrugging at Mercedes's puzzled look. "See you then."

She set the receiver down. "I didn't think Emma Von Albrecht could keep a secret from me, but I guess she can if she thinks it'll make a nice surprise for me. I wonder what it could be."

"A cake?" Mercedes said.

Pagan shook her head and put her trench coat on over her dancing togs.

The phone rang again and Mercedes picked it up again. Pagan knew who it would be.

"Hi, Devin," Mercedes said, eyeing Pagan questioningly.

Pagan shook her head, mouthing, "I'm gone."

"She left for rehearsal," Mercedes said. She listened and

frowned. "I can't help it if the car's still downstairs. She's not here."

Dang. He knew she was here, avoiding him. Pagan walked over and Mercedes handed over the phone.

"What?" she said.

"How are you this morning?" Devin asked, as if nothing had happened.

"I had a dream about you," she said. "Something involving a boa constrictor."

"How sweet," he said. "I can't talk much right now…"

His tone changed into almost a warning, and she remembered that they'd found listening devices in the room. Did that mean the phone wasn't safe?

"But I'll pick you up after the shoot," he finished.

Should she tell him about Emma's invitation now? If someone had tapped the phone, they'd have heard that conversation so…

"I have to go," he said with a sudden urgency. She heard voices in the background.

"Bis bald," he said, and hung up.

She put the receiver down on its cradle slowly. *Bis bald* was German for *See you soon*, and he'd said it to her one night back in Germany. That was the night she'd danced with Thomas, and Devin had told Nicky to stay away from her. The night Pagan had taken a drink for the first time since the accident and gotten fired off her comeback film. That was the night she'd first really thought about being with Devin, about walking up to him and kissing him and pushing him onto the bed and…

Stop it! Or as that cute girl in the Jewish gang had said,

Para! Para! Pagan had a full day of dancing with Tony Perry to soldier through before she wrestled, not literally unfortunately, with Devin again.

Pagan arrived only two minutes late to the set at the Colegio, allowed Rada to envelope her in her white dress again for the big embassy ball and found Tony and Victor Anderson whispering with their heads together while the extras practiced.

"Sorry I'm late," Pagan said, although two minutes really didn't count and she wasn't sorry at all.

"Miss Jones," Victor said in an acid tone that made Tony grin. "So glad you could make it."

"Stopped to take a little hair of the dog before she got here, I suspect," Tony said.

It didn't take Pagan by surprise, but Jared the choreographer gasped. Victor Anderson, however, only frowned and leaned in toward Pagan, as if trying to sniff her. So he was already suspicious, no doubt thanks to Tony Perry.

"How are you, Mr. Anderson?" she asked, breathing out the *H* as much as possible so he could smell the Pepsodent, and favored both him and Tony with her own blinding smile, which only experts could detect as fake. "Tony's such a joker. Too bad he can't stop stepping on my toes."

It got worse from there. Victor ran them through a rehearsal with the music running and the extras standing around watching. Tony behaved himself the first two times they did it. After that, when Victor began making changes, Tony began to sabotage Pagan.

First he pushed her in the wrong direction in a move they'd done a thousand times, throwing her off beat. Then he shoved too hard on a turn and sent her too far, so she missed grabbing his hand and messed up the whole move. It made her look clumsy, off-kilter.

Drunk.

He was making her nightmare come true—being branded a hopeless, unreliable alcoholic all over again. She thought carefully about kicking him between the legs again, then shoved the thought down into her rage-barrel and rehearsed again. Acting out physically now would be unprofessional. She could get through this. Even Tony wouldn't want to ruin every single take.

Jared walked them through it again in half-time, and Tony was perfect then, of course. But when they had to do it on the beat he let her hand slip through his at the wrong moment on a hold, and she took an awkward extra step.

"Goddamn it!" she yelled, and then held her breath. She'd just screamed on set. She was becoming the raving bitch Tony wanted her to be.

Victor shook his head. "Once more, Miss Jones, and get it right. You're keeping everyone waiting."

Again in half-time. Perfect. Again to the beat—and perfect.

"Let's roll it," Victor said. "Before Miss Jones forgets the steps."

"If she does, she can just lift that skirt and spread her legs," Tony said.

Pagan's cheeks blazed as Victor laughed. He actually laughed! Two of the grips chuckled, too.

"That's something girls always know how to do, right?" Victor said.

Pagan had heard men joke like this about women before on the set, but it had never been aimed at her. Mama had made sure of that. How did women deal with this without becoming homicidal?

And she was putting up with it to shoot the biggest pile of garbage to ever stink up Hollywood. A movie that, if it made it to the theaters, would only poison the reputations of everyone involved. Pagan was the only halfway big name actor in the ridiculous thing. Her agent had begged her not to do it. He'd even offered to get her out of it.

It was a movie that would die unmourned by anyone but Victor and Tony if for some reason it never got made. The thought made her smile. There was power in doing precisely…nothing.

"Now, Pagan." Victor got up from his chair as if he hadn't just been joking in the most disgusting way ever and clunked over to her in his riding boots. "Stop fighting Tony on every move. You must learn to surrender."

"Surrender?" she asked with a savage little laugh. "That's all girls ever do! And it's old, it's square, it's uncool. You're falling behind, daddy-o, so I'll clue you in. It's 1962. The tango is tired. If you want the kids now to dig this picture, we need to modern this puppy up and go from tango to the Twist. This sad little script and your pet boy Tony are No-wheresville."

Victor looked more confused than angry, as if he was still translating her hepcat lingo into English. "What the hell do you know, little girl?" he said. "Let the adults do the think-ing."

"Adults?" She rolled her eyes. "You're a walking farce, a

cliché in terrible pants. I've worked with real directors, people with actual talent. And you are *not* one of them."

"How dare you!" Victor drew himself up to his considerable height to glare down at Pagan. Too bad he hadn't brought his riding crop, or he could have smacked it threateningly against his riding boot at her. "I'm in charge of this film, Pagan Jones. Not some silly, drunken flibbertigibbit!"

Pagan laughed. She couldn't help herself. Compared to the head of the East German Stasi and Von Albrecht the notorious Nazi war criminal, Victor Anderson was a joke.

"You know what?" she said, still smiling. "I don't feel so good."

Victor's eyes narrowed. "You wouldn't."

Pagan put the back of one hand to her own forehead. "I may be coming down with something serious. I hope it isn't the movie set flu."

Victor's face slowly reddened. "If you do this to me, you'll never work in this town again."

She patted his arm. "You're cute."

The extras and the assorted grips and assistants were all watching, transfixed. She raised her voice so they could all hear clearly. "You all can go home for the day. And tomorrow, too."

She gave Victor one last blinding grin and walked away, big skirt swinging.

"She can't do that, can she?" Tony asked Victor, a desperate edge to his voice. "This is my first movie!"

"You come back here, you little bitch!" Victor shouted after her. "I won't allow it!"

"Fire me, then," she said, and turned on one foot to look

back at them gaping at her in the most marvelous way. "But I'm the only star you've got."

And she walked out.

Devin was waiting for her outside the Colegio, leaning against a long black car in his perfect summer suit and his Italian race-car-driver sunglasses.

"Don't you look like the cat that got the cream," he said, pushing away from the car.

She let her grin take over her face, and did a little tap dance on the sidewalk. "I told Victor Anderson he could get bent and played the sick card," she said. "I hope he fires me."

"I heard," he said, and held the door open as she got inside. "Should I arrange his mysterious disappearance?"

"Tempting." She settled back into the leather seats of the cooled car. "But he'll disappear not-so-mysteriously from Hollywood soon enough."

"I have a report to make in half an hour," he said. "I may get clearance after that to send you home, at which point you could quit the movie and never look back."

"Send me home?" Her good mood faded around the edges. She still harbored anger and resentment at Devin for keeping her at arm's length, but she didn't want to see the last of him just yet. "But there's a lot more I could do."

"No," he said flatly. "You've done what we needed. It's time to let the professionals take over."

That rankled her. They might not be paying her, but she'd done okay so far. Better than okay. "But Emma called me and invited me over for something secret she says will be really fun. I think I should go."

"That's not a good idea," Devin said. "We have no idea

what Von Albrecht's keeping in that basement, or who else he's collaborating with."

"But that's exactly why I should go back," Pagan said. "They still trust me, so I'm the only one who can get inside without blowing the whole thing. I might even be able to get into Von Albrecht's main office on the ground floor."

Devin shook his head. "You've endangered your own life enough. Don't you want to be done?"

"No, because it's not done! If you're making a report today, that means they probably won't do anything until tomorrow at the soonest, and who knows what I could find out in the meantime?"

"It's not safe," he said. "Every time you go there, you risk Von Albrecht getting suspicious. I know you told him that you sought him out because of your mother, but he and Dieter are in the middle of plotting something dangerous. They might get paranoid about you."

The more he protested, the more she realized she had to go. That poor dog was still down there, and all the other animals.

"It wasn't safe yesterday, either," she said. She hadn't told Devin about the near-fight she'd witnessed between Dieter's gang and the Jewish kids because she'd nearly ruined the whole mission by overhearing it. But Dieter's ominous words about "tomorrow night" kept repeating in her ears. That tomorrow night was now tonight. "And the clock is ticking. January 30 and whatever Von Albrecht has planned isn't far away. The sooner we know what he's doing, the sooner I can be done."

"What if I asked you, as a personal favor to me, not to go tonight?"

He was serious. He really didn't want her to go. For some reason that was upsetting.

"You wouldn't," she said. "Because you know better."

"I don't want anything to happen to you," he said in the same flat voice that gave nothing away. But she wanted to think that his words were telling. "You've done more than your share already. I told Mercedes I'd do what I could to keep you safe."

"No one is ever safe," she said. "And you can't make me safe by squashing me down, telling me what to do."

Devin's blue eyes were stark as they gazed at her, and he nodded. "I have to trust you."

Trust her. There was the rub. How could anyone ever really trust her again after what she'd done to Daddy and Ava? She could've saved all of East Berlin and still it wouldn't blot out that stain on her soul.

"I can understand why you wouldn't."

It came out very quiet.

He was frowning at her. "This isn't about the past. This is about the very dangerous now. Even fully trained, professional agents wouldn't be safe if they went undercover in that house. Both Von Albrecht and his son are dangerous." He moved restlessly, something she'd never seen him do before, always so self-contained and in control. "But I know, I know. You've proven that you can more than handle yourself."

"I won't stay long tonight," she said. How odd that she was reassuring him for once. "I'm going over at seven thirty. I'll be out by ten."

His eyes met hers, and the look of worry there disturbed her. "One minute later than ten o'clock and I'm coming in after you."

CALESITA

Merry-go-round. A move where the lead
dances around the follower.

Pagan knocked on the Von Albrecht front door exactly at
7:30 p.m., dressed in a casual gingham dress. Whatever secret thing Emma had planned better not be formal. It was a
relief to see Emma as she opened the door, grinning, wearing capri pants and white Keds like the ones Pagan had worn
the day before.

"You look so cute!" Emma walked onto the front stoop
holding her purse and gave Pagan a hug.

Pagan hugged her back. "So do you. Love the ponytail."

"Got your things?" Dieter said in his Argentine-German-
accented English, standing in the doorway, with his hand
on the knob. He was wearing jeans, a white T-shirt and a
red leather jacket that made him look like a blonder James
Dean in *Rebel Without a Cause*.

"All set," Emma said.

"Good," said Dieter. He looked energized. He turned a
rare smile toward Pagan. "Good evening, Fräulein Jones. I
hope you enjoy our little entertainment tonight." He closed
the front door and trotted down the steps past Pagan.

She stood there for a moment, confused.

"Come on," Emma said, following her brother. "They're waiting for us down the block."

Pagan stayed rooted on the stoop of the Von Albrecht house. Getting inside it was the main reason she'd come over. The animals. The tunnels. "But I thought…"

"We're going out!" Emma took her hand and tugged on it. She was wearing cherry-red lipstick and her blouse had little cherries printed on it. She lowered her voice. "Dieter made me promise not to tell you till we got there. It's one of his gang's secret outings, and it's going to be amazing!"

An outing with Dieter's gang sounded about as fun as a strip search in reform school. Did this mean the "something big" Dieter had chortled about was happening somewhere else, maybe something to do with the meeting with the Jewish kids? Von Albrecht had said that Dieter was integral to his plans, and he was also the ringleader of the gang. So wherever Dieter went, much as it galled Pagan, that was the place to be.

She hated leaving that poor tortured dog in the basement a moment longer, but it was better to stick to Dieter like glue to see what he was up to.

Later, if she had to break into the house or start a dang fire to get those animals free, so be it.

Pagan let Emma drag her down the steps and along the sidewalk after Dieter. "Is it far? How late do you think we'll be out?" She sounded like a total stick in the mud, but she needed whatever info she could get.

Emma shrugged. "Not far. Come on!"

Two cars full of teenagers were idling on the street waiting for them. The wide-open windows had way too many feet and elbows already poking out of them. Dieter shoved one of the boys over so he could drive the Mercedes Benz, while Emma pulled Pagan into the same car. She ended up half on the lap of a boy briefly introduced as Wolfgang and half on top of Emma, who put her arms around Pagan's waist quite contentedly.

The drive only took around twenty minutes, but it felt like a century with Wolfgang's knees jabbing into her backside. At one point he and the boy next to him got into a play fight, smacking and punching each other, laughing and yelling at each other in German as they did so. Pagan nearly got an elbow in her eye and said, "Hey, if you don't mind," in English.

Wolfgang slapped one more time at the other boy and angled his head toward Emma. "Doesn't she speak German?"

He said it in that Argentine-inflected German this group tended to use.

"Do you know any German?" Emma asked Pagan in English.

"I shot a movie in Berlin this summer, so I learned how to count to five," Pagan said. She'd learned during that time how handy it was to have people think you couldn't speak their language. "And say thank you, but I don't think that counts."

"She doesn't," Emma said to Wolfgang in German. "But she just shot a movie in Berlin."

Wolfgang's eyes got big, and in the rearview mirror, Pagan saw Dieter give her a long hard look. "Were you only in West Berlin?" Dieter asked her in English. It was the most interest he'd shown in her so far. "Or did you go see our Red friends in the East?"

"I went to East Berlin once before the wall went up," she said. "It was a mess."

"Well, first the damned Americans bombed it," Dieter said, and everyone else in the car nodded. "Then the damned Russians stole half of it. That's not an equation that leads to success."

He wasn't wrong. Dieter was a bit smarter when he wasn't in some frothing racist rage. She could see why the other kids followed him. But he didn't have the whole story, and she wasn't about to tell him that West Berlin was flourishing, thanks to the Allies that had defeated Hitler.

"The Führer would weep if he saw the Fatherland now," Wolfgang said.

Dieter's sly smile, intended only for himself, was visible to Pagan in the rearview mirror. "That's why we do what we do," he said. "That's why we do what we're doing tonight!"

Everyone in the car except for Pagan yelled out, *"Jawohl!"* Emma, too.

Lovely. She was stuck in a car with a bunch of Nazi kids. She'd rather dance twelve tangos with Tony Perry.

Twilight darkened to night as they moved through a neighborhood with narrow cobblestone streets to a deserted area filled with warehouses. Between buildings, Pagan caught sight of the river.

The car angled down, and something blotted out the sky. The car rattled and jumped over rougher terrain than cobblestones, and came to a stop. They poured out of the car, and Pagan found herself once again underground.

This tunnel was larger than the one she and Devin had been in the night before, and it looked carved out of the bedrock rather than lined with brick. Several of the boys had flashlights, and they moved around the floor like reverse shadows as everyone tramped farther down the tunnel.

"Where are we?" Pagan whispered to Emma.

"Look out for the tracks," Emma said, pointing with one hand, and taking Pagan's hand with the other. Twin metal lines emerged from the rock and then disappeared again a few yards on.

Pagan stepped over them carefully. "Is this an old metro tunnel?" she asked.

Emma shrugged. "Something like that, we think. But it gets cooler. Look!"

The tunnel narrowed sharply up ahead, and light shined through it from multiple sources. Pagan had to duck to get through the opening, and stepped down, blinking as the space then opened up wide around her once more.

Hundred of candles and a few oil lamps had been lit and placed in the nooks and crannies of what looked like a very fancy, very large basement with a high vaulted ceiling and Greek pillars lined up and down both sides. In the central area was a raised stone, almost like an altar. Off to the side the remains of human-size statues, clad in long marble robes, their feet in sandals, watched in silence. A dozen teenagers, mostly boys, were already there, lighting the candles and shouting up at the ceiling to hear the echoes.

"It's the crypt of an old church," Emma said.

They were standing on the top step of a staircase marching down to the crypt's floor. It must have once led up to the ground floor of the church.

"What's above us?" Pagan asked as Emma guided her down the steps. They were uneven from years of erosion. "Is the church still there?"

Emma shook her head. "It's a warehouse for old trolley cars," she said. "Nobody else but Dieter and his friends know this place exists down here! Isn't it the coolest? I wish we could open up the tombs in the side chapels, but Dieter thinks I'm disgusting."

Pagan was with Dieter on that one, but she smiled encouragingly. Curiosity was a good thing. She was someone who couldn't leave a mystery behind; only for her, the mystery was usually a little more current. "You probably like history in school."

"I love history," Emma said. "I told Papa I wanted to be a history or archaeology professor when I grow up. But he said it was important for good German girls like me to get married to German boys and have lots of babies of pure German stock."

Pure. There was that word again. "Do both," Pagan said. "That'll show your father."

Emma wrinkled her nose and looked down. They'd reached the flagstones on the floor of the crypt. "I don't want to get married. Boys are…" She looked over at the young men shoving one another and dripping wax on the pillars from the candles and shuddered. "Boys are awful."

"Some of them," Pagan said carefully. "You know, Gertrude Stein lived most of her life with her best friend, Alice. You don't have to get married."

"Do you want to get married?" Emma said, slinging a look over at Pagan before ducking her head down again.

"I don't know," Pagan said, and meant it, but probably for different reasons than Emma. Maybe it was the way her mother had dominated her parents' marriage, or all the divorces she'd seen in Hollywood. Maybe she'd spent the first twelve years of her life doing every little thing her mother ordered her to do and couldn't imagine bending that way again to anyone.

But maybe there was someone out there who was more like a partner than a husband. Someone who didn't expect you to obey but who was looking for a companion in adventure. She'd never thought men like that existed. Not until very recently...

But she couldn't tell Emma that. She had to keep up the illusion that Emma might stand a chance with her, if only for a little longer. Best to stick close to the truth, just not the whole truth.

"I like kids, but I never dreamed about my wedding the way other girls do. I don't want to answer to some guy every day, you know?" She narrowed her eyes, considering. "Might be worth it, though, if I could get Dior to custom-make my dress."

Emma laughed. "*Ja*, get the dress and the presents. And then get a divorce!"

"Believers!" Dieter had leaped up onto the stone platform in the center of the room. Towering over them in his red jacket, his golden hair gleaming in the lamp and candlelight, voice echoing back through the vaulted stone chamber, he looked every inch the young, charismatic leader. It made

Pagan uneasy. He was speaking in German, so Emma quietly translated for Pagan. "We're here for our monthly contest against the Yids, the Reds and the Negros. Are you ready?"

The assembled group let out a roar.

"Are the cars ready?" Dieter turned and pointed at Wolfgang.

"The cars are ready!" Wolfgang shouted.

Cars? That was the last thing she needed.

"Is the racecourse ready?" Dieter swiveled on top of the platform and pointed at another boy.

"The racecourse is reserved, marked and ready!" he shouted.

These idiots were going to race cars in the deserted warehouse district of Buenos Aires? The thought made her queasy. She'd done enough crazy driving to last a lifetime, thanks. Pagan nearly turned on her heel and ditched them then. But she had no idea where she was, or how to get back to the hotel. The neighborhood hadn't exactly been overflowing with taxis, either.

And she had to stick with Dieter. If these races happened every month, and if she was right that he had something big planned for tonight, then this wasn't the whole story.

She took Emma by the hand and walked her down the church steps to stand by the altar at Dieter's feet, a suitably reverential expression on her face, the better to overhear anything or follow him.

"I know that normally I am the first driver to win the first race against our enemies," Dieter was saying. "But I've been showing the ropes to my best friend, Wolfgang, here, and

I think he's earned the right to take the wheel in tonight's first race. What do you think?"

"Jawohl!" One of the boys shouted, and the others took up the call. *"Heil Wolfgang!"*

"Are we going to win?" Dieter held his arms out to the crowd of maybe three dozen teenagers.

"Jawohl!" they shouted as one.

Emma shouted with them, laughing and clapping. She grabbed Pagan's hands and clapped them together while Pagan manufactured her best delighted giggle. "See? Drag races! Just a block from here. I read those stories of how you and Nicky Raven were caught racing down Sunset Boulevard, so I knew you'd enjoy it!"

Poor, silly Emma. She must've also read the stories of Pagan driving her Corvette off a cliff, but it hadn't occurred to her that might've led to a change of heart when it came to drag racing. Pagan couldn't imagine a more asinine activity, or one more likely to give her an anxiety attack.

Dieter had jumped down from the altar, and leaned in to say something to Wolfgang quietly. Pagan was close enough to hear: "…give you my jacket in the tunnel."

Wolfgang nodded and then they were all headed back up the steps, out of the sunken church.

Dieter was going to give Wolfgang his jacket, but why? Were they more than switching roles in the driver's seat?

"We don't have to drive the cars, do we?" she asked Emma to keep her busy. She knew Dieter would never let a girl drive in a race. Around them, the kids were streaming back up the stairs and out through the narrow opening into the metro tunnel. This then must be their gang meeting place, where Dieter gathered them first to get them all stirred up.

"No!" Emma laughed as they walked up the steps. "Dieter and Wolfgang have two special, fast cars they work on between races. Only Dieter, Wolfgang, and maybe Fritz and Heinz have been allowed to drive them so far. I'd like to see Dieter's face if I tried to drive one."

They followed Dieter out of the crypt and walked past the parked cars inside the metro tunnel. Pagan could see now with more flashlights at work that there were actually ten cars parked in different spots. Someone in a red jacket was revving one engine of a hot rod with flames painted on the side, and someone in a black jacket was starting up the other. It wasn't light enough to tell whether Dieter was still wearing the red jacket or not. The rest of the kids kept on walking out of the tunnel.

"The races happen nearby," Emma said. "We park the cars underground so the other gangs don't spot our meeting place."

They emerged from the tunnel in a gravel-strewn area with a fence around it. Two boys had unlocked a gate and dragged it open to let the hot rods drive out. One went right. The other left, and the kids walking along behind them split up, too.

"You split up so the other gangs don't know where you're coming from?" Pagan asked. They were half jogging along now, angling right after they made it through the fence.

"Exactly. It's all Dieter's idea. He's the leader, you know. He's very clever."

Pagan didn't say that anyone truly determined to find their

hideout had only to follow some of them after the race to find their secret spot.

But maybe most kids didn't think like that. To Emma this was all crazy fun, something the adults didn't know about. The secrecy, the hiding place, it was part of the festive atmosphere, something to make them feel special. The other gangs couldn't be much of a threat to them then. Maybe they got all their aggressions out via these drag races. Races were dumb, but they were better than fighting.

"Where are we?" Pagan asked.

"South of the main city," Emma said. "It's called Dock Sud, or South Dock, because the southern docks are right through there." She motioned at the water gleaming between two large warehouses on their left.

"So Buenos Aires proper is—that way?" Pagan picked a direction at random.

Emma laughed and pointed back behind them. "More like that way. There's a bridge a block or so over there to get you across the Riachuelo. That's another branch of the river."

A bridge over *there*. Pagan made a point to remember that, in case she needed to get the hell away from this madness. With luck, if Dieter went anywhere in Wolfgang's black jacket, she could follow him.

After three long blocks they arrived at the dead end of a long wide street that ran straight for several hundred yards along the water. Warehouses, silent and dark, lined the other side. It might have been beautiful with the moon sparkling on the river if it wasn't for the jostling clumps of smoking teenagers and the trash littering the sides of the road.

Four cars were parked, headlights on, at the end of the

street. The two hot rods lined up one behind the other. So the other two—one with tiger stripes, the other with an oh-so-subtle dragon's head roaring out flames—must belong to the other gang.

The guy in the red jacket didn't get out of his car, and Pagan couldn't see his face. But the other guy, in the black jacket, climbed out. It wasn't Wolfgang or Dieter. Did that mean Dieter was the other driver, still wearing his red jacket?

Pagan pushed her way through Dieter's followers, boys and girls, to get a better look, but Emma grabbed her wrist and shook her head. "That's their side," she said, gesturing to the water side of the street. "This is ours."

Pagan craned her neck. The kids on the other side looked a lot like the kids on this side, dressed in the same jeans and T-shirts or cotton dresses, the boys with their hair gelled back and the girls sporting teased bobs and winged eyeliner. Like Dieter's crew, they were talking to one another in low voices, throwing narrowed glances over at their rivals. Up near the cars, which had their hoods up, boys were bent over the engines while girls held flashlights. "Who are they?"

Emma shrugged. "Jews, mostly. Other nights we race the Negros, or this really stupid group of pinkos from San Telmo. But mostly we race the Jews. Dieter says there are way too many in BA. Perón let Germans immigrate to Argentina, but he let the Jews in, too. It doesn't make any sense."

"It's easier to get along in the world if you give up hoping people will make sense," Pagan said.

It was the Nazis that didn't make sense to Pagan, and Mama, too. She was still trying desperately to understand her mother's actions to help Von Albrecht and maybe others, and now here she was in the midst of people who thought a lot like Mama.

Maybe there was something to be learned here. She let Emma lead her closer to the first hot rod. The hood was open, and the guy she didn't know in the black jacket was making some last-minute adjustments to the engine while another boy held a flashlight so he could see.

"We're starting soon, *ja,* Franz?" Emma yelled to the mechanic in German over the noise of engines.

"In a minute," Franz said without looking up.

Pagan stepped away from Emma and peered inside the car at the driver in his red jacket. It was Wolfgang. He *had* taken Dieter's jacket. Then where the hell was Dieter?

She craned her neck, looking over the milling throng of the fascist gang. The car headlights were the main source of illumination, and they were pointed the other way, so all she saw at first were dark human shapes and glints off eyes and teeth.

A flame sparked near the back of the crowd. A lighter. As Emma talked to Franz the mechanic, Pagan drifted toward that flame, squinting. A big hand cupped the light. A flash of blond hair. Flexible lips pursed around a cigarette as the tip smoked, and a mole flexed next to a dimple on a cheek.

Dieter. He now wore a black shirt she hadn't seen before and black pants and a jacket. Ranged around him were maybe half a dozen other boys, also dressed in dark colors.

Dieter shot a look back at the cars, and Pagan shrank back, using a cluster of five other girls as cover. But Dieter wasn't looking for her. Pagan turned to follow the direction of his gaze and saw the girl from the Jewish gang, her hair still in that fabulous bouffant, kissing her boyfriend, Hector, in front of his car's headlights.

Dieter's hand curled tighter around his cigarette as he stared at them.

Naomi, that's what they'd said the girl's name was back in the stairwell below the observatory. Something about her really had Dieter on a string.

Back by the hot rods, Franz shouted something at Hector. He shouted it in Spanish, but Pagan could only recognize about one in three words. He must be using some kind of Argentine slang.

Hector understood it well enough, though. His chest puffed out and he shouted back, "Keep your fascist eyes off my girl, jackboot!"

"But it's impossible to see anything else when her nose is that big!" Franz shouted back. The boys and girls around him laughed. "I could keep my fireplace going all night long with that much firewood."

Firewood. A Nazi reference to Jews burned in the crematoria in the camps. Pagan felt sick.

Hector lunged violently toward Franz, but Naomi grabbed his arm. "Hector, no! Nobody cares what he says."

Pagan looked back at Dieter. He was backing away from the crowd slowly, staring at Naomi. The other boys who had been ranged around him were now nearly half a block away, but Dieter was having a hard time leaving, and his eyes had the same strange glint she'd seen when he looked at Mercedes.

Pagan wound her way as seamlessly as she could through the crowd, getting closer to Dieter. If she was going to follow him, she needed to be quick and careful. Emma was bound to come looking for her soon.

Franz was still taunting the Jewish girl. He caught her wrist in one large hand and jerked her body toward him.

Naomi wrenched her arm away and slapped him across the face.

His cheek reddened. "You're asking for it," he growled, loud enough to hear over the roaring engines.

Hector yelled something angrily and got between them. Behind him, his friends surged forward to surround Naomi protectively.

Pagan looked back again at Dieter. Still gazing at Naomi and her friends, he spat on the ground, smiled and said, low, "You'll all find out who's in charge soon enough."

There it was again, the hint that something big was happening. Where the hell was he going, leaving most of his gang behind?

Pagan kept one eye on Dieter and got closer to the clutch of girls she'd been using as cover. "Who is that girl who slapped Franz?" she asked in English. "She's such a trouble-maker."

"That's Naomi Schusterman," a girl in a poodle skirt said in heavily accented English. "Her father and mother work in the Israeli embassy."

"Do you know her that well?" Pagan asked. For rival gangs, they knew an awful lot about each other.

The girl shrugged. "Everybody knows Naomi and her boyfriend."

"And Dieter knows who all the Jews are who work in the

embassy," another girl piped up. "We need to keep watch, he says."

Well, that was disturbing. The other girls were nodding, staring at the fracas, as if it wasn't strange at all. They hadn't seemed to notice that Dieter and his six friends had broken away. The drama up by the cars was too fascinating.

Hector slammed the hood of his car down with a loud clang and shouted something at Franz, who screamed back.

The boys on both sides were yelling things Pagan couldn't decipher. Chins were pulled in, fists clenched. This wasn't posturing. They were getting ready to fight.

Pagan backed away as the girls and everyone else flowed toward the conflict.

The Germanic crowd around Wolfgang's car was chanting, *"Sieg! Sieg! Sieg!"*

Victory. A chant painfully close to the Nazi *"Sieg heil"* everyone remembered from the war.

The headlights from the two hot rods shined down the long naked roadway before them. Taunting teenagers knotted behind each car as Hector got in his car and revved the engine. Naomi gave him another kiss through the open side window.

Dieter had finally turned his back and was walking away, fast. Pagan took the navy silk scarf from around her neck, threw it over her bright hair and followed him.

She took one last look back as Naomi Schusterman walked up to stand like a sleek statue in the headlights, both hands in the air, about to signal the start of the race.

Naomi reminded Pagan a little of herself, before the accident. A bit foolish and fearless, and fierce.

The girl's arms swung down, and the cars surged forward. Pagan caught one last glimpse of Emma, cheering, before she turned and ran as quietly as she could after Dieter.

ESPEJO

Mirror step. When one dance partner mirrors the steps of the other.

Pagan followed Dieter and his six cohorts back to the mouth of the tunnel where their cars were parked. None of them seemed to notice her hanging back in the shadows. Dieter did look over his shoulder, but it looked like a reflex. And each time, Pagan was hugging the long wall of the warehouse, and his eyes skimmed right past her. Her navy dress with its white polka dots turned out to have been a good choice for skulking. She made a mental note in case she needed to lurk in the future.

All six boys piled into Dieter's car, talking among themselves as she crouched behind a different parked car, listening hard. She couldn't catch a lot of it, thanks to slang and their local accents, but she could tell that Dieter was laughing at how easy it was to distract their rival gangs on this important night.

"They try to watch us," he said, finishing up his cigarette as the others jostled into the car. "They think I don't see them spying, but I do."

"They watch us, and we watch them," said a large boy in the backseat.

"*Ja, ja,*" Dieter said. "It's part of the deal. But right now the idiots are back there, thinking we are there, too. They think I love racing so much that I must be there, that we all must be. They could never imagine we'd use this night for something more important than any race."

"They'll never know we helped change the world," the large boy said.

"After, we'll make sure they know," Dieter said, and tossed his cigarette into the darkness before he got into the car.

As he started the engine, Pagan opened the door to the car she was crouched beside and crawled inside. She was going to have to work fast if she wanted to follow them, although she had a sinking feeling she knew where they were headed.

Above her lowered head, the lights from Dieter's car cut a swath across the rough rock walls of the tunnel. Dieter had even turned on the radio, albeit at a low volume. Elvis was singing "Rock-a-Hula Baby" as they drove past.

She felt for and found the steering column. She didn't have a screwdriver or anything like it to help her rip the plastic cover off the steering column. Back when they were in Lighthouse Reformatory, Mercedes had drawn a diagram on a napkin stolen from the cafeteria to show her where the clips holding it in place were. They'd been planning an escape to Mexico at the time, and once they were free, they'd need to steal a car. So Pagan had memorized everything Mercedes told her, and the information had stuck.

Pagan had no idea what kind of car she was in now. She'd stopped paying attention to makes and models after she crashed her Corvette. But Mercedes had stolen pretty much every kind of car on the planet in her day, and her lessons had been comprehensive.

Pagan's hands fumbled around in the dark, until she found a clip, and then another. In two quick rips, the steering column was exposed. Or at least, it felt that way. Mercedes had said you often needed to steal a car in the dark, so it was best to feel for the wires leading straight up into the steering column.

As Dieter's engine faded into the distance, the blackness and silence became total except for Pagan's own breathing. She sat up and flicked her Zippo lighter to life to see what she was dealing with. Looked like an automatic transmission, maybe a Turboglide.

Battery wires—red, right? Better be. She had to strip the dang things with her teeth, since Mercedes wasn't here with a handy pocketknife. Twist those, then connect the ignition wire, then the stripped section of the starter.

Careful now. Don't electrocute yourself.

How embarrassing it would be if Emma and company came back to find her dead body, hair on end, smelling of burned skin, lying on the front seat of the car. No, thanks.

She barely touched the starter wire to the battery and the ignition stuttered to life.

Her heart was hammering louder than the engine, but a wide smile spread across her face. Just wait till Mercedes heard she'd hot-wired her first car!

She tapped the accelerator to rev the engine, shoved the thing into gear and reluctantly flicked on the headlights. She needed them to get out of this dark hole, then she could turn them off for stealth.

 Her hands were shaking as she hauled the wheel around and bounced up the uneven floor of the cave toward the open air. Ever since the accident that killed Daddy and Ava, even being in the front seat of a car was enough to make the back of Pagan's neck sweat. Driving was like traveling back in time to the night she'd drunkenly driven them off that cliff. Red convertibles were the worst, of course. She'd driven one since the accident, and only because she had no choice. Never again.

 But this car was gray, inside and out, and had no drop-top. It was huge, with spiky fins and a vast hood.

 Nothing like her cherry-red Corvette. Not at all. This was not that night. It was something else. Tonight she was driving to make things better, not worse. Helping not hurting. That was her driving mantra, and it damn well better keep her steady, damn it, or the panic would win.

 Dieter's crew hadn't closed the gate behind them, so she was able to click off her headlights and gun the car out of there to follow their distant red taillights off to her left.

 Now she was the one following someone else in a car. It made her wonder—what had happened to Alaric Vogel? Was he still out there, possibly a block or so behind her, doggedly watching her every move?

 No headlights appeared in her rearview mirror for blocks, and she could hear no engines other than Dieter's in the distance. If Vogel was still following her, he'd changed his tactics.

 For a couple of miles, she had no idea where she was. She

followed as they crossed a small arm of the river and wound through narrow cobbled streets that reminded her of San Telmo, where they'd first found Dieter in the café. But then the streets widened, the buildings grew taller and more gracious and a park appeared on her right just as Dieter pulled over and parked in front of a brick building.

They were back at the Von Albrecht home.

Pagan turned right, losing sight of Dieter's car. But she didn't want to pass Dieter and his boys as they piled out. She knew where they were headed now. She parked on the side street and reluctantly tugged the wires she'd rigged apart. The engine sputtered into silence.

There were no lights on in any of the Von Albrecht windows as Pagan slunk up the back alley where she'd seen Dieter parking his bicycle from Emma's window the day before. The bike was still there, chained to the steps leading up to the kitchen.

She flattened herself against the building and peered into the window in the doorway that led to the Von Albrecht kitchen. It lay dark, but through the doorway into the dining room the hall light shone, and three tall male figures were walking quickly in her direction before an abrupt turn that signaled they were going exactly where she'd guessed.

Into the basement.

They must have all gone down there. She'd gotten there in time to see the last three.

Time to pick another lock. Hairpins in hand, she glanced up and down the alley to make sure she was still alone. The windows above remained dark. Nothing but the smell of rotting garbage.

The lock on the back door was a simple one. She eased the door open.

A bell clanged overhead. She crouched down and froze.

The empty house gave no answer. She stood up slowly, and saw the bell, a simple dangling thing, hanging from the door frame above her. She stood on her tiptoes to hold the clapper still as she shut and relocked the door.

Something about the way the sounds bounced around told her that the building was now profoundly vacant. She wasted no time, running lightly down the stairs to Von Albrecht's basement to press her ear against the door there and listen. Nothing but her own pulse came back to her. Of course, it was soundproofed. Still, somehow she knew no one would come running as she plied the hairpins again.

She'd picked this lock just yesterday, so now it opened to her in seconds. She creaked the door open to stand in the dark, holding her breath. No sounds, no movement. Nobody would work down there without light. Dieter and his boys must have gone down that second set of stairs she'd seen yesterday. They were using the tunnels.

She flipped on the lights to find the laboratory nearly empty. The cages with the animals inside, the lead box, the pile of notes, the measuring equipment—they were all gone.

This was bad. That was all Pagan could think, over and over. *This is bad.*

Her impulse was to run after Dieter, to follow him every step of the way. But how could she stop him and six of his most muscular friends? She needed help.

She left the lights on as she ran back upstairs, found a phone in the kitchen and dialed the Alvear Palace Hotel.

The phone in Devin's room rang and rang, so she hung up, called back and this time asked for her own suite.

Mercedes picked up the line. "Hello."

Pagan exhaled in relief at the sound of her best friend's voice. "M, it's me. I need your help."

"Tell me," Mercedes said without hesitation.

"I'm in Emma's house, alone. But...I can't be specific in case this line is tapped, but the basement's been cleaned out. Everything's gone. Everything. I called Devin's room, but he's out. So I need you to leave a note for Devin—not with the hotel clerk. Put it under his door. Don't be specific, in case someone else finds it. Tell him... Just tell him..." Her chaotic thoughts weren't giving her an easy way to tell Devin what was going on without revealing everything.

"I'll tell him you're at your friend's house, and it's been cleaned out," Mercedes said, calmly filling in the blanks. "Do you need him to come there?"

Did she? She might not be here long herself. "He'll figure out what to do. He may be on his way here now—he knows I came over tonight, and he didn't want me here later than ten."

"It's nearly that now. Do you think...?" Mercedes stopped herself, remembering that they couldn't really talk openly on the phone. "I'm coming there right after I leave the note."

"No! You're not getting involved again, remember? Not like that. Anyway, I need you to stay there so I can call you if I find out where they went."

"You can't stay there." Mercedes's voice was low and urgent. "What if that man comes back?"

"I've always been good at improvisation," Pagan said. "Gotta go. Wish me luck."

"Luck," Mercedes said as Pagan hung up.

The floorboards creaked as she ran back down the hall and, on a whim, tried the door to Von Albrecht's office. To her astonishment, the knob turned beneath her hand. It was worth a quick look.

She entered to find a musty, airless room, the windows shuttered, filled with bookcases and a desk. But it took only a moment to realize that the desk was empty. The drawers held nothing but a few pencils and a writing pad with half the pages torn away. Pagan moved to the filing cabinet, and it trundled open easily to show her its empty drawers.

This was worse than bad. Von Albrecht was done with his experiments. Either he knew he'd been found out and was burning bridges, or he'd moved his project along to the next phase.

And the next phase might involve something nuclear.

She left the office and went back down to the cleared-out laboratory. The actual cages and the big black box were gone. All of them would have been heavy, and far too noticeable to have hauled out the front door or the back alley, where prying neighborly eyes would see.

They must have taken everything out through the second staircase leading down. Through the tunnels.

She stared at a large half-empty bag of dog food that still rested there. That poor dog and the other animals could be dead now.

Maybe not. Despair was no earthly use to them or anyone else. But she had to know. She had to try. She couldn't wait for Devin to come. She'd follow the Nazi boys and skulk, sneak, lurk. She'd play it smart and be Devin's eyes and ears and hang back till help arrived. But she couldn't stay here a moment longer.

Pagan sprinted to the narrower, older brick staircase in the basement that led farther down. The bricks reminded her of the tunnel she and Devin had walked through last night, from Julieta to Romeo.

This house wasn't very far from the place she and Devin had exited using "Romeo," and Julieta and Villa 31 were less than a mile from that, literally across the tracks. How many old tunnels were there and how many people were using them for their own secret purposes?

She padded down the brick stairs and pressed an ear to the door. Silence. And the knob turned beneath her hand. Clearly if you made it this far, Von Albrecht figured you had permission to go farther.

The door hinges squealed as she opened it, pushing her back to hide against the door frame, waiting for someone in the darkness to notice.

Water dripped and splashed somewhere in the distance. Air stirred faintly, signaling a wide-open space around her. But no one called out. No footsteps came running.

Pagan fumbled around for a light switch. She really should carry a flashlight or something when she went snooping. She moved blindly down the wall, feeling. Something tick-led her forehead.

She ducked, swiping at it, fearing bats or bugs. But her hand grabbed hold of a small chain. She gave it a pull. Some-thing overhead buzzed, and a light went on.

She was indeed inside another brick tunnel, one wider than Julieta's. Lights had been strung haphazardly from arch to arch around the fifty-foot-wide space, which was empty except for one large metal table she recognized from the lab. Shards of glass littered the floor beneath it. This must be the last of the equipment they were moving tonight.

The air was warm and oppressively humid. Mold and dank lived here. To her right, the tunnel narrowed sharply to an archway. Rumbling echoes traveled through it. That must be Dieter and the boys, moving the last of the equipment through the tunnels. But to where?

She ran to the arch and paused, looking toward the rumbling sounds down a long, narrow brick tunnel, dark but for bobbing lights far in the distance.

Praying there were no open pits or random boulders between her and them, Pagan set off down the tunnel at a quick walking pace. She needed to get closer, but it was stupid to run when you couldn't see what was under your feet.

But her pace must have been faster than theirs, slowed by their cargo. She neared the lights and heard one of them calling something that sounded like, "How's the loading going?" in German.

She slowed. Faint light etched seven large male silhouettes ahead of her pushing large rectangular things—carts, probably—loaded with boxes. The wheels made grating noises on the uneven ground.

"Nearly done," someone else said, and an eighth male shape walked up to Dieter's crew. He was also carrying a flashlight, and his beam just brushed her shoe before continuing its arc over the tunnel as he turned to walk with the others.

"The object is aboard the ship," he continued. "We should be ready to weigh anchor as soon as you lot are done with this and the area is secured."

Ship? That's where the lead box had gone. That had to be the "object" this guy was talking about.

Cart wheels squeaked.

"The traitors in Berlin will get a nice surprise in a couple of weeks." A familiar voice, low and full of contempt. Dieter.

Wait, wait—Berlin? That's where they were taking their nuclear present?

Of course! The date of January 30 was weeks away, but it would take a ship at least a week to get anywhere near Germany, and more time to transport something overland from there to Berlin. That's why everything was being moved now—to make the January 30 deadline in Europe.

"Using the Americans' own plutonium to poison them and the rest who occupy Berlin," the first boy said. "Your father's a genius."

Using *American plutonium*? Had she heard that right? Somewhere she'd heard that plutonium was even nastier than uranium. Maybe Von Albrecht had a way to get it into the water supply in Berlin or something, to poison people. That was no better than a bomb. But how could it be American?

"I know he doesn't want me to go with him, but I'm hoping to persuade him otherwise," Dieter was saying.

"Americans are idiots," the first boy said. "They recruited him to come work for them in the first place!"

"Arrogant, more like," said Dieter. "They thought he'd be grateful they didn't hang him at Nuremburg."

"Arrogant idiots," the boy said with a laugh. "On that perhaps we can agree. Nearly ten years since he stole their plutonium and still they couldn't find him."

"They underestimate him," Dieter said. "After the anniversary, they won't do that again."

Pagan couldn't quite believe what she was hearing. From what these boys were saying, the Americans had recruited Von Albrecht after the war and he'd stolen their plutonium and gotten away with it. No wonder the CIA had been so eager to get her here to identify him. They needed to find him to cover up their own mistake.

But if they were so anxious, why hadn't they moved instantly to recapture or kill him once she'd told Devin he was their man?

Then she remembered the lead box. Maybe after her report indicating the nuclear material still being in his possession, they'd decided to approach with caution.

And her snooping had given them the January 30 date. They'd all thought they had more time. Maybe the CIA was hoping to lure Von Albrecht from his home, away from his plutonium, to nab him.

Instead, he was setting sail for Berlin with that plutonium, tonight.

It was easy to follow Dieter and the boys now that they were talking. They weren't even trying to be stealthy, and the rattle and squeak of their carts covered any possible sound from her footsteps. Apparently the Americans weren't the only arrogant idiots on the planet.

★ ★ ★

The brick tunnels transitioned to cement for a few hundred yards, then to rock. Moss and stranger growths sponged over the walls. The farther they went, the wetter everything got. She couldn't be far from the river now.

The reality of what she had overheard was still filtering through her thoughts. How could the US let a man guilty of atrocious crimes like Von Albrecht off the hook? Could any contribution he made to the US nuclear program possibly justify that? Maybe they hadn't known the extent of his crimes when they first recruited him. That seemed unlikely. At best.

It got worse.

Mama hadn't only helped a Nazi escape the US. She'd helped a Nazi carrying stolen American plutonium.

A wave of dizziness overtook Pagan. She stopped dead and had to lean against a wet wall.

Had Mama known about the plutonium? Had she known about Von Albrecht's experiments? Or was she simply being a good German?

Pagan didn't want those facts to matter. Mama was dead. Her crimes were done and paid for, one way or another, with her suicide. But knowing what had been in her mother's mind mattered to Pagan. It mattered more than anything.

Well, it didn't matter more than stopping Von Albrecht's shipment from going out. Later on she could suss out the dark meanings behind this all. She had to keep track of them until Devin or someone with authority could arrive.

Pagan pushed herself away from the wall and doggedly kept walking after Dieter's crew. Her mother had helped make Von Albrecht's schemes possible. It was fitting that her daughter was trying to stop him.

A gray spot appeared in the blackness ahead, and the tunnel around her gradually lightened. When the floor became cement and she spotted a lightbulb glinting in the ceiling ahead, Pagan hugged the wall even closer and slowed her pace. If Dieter or his boys looked back, she might be visible now.

Finally the tunnel sloped up, the floor slippery with mud and mildew. Pagan stopped and watched the boys try to shove their carts up the ramp, only to slide back down. Dieter and the eighth boy disappeared, then ran back down with buckets and sprinkled sand on the floor.

Once they had completely disappeared, she ventured forward and looked up.

She made her way carefully up the ramp into what appeared to be a warehouse, as Dieter's carts clattered farther away. The walls here were corrugated metal and wood. Metal shelves, most of them empty, towered toward the ceiling. Voices floated down to her, and an engine rumbled distantly.

"Better hurry," she heard the eighth boy's voice echo. "We're about to lift anchor."

Pagan startled forward and nearly tripped. About to lift anchor? Once they were at sea, the ship and its deadly cargo would be tough to trace. She had planned to hang back, to play it safe. But if they were about to lift anchor...?

Don't be stupid. If Mercedes had alerted Devin, he must be either following her through the tunnels by now or he'd sent his helpers through the city looking for her and for Von Albrecht. She was going to play this one smart. One girl against all these armed boys—even Pagan knew better than to tempt fate that way.

Her skin crawled with anxiety as she paused on the ramp and poked her head up. Her eyes were at ground level of a warehouse floor, mostly empty again. Dieter and his friends were walking away from her toward a large open door.

Sounds filtered through the door: the low snarl of a large engine, and voices. A cool breeze that smelled like oily water stirred her hair.

Keeping low and in the shadow of the doorway, Pagan followed the boys wheeling their carts outside.

The deep call of a foghorn blasted the air with a chest-shaking grumble. She peered around the edge of the door-way to see a ship, its masts looming not fifty yards to her left. She was at the docks, with the water chilly and black stretch-ing out before her. Cranes like giant insect legs groaned and swung crates onto the ship, which was big, but not some enormous cargo-carrying thing owned by a shipping line, small enough to be privately owned. Either Von Albrecht had leased it, or he had some big pockets behind him, help-ing to get the plutonium to Europe.

The wind lifted her skirt and scattered goose bumps over her arms. Men dotted the dock leading up to the gangway, and Dieter and his thugs were now approaching the crane with their carts. She needed to alert the authorities, have them stop the ship. But how?

The area was lit only in spots—the warehouse door, the crane, the gangway and the section of the ship's deck where the cargo was being loaded. No sign of a pay phone to call Devin or the cops.

She ducked back into the warehouse and did a quick survey. No phones in there, either. No office where a manager might have a phone. Nothing but shelving and crates, and a tunnel that led to the Von Albrecht house.

She could go back. Now that she knew where the cargo was going, she could tear all the way back to that terrible basement and call Mercedes or the cops from there.

But that was a mile or more away and would take her at least another half an hour. The eighth boy had told Dieter they were nearly ready to lift anchor. By the time Devin or anyone else reached the dock, the ship would be long gone.

If only she could sink or scuttle the damned boat. Where was a torpedo when you needed one?

No, no. Play it smart. It's a huge ship swarming with evil men. Leave it alone.

The warehouse doors swung open, and she ducked back behind a shelf.

"Just a few more crates to go," a man said. "Then I must say farewell to you, my son."

That voice.

The high, nasal tones could belong to no one else.

"Don't make me stay here while you go to glory, Father," Dieter said. "Let me come with you. I could be useful in Berlin."

They walked up to a set of crates and a cage very much like the one that had held the dog, one shelf over from Pagan. She peered through the shelving at Von Albrecht's stoop-shouldered form, clad in a khaki trench coat and gray fedora as he walked by his son's side. Behind them came three of Dieter's boys, pushing a cart.

"You have already proven yourself to me," Von Albrecht said. "You and your friends have been instrumental in guarding the house and obtaining and moving materials. Before that you kept any spying eyes from the house and monitored the behavior of the Jews and others who might have been searching for me. You've done more than enough."

Dieter was smiling that open, delighted smile again. It was chilling how it only appeared when his father gave him validation. How different might Dieter have been if he'd been born to another father? One that gave him warmth and love without condition. One that respected other people.

Pagan realized she was clutching the cloth of her dress over her heart, trying to ease the pain there. She missed Daddy. He had given her the things Dieter's never had. And Daddy was still there, inside that ache behind her heart.

"I want to do more than enough, Papa," Dieter said. "I want to be there when the Führer is avenged."

Von Albrecht gave his son a slit-eyed smile and shook his head. "Too dangerous. It may require that I sacrifice myself in the blast. I could not sacrifice you, as well. You must carry the work further if I do not survive. When Berlin is a wasteland, and the Allies begin to bomb one another into the Stone Age, you must be here to lead. You must be one of those who lifts humanity from the ashes to begin the Reich anew." His pale blue eyes glittered as he scanned his son's tall, broad-shouldered form. "You are the embodiment of all I have worked for. You serve me and the Führer best when you live on and lead your race to rule."

Pagan was shaking so hard she had to pull away from the shelf so it didn't rattle along with her bones. So Von Albrecht wasn't poisoning people with the plutonium. He really was sending a nuclear bomb to Berlin.

And if a bomb went off in that divided city, the Soviets would think the US had done it, and the US would blame the Soviets. If either one launched a retaliatory strike…

She couldn't think about that. She couldn't worry about something a couple of weeks away when she was here, trapped in a warehouse with the man who'd built the bomb and his bruiser of a son.

Devin had told her he'd come for her if she wasn't back at the hotel by ten, and it had to be past that now. Mercedes was trying to reach him, too. He knew about the basement. He'd find the entrance to the tunnels. She had to believe that he was on his way.

But what if he didn't make it in time?

Von Albrecht and Dieter were turning back toward the door to the warehouse.

"Why did you bother loading those animals onto the ship? Why not just put a bullet in them?" Dieter asked.

Pagan perked up. The animals were on the ship? And they weren't all dead?

"Waste of good bullets," Von Albrecht said. "Tell your boys to dump their cages into the water before we weigh anchor."

A nuclear bomb on a ship full of fascists, minutes from setting sail for the open ocean. Trapped, abused animals about to be thrown in the ocean.

Pagan looked down at her once-white Keds, her bare, mud-splashed calves and the damp hem of her polka-dot dress. This was no place for a teen girl movie star. But here she was. There was no one else.

She wasn't going to play it smart, after all.

Dieter's friends were piling crates and boxes onto a pallet on the cart. That pallet would be lifted by the crane onto the ship. That was how she could do it without being seen. If she was lucky.

It was idiotically dangerous, but few people had ever accused Pagan Jones of being smart. She'd walked into danger before. She'd pranced right up to East German soldiers with orders to shoot, to help Thomas and his family escape East Berlin. She could do this. If she couldn't scuttle the engine, maybe she'd distract the pilot…or whatever people who drove ships were called. She had to try.

The long side of the last pallet being loaded was pressed up against the shelves, including a narrow open space between shelves. The boys were still stacking crates on the far side. Dieter and Von Albrecht had turned to let them finish, heading outside. Only a few more boxes to go, and the pallet would be wheeled out to the crane.

Pagan crouched and, using her hands for balance, crawled into the narrow space between the shelves and onto the crowded landscape of the pallet. The boxes and crates were crammed together more haphazardly than most shipping containers would be. These guys were in a hurry, and all these boxes of animal kibble, empty cages and lab equipment were now trash, evidence of Von Albrecht's activity that would very likely be dropped off the side of the ship once they got to sea. So they hadn't bothered to stack it with care. There was just enough space between a large cage, filled with animal dung and dirty newspaper, and a metal tank marked Propane for a girl to squeeze in.

Pagan had always wanted to be tall enough to be a real model. Clothes just looked better on those long, elegant bodies. But now even her five-foot-six felt enormous. She slotted her head into a space between two higher level crates and hoisted her hips to sit on the cage, her legs, dirty and bruised, wedged between it and the propane.

The angle she was forced to lie in sent a stabbing pain down the small of her back. The foul smell of old animal urine and feces was cut with the nostril-curling odor of gas.

She thought of her mother's favorite perfume, the soft, romantic L'Heure Bleue by Guerlain. Bergamot and tuberose this was not. Mama would not approve.

Just another reason to do it.

With a jolt, the cart began rolling. Pagan's head jerked forward, banging her nose on the crate in front of her face, and she stifled a cry of pain. Above the grating sound of the wheels and the creak of the cargo around her, she heard the voices of Dieter's crew shouting to get the warehouse doors open. The last pallet was coming through.

The last pallet and one very cramped girl.

VOLCADA

To tip over, capsize. A falling step.

The temperature dropped as Dieter's boys rattled the cart carrying Pagan's pallet outside, and the ride got rougher. Pagan was grateful for the darkness, and flexed one foot experimentally to keep the muscles from seizing. If she skewed her eyes way to her left, she could just see a slice of night, which lightened and then was blocked out by the brown painted metal of the crane.

Loud male voices shouted, and the pallet shook as they slung things around it and hooked cables to it. Pagan couldn't see exactly what they were up to, and it was taking forever. Her neck was on fire from the strain of holding it at this absurd angle.

It's only been a minute. Calm down.

The pallet lurched upward and swung like a carnival ride. Pagan's stomach dropped as her entire body slid and bumped toward the edge of the pallet. She caught a glimpse of the ground falling away, before she grabbed the edge of a crate and jammed her foot between two boxes to stop her fall.

Air rushed down at her. Cable groaned. A view of the

ship flashed past as the pallet spun in midair. Pagan loved roller coasters and every sort of carnival ride. She shrugged at heights. But she'd never before lain on a pallet as it swirled and threatened to tip her out like a fried egg from a buttered skillet.

Her head swam. Gorge rose in her throat, and she swallowed hard.

Just another few seconds. Hang on.

The pallet hit the deck with an earsplitting smack. Pagan bounced up at least six inches and slammed down onto the crates beneath her. The edge of the cage cut into her ribs. She squeezed her eyes shut to keep from screaming.

A man circled the pallet, disengaging the hoisting cables, and she stayed as still as she could. Each breath sent a jab of agony through her. Could you tango with broken ribs? Just as well she'd all but quit the movie.

The man yelled something in Spanish she didn't understand and threw his arms up. The crane lifted the cables away from the pallet. They vanished into the dark of the night sky above her. Heavy boots walked away, and it got quiet.

She yanked her foot out of the crevice she'd jammed it in, and experimentally wiggled her toes inside her shoe. At least those weren't broken. The pain in her ribs had calmed to a red growl in her side. Maybe it was only a bruise. She sat up, one hand easing her neck, and peered over the top of the nearest box.

She was seated pretty high up on the crates and had a view out over the front half of the ship, piled haphazardly with other pallets. It looked like a cityscape in miniature, the towers of boxes like skyscrapers with deep alleys zigzag-

ging between. She was King Kong, with a view of a miniature New York.

No sign of Von Albrecht or Dieter. The ship's bridge lay
behind. A knot of men was busy doing something to some
crates over on the…port side, was it? All her knowledge of
shipping came from watching pirate movies. That might
be where they were going to dump the animals overboard.

"Que demonios esta hacienda aqui?"

Pagan's throat closed and her head swiveled around. A
skinny man in corduroys and a work shirt scowled below at
her. He had a gun tucked into his belt.

But he wasn't pointing it at her. She was young, female and
rumpled enough that she probably looked like a runaway, or
a drug addict who'd fallen asleep in the wrong place. Cer-
tainly no threat to a dockworker moving illicit cargo for a
once and future Nazi.

"Lo siento," she said, trying to imitate Emma's German-
Argentine accent. It wasn't easy. "Please don't tell anyone."

He snorted. "Come down from there," he ordered, flap-
ping his fingers at her. "You can't stay on the ship."

She stood up, but took care to keep the top of her head
from going past the top of the crates around her to avoid
anyone else seeing her. She had to get rid of this guy somehow, without anyone else noticing.

And without getting shot. One of the smaller empty cages
was piled up to her left, towering over the skinny dockworker. She put one hand on the back of it and pressed. It
was heavy, but it shifted slightly when she pushed.

"But I'm Dieter Von Albrecht's girlfriend," she said. Oh,

crap, maybe she should've claimed to be Emma instead. "I just want to say goodbye to him."

The man's eyes narrowed. "They why not drive here and wave? No. No stowaways. Come down."

He put one hand on the grip of his gun, flicking off the holster snap that held the pistol in place. "Hey!" He looked off to his left, shouting to his fellow sailors. "Come look what I f—"

Pagan shoved the smaller empty cage with all her strength off the crate beneath it. It shot forward and fell with a horrible rattling thump right on the dockworker's face. He crumpled in a flurry of flailing arms and legs. The cage tumbled off him to the side.

In two bounds, she was beside him, pulling his gun from its holster. He stirred, blood oozing from a cut on his forehead.

"Sorry," she muttered, and smacked him between the eyes with the pistol.

He fell back and lay still. She put one shaking hand to the vein in his throat and felt his pulse beating beneath her fingers. He'd live.

But had anyone paid attention to his shout? They were in a pool of darkness in the middle of a crate-filled deck. It wasn't easy to pick out anyone unless you were up high. But the sound of the falling cage would draw attention, too.

"Juan?" a man yelled.

"Something fell. Over there."

"I heard it."

The voices were coming from *that* direction. So Pagan backed up between her pallet and its neighbor in the opposite direction, then rounded a corner and began winding her way through the jungle of crates in what she thought was the direction of the bridge.

Once she got to the bridge… What the hell was she going to do then? She had a gun now, and that should help her intimidate the ship's captain into keeping the vessel here. If that didn't work, maybe she could shoot the steering wheel or whatever steered a ship. Even her appearance there might stall them long enough.

The faint thrumming beneath her feet whirred into a full-body vibration, and someone sang out the Spanish version of "All ashore that's going ashore!"

Pagan began to run, darting in between stocked pallets and piles of crates. Behind her, a man called for a doctor. Her unconscious dockworker had been found.

Maybe transporting the injured worker off the ship would stall them a few minutes.

She rounded the corner of a very large crate to see the edge of the ship with animal cages piled high along it and Dieter and Von Albrecht standing only ten yards away. Two other men were busy with the cages. Two went splashing into the water as she watched. She couldn't bear to think that they'd contained any animals. The gangplank cut a line from ship to shore ten yards beyond. She'd gone in completely the wrong direction and ended up on the dockside of the ship.

She managed not to curse out loud and darted back between two crates, crouching low. Her heart was pounding so hard it hurt her injured ribs.

Had they seen her?

"Enough begging!" Von Albrecht was saying to Dieter.

Oh, good. He was still arguing with Dieter, which meant he hadn't spotted her. "I'm tired of your selfish pleas. Get off this ship and go look after your sister. Wait for my signal."

"Yes, Papa," Dieter said, disappointment heavy in his voice. "Just say the word, and I'll organize a revolt right here. All of South America..."

His grandiose dreams were interrupted by a sharp barking sound and a ferocious growl.

"Stupid cur," Von Albrecht said. "Hurry up and throw it overboard before I do it myself."

The dog. It was still alive. And about to be killed.

She looked around, gun in hand, for something, anything, to help. With Von Albrecht, Dieter and those two men there, her gun couldn't keep them all at bay. She needed a distraction to pull some of them away. That would keep them from killing the dog for now. Then, if she could get Von Albrecht in her sites with only Dieter as backup, she could order him to stall their departure.

Hell, she hated him so much she might even be able to shoot him if he said no.

All around here were boxes, crates, cartons and bins labeled Glass, Instruments, *Gasolina* and Waste. One, more pristine, painted white and strapped to the deck itself, was labeled *Emergencia* and had a bright red stripe across it with smaller writing on the lid. But all it probably held was life jackets or inflatable boats or something.

Wait. Gas.

A large metal tank sat under a pile of wooden boxes with the word *Gasolina* stamped across it in big black letters. Would a bullet penetrate the tank? How big of an explosion

would it make? Big enough for any nearby police or firemen to come running? Big enough to set the ship on fire?

At the very least it should make a fine distraction.

Pagan backed off twenty feet, ready to run, aimed her
pistol and fired.

Clang! The bullet slammed into the metal tank, and Pagan
turned to run.

"What was that?"

She was halfway around the corner of a huge pallet of
boxes when she realized. No explosion. No fire. Nothing.

But the gun had banged loudly. That would draw at least a
couple of them away. Heavy footsteps were moving around,
searching. She circled the crate next to the gas tank to approach it slowly from another angle and peered around a
corner.

The bullet had punched a large hole in the side of the
tank, doing more damage than she'd thought. Liquid spilled
out, pooling on the deck. The nose-curdling tang of it indicated that indeed it was gas. But shooting it hadn't ignited
diddly-squat.

Served her right for learning everything from the movies.

The heavy footsteps were still searching. They hadn't
found her yet, and they probably hadn't had time to deal
with the dog. Still, she needed to set that fire. It could be
both signal to the authorities and a chance to stop the ship
from leaving, if she could just get the dang thing to light.

The liquid, spilling from the tank. If she could light that…
She fumbled in her pocket for her Zippo, the lighter she'd
stolen from Alaric Vogel. She'd have to throw it into the big-

gest puddle of gas from farther away or risk getting burned herself. She flicked the flame to life.

"You're a fool, Pagan Jones."

That horrible voice.

Pagan turned to see Von Albrecht standing ten feet away between towering crates, looking down his long nose at her.

She raised the gun. "Who's the bigger fool?" she asked. "The fool, or the fool who calls her names when she's carrying a loaded gun?"

A large hand reached out from the darkness beside her and grabbed the gun.

Dieter. Sidling with eerie quiet down a narrow trench between crates.

Pagan gasped, but managed to kick his shin as she tried to twist away. Her toe slammed into bone, and Dieter grunted. But he didn't flinch. With ridiculous ease, he wrenched the pistol from her fingers. She stared at it helplessly as he backed off a step and pointed it at her.

His thick lips curled smugly, and he gave her one hard shove on the shoulder. She stumbled backward and sat down hard on the white *emergencia* box.

"Idiot," Von Albrecht said. Smoke curled around his head from the cigarette in his mouth as he walked up to stand next to his son. She'd been so busy tracking the other men's steps she hadn't heard these two come at her from different angles. And now her gun was in Dieter's hand.

But she did have a tank spilling propane and a lighter. Hands trembling, she managed to flick the lighter back on and held it out over the puddle of gasoline growing larger every second, on the other side of the *emergencia* box.

"Hello, Dr. Van Alt," she said.

Von Albrecht raised his gray eyebrows at the sound of his real name, his Nazi name.

"Yes, I know who you really are," she said. "And all the terrible things you've done. One step toward me and I'll light us up," she said.

Von Albrecht made a scornful sound in the back of his throat. He removed the cigarette from his lips and threw it right into the stinky puddle of gas.

Pagan exclaimed, and jumped, scrambling for cover. Dieter moved sideways with amazing speed for someone so tall, and shoved her back down onto the white box.

The cigarette sank into the puddle of gasoline and went out.

"Go ahead and throw the lighter," Von Albrecht said. "You will only prove that you're as stupid as you look."

She stared down at the growing puddle, not understanding. "But…it smells like gas."

"It is gas," Von Albrecht said. His smirk showed how it pleased him to lecture her. "But it is the vapor which explodes at low temperatures, not the liquid. The liquid requires higher temperatures or a larger spark for ignition."

So the movies had lied about both guns and cigarettes setting gas on fire. She really needed to have a chat with those screenwriters. If she got out of this alive.

"Where's a blowtorch when you need one?" Pagan said. Her voice was miraculously steady. "Look, I'm all for your plan to blow up Berlin. Mama would've loved it. I just don't like it when people hurt animals. So let me take the dog in that cage with me, and you can lift anchor. No hard feelings."

Von Albrecht considered her without emotion, but Dieter snickered. "Let's take her with us, Papa," he said. "She has been to East Berlin before. Let her die there."

"I believe in what you're doing!" Pagan said. Her voice had a desperate edge that was real, but it seemed appropriate. "I told you before, Doctor. Mama told me all about you. She taught me well. I won't give away your secret."

Von Albrecht pursed his lips and shook his head slowly. "You are not your mother."

"I…" Pagan couldn't speak for a moment. Even now, in the midst of insanity, with a Nazi's son pointing a gun at her head, his words struck her. Von Albrecht meant that she wasn't like Mama in a bad way, of course. But it didn't matter. All that mattered was that in this one thing, he was right. Pagan was not her mother. She was herself. That was all. That was enough.

And she was damned well going to stop him and get out of this alive.

"I only came here because I saw Dieter and his friends leaving the drag race," she said. "He's just…so big and strong." She fluttered her eyes the tiniest bit at Dieter, who frowned down at her. "I wanted to know what you two were planning, to be part of it. But then I saw the dog. I love animals, you know? I thought maybe if I distracted you by shooting the gas tank, I could get him free somehow."

"You're not a bad actress," Von Albrecht said. "But you're a stupid girl, and I think we will put you into the water along with the mongrel."

Dieter snorted a laugh, and it chilled Pagan to the bone.

NINA BERRY

Who cares if you're cold. Keep them talking. Stalling them was all she had now that the gas didn't start a fire.

"I don't believe you've really got a bomb," Pagan said. It was the only arena she could think of that might provoke Von Albrecht. And Dieter wouldn't dare interrupt his father talking to shoot her. "Everybody knows the Germans tried to build an A-bomb during the war, but none of you were up to the job. And then you lost! I bet you can't even get your revenge right."

Von Albrecht's narrow lips smiled. "More stupidity. I learned a lot while I was working with your government after the war. Guards at the camp where I did my experiments were hanged for war crimes—guards who only did their job because I told them to. They died, yet your government gave me a house, and a car—your American way of life. All because the US thought they could use me to create better, bigger machines of death. Instead, I used them. They taught me to make bombs, and then I took their plutonium, and I made a better bomb. Berlin's buildings and avenues won't be destroyed, you see. My bomb will not explode the same way the ones at Hiroshima and Nagasaki did. Instead, it will rain radiation down on everyone within a twenty-mile radius. Enough to kill them within minutes or hours. But the city of the Führer will remain, washed clean of filth."

He was enjoying it, talking down to her like this. Every second he talked was another second closer to Devin or the authorities arriving.

But still no one was coming. They might never come. The United States had made Von Albrecht's horrific animal experiments possible. They'd given him all he needed to destroy a city, and maybe start a war. How could she rely on them to get here?

Devin. She could rely on him. He would come.

"Your government is an accomplice in this special mission," Von Albrecht said, as if reading her thoughts. "You would do better to follow your mother's way. We are pure."

There was that stupid word again. Unless you were referring to drinking water or a diamond, it was pretty meaningless.

"Pure isn't so great if it's pure evil," Pagan said. Her voice was strong, but her heart was sinking into a pool blacker than the water around the ship. This was the man her mother had helped.

"Disease always believes its cure is evil." Von Albrecht's eyes were alight with horrible glee. "Your mother would have loved my creation. They call it a dirty bomb, Imagine—no explosion! No blast wave to destroy the few buildings you and your Allies left us after the war. Just dead Communists, dead Americans, French and English. Dead, dead, dead!"

Pagan stared up into his pale eyes, wide with excitement. Excitement at horrific destruction. It was insane. But if you planned your insanity systematically, when did it cease to be insane? When did it simply become evil?

From the very beginning. From the first moment you looked at people and saw things.

It was too easy. All you had to do was look at the dog in the cage, and see not an animal capable of suffering, but an object to be used and thrown away. Once you looked at a single human being that way, what was to stop you from seeing them all as disposable? They became a disease to be cured, perhaps with a cleansing bomb, chemotherapy attacking a cancer.

The hotel clerk hadn't seen Mercedes the girl. Neither had Dieter. To him Mercedes and Naomi Schusterman weren't human beings; they were vessels into which he could pour his hate.

Mama had thought that way about Jews. She'd helped this man. Only one question stood out in Pagan's mind now.

"Did Mama know?" she asked. Her nose and eyes were running, and she wanted to throw up, but she wiped her face with the back of her muddy hand and stared at the Nazi. "Did she know about all the things you did during the war? Did she know what you were planning to do here?"

Von Albrecht's thin lips curled up in a smile of condescension so complete it was its own kind of madness. "So the little girl wants to know if her beloved mother was complicit in my so-called crimes? You look to *me* for reassurance? Well, don't look here. Because your mama didn't care what I'd done, or what I was planning to do. She only cared that I achieved my result."

A weird little sob came out of Pagan. A wave of dizziness made her sway there on top of the white box. "Did she tell you that?"

"We didn't need to speak of it," he said. "We were alike, your mama and I, in one very important way. Anything blessed by the Führer was to be applauded. Anything that furthered his Final Solution was sacred work. She knew it as well as I did. And now you know it, too."

He and Mama—true believers both. This was the disgusting place she had come from. What was there to make her any better than them?

The dark world swam. What was the point? One stupid little girl could never stop such a legacy of hate. A stupid girl who had been born from that legacy. She worked for those who sheltered Von Albrecht and inadvertently provided the plutonium. She was part of it.

Dizziness spiraled over her. She leaned both hands on the *emergencia* box, head down, staring at the red stripe. The list of contents printed in black between her thumbs swam before her eyes.

Off in the distance, through the swirling dark, short, sharp, furious barks cut through the roar in her ears. The sound of a dog's focused rage.

Focus.

Pagan blinked, and the words on the box beneath her sharpened as if she'd put on glasses. Von Albrecht was still talking, but she wasn't listening. The dizziness began to lift, like fog at sunrise.

If she gave up now, who would save the dog?

She gulped in air and listened to the dog barking, calling to her. Her eyes ran automatically over the list of contents in the box beneath her. She concentrated, pushing her despair aside. Breathe, focus, read the list.

10 *chalecos salvavidas.* Life jackets.

5 *luces de emergencia.* Emergency lights.

2 *pistolas de bengalas.* Flare guns.

2 *purificadores de agua.* Water purifiers.

Her eyes skipped back up a line.

Pistolas de bengalas.

Flare guns.

Von Albrecht was still gloating over her hopelessness and stupidity. Something about the Führer and mongrels and war. It didn't really matter. She glanced at Dieter. He'd lowered the gun while he listened to his father, but he could easily raise it and shoot her if she moved. She needed them both to stop concentrating on her, to be certain she wasn't even a small threat, if only for a few seconds.

She narrowed her eyes, staring back down at the emergency box's content list. These men were going to kill her and then kill tens of thousands more.

Also, Dieter had a gun and big meaty hands that enjoyed hitting people. What she had in mind wouldn't be fun. It would hurt. But it might work.

"You're not as strong or as smart as your mother was, are you?" Von Albrecht was saying. "Stupid, spoiled little American girl. But then it should be no surprise. Your silly father wasn't German. You're a mongrel."

"Damn you," she muttered, teeth clenched.

She looked up at Von Albrecht. He was shaking his head at her in amused disgust, ready to turn away. Good.

She glanced up at Dieter, sweat-soaked hair falling in her eyes. Her hands on the lid of the box clenched into fists. She channeled all her anger, all her volcanic hatred, into her voice. "You arrogant, murdering sons of bitches—damn you!"

She launched herself at Dieter, fists raised.

She must have taken him off guard, in spite of her angry words, because he barely raised his hands in time to fend off her jab and right cross, aimed at his face.

"What…?" he started to say.

"I'll kill you both!" Pagan screamed. It sounded appropriate, and right now she wished she could. And she rammed her knee into his crotch.

The blow was slightly off, landing mostly on his inner thigh. But it must've hit something vital because Dieter's face transformed with a look of agonized surprise.

"Oof!" He exhaled hard, eyes screwing themselves into red points of rage. "You bitch!"

He backhanded her across the face. The impact sounded like a wet fish hitting the pavement. Her bones liquefied.

Pagan found herself sprawled across the top of the *emergencia* box almost before she even knew she'd been hit. Her head was a scarlet bowl of pain. A strange low hum had taken over the world. But she was awake, and alive. And she'd gotten what she needed. *Emergencia* boxes were never locked, right? They'd better not be.

She lay still, eyes shut. She'd never acted unconscious before, but it couldn't be that complicated.

Von Albrecht chuckled as Dieter cursed.

"Bitch!" Dieter spat. She heard him put the gun down on a crate. "That hurt."

"Even gnats can bite," Von Albrecht said. "Here. That cage looks about right. Get it down for me. She'll fit inside it. We'll put her into the water with the cur she loves. Even if she wakes up, she'll sink to the bottom."

"Good." Dieter shuffled away and grunted as something metal shifted a few yards away.

"That one," Von Albrecht said.

Pagan barely opened her eyes. Through the curtain of her lashes and hair she saw Von Albrecht about five yards away, back to her, pointing up at a large cage on top of a crate. Dieter was climbing up a nearby box to start lowering the cage down.

Perfect. As quietly as she could, she slipped off the *emergencia* box, slid the latch open, unsnapped a second catch and lifted the lid. Lying on top of a pile of life vests were two fat-barreled flare guns.

"Hey!' Dieter said from atop his crates. "She's awake!"

Pagan grabbed a flare gun in each hand. They were big, and heavier than she'd thought, but close enough to what she'd fired when she'd played *Young Annie Oakley* for the purpose she had in mind.

"What is she…?" Von Albrecht's eyes got round behind their glasses as Pagan lifted the gun in her left hand to point at him. "Help! Heinz! Lars!"

"Will this work, Doctor?" she asked, and aimed the flare gun in her right hand at the growing puddle of gas and pulled the trigger.

She had time to see Von Albrecht's lips start to form the word *No!* before she dove for cover.

The tank exploded in a fountain of fire. A wave of heat scorched her back. The air filled with the pungent smell of gas and charred wood. Splinters and metal bolts rained down.

She lifted her head. The pallet of crates where the tank

had been stored was on fire. Flames reached toward the sky and licked the crates nearby.

Far away, men were shouting. Attention was being paid, at last. Von Albrecht and Dieter must have run for it. In the sea of packing crates with the flames starting to take over, she couldn't see them anywhere.

Pagan coughed and got to her feet. Her ribs were screaming at her, her head rang and the bottom of her shoes and the hem of her dress were singed. At least she hadn't gone up in flames.

Feet were pounding toward them. Von Albrecht's high, nasal voice was shouting orders, getting farther away.

"Come on, Papa," she heard Dieter say. "We must get off the ship."

The right side of Pagan's body was hot from the flames. She gathered her wits and stumbled away. A sailor ran past her, carrying a hose, shouting.

She got to clearer air and took a deep breath. Before her the black sea rippled with reflections of red. A large cage sat by the edge of the ship. The creature inside it whined at her and whapped its tail against the bars.

"Hey there," she said, limping toward the dog. Her left calf was shouting at her. She'd wrenched it somehow. She laid one of the flare guns down so she could put her hand through the cage bars to stroke the dog's head. He licked her hand.

Pagan looked back at the now-raging fire. Two groups of men were fighting it with water hoses. They might get it under control.

Off in the distance, a siren wailed. A second siren joined it.

"Not bad for a stupid little American mongrel, eh?" she

asked the dog. "Never before has any girl been so happy to see some rocket's red glare."

Something caught the dog's remaining eye. It growled, tail rigid.

Von Albrecht and Dieter were hustling down the deck. The gangplank had actually been partially retracted from the dock while she wasn't looking, and Von Albrecht was shouting for a sailor to hurry up and put it back. The man was hastening to obey, so they could all abandon the burning ship.

Pagan hefted the flare gun she still held in her right hand. She wasn't a great shot, but she could fire it at them. See what damage it might do. Hurting Von Albrecht and Deiter sounded wonderful right now. But killing was something else entirely. She'd killed two people she loved with a single turn of a steering wheel. That was enough blood on anyone's hands.

But if she could delay them, maybe the cops would arrive, and the CIA could get them into custody and mete out a little justice.

She leveled the gun at the gangplank, her finger tightening on the trigger. She might get lucky and set it on fire, too.

But that would trap them all on board with a fire blazing. And with her luck she'd fire it straight into the water or blow Von Albrecht's head off. Or hit the poor sailor trying to extend the gangplank.

Her hand holding the gun shook. She lowered it.

Von Albrecht shouted something to one of the men rushing over to help with the gangplank and waved toward Pagan. The man took something black from his hip, and raised it. A loud crack, and a bullet whizzed past Pagan's head. Another crack, and she ducked to see a chunk jump out of the wooden deck at her feet. Von Albrecht wasn't backing off.

The sirens were closing in. But would they get there in time? A shot ricocheted off an empty cage next to Pagan. There were no other animals left on deck. Von Albrecht's bastards must have killed all but the dog.

Good thing this particular bastard wasn't a good shot. But he was walking toward her, taking aim again.

The gangplank was nearly to the other side. Von Albrecht and Dieter waited impatiently. The moment it was locked down, they would get away. He who had inflicted so much suffering was about to escape justice once again.

Beside her the dog was still growling. The few hairs left on his neck stood straight up. The bleeding lips were pulled back to show his fangs as he stared balefully at Von Albrecht.

Pagan unlatched the cage.

"Get him, boy," she said, and she swung the door open.

Like a guided missile, the skeletal form took off after Von Albrecht.

The man firing at Pagan lifted his gun and yelled, "Look out!"

The dog shot past him. He fired at it, taking another chunk out of the deck.

Von Albrecht turned, blinking at the blur of raw skin and teeth bearing down on him.

"Help!" He threw his arms up to shield his face. The dog launched itself at him in a great arcing leap.

Dieter screamed and lunged forward, then flinched back as teeth flashed at him. The man who had been shooting at

Pagan raced back toward Von Albrecht. Damn it, they might hurt the dog. Pagan broke into a run.

Lights were flashing, red, blue and white. The gangplank wavered, not yet secure. A siren wailed closer, and men's voices shouted. Police cars and an ambulance screeched to a halt alongside the dock. Men in uniform were pouring out, shouting questions and brandishing guns. Firemen pulled a hose from their truck.

Von Albrecht was on the ground, screaming and wrestling with a fury of white teeth and raw flesh. Dieter's face was contorted in an agony of indecision. He reached toward the dog again, then drew back to avoid being mauled. His cohort had his gun up and was trying to find a way to shoot the dog without hurting the man beneath it.

"Get away!" Pagan shouted, and fired the flare gun over Dieter's head. The round sparked and hissed up and into the black sky, leaving a trail of smoke.

That should bring the cops right to them.

The man spun around, yelling. Dieter was staring at her as if she'd popped up out of her grave.

"You," he said. His face was wet with tears. Being unable to help his father was tearing him apart. In a way, she knew how that felt. As he stared at her, his face hardened.

"Drop the gun!" she shouted, aiming at the man who had one. The wet sounds of cloth and flesh ripping continued as the dog ravaged Von Albrecht. His screams were growing more frantic.

The man dropped the gun, his gaze torn between her and the uniformed men pelting toward them.

"Get down on the ground!" Pagan shouted at him and

Dieter. When they didn't react, she repeated it in German. "I said get down on the ground!"

Bewildered, the man obeyed. Dieter did not. The cops were only thirty feet away, feeling for their own pistols now and shouting at her in Spanish. One of them was grabbing at the gangplank, trying to bolt it to the dock.

Pagan aimed the flare gun at Dieter. "It's over."

He looked up from the writhing, bloody mess that was his father and the dog and shook his head at her. *"Nien."* His eyes were like stones. *"Nien!"*

And he dove into the sea.

Pagan stood there stupidly for a moment, flare gun still pointed where Dieter had been.

"Drop it!" a uniformed man shouted at her from the dock, pointing his own gun at her. Other men were shouting down at the water, ordering Dieter to stop.

Pagan dropped the flare gun as the gangplank was finally affixed. The cops swarmed toward her.

Let them come. She patted her thigh and said to the dog, "Leave him, boy. Come here."

The dog lifted his head. Von Albrecht was moaning, flailing. He shoved at the dog, and the animal left him, trotting over to Pagan. His muzzle was smeared with blood, but his tail was wagging.

Pagan knelt down and put her arms around the dog, not caring about the cops surrounding them or the mud and blood now smeared over her face.

"It's okay now," she said to him as she pulled the wiggling body closer. "It's all right."

ENTREGAME

Surrender. To give oneself up to the leader's lead.

Pagan wouldn't let go of the dog, and the cops finally gave up trying to pry the gaunt creature from her arms. Someone handed her a rope, but she didn't have the heart to tie it around the poor thing's raw neck.

She tried to answer the questions the cops were throwing at her, until a nurse scolded the men, threw a blanket over her shoulders and led her and the dog away to sit near the ambulance.

She watched them load Von Albrecht, still moaning in agony, into that ambulance. So he was alive, if badly bleeding from dog bites. Pagan was about to protest, until, through the press of uniforms, she saw Devin Black speaking to the ambulance driver.

A wave of relief, of peace, overtook her. She waited and sipped the water and took the aspirin the nurse gave her. When the woman wasn't looking, Pagan lowered the cup and let the dog have a drink.

Eventually, the nurse asked Pagan to get into a second

ambulance. She and the dog climbed inside the back to find Devin sitting there, smiling at her.

The dog walked up, tail wagging, and licked Devin's hand. His dark brows came together in concern as he carefully stroked the dog's battered ears. "Good work."

Pagan sat on the bench opposite him. It took everything she had not to throw herself on him and never let go.

But the doors were opened, with men and women coming and going outside. She wasn't sure if anyone was supposed to know who she was, or who Devin was. But if she could've wished them gone anywhere else on earth in that moment, they would have vanished forever.

"It's so good to see you," Devin said, his voice low. His expression resembled something like pure happiness.

"Dieter," she said. "Did they get him?"

His eyebrows quirked up. "No. I didn't know he was here. Was he the one the police saw jump into the water?"

She nodded. "He and some of the members of his gang were helping his father. You have to get him. He saw me, and he's, well, angry doesn't quite cover it."

"He's very dangerous. Hang on." Devin jumped out of the ambulance and walked over to a very thin man whose pale scalp shined between long, carefully combed strands of hair. Blue and red lights flashed around them as Devin spoke to him. The thin man threw both hands up and hustled out of Pagan's view, shouting at someone.

Devin climbed back into the ambulance and sat down opposite her again without touching her. He was wearing a black shirt with no jacket, black pants and soft-soled shoes. He looked like a cat burglar.

"How did you find us?" she asked. She really wanted the ambulance doors to close. She needed to be alone with Devin. Even if he didn't love her back.

He glanced over at the outside world as if he, too, was waiting for it to go away. "Mercedes told me you'd gone to the Von Albrecht house, so I went to the basement, saw the entrance to the tunnels, and followed it to the docks."

"Mercedes." Pagan straightened. "She'll be worried."

"I just called and told her that you're all right," he said. "How are you feeling? The nurse said you didn't need to go to the hospital, but…"

"I'm fine," she said shortly. She didn't want to talk about what she'd learned about her mother, or about anything else right now.

Devin was so close. But she schooled her voice to stay clinical. "They got Von Albrecht, didn't they? Your friends?"

His eyes kept moving over her face. "He's heading for one of our safe houses now. After he's been stitched up a little, they'll question him."

"What about the bomb? It's on the ship."

"So it *was* a bomb," he said, and sat up straighter as the skinny balding man walked up to the open back of their ambulance. He was younger than his hairline indicated, and so thin that his bland suit hung from his shoulders like a sack on a stick doll. He had an intense nervous energy to him. An eye twitch wouldn't look out of place.

"There's news," he said to Devin as he cast a wary glance at Pagan.

"You can talk. This is Pagan Jones," Devin said tersely. "Pagan, this is my colleague Reggie Pope."

"Nice to meet you, Miss Jones." They were speaking in English and Reggie Pope had a flat Midwestern US accent. His eyes traveled over her dismissively before he turned back to Devin. "The fire's completely out. The Argentine police have impounded the ship and all its contents."

"When do we get it from them?" Devin asked.

"Officially, negotiations should take a few days," Reggie said. "But they've already asked for our help to store the… object in question. They're not equipped to deal with it safely. But we're still not sure exactly what it is."

"Von Albrecht said it was a dirty bomb," Pagan said.

Devin's head came up, and Reggie Pope's eyes went round. He said very carefully, as if speaking to a child, "Did he use those exact words—dirty bomb?"

Pagan shot Devin an *are you kidding me?* glance, which made him smirk. She said, "I believe Von Albrecht's exact words were that there would be—" her voice took on Von Albrecht's relentless tone ""—no blast wave to destroy the few buildings the Allies left standing after the war. Just dead Communists, dead Americans, French and English. Dead, dead, dead.'"

Reggie blinked at her, confused.

"And he said he was working for the United States before he escaped. You let him get away with some plutonium."

Reggie's twitchy face became positively pale.

"I don't think you heard me, Pope," Devin said. "This is *Pagan Jones.*"

"Oh!" Something clicked inside Reggie's brain. "I'm so sorry, Miss Jones. I wasn't expecting someone so—" he hesitated "—young."

"You better go tell them what they're dealing with," Devin said. "It's time for us to go."

"Yes, yes, of course." Reggie pulled at the ambulance doors. "A dirty bomb. Good Lord!"

He slammed the back doors shut, and the ambulance took off.

Pagan and Devin stared at each other in the dim gleam of the ambulance's greenish overhead light. The dog laid down at Devin's feet and sighed. The gurney between them rattled.

"I told them to stop by a veterinarian near the hotel first," he said.

"Thanks." Her mouth was dry. She couldn't stop staring at him.

He was staring back. "Who hit you?" His voice was low with controlled anger.

There must be a bruise forming on her cheek, and it warmed her a little to think the sight of it made him angry. "Dieter. But I wanted him to."

He gave her a puzzled little smile. "You're going to need to tell me a little more."

So she outlined it all for him in short, unemotional sentences that left out any thoughts about her mother: how she'd gotten on the ship, started the fire and stopped Von Albrecht.

He listened without interruption. A faint, thoughtful line creased his forehead. "You are the most extraordinary creature, Pagan Jones," he said. "Just when I think I've grasped the depth of your courage and resourcefulness, you surprise me."

Pagan's throat tightened. She opened her eyes wide against the tears threatening to spill over. "I tried to play it smart and stay low," she said. Why had his words made her want to cry like a child? "I knew you were coming, that there were too many of them, that it was stupid to go on board. But they were going to lift anchor. They were drowning the animals. I couldn't wait."

Her face was wet, damn it. In spite of the blanket over her shoulders, she was shaking. "I'm sorry," she whispered.

In a breath, Devin crossed the space between them and took her in his arms. She sank into him and gave in to several shaking sobs. Devin said nothing, only rocked her slightly.

As she calmed, she realized that the dog had moved to lie on her feet, and that Devin smelled like fresh tobacco leaves and musk. It was so warm and safe in his arms. She closed her eyes, pressed her forehead against his neck, praying she'd never have to leave.

Devin said, "What Von Albrecht did to those animals and to his victims during the war, the terror he had planned for Berlin, that's no one's fault but his, and the devils who helped him. Don't you ever apologize to me, Pagan Jones, *mo grádh*. I won't stand for it."

The ambulance came to a halt, and the driver tapped on the window between them.

"We're at the vet," Devin said.

Pagan nodded, and pulled away, sniffing. Devin produced a handkerchief from somewhere. She took it, and felt cold again as he left her to open the back doors.

While she blew her nose and talked softly to the dog, Devin spoke to a sleepy man who opened an upstairs window. Shortly after that, the man, now in a white coat, was accepting a wad of bills from Devin and frowning over the dog's many wounds.

"The blood on his mouth isn't his," Pagan said in Spanish, giving the dog another careful hug. "Go with the nice vet, sweetie." She really needed to give him a name.

"Give him food, too, whatever he requires," Devin said. "We'll send someone for him in the morning."

She watched the vet walk back into his dark office with the dog. She didn't want to let him go.

"Rocket!" Pagan said suddenly. She dropped the blanket that was wrapped around her, ran up to the dog and kissed the top of his head. "Your name is Rocket. *Su nombre es Rocket*," she added to the vet.

"*Sí?*" he said, smiling and blinking sleepily. "*Buenos noches, señorita.*"

"*Buenos noches, señor. Gracias,*" she said. "*Buenos noches, Rocket.*"

She walked back out to Devin, who stood by the ambulance. When he tried to drape the blanket over her shoulders again, she shied away.

He lowered the blanket. "Are you all right?"

She couldn't look at him, but she shook her head. She wanted yet didn't want him to put that blanket on her, so he'd put his arms around her again. She wanted to snuggle in that embrace, knowing she could stay. She wanted him to bring her a martini wearing nothing but a smile. But she didn't get a lot of things she wanted in this world. Hell, she was lucky just to be alive.

"You can tell me anything, you know," he said, and waited.

"Okay." She inhaled and tried to put all the awful things in her brain into a sentence. "You and me in there, just now." She jerked her head toward the open back of the ambulance. "What did that mean?"

His eyes flicked over her face. Then he tossed the blanket into the ambulance, closed the doors and banged on them twice.

The ambulance engine stuttered to life, and it pulled away, rattling off down the street. Across the way, a light in an upstairs window was extinguished. The quiet of the night filled all the cracks in the cobblestone street and infiltrated the fog. They were alone.

Devin paced away from her, hands jammed in his pants pockets, then pivoted around to face her. "When I held you in my arms just now, it meant that I wanted to comfort you, to keep you safe. I didn't do it to keep you as an asset. I did it because I care. You know that."

She was frozen in place. The words sounded right. They sounded pretty darn great actually. But…there was always a "but."

"You comforted me in Berlin, too," she said. "You kissed me. But then you went away. Tonight, you said nice things, and you held me, but it doesn't mean what I want it to. So I can't let it keep happening. I can't keep hoping for something that isn't true. I probably shouldn't see you again."

His eyes flicked at her, mouth moving into a determined line as he came to some kind of decision.

"Listen to me," he said, taking her shoulders in both hands. "Sometimes the kissing and the flirting is fun, but most of the time it's not. I like Julieta, but kissing her didn't mean anything to me. She and the others—they're not like the time I kissed you. Back in Berlin." He took a deep breath and his eyes got very bright. "Nothing else in my life has ever been like that."

Pagan swayed. Had she heard him correctly?

"It hasn't?" It was the only thing she could think to say.

"You're like no one else, Pagan. But I couldn't do anything more, or say anything, because you were working for me. It wouldn't have been right. And I didn't want to make a mistake."

She nodded. "I know it's important you don't mess up at your job. Lives are at stake…"

"Yes, but that's not what I meant. I meant that you're important." He gave her shoulders a tiny shake, as if trying to awaken her from a bad dream. "I didn't want to make a mistake at the beginning because I knew very early on that I…" He swallowed, his face drawn. "I didn't want to be like Nicky."

Nicky. The boy who'd scooped her up when she was at her lowest and made her feel loved. There had been no waiting with Nicky, no careful consideration of what was or wasn't right.

"You didn't want to be my boyfriend?" she asked, her voice small.

"No!" He shook his head vehemently. "I didn't want to take advantage of you. I don't think he meant to, but when he first met you, Nicky swept a very unhappy girl off her feet."

Pagan had been drinking secretly every day when she met Nicky. Nicky had come along and made her feel like maybe life wasn't so pointless, after all. Some of her choices after that had been terrible, but being with Nicky, until the end, wasn't one of them.

"I might've loved Nicky," she said. "Or maybe I loved how he made me feel—I don't know. But I did what he wanted, you know?" She looked Devin dead in the eye and pulled her courage up from somewhere. "And that's why you're hesitating with me. Because I went all the way with Nicky."

"What?" He dropped his hands from her and took a step back in astonishment. "You think *that's* why…?" Overcome with something like disgust or anger, he turned away from her. The line of his shoulders were taut as a piano wire.

Was he angry with her, or…? "You didn't know that I… that he and I were together like that?"

"It's got to be said, then." He was speaking low, as if to himself. He turned back to face her again, slowly. "I can't allow you to go on thinking that matters to me. Don't you see?"

When she stared at him, he threw up both hands in a fury. "Oh, goddamn this great, wide, stupid world and all its stupid ways. It's heels-owre gowdie."

She had no idea what he was talking about, only that whenever he descended into unintelligible Scots, it was a sign of real emotion.

His eyes were burning as he put his hands on her shoulders again. A tremor ran through his fingers deep beneath her skin. "How I behaved toward you has nothing to do with your time with Nicky. When we were together in Berlin, you were vulnerable, on the edge and maybe still in love with him. And until the other night, I wasn't sure how you felt about me. So I kept my distance not only because I was your guardian. I did it because I didn't want you to take me out of sadness or as a distraction." He was looking her dead in the eye, as she had with him, moments before. "I wanted you to love me as much as I love you."

She stared at him, dumbfounded. Her knees appeared to be made of pudding, and her head seemed to have floated off her shoulders like a helium balloon.

"Yes." He pulled her closer, fingers digging into her arms hungrily. "I love you. You said it first, but I felt it first. I felt it the morning in our hotel suite at the Berlin Hilton when I quizzed you on your lines and you were so…strong after all you'd been through, and so funny. And the night Nicky tried to get you back, I wanted to kill him, really kill him. I knew then I was in way too deep. And when you took a drink later, I wanted to hold you, to make it all better, although I knew I never could."

It was his fierce grip on her more than his words which brought her down to earth. It was the line of his throat, the movements of his mouth, saying these words to her that made it feel real. That made her think it might be true.

"You helped me," she said. Her face was wet, but she wasn't crying. Her eyes were brimming with something like joy. "You found Hans and Matthew so I could have an AA meeting with them the next day. It's the most amazing thing anyone's ever done for me."

He put his palms to her cheeks, fingers sinking into her tousled hair. The storm in his eyes calmed as he gazed down at her. "When I got the phone call telling me that Thomas and his family were safe because of you, that you had stayed behind so they could escape. That's when I knew I'd found the most magnificent girl in the world." His voice was husky, his Scottish burr purring like a panther. "The only one for me. Pagan Jones. *Mo grádh.*"

He bent and softly kissed her lips, as if she were the most precious thing in all the world.

"Mo grádh," she repeated against his mouth, getting the lilt right this time. "I know what it means now."

"My love," he said, and her lips opened as he kissed her more deeply.

Everything went dark as her arms wound up around his neck. His fingers stroked the soft skin of her neck and his touch sent shivers along her skin like ripples in silk. He traced kisses down her jawbone and below her ear.

"I want to devour every inch of you," he breathed in her ear, and then lowered his head to sink his teeth softly into her neck.

A sound she'd never heard before came from her throat. The streetlight cast not two shadows, but one, onto the cobblestones.

Devin's lips were on her shoulder, her collarbone, and her mind was hot, black and red. She dug her fingernails into his back, wanting to destroy what little space there was between them. The past, the fear, the whole world that was always there, always looming over her, was vanishing now. Together she and Devin would tear it all apart.

"We can't, we can't," he murmured. "Not yet." He kissed her mouth again and pulled away. His lips were reddened, his dark hair every which way.

"Not yet?" Language came strangely to her. Words were foreign, conversation overrated.

"Not yet," he said with more conviction, and kissed her again as if he couldn't help it.

"My mission with you is over," she said, her hand on the back of his neck. "You're not my supervisor anymore."

He kissed her again. "Dieter's still out there. He's dangerous."

She interrupted him with another kiss and shook her head. "We'll get him in the morning. I don't want to wait for you any longer."

The two-block walk to the Alvear Palace Hotel took longer than it should have because Devin kept pulling her into shadowy niches and alleys to make out. By the time they stopped at the concierge desk, the blood in her veins was thrumming. She tugged on his hand, pulling him toward the elevator. But Devin paused long enough to put a wad of bills in the surprised man's hand. "Please leave a message for Miss Duran that Miss Jones is quite safe and not to worry. And in the morning, please send a man to get Miss Jones's dog at Dr. Fernandez's office and then bring the dog to her suite."

Pagan favored the man with a giddy smile. "Thank you so very much."

The concierge smoothly slid the money in his jacket pocket. "Of course, *señor. Señorita.* It is as good as done."

It took years for the elevator to arrive. Pagan couldn't quite believe it when she saw an older couple already inside it, also going up.

"Don't they know we need to be alone?" she whispered in Devin's ear as they pressed the button for the seventh floor and leaned against the back wall, side by side. The lift groaned and rose so slowly Pagan considered getting out to push.

Devin let go of her hands long enough to push aside a stray lock of her hair, his fingertips brushing her eyebrow, her cheek, her lips.

"I'm a muddy mess," she said softly.

His flexible mouth turned up in a knowing smile. "I could give you a bath. No extra charge."

She was going to burn a rift in the elevator floor, sending them both plummeting into the depths. And she didn't care.

When they were in his room, with the door shut and locked behind them, Devin slid her clothing off one piece at a time. Then they were in the tub together. She couldn't help splashing him until he grabbed her and slid her body, slick with soap, on top of his. The water splooshed over the sides of the tub, and Devin took in a mouthful of water that sent him spluttering with laughter.

"Clean enough!" he said, and in three decisive moves had her out of the tub, wrapped in a huge soft towel and thrown, giggling, onto the bed.

What followed was both more serious and more fun than she expected. Devin kept finding places on her body she hadn't paid nearly enough attention to. He was patient; when her breathing began to come fast and shallow, she didn't have to ask him to keep doing exactly what he was doing. He knew.

Later, Pagan opened her eyes to find Devin propped up on one elbow in bed beside her, looking at her, a tiny smile on his lips.

"Well, hello," she said, stretching luxuriously. Most of the pillows were still on the floor, but the sheets and bedspread, which had been wrenched out of place, were now thrown haphazardly over her.

"You sleep without a pillow," he said.

"Miss Edwards took away my sad excuse for a pillow to punish me for insubordination my second day in reform school," she said. "I got used to sleeping without one."

"Insubordination—from you?" He frowned, pulling her in close for a kiss. "Not possible."

There was more kissing, until he broke away and said, "I've always wondered. Why did your parents name you Pagan?"

She turned over restlessly onto her back. "I don't know. It was Mama's idea."

"Doesn't mean it wasn't a good idea," he said, and kissed her shoulder.

She turned her head. She'd never seen him so sleepy and warm and sweet. But the thought of her own name now set her teeth on edge. "I don't know if I like it anymore. Not after what I found out about her."

"She did at least one good thing," he said. "She made you. And I think she named you perfectly."

She turned back on her side to face him. "Someone asked her about it once for a magazine interview. She said she chose the name because her daughter was not one to believe everything she was told. That she—that I—would follow my own creed. I don't know. Maybe she made all of that up. And when I think about it, I did everything she told me. Some pagan I turned out to be."

He laughed. "But that's changed. No one knows what

you'll do next. We just sit back and marvel. It's the perfect name."

Pagan wasn't so sure. "But if Mama believed all these horrible things like Von Albrecht says, if that was her idea of following her own creed, then it's a horrible name."

He smiled. "Your mother may have given you the name, but she wasn't the pagan, the disbeliever. You are."

Mama had been a true believer. That's what Von Albrecht had said. Was Pagan all that different? She wasn't sure of that, or of anything.

"Right now the only thing I believe in is that you're the best kisser in the world," she said to him.

"Allow me to demonstrate," he said.

The kissing went on, until he had to pull another one of his English Durex condoms out of the nightstand.

Sometime later she stirred to find him standing over by the desk in his room, wearing only his pants, going over some papers.

"Do you ever sleep?" she asked.

He turned, smiling. "I don't want to sleep while you're here. Every second is precious."

She blushed and shook her head at him in mock accusation. "And whenever you don't have a Nazi war criminal newly in custody with his gang leader son still at large."

"Dieter." Devin shook his head. "I checked in, and no sign of him returning to his house. Emma's going to wonder what happened when she wakes up."

"You should put a watch on the gang's underground headquarters, down by the South Docks," Pagan said, sitting up. "Where they have their drag races."

"I'll tell our contacts in the local police," Devin said. "Our numbers are stretched a bit thin now that we have Von Albrecht in custody."

He was still frowning over the paper in his hand. "What's wrong?" she asked.

"It's a little odd." He walked over, papers in hand, and sat on the bed beside her. "I've been going over the files they gave me, and none of them say that Von Alt was working for the US Nuclear Program, much less that he was specifically working on a dirty bomb."

"They kept it from you," she said.

He threw the papers down. "Which leads to my next question…"

"What else have they kept from you," she finished for him. "Von Albrecht told me he stole the plutonium for the bomb from the American program he was working on. He said he'd created something they'd been trying to make, but hadn't succeeded."

Devin leaned back against the headboard. She couldn't help watching how his abdominal muscles bunched up nicely as he did it. "The Americans, the English and the Soviets all recruited Nazis they thought might be helpful after the war."

"Helpful?" Pagan said. "Look at what he did to Rocket. He did worse things to people during the war."

Devin stared off into the distance, shaking his head a little at the thought. "That kind of decision is way above my pay grade," he said. "I'm not saying I agree with it, but he might've had vitally important information at the time, something that would do more good than his death could ever do."

"But he should have gone to jail at the very least!" She moved restlessly under the sheets. "You can't pat men like him on the head and say, 'Bad boy, don't do it again,' and expect him to behave. His victims deserve better than that."

"I agree," he said, reaching out to touch her cheek. The contact soothed her. "But at least we prevented him from creating more victims."

She scooted over to lie against him, her head on his chest. He put an arm around her, and she took a deep breath, inhaling every particle of him that she could. The even drumming of his heart, the warm scent of his skin, the way one corner of his mouth indented a little farther than the other when he smiled. She'd waited so long for this; she needed to savor every second.

"I asked Von Albrecht if Mama knew what he'd done," she said. "And what he planned to do."

He pulled her in closer. "What did he say?"

"He said she didn't care what he did, as long as it helped the Führer's dreams come true. He said she was a true believer, like him. Basically he said that my mother was a monster."

He pressed his lips against the top of her head. "How could she be a monster and still have created you? People are complicated."

She pulled away from him a little to look him in the eye. "You never talk about your father. Yet he's part of who you are."

"My father was not a good man." He looked down, his

face carefully blank. "I don't know whether or not he loved me. Not the way you know your mother loved you."

The only thing Pagan knew about Devin's father was that he'd been an expert art thief who had used his own son as a decoy and a helper until, somehow, it all came to an end, and Devin had been recruited by MI6.

Being with Devin was somehow safe and exciting at the same time. It allowed her to finally say the dark thing that had been gathering strength in the recesses of her mind. "But Mama was such a bad person…" She'd said those words to Mercedes back in Los Angeles. She hadn't known how to finish the sentence then, but she knew now. Still the words did not come easily. "Does that make me bad, too?"

He shifted away so he could look down at her, dark brows drawn together in concern. "Of course not."

"But I've done terrible things," she said. "I don't want to be like her, but part of me is. I can't help it."

"You can be like her in many ways and still be a good person," he said. "You can take what you loved about her and use that to make things better."

"Mama did love us," Pagan said, and put a hand on Devin's chest. His heart beat beneath her palm. "And your father must have loved you, somehow, some way. How could he not?"

He put his hand over hers. "This isn't about me. Or my father. I want you to know that I don't take your feelings lightly when I say I don't believe in monsters. Your mother was a human being. She had many sides to her—one side was ugly and wrong, but another was beautiful and right. That's the side of her that loved you and your sister. The bad and the good don't cancel each other out, you know. They live, side by side, in all of us."

Pagan knew all too well the weak side of herself. It was finding the good that was challenging. "If it's all so damned gray," she said, "how do we decide who's right and who's wrong? How do we choose a side?"

"I second-guess myself a lot," he said, interweaving his fingers through hers. "And then I go with my gut."

"I guess we have that in common," she said.

He put his arms around her again and buried his face in her hair. "I still can't quite believe you're here with me. Like this. I never want to leave this room."

"Scared you tonight, didn't I?" she said. "Sorry."

"Never be sorry," he said. "It's one of the reasons I love you—that you risk yourself for what you know is important."

Those three words. He said them again. She kissed his chest. "You're the one who made it all possible, Devin Black. You're the one who gave me the chance to see what I could be, what I could do." She scooched up and kissed him twice.

He kissed her a third time, long and hard and deep. It left her breathless.

"Let's see if we can tire you out enough to get you to sleep," she said.

Later, she woke to find him passed out beside her. She couldn't help staring down at his long black eyelashes and his mouth, softened by sleep. Then she wrapped herself in his robe and padded into his bathroom and closed the door before turning on the light. He needed every minute of sleep she could give him.

There beside the sink lay the hair gel and the Pepsodent she remembered from her visit to his bathroom in the Berlin Hilton. Everything was spotlessly neat and organized, set in straight lines and right angles. Someone had drilled order and neatness into him. Maybe that had been his father.

There were two other things he'd brought with him in Berlin that she'd found after searching his rooms. Had he stored them in the same, secret place here in Buenos Aires? She lifted the top off the toilet tank and set it on the seat.

Sure enough. A black waterproof bag lay at the bottom of the tank. She put her hand into the cold water and pulled it out. Time for him to share with her as much as she had with him.

When she woke up it was late afternoon, and Devin was in the shower. Well, they hadn't gotten in from the night's craziness until close to 5:00 a.m. She dialed the number for the suite she shared with Mercedes. The number rang and rang until an operator picked up.

"Any message?" the woman asked.

Maybe the vet had brought Rocket by, and Mercedes had taken him for a walk or something. "No, thank you," Pagan said. "Can I have room service, please?"

She ordered coffee and breakfast, and it arrived as Devin walked out of the bathroom, buttoning his pants, his dark hair spiky and damp.

"Any word on Dieter?" she asked.

"No sign of him yet. The cops have been alerted, but they're a bit overwhelmed right now."

Pagan wheeled the food cart over to his side of the bed. "Time for breakfast."

"You shouldn't have," he said as he sat down.

"This is as close as I get to cooking," she said, fanning a napkin onto his lap. "But I know you like your coffee black." She poured him a cup and set it down on the saucer.

"Bacon, sausages, eggs, mushroom, tomato and porridge?" He flashed her a grin. "You must love me if you ordered a full breakfast."

"I guess I must," she said. He looked like the boy he was, sitting there with his hair wet and messy, his bare chest still damp from the shower. It was blissful just to look at him.

He stuffed a large bite into his mouth. Through the food, his accent was waxing Scottish, which meant he was relaxed, and happy. "I'm starving, and you're amazing."

"Had to butter you up, along with the toast, before asking you all sorts of personal questions," she said, pulling a chair over to sit on the opposite side of the food cart.

"No black pudding?" He made a tsking noise before taking a large bite of toast. "Can't answer personal questions without beans and black pudding."

"Couldn't find either one in Buenos Aires," she said. "Although any food where the main ingredients are blood and intestine might not ever make it to my breakfast table."

"What in heaven do you think sausages are?"

He couldn't stop smiling at her, which made her smile, which made him smile, in a wonderful endless circle. It would've been kind of sickening if she wasn't so damned full of joy.

"Here come the personal questions," she said. She hated

to break the mood, but she might not get another opportunity to ask him about what she'd found in the bathroom. "Are you ready?"

"Fortified, anyway," he said, eyes narrowing with joking wariness. "One can never be fully prepared for an ambush."

"I found this," she said, and took the plastic Baggie from where she'd put it in the nightstand.

His chewing slowed down as his face smoothed into a familiar suave blandness. "Had to look again, didn't you?" He shrugged and began to cut up a sausage. "It's the best place to hide things in a hotel room."

She opened the black bag and pulled out a second plastic bag. "You are so thorough. Did someone beat you to make you tidy?"

"My father smacked me a few times," he said readily enough. "He was a stickler for organization, so it became a habit. Mum knew better than to hit me."

"Mama never hit us," Pagan said, thinking back. "Daddy, neither. But I think we pretty much always did what we were told." She pulled his pistol out of the second bag and laid it carefully on the tray. "What kind of gun is this?"

"Walther PPK," he said, still eating, but getting more serious by the moment. "Standard issue, no serial number."

"And this." She pulled out a small glass vial stopped with cork. Inside it a shiny, squashed bullet rattled around. "Who shot this at you?"

It was a guess. She had no idea why he kept a flattened bullet with him wherever he traveled.

He finished chewing and swallowed his egg, looking at the bullet in her hand. When he looked up at her, his blue eyes were almost black, his jaw tense. "I'm the one who fired that bullet." His voice was low. "I shot my father."

Pagan set the glass vial with the bullet down gently on the food tray. This was why he never talked about his father. This was why he identified with her so much. They had both hurt their fathers. Pagan had accidentally killed hers. Maybe Devin had done the same.

She wanted to put her arms around him, but she sensed that might either break him, or shut him up. "What happened?" she asked.

Devin put his fork down and spoke with careful emotionlessness. "It was during our last heist, on a large estate in the south of France. A buyer had asked my father to acquire several paintings being kept there as part of a private collection. What we didn't know was that the buyer was working for the French police and Interpol. My father had long been an irritant to many police forces all over Europe, and they had decided to get him once and for all."

"How old were you?" she asked.

"Thirteen," he said. He was speaking in a crisp English accent now, one that enabled him to control every syllable he uttered. "I was better at climbing than my father, so he sent me in first, over the fence, and then up the wall to the second-story window, to cut the alarms. It was after I let him inside that the police surrounded us."

He got off the bed with an abrupt movement and walked over to the closet to take a shirt off its hanger. "My father wouldn't surrender. They had us with our backs to the wall, guns out. We had nowhere to run, and he wouldn't stand down. Instead, he…" He drew a breath in sharply. "He grabbed me and held me in front of him. As a shield."

Pagan was standing up, hand over her mouth, like some melodramatic silent movie actress of old. But she couldn't help it.

Devin unbuttoned the shirt and slipped it on. "He managed to get through two rooms that way, holding my arm up behind my back, right on the edge of breaking it, pulling me with him. The police followed us every step, waiting for him to make a mistake." His English accent was fraying into Scottish as he spoke. His once-vacant expression was pinched with pain. "But I knew him. No one ever executed his plans with more precision and discipline. He wasn't going to make a mistake. So I made it for him."

"You took his gun," she said. She didn't know how she knew that, but she could see the scene in her mind with perfect clarity. Young Devin would have been tall and very thin, his father taller, more solid and utterly relentless.

His eyes met hers for the first time since he'd started telling her what happened. In them, hurt mixed with a strange satisfaction. "I had to break my arm to do it, but yes. I got his gun. He'd positioned himself right near a window, and he would probably have made it through because I was still blocking the police from getting a clear line of sight. So I shot him."

She sat there, trying to absorb what he said. No wonder MI6 had recruited him. "What happened to your father?"

"They took him to a hospital, and he died while they had me in custody."

He was looking blankly at his ties as she walked up and

took his hands in hers. "I'm so sorry," she said. "I knew we had a lot in common, but I didn't know how much until now."

He met her eyes, but there was no forgiveness in them, for himself or for his father. "The difference is that you didn't mean to hurt anyone," he said. "I aimed for my father's heart. Missed it by an inch or two, but my hand was shaking."

"I might've done the same if my father had used me as a shield," she said. "He trained you to be a thief, used you to make a profit and then he betrayed you. You were a child. He's to blame, and you know it."

"I know it," he said. "And I don't."

She knew exactly what he meant. All too well. "So you went to work for the British government. To be as different from him as possible."

"Am I really that different?" He released her hands to grab a tie. His nose was wrinkled again in self-disgust. "I recruit and use people, the way my father used me. I utilize the skills I learned from him to blackmail, strong-arm and spy. I continue to steal, only now it's information instead of art."

"But you don't do it to profit yourself," she said. "You do it for your country, for a higher purpose."

"That's what I tell myself," he said. "Sometimes I even believe it. When I read your story and saw your talent on screen, I thought, 'There's a girl who's also looking for redemption. I can use that.'" He shook his head. "I didn't see you as a person with a painful past. I saw you as a tool to use in our cold little war against Communism."

There it was again. Thinking about people as if they were

things like tools instead of human beings. She'd seen how that turned into evil.

But this was Devin, not some Nazi war criminal or Communist dictator. Heck, Pagan herself had used Emma Von Albrecht as a way to investigate her father. Did that make her evil?

"Why you do it makes a difference," she said. "You do it to help, not to hurt."

"Help us. Hurt them," he said. "It's two sides of the same coin, and I'm constantly flipping it, not sure which side I prefer."

"You could quit," she said. "We both could. You could finally be a self-important studio executive. Just like you always dreamed!"

In spite of himself, he laughed. "How do you do that?" he said, taking her hand again. "You could make me laugh at the end of the world."

She lifted their hands so that they stood palm to palm, and interlaced her fingers with his. "We stopped a nuclear bomb from going off in the middle of Berlin, Devin."

"Okay, so it's hard to see a downside to that." Keeping hold of her hand, he selected a narrow black tie from all the other narrow black ties. "Gold stars for all. But most especially for you—for going to see Emma last night. If you hadn't, we might not have caught them."

"You can always rely on me to defy your orders," she said.

"You are dependable in that way." He dangled the tie around his neck, and kissed her. "But I can recall several things you did last night exactly as I asked you to do them."

"I take requests in bed," she said, kissing him back. "With you. When I feel like it."

"Noted." He was smiling in a way that put the Cheshire cat to shame as she took the ends of his tie in her hands and began to tie it for him.

"Why January 30, 1933?" she asked, remembering the handwritten note in that terrible basement that said, *Twenty-nine years to the day.* "Did you ever figure that out?"

"Pope did. He's good for something. January 30, 1933, was the day Hitler became chancellor of Germany. A strange way to commemorate something—killing everyone in Berlin."

A jarring ring cut through his words, and she startled. He steadied her, hands on her shoulders, and she laughed at herself. "Guess I'm a little jumpy."

He kissed her nose. "After what you did last night, I'd be jumpy, too." He walked over to the phone as it rang again insistently. "Yes?" he said into the receiver.

He stood up straighter, coming to attention. "When?" His voice held an urgency that made her walk over to stand beside him.

"Of course. Where?" He listened. "All the way out in Tigre? It'll take me a little while to get there, but I can leave shortly. Thirty-five Avenida Garibaldi. See you soon."

He hung up, repeating the address to himself silently a second and third time before saying, "I'm sorry, but I have to go."

"What's wrong?" She tightened the belt on her robe, wishing she had fresh clothes of her own to put on so that she could force him to take her with him.

"A group of thugs tried to kidnap the Israeli ambassador

from his home last night." He finished tying his tie in the mirror as he spoke. "But his guards drove them off. None of the Israelis were hurt, but Pope thinks it was an attempt to retaliate for Von Albrecht being taken."

"Dieter?"

He shot her a look. "Maybe."

"So Dieter blames the Israelis for everything?"

"Nazi habits die hard. It's good for us, but it's too bad for the Israeli ambassador. And ever since their Mossad agents kidnapped Adolf Eichmann here a year and a half ago, they're the first to get blamed and attacked for anything like this."

"At least they didn't get him." A vague uneasiness was stirring in her gut. Dieter was out there, and he hated her. What would he try now that his attempt to take the Israeli ambassador had failed? "Where are you going?"

"We're running short on men, and Von Albrecht's guards need a break. I'll help out until they get some more men. They weren't prepared to take him into custody yet, so they're scrambling a bit. And he's too badly injured to fly him out. He'll need at least a week to recover."

"Good old Rocket," Pagan said. "So they're going to take him to America eventually, then. To stand trial like Eichmann did in Israel?"

"He'll be taken to America," Devin said, finishing up his tie. His eyes in the mirror were troubled. "But probably not for trial."

"They wouldn't kill him," she said, not sure that was the truth. "Why save him only to kill him in secret?"

"Pope told me last night," he said. "He's pretty sure they'll get Von Albrecht to come back and work for them again."

"What!" He had to be kidding. Except that right now he looked like someone trying to squash down a poisonous anger. "But they tried that once already—and look what happened!"

"I know," he said shortly. "I know."

She walked around to face him. "This is a man who tortured and killed thousands during the war, then stole plutonium from the United States and tried to kill the entire city of Berlin and start a nuclear war. He needs to be punished!"

"I agree," he said. "But it's not my call to make. And you said yourself that we do it for a higher purpose—for our countries."

"No, but you have to make them see, Devin!" She couldn't believe he wasn't more outraged. He was angry, yes, but she could see the resignation in his face, in the resolute set of his shoulders. "If you told them that he'll try to escape again, that he's slippery and dangerous and..."

"They know all of that," he said. "And they don't care. They might put extra security on him, limit his access to nuclear materials. That kind of thing."

"He's guilty of attempted genocide. You saw what he did to Rocket. He did that to people, Devin!"

"You have to understand," he said. "They don't care about his integrity or his character. They don't care about punishing his crimes as long as he can be useful to them. And now that he's succeeded in building a dirty bomb that works—or so he says—they're going to want him more than ever. And he'll say yes, of course. It's better than prison or hanging."

"Oh, my God." She couldn't stand to look at him any longer. She walked over to the ravaged bed where they'd been so happy moments before and sat down. "You're going to help them do it."

"That's my job," he said, walking to his closet to take down a suit jacket. "It's what we were talking about. The world is messy, Pagan. Gray."

He was right, and yet...she could not accept this. She'd seen the look in Von Albrecht's eyes, witnessed the tortured animals in his basement.

To think she could've killed Von Albrecht herself, but hadn't because she assumed the CIA would punish him. She'd always opposed killing people, but if governments like the United States didn't punish the guilty, who would?

"Some things are black and white," she said. "Otherwise, what's the point of anything?"

He swung his jacket on, pulling the perfectly tailored sleeves into place over his shirt cuffs. "Sometimes we stop the bad guys. And sometimes we get them to come work for us. Even if I wanted to stop the CIA from recruiting him again, I couldn't. It's out of my hands."

"So you're just following orders," she said. Her heart was as heavy as Von Albrecht's box of lead. "The men working for Von Albrecht could say the same."

He pivoted toward her. "I'm not plotting the death of millions, Pagan. I'm going to guard a man to keep him from doing that. That's all I can do. I'm not a politician, or a general. If and when they ask me to do something against my conscience, I'll say no. But keeping Von Albrecht in a safe house until he can be moved is not a war crime."

She stood up. "You've always been a rule-follower," she said. "At first it was your father who made the rules, but MI6 and the CIA are your daddy now. You'll do whatever they say until they betray you."

His eyes were like blue radiation. "Don't be a hypocrite. You were happy to deceive Emma Von Albrecht for us if it meant you could discover more about your mother. Did you ever think about what will happen to her now that her father is gone and her ape of a brother is on the lam? No. You gave her a wink and set a dog on the only parent she has left. You destroyed her life, and she'll never know it was you. But you probably saved a million people in Berlin. Was that worth it, Pagan?"

"I don't know," she said. Poor Emma. Pagan really hadn't thought about her much, had she? She'd been so caught up in her own mission the wreck it might leave behind hadn't entered her mind. That wasn't right.

Then she remembered the smug look on Von Albrecht's face as he told Dieter to put her in a cage and drown her.

"Thousands of lives saved for one life upset," she said. "That's worth it. But you helping to send Von Albrecht back to the American nuclear program won't save anyone. If anything, he'll help them build better bombs to kill more people with."

His fists had loosened. His stance became distant, casual. The superior, sophisticated Devin Black was back, and he spoke to her as if she were a child in need of a lesson. "Nuclear material is used in treatment against cancer—did you know that? What if Von Albrecht's research leads to a new treatment that actually saves lives? We can't know what part he has to play, but maybe…"

"Maybe? You're going to help a war criminal live a cozy

life in the States based on a maybe? I can't believe I helped them do it."

"Cozy's a bit of an exaggeration. If it will ease your conscience, think of it as prison, with benefits."

Putting it that way made it sound like a viable option. But people who'd done far smaller things were in real prisons, without benefits. She'd thought so highly of the United States that she'd been eager to go work for the CIA. But instead of working for the good guys, she'd helped out the gray ones. Was there anything left in this world she could believe in?

"Does it ease your conscience?" she asked.

He paused, and the polished mask of cool slipped. "Nothing ever quite succeeds in that. Don't you have a movie to shoot today?"

"I told them yesterday that I'm sick," she said. "They can shoot around me until I'm not."

"If you decide to pull out of this movie completely, I'll have a word with the head of the studio," he said. "So they don't penalize you."

She was having a hard time giving a damn about any of that. "What will happen to Emma?"

Devin shrugged. "We have no plans to interfere with her," he said. "She can live out her life here, such as it is."

"Maybe I should go over there, ask Emma if she's seen Dieter, find out where he might be."

He gave her warning look. "She may have heard about your role in all this. It's better you stay away. You're done, remember?"

"Then can I come with you to the safe house?" She knew the answer, but she had to ask.

He gave a mirthless little laugh. "I can just see the look on Pope's face if I brought you there. No. You're off the case. Go shopping, see the sights."

It made perfect sense, but a wall was going up between them, a nebulous boundary of clashing ideas and agendas. Some part of her longed to climb back into bed with him and forget they'd ever had this discussion. Another part of her wanted to punch him in the nose.

He was looking at her, a faint line between his brows, as if trying to solve a riddle. "You know that I love you," he said. "No matter what else I say or do."

Her resistance, her annoyance and anger at him, melted before the warm fondness in his eyes. But why did it feel like he was saying goodbye? "I love you, too," she said. "No matter what."

His lips edged into a smile. "I'll call you later," he said. "I don't know if they'll let me out tonight, but I'll do my damnedest to get back and see you."

"I'd like that," she said, and watched as he walked out of the room and shut the door behind him.

CASTIGADA

Punishment. A move in which the lady's leg kicks forward and around, stroking her standing leg.

Devin's phone rang after she showered and was getting dressed. She stared at it for a few rings, then shrugged and picked it up. *"¿Hola?"*

"Oh, uh, forgive me, *señorita*." She recognized the smooth voice of the concierge. "But I thought there was someone there to help me with a little problem."

"Mr. Black is out," she said. "I could take a message for him."

"It's a bit more urgent than that." His voice was still smooth, but underneath she could hear an edge of anxiety. "You see, we brought your dog in around eight o'clock this morning, and per Mr. Black's instructions, we took the beast up to your suite, but no one answered the door. We rang the room again around noon and once more, just now, but no one has answered."

That wasn't like Mercedes, to be out all day. "Has Miss Duran left any messages for me?" she asked.

"No, *señorita*. No one has seen Miss Duran since yesterday."

Something about the way he said "since yesterday" made the hair on the back of Pagan's neck stand up. She hadn't spoken or talked to her friend since that frantic phone call to her from the Von Albrecht house.

She must be out all day sightseeing. It couldn't be anything else. Mercedes, of all people, could handle herself. Still, it was very unlike her not to leave a message. "I'll be there in two minutes. You can bring the dog up to me then."

"Gracias, señorita."

Pagan left Devin's suite and walked faster than usual down the hall toward her door. Nothing bad could've happened. Mercedes was probably squeezing a few more hours of boring museums and historic buildings in before heading back to her comic books.

"Mercedes?" The suite door opened to her key, and Pagan's heart gave a jolt and her breath stopped. A bronze flat shoe belonging to Mercedes lay upside down on the Persian carpet next to the overturned coffee table.

"Mercedes!" Pagan threw open the door to her friend's room, but it lay quiet and neat. No one in the bathroom, no one in Pagan's room, either...

"Señorita?"

She whirled, hand on her throat, to see a bellboy standing in the doorway to the suite, holding a leather leash connected to a brand-new collar around Rocket's neck. The dog, bandaged and smelling of iodine, wagged his tail warily, sniffing the air.

The bellboy's eyes were wide. "Is everything all right, *señorita?*"

"No," Pagan said, her mind racing. Mercedes was gone,

taken, perhaps, with a fight. It had to be Dieter or members of his gang. She didn't see any blood, so...

She sank down on the couch as her knees gave way.

The bellboy was beside her. The dog was licking her hand. She looked into Rocket's one good eye and took a deep breath. "My friend has been taken away by Dieter Von Albrecht," she told the bellboy. "You heard about the fire down at the docks last night? Well, one of the boys involved has kidnapped my friend. I need you first to call the police and tell them what I just said. Second, leave an urgent message for Devin Black in suite 736. Third, take the dog and keep him safe until I return."

She was up and pushing him toward the suite door. There was no time to lose. "Return?" the boy said. "Where are you going?"

She looked him dead in the eye. "I'm going to find my friend, and I'm going to make anyone who hurts her pay."

He swallowed, trying to find a reply.

"Go! Call the *policía* and tell them now that Miss Duran was taken by Dieter Von Albrecht. *Entiendes?*"

"*Sí,*" he said, and ran down the hall with Rocket jogging alongside.

Pagan slammed the door, and in a blur she ripped off her muddy dress from the night before and changed into sneakers, stretch pants and a dark shirt. What she was about to do was better done in flats.

Carlos was reading the paper in the lobby. She hadn't expected to see him, and the sight energized her. "Carlos! I need to get to the Von Albrecht house, now."

She tersely told him Mercedes was missing during the

brief drive there. It took less than five minutes, and Carlos intimated that he knew how to get ahold of Devin, better than the concierge. "I'll have to drive to where he is," he said. "But I'll get him as soon as I can."

She thanked him, put a scarf over her bright hair and made Carlos drop her across the park from the Von Albrecht house, to make her arrival less obvious, in case Dieter's thugs were watching.

As she ran across the park she became aware of an echo of her padded footsteps in the distance.

Alaric Vogel. Pagan had almost forgotten about him. But of course he was still following her. Why would he stop? If he'd been on the job last night, he must have seen her enter the Von Albrecht house and never come out. Now, with Von Albrecht "missing," he and the Stasi must suspect she was somehow connected. Well, he could follow her now till the end of time. He was irrelevant.

She rapped on the door, waited, then pounded harder. She needed to keep her cool with Emma, string her along a little longer, so she could find out where Dieter had taken Mercedes. She inhaled a breath that did nothing to soothe her and arranged her face carefully into a smile.

Emma, her eyes red, whipped open the door. "Pagan, oh, my God!" she said, and flung her arms around Pagan's neck, crying.

Pagan patted her with hands heavy as lead. "Emma, honey. What's the matter?"

So much. So very much was the matter.

"Come in, come in. I can't talk out here." Emma pulled away, sniffing, and tugged Pagan inside. She shut the door and pulled a handkerchief out of her skirt pocket. "They took Papa! He's gone!"

"What?" Pagan took her by the hand and led her down to the kitchen. "Who took him? Why? Here, sit down."

Emma sat in a kitchen chair, tears streaming anew down her cheeks. "It's got to be the Israelis. That's what Dieter thinks. Papa was in the German army during the war, and the Jews think he did all these crazy things. He disappeared last night, and Dieter says he was kidnapped. Just like with Adolf Eichmann. Dieter says the Jews will put Papa on trial, too. If they don't kill him instead."

Her own last words brought forth a fresh bout of sobbing. Pagan didn't like the way Emma's mouth curled with disgust when she said, "Jews," but she grabbed some paper napkins for her to use as tissues and poured her a glass of water.

"That's insane," Pagan said, setting the glass down. "When did Dieter tell you all this?"

Emma waved her hand in the air. "Earlier. Papa told him all kinds of things he never told me. I always knew that Papa thought I couldn't handle it because I'm a girl. And it turns out he was right!"

Pagan patted her arm and asked the question burning on her tongue. "Where's Dieter now?"

Emma blew her nose on a napkin. "I don't know. He called me this morning and told me about Papa. He kept shouting about revenge and told me to stay here and I haven't seen or heard from him since then! He left me here all alone. First we lost Mama, and now Papa. Oh, God, what if they come after us?"

Revenge. Dieter had been shouting about revenge. Dieter

must have organized the attack on the Israeli ambassador first. And when that hadn't worked, he'd turned to a more personal vendetta. He knew from Emma where Pagan was staying and must have gone to Pagan's suite this morning to get that revenge. Only he'd found Mercedes there instead. He already hated M for standing up to him, for not being a blond Aryan idiot like him and his friends. He must have had backup if he'd succeeded in taking Mercedes without bloodshed. "I don't think you need to worry about them coming for you," she said. "They didn't go after Eichmann's family, did they? You're innocent. You can't be held responsible for your father's crimes."

"Papa is innocent, too," Emma said indignantly. "He fought for his country. You can't kidnap him because he fought for his country!"

Pagan swallowed down a blazing response and shook her head. This was not the right time to tell Emma the truth about her father. She needed to know how long Dieter had had Mercedes. He wouldn't kill her outright, would he? No, he'd keep her so he could use her against Pagan. He was probably calling the hotel right now to taunt her. "Of course not. I didn't mean that. What time did Dieter call you?"

She'd slipped it in as casually as she could, but it hadn't been invisible enough. Emma's frown deepened. "Around lunchtime, maybe. I don't know. Why do you care? Whatever he's doing is justified. Whatever revenge he takes, it won't be enough to compensate us for them taking our father!"

Lunchtime. That was *hours* ago, enough time for all kinds of terrible things to happen. But she knew where Dieter must have gone to do them. "No, no, of course not," she said automatically. "Sorry. I just need to make a quick call."

She left Emma and trotted over to use the hall phone to call the concierge at the Alvear.

"I need to leave a high priority message for Devin Black," she said in English when the concierge picked up the phone. "Let him know that Pagan Jones is going to the South Docks area. I don't know the exact street, but it's a block from the river near those docks."

"Of course, *señorita*," the concierge said smoothly.

"Tell him it's about Dieter and Miss Duran."

"What are you doing?" Emma ripped the receiver's cord out of the phone with one jarring pull. "Who are you talking to about my brother?"

Oh, hell. Once again, Pagan hadn't paid quite enough attention to Emma. She'd overheard the whole thing, of course, and she understood English perfectly. Her small fists were clenched, her wet face flushed with horror and rage.

"Dieter's about to hurt someone, Emma," Pagan said, and handed Emma the detached phone receiver. "I have to stop him. You see that, right? If he hurts someone, it will be worse for him once the police get him, and then you'd really be all alone."

"What Dieter does is none of your business." Emma advanced on her, and Pagan backed up two steps. She wasn't afraid exactly, but she also didn't want to waste time in a fight. The front door of the house was fifteen feet down the hall. "You gave away our hideout."

"If people are getting hurt, it's everyone's business," Pagan said. "Open your eyes, Emma! Your father was no saint."

Emma cocked her head. "I don't know what Papa was doing. How could *you*?"

"It's going on right under your nose, Emma!" God, if only the girl could see the truth, she might be saved from becoming like her father and brother. Pagan turned away from her and walked down the hall. "Haven't you ever wondered what your father was doing in that basement of horrors?"

"It's research for his classes… Are you saying— Do you know what he was doing down there?" She grabbed Pagan's shoulder and turned her around, her eyes searching Pagan's face. "How could you know?"

Oh, hell, she'd really messed this up. "You said your father was kidnapped, like Adolf Eichmann. You know what Eichmann did, don't you, Emma? He's directly responsible for the death of millions of people."

"That's a lie," Emma said in the flat voice of someone who had heard the story and rejected it many times before. "Jewish lies to defame great men like my father. " Her look and her voice sharpened. "Are you a Jew?"

"What if I was, Emma?" Pagan stared back at her. "Would that change how you feel about me?"

Emma stopped dead, her face going pale. "Dear God, you're a Jew. That's why you came here in the first place, isn't it? You don't care about me at all."

"I do care!" Pagan shoved aside a stab of guilt. "I want to stop Dieter from doing something terrible, from becoming just as bad as your father."

"Oh, Papa!" Emma crumpled right before Pagan's eyes. One minute she was standing there, angry and righteous.

The next she was curled up on the floor of her own hallway, hugging her knees and sobbing. "I need my papa!"

Pagan had curled up like that in the hospital, after she killed her father and sister in the accident. She'd wanted to curl up so tight that she'd disappear.

She knelt down beside Emma. "I'm so sorry, Emma. I lost my father, too. And it's so hard, the hardest thing there is. But your father's gone, not dead. And it's not the end of your life. You'll find your way."

Emma kept sobbing. Pagan's words were empty, and she knew it. What use was it to say anything now, when Emma had lost all trust in her and could feel nothing but the loss of her father?

It was Emma's job now to mourn, for however long it took. Knowing that was freeing in a way, for Pagan. She could leave Emma and try to stop Dieter from hurting Mercedes.

"I'm going to leave now, Emma," Pagan said, putting a hand on the girl's shuddering back. "Every second that goes by means Dieter might hurt someone else."

She couldn't be sure that Emma heard her. It was horrible to stand up, to pull away from the raw need of the weeping girl in front her. But something far more urgent lay ahead.

"I'll come back to see you," she said, pushing herself toward the front door. "I'll check on you, I promise."

"Get out, you lying Zionist bitch." The words were muffled, wet. Emma uncurled and got up on her hands and knees, screaming. "Get out of our house!"

Pagan fled. The door snapped shut behind her with a sound like a gunshot, and she ran across the park for the nearest taxi stand, not looking back. She couldn't. She'd never broken anyone's heart before, except her own. It was far worse than she had ever imagined.

Between buildings, a violent orange stripe of sky glowed menacingly. It would be dark soon. Her black cotton capri pants, sleeveless collared shirt and flats weren't going to keep her very warm after the sun went down.

"Dock Sud, *por favor*," she told the cabdriver as she climbed in breathless and slammed the door.

The man made a face at her in the rearview mirror. "Dock Sud? Why would pretty girl wish to go to…"

"Get me to Dock Sud, as fast as you can!" Pagan interrupted. She had no time or patience now for men telling her what she wanted. The driver clamped his mouth shut and looked impressed. "There's a street parallel to that part of the river, two blocks in. I can't remember the name. Just get to that area and I'll tell you where to go."

"*Sí, señorita*," the driver said, putting the car in gear with a shrug. "If you insist."

"Here." She leaned over the back of the seat and put some bills beside him. "And more if we get there fast."

"*Sí, señorita*," he said with more enthusiasm, and hit the gas.

The early-evening traffic was maddening, and it was well and truly dark by the time they crossed the Riachuelo branch of the river. Pagan thought she saw the same set of headlights behind them a couple of times, but then they disappeared, and she couldn't be sure. There were fewer cars here, since the workers had all left for home, and Pagan rapidly recognized the long straight streets lined with two-story buildings and warehouses.

"To the right! Here. Drop me here."

The cab pulled over half a block from a chain-link fence she recognized. She threw a wad of money at him and let herself out.

"I will wait for you," he said. "This is not a safe area."

He was clearly concerned, which was nice. She started to tell him to go, anyway, and then thought of something better.

"I have a special request for you," she said. "Double your usual fee, if you drive to the Alvear Palace Hotel and tell the concierge exactly where you dropped me. Tell him I'm going into an underground area next to that warehouse there and to tell Mr. Black. Then come back here to get me."

The driver blinked. "Of course, if you wish. But you should not be down here alone."

"Then get back soon." She gave him her most blinding smile. "And thanks."

She left him staring after her as she half ran down the block toward the door in the fence. The cab's headlights reached far enough to illuminate the padlock on the fence.

Damn it. This was the place. She was sure of it. She could take forever to try to pick the lock or...

She craned her neck, assessing the fence, a normal chain-link affair about ten feet high. No razor wire curled or strung across the top, and it was shorter than the fence around the Lighthouse Reformatory for Wayward Girls, her old reform school. She'd succeeded in scaling that fence and crossing its barbed wire, with the help of Mercedes and some tough wool blankets. This shouldn't be as tough as that.

Of course, she didn't have Mercedes to give her a boost, and she'd been living a pretty soft life since Lighthouse. Three feet up, her foot slipped, and she fell with a jarring thud to the sidewalk. She bent her knees, though, as Mercedes had taught her, and rolled back onto her butt to absorb the shock. It wasn't that far, really, but the last thing she needed was a twisted ankle or a bum knee.

The cab had gone. No headlights to help her now, and the front yard of the warehouse wasn't lit for security the way it might have been back in the States. Her fingers were aching from the chain link digging into her flesh, and she'd scraped her palm when she rolled back.

At least no one was shooting at her, like the night she'd been chased through East Berlin by a vengeful, armed Alaric Vogel. How must he hate her still to be following her every move. He was probably standing out there in the dark, smirking at her sad attempt to scale the fence this very moment.

The thought gave her a boost of energy. To hell with him. She had been training as a dancer the last month or so, and she was fit. She stretched out with a few high steps, then lifted one foot carefully and dug the toes into a link in the fence, both hands reaching high, and hoisted.

Her legs were strong from the dancing. She lifted herself with ease and carefully found the next foothold, then the next. Then she was at the top, bending at the waist to swing her right leg over. Rather than drop and risk her previously injured ankle again, she took the extra time to climb down and land lightly on the ground.

The yard here was dirt. With the stars her only illumination, she could see the black bulk of the warehouse in front of her. She jogged lightly to its right, sticking to the side of the warehouse in case Dieter had posted any guards, and finally saw the ramp sloping down into the earth. No sign of Dieter's thugs. She sent a thank-you to the goddess of girl spies for Dieter's arrogance, and trotted as quietly as she could down the ramp.

It became very dark very fast, so she stuck to the wall. If she remembered it right, the tunnel eventually narrowed to the doorway, and that led to the stairs down into the sunken church.

She'd only been there the night before, but without Emma chattering and multiple flashlights illuminating the way, the tunnel was like the lair of some giant worm waiting to thrust its way up through the dirt and swallow her whole.

Thunk! She bumped into something so hard that her body recoiled and she landed on her butt again, hands scraping the rock of the tunnel floor.

What the hell? She got achingly to her feet, dusting off her hands. Her palms were now wet with what was probably blood. She moved forward carefully, feeling her way.

Her knee hit it first. Metal. She lowered her hands and touched the smooth horizontal surface of a car trunk.

Of course. They'd parked here and walked farther down. Feeling around to the driver's side of the car, she tested the door and it clunked open. No point in locking your car inside your secret hiding place, was there?

She opened the door and slid into the driver's seat, feeling for the steering wheel, and then the dashboard. Where was it in this type of car? There was no way to know the make and model, but it was a sedan and…there it was. She tugged on a knob and the headlights turned on.

Parked cars humped before her like a pod of sleeping whales. The tunnel arced unevenly downward. She would have to pray that Dieter and his friends were too far down in their lair for the light to leak down to them. With the light, she was able to run at nearly full speed past the cars, avoiding uneven footing, to arrive swiftly at the narrow doorway and the steps.

She paused to one side of the doorway, trying to keep her breathing quiet, and listened.

"Who taught you to build a fire?"

An irritable and irritating voice filtered up from below. Dieter.

"Klaus didn't bring enough kindling," another voice said. It sounded like Wolfgang.

Pagan edged around the door to peer down at the chambered space below. As before, steps led down to a hard stone floor with some kind of altar in the middle and side chapels disappearing into the darkness on either side. Candles had been lit and positioned on the bases of broken statues and over the floor to show about ten young men clustered around two piles of wood off to one side. One of them had a lighter, and was trying to get the fire started in front of one of the side chapels while Dieter, noticeable for his height and his honey-blond hair, stood over him, haranguing. Another boy stood by holding some kind of long metal rod.

What were they messing about with? And where was Mercedes?

Pagan walked with silent care down a few more steps,

squinting in the wavering candlelight. Maybe they'd stuffed Mercedes in one of the pitch-black side chapels. There was no way for Pagan to get down there and search without being seen, and it would be ten boys against the one of her. But if they weren't actively engaged in hurting Mercedes, then Pagan could wait and watch until help arrived.

"She's moving," one of the boys said, and poked the larger pile of wood with his foot.

Only it wasn't a pile of wood. An invisible hand squeezed Pagan's heart, and she froze in her tracks as one of the boys leaned down and turned Mercedes over onto her back. In the flicker of the shadows, crumpled there on the floor, she'd looked like just another jumble of firewood.

Blinding-hot fury suffused Pagan. She nearly catapulted down the stairs into the clutch of evil boys then and there. She forced herself to crouch down and take a deep breath.

Stop. Look. Think, Pagan. It was a drunkard's training, and it came in handy at times like this. Don't just grab the martini because it's there. Stop. Think.

Mercedes was barefoot and wearing her flannel pajamas, now scuffed with dirt, but their pinstripes were still visible. They'd tied her hands behind her back, and when they turned her over, she laid quite still, eyes closed. Pagan didn't see any blood or evidence of broken bones, but that didn't mean they weren't there.

The boy had said, "She's moving," which implied that they knew she wasn't dead. She wasn't moving now. Another boy had knelt down and was feeling her neck, as if for a pulse.

"She passed out again," he said. "That stuff you gave her is potent."

They'd drugged her. Of course. Mercedes was too dangerous to leave conscious for long.

"Keep a close eye," Dieter said. "She should be waking up soon, and I want her to watch everything we've got planned."

A low moan reached Pagan's ears. On the altar, something writhed.

With no candles nearby, the altar lay in darkness. Only one boy stood beside it, and he was focused on the group around Mercedes, so Pagan hadn't seen the person lying on top of the bare stone slab.

The hair on her arms lifted, her skin prickling, as her eyes adjusted to even greater lack of light. There were ropes, and long dark hair, a gag and a familiar pair of dark brown eyes, opened wide in terror.

Naomi Schusterman was tied to Dieter's altar.

CHAPTER TWENTY-THREE

DOCK SUD, BUENOS AIRES

FRICCIÓN

A move where the woman is pulled, dragging her toes along the ground.

Naomi Schusterman was alive, but she had a black eye and her flesh was rubbed raw across her legs and arms, where the ropes bit tight. Her dress was torn at the neckline, as if a meaty hand had grabbed it and ripped downward, exposing her white bra and more bruised flesh.

Pagan hadn't thought it was possible for her to be even angrier. Staring down at the girl, laid out and prepared for whatever horrors Dieter had, she stood up and ran down three steps before she realized—she had nothing to fight them with.

No gun, no knife. She had some money, a tube of lipstick and the lighter she'd stolen from Alaric Vogel in her pocket. Unless someone had left a stick of dynamite lying around she could set alight and hand to Dieter, like some Bugs Bunny cartoon, that wasn't enough to defeat Dieter Von Albrecht and nine of his thick-necked friends.

She ducked down and prayed they hadn't heard her footsteps. There were too many of them for her to sneak down and somehow untie the ropes unseen. She didn't have a knife to cut either Naomi or Mercedes free, and if she was caught, then they were all sunk.

All three of you will die if you go down there. She had to tell herself that three times before her desire to wade in and start screaming came under control.

A deep tremor took over. She made herself breathe in deeply three times, waiting. There had been no outcry, no one calling out, "Hey!" She hadn't been spotted.

Trying to ignore her rattling insides, she peered down cautiously. No one was looking in her direction. She'd gotten lucky.

Dieter had wandered over to the altar and was checking on the ropes tying Naomi down. As he got close, she recoiled as much as the ropes allowed. And as he ran his hands over the bonds across her chest, he ran his hands over her body, too.

"You should have stayed inside tonight, you stupid Jew," he said, his voice thick as syrup. "Didn't you know I'd come to take revenge for what you did to my father?"

Naomi shook her head, trying to speak against the gag.

Dieter looked down at her with a smirk. A moment later, his face morphed into a mask of anger and he slammed his fist down into the altar, an inch from Naomi's head. "Why would I listen to your lies?" He brought his face close to hers. "Poor, filthy creature, lies are all you can speak."

Horrible echoes of what Emma had said. Pagan closed her eyes against her rising nausea, clenched her fists and chanted silently, "Don't be stupid, don't be stupid," to herself. It was she who was responsible for the disappearance of Dieter's father, not Mercedes, not Naomi, not Naomi's fa-

ther at the Israeli embassy. By rights, it should be Pagan tied
to the altar down there.

But Dieter wasn't obsessed with Pagan the way he was
with girls like Naomi and Mercedes—girls he hated and
wanted. If she stood up and admitted her fault in the Von
Albrecht affair, it would do no good. Dieter would find a
way to blame Mercedes, the Jews and Naomi herself, and
goodbye everyone.

Anger and heroics were luxuries Pagan couldn't afford
right now. She had to think. She had to get help. Somehow.

But help was miles away. If Devin had left soon after Pagan
did, which was doubtful, he would only know to go to the
general South Docks area. If the taxi driver's message got
through, he'd know where to come, but be farther behind.
Pagan couldn't tell what Dieter was planning with the ropes,
the altar and the fire, but it had to be horrible. And once
they got the fire lit, it would happen soon.

Devin would never get here in time.

"I think I got it," Wolfgang said, feeding a twist of newspaper to the tiny flames now licking the pile of sticks on
the floor.

Dieter left Naomi to pace over to him. "Finally. It needs
to get a lot bigger and hotter before we're ready."

So she had a little time. To do what? Maybe she could
bang on doors of the buildings outside or something, get
some help, find a phone, call the cops.

She backed up slowly, knees bent, head down, trying to
stay as small as possible.

Something slipped along her thigh and clacked onto the
stone step.

She halted and stared at the boys milling around below.

One of them glanced up in her direction. She held her breath and got ready to bolt.

But then Wolfgang said something to him, and the boy looked down at the fire again, and the moment had passed.

But what had clattered? Her fingers tapped around until they encountered a small smooth metal rectangle. The lighter she'd taken from Alaric Vogel was lying on the step with its red-and-yellow East German *volkspolizei* symbol facing up.

Damned thing had slipped out of her pocket. She scooped it up and got the hell out of there.

The car headlights lit her way back up to the world above. Her mind was racing, but no answers appeared. Where could she get help? This was a warehouse and shipping district. Businesses closed up shop around 5:00 p.m. and the streets became deserted. That's exactly why Dieter had chosen this area for his gang's hideout. So banging on doors was unlikely to help. There were no public phones, either. It wasn't a place meant for pedestrians, or tourists, or people who urgently needed the police.

She put the lighter back in her pants pocket, paused and then pulled it out again. She ran her thumb over the raised black, yellow and red symbol on one side with its oak leaves, hammer and calipers. The former owner of this lighter had been following her for days now.

Had he followed her here?

Standing near the entrance to the tunnel, she looked around at the bare dirt yard and the blank mass of the warehouse beside her. Nothing moved. No footsteps echoed hers.

She paced deliberately to the corner of the warehouse,

not trying to conceal herself. A few yards away lay the fence she'd climbed over and a bit of the road on the other side. The evening summer breeze blew an empty box tumbling down the sidewalk. Everything else lay still.

"I know you're there." She spoke in German, pitching her voice so that it carried. "Come out. I need to ask you a favor."

Her voice died in the empty air. The box kept thumping down the sidewalk out of sight. She stepped away from the building so that the feeble starlight fell full upon her.

"I know you remember that night in Berlin," she said, lifting her voice to project out into the dark. "The night you hunted me. I knocked you out cold. I could have killed you then, but I chose not to. That means you owe me."

The fence creaked in the wind. Pagan shivered and resisted crossing her arms against the chill. She needed to look confident, assured.

If there was anyone watching, that is. Maybe she was crazy.

A shadow moved. Alaric Vogel was standing by the far corner of the warehouse, eyes glittering at her under the brim of his hat.

He was still tall, with broad shoulders and a strong, slim build under the belted gray trench coat. And he was handsome still, too, the arrogance of his hawk-like nose softened by the dimple between his full lower lip and his square chin.

The cute one. At first that's how she'd nicknamed him in her head, on the night the Berlin Wall went up. Then, when he'd hunted her through the midnight streets of East Berlin for miles, she'd changed that to *the relentless one.* His being here proved that name was all too appropriate. The question now was, how much did he resent the little trick she and

Devin had played on him in Villa 31? Was he nothing but a ruthless monster, or did he have even the slightest sense of right and wrong?

Vogel didn't speak. He stood there, hands in his coat pockets, staring. Waiting.

"Do you have a gun?" she had to call out against the wind.

He thought about his answer, eyes shifting. "Yes."

That was good. She wanted him to have a gun. But it made her stomach flutter thinking he was armed and she was not.

"Why?" He asked it casually, as if her answer didn't matter.

"Because I don't have one," she said, and walked cautiously toward him, her hands out, empty. "And Dieter and his fascist friends are about to do something awful to two girls, one because she's Jewish, the other because she's got darker skin. We have to stop them."

His lips curved up in a derisive smile. "We?"

She kept moving toward him. She was more persuasive up close, and she wanted to see his face, gauge his reactions. "You're a Communist, so you hate Nazis and fascists as much as I do."

"Fascists like your mother?" he asked.

That stopped her in her tracks. Handsome though he was, his eyes were cold, waiting for her reaction. She didn't want them to, but those words hurt.

"How do you know about my mother?" she asked, her throat tight. "Did everyone know but me?"

Her emotion seemed to please him. "We have the file the Nazis kept on her during the war. Our Russian friends found it in the archives when they swept into Berlin. As your father fought for the Allies, his wife was doing her best to spread Hitler's message back at home."

She paced closer again. He didn't seem to mind. "And Von Albrecht? Was he in her file, as well?"

"I found out about Von Albrecht by following you." He gave her a shallow, mocking bow. "Thank you."

He was being sardonic with her now, but when she'd called for him a few moments ago, he'd stepped out of the dark. He didn't have to do that. Something was driving him to talk to her, to tell her a little about himself, to boast. Perhaps he did feel some sort of obligation, or maybe he had a strange appreciation for the nerve it had taken her to call him out. Either way, he was still talking to her. The longer that happened, the likelier it was that he'd help her.

But every second counted.

"Sorry about the other night," she said. "It wasn't my idea. But I needed to see who you were, and you seem to have recovered well enough."

"You should have known it was me," he said. Behind the ice in his eyes, amusement flickered. "Long ago."

"How long have you been tracking me?" she asked. "Was that you following us after Frank Sinatra's party in Los Angeles in December?"

"Perhaps," he said with a lift of his eyebrows that told her the answer was yes. "It didn't take me long after the wall went up to realize who you were. It wasn't difficult to persuade Comrade Mielke to promote me and let me build a file on you. He hates you after what you did for the traitor Thomas Kruger."

Mielke was the head of East Germany's security service,

the Stasi, and a humorless, ruthless man. Pagan had acted like the silliest creature on earth the night he questioned her, and he'd decided she was harmless. He'd been wrong.

"How is Erich?" she asked, still sauntering toward him. She was only six feet away now. "Please say hello from me when you see him next."

His eyebrows lifted, bemused at this insolence. "I may not phrase it quite like that," he said.

Pagan had been sexy and cheeky with Alaric Vogel the night they met, at first. He'd liked what he saw. She'd flirted and deceived, and then humiliated him, and he hadn't hesitated in his hunt after that to kill her. It was absurd that they were here now, talking almost like allies. But here, now, in this one thing, they had a common purpose. The Communists had been instrumental in defeating the Nazis, and their ideologies were directly opposed. Vogel was as predisposed to hate the likes of Dieter Von Albrecht as Pagan was.

And Vogel's doggedness had wrung from Pagan a strange, grudging respect. So far it looked like her shenanigans had made him feel the same.

"Maybe you won't tell your friends in the Stasi about tonight at all," she said.

The smile faded. "Comrade Mielke only agreed to let me follow you because he despises you almost as much as he despises loose ends." He shrugged. "But you've proven quite valuable."

"Too bad your team didn't get Von Albrecht," she said.

"I would have shot him if he'd had the courage to leave his hole," Vogel said. "Fascists destroyed my country. I have more reason to hate them than the daughter of a Nazi sympathizer."

She ignored the dig. "Then help me keep the next generation of Nazis from hurting anyone else."

He pulled a pack of Winston cigarettes out of his coat pocket. Her old brand. He removed a cigarette from the pack and tapped it on the back of his other hand. "You think I owe you my life because you didn't kill me back in Berlin?"

"You nearly killed me," she said. "I had your gun in my hand, and no one would have blamed me if I killed you. It would have been so easy, and I wouldn't have to deal with you following me now. But I didn't."

"But if you had killed me then, I wouldn't be here listening to you ask for my help." He put the cigarette between his lips and reached into his pocket for a match.

Pagan pulled her lighter out of her own pocket, stepped closer and flicked the flame to life.

He squinted against the light, leaning in, and saw the *volkspolizei* insignia on the lighter. The lighter she'd taken from his unconscious body the night he'd tried to hunt her down.

His condescending sneer dropped. His eyes flicked up to hers, infuriated.

She gave him her most impudent smile, and moved the lighter closer, offering it again.

As his gaze shifted from her left eye to her right, his anger leaked away. His lips curled around the cigarette in a reluctant appreciation. His eyes narrowed again, but this time with conflicted amusement and respect.

He bent in close, very close, and put the tip of his cigarette to her flame. He lingered there a moment. His dark auburn hair was cropped precisely around his ear, but a faint stubble was emerging on his cheeks. She could smell the waxed cotton of his trench coat, his musky skin and the powdery pomade he used in his hair.

He straightened, towering over her, and blew the smoke up into the air. He pulled aside his trench coat to draw a long-nosed pistol from his shoulder holster. She couldn't help taking a step back, which made his smile widen.

"If I help you tonight," he said. "My debt is paid."

She stared at him. This was really happening. "If we save Mercedes and Naomi Schusterman, the debt is paid."

He nodded, dropped the cigarette and stomped it out. "How many of them?"

"Ten," she said.

"Ten?" he said, amused and taken aback.

"Ten boys." She gave a little wave of her hand to dismiss his skeptical look. "You can handle them. Unless you've only got blanks in that gun."

Another reference to the night she'd shot his own gun at him, knowing the first few bullets were blanks. Reminding him of that moment was a risk…

He gave a tiny snort. "No blanks this time."

So he appreciated the in-jokes. Good. "I'll help. They're down that tunnel you probably saw me go into. They parked their cars in there. Past the cars there's a narrow opening, down some steps, in a kind of sunken, ruined church. Naomi's tied with ropes to an altar in the middle of the floor, and to the right of that, Mercedes is tied up and knocked out with drugs near the boys who are building a fire. There are candles and broken statues and side chapels…"

He'd been checking his gun while she spoke, and before she finished, he bent over and pulled a thin sharp knife from his boot.

"Here." He handed it to her, hilt first.

"Oh," she said, not taking it. "Stabbing someone…too personal for me."

"Not for stabbing," he said in a long-suffering tone. "To free the girls. You said there were ropes." He offered her the hilt again.

"Oh!" She took the knife gingerly. "Good thinking."

He strode around the corner of the warehouse, back the way she'd come, and she scurried after him. She hefted the knife and stared at his gray trench-coated back. Clearly he wasn't the slightest bit afraid of her stabbing him. She didn't know if that was good or bad. As they entered the tunnel, he stuck to the wall, as she had.

"Light up ahead," he said. "They may be coming out."

"No, I turned on the car headlights," she said. "So I could see."

"Hmph." He let out an appreciative sound and they picked up speed. "Can you get down there ahead of me, quietly?" he asked.

She couldn't remember the German word for *sneak*, so she said, "I'll try."

"Get as close to the girl on the altar as you can, then I'll distract them while you cut her free. Then we get your friend by the fire."

He was good at this. She was strangely reassured yet nervous as hell. "An excellent plan."

They slowed as they neared the doorway and aligned themselves on either side of it.

Pagan shot a look over at Vogel, breathing hard from the run down the tunnel, and from nerves. He had his gun pointed up, and his chest was rising and falling in sync with her own. Their eyes met.

"Don't kill anyone," she whispered. "If you can help it."

"And why not?"

"I don't want any more blood on my hands."

That gave him pause, but he nodded curtly. "If I can help it."

She had stepped through the mirror into the reverse of her adventures with Devin Black. Now she was working with a man who had once tried to kill her and followed her halfway around the world.

And it had gotten him promoted. Alaric Vogel might be nutty, but he was no fool.

From below, voices.

"I think it's ready," Wolfgang was saying.

Vogel peeked one eye around the frame of the doorway. Pagan did the same from her side.

The fire was larger now, burning brightly. The boys were still mostly clustered around it and Mercedes, except for Dieter, who stood by the altar, hands behind his back, waiting.

Naomi was lying still. It was too dark to see how she was doing, but they had to assume that she was still alive. The alternative didn't bear thinking about.

Wolfgang crouched by the fire and took hold of something in his right hand, which wore a thick, padded glove.

He lifted what looked like a stick, glowing at one end, and showed it to Dieter. "What do you think?"

The stick was a metal rod. It had been heating in the fire while Pagan spoke to Vogel, and now it glowed orange hot. She couldn't see the symbol on the other end of it, but she knew its purpose now. Dieter and his friends were going to brand Naomi Schusterman.

"Make sure the other one is awake," said Dieter.

Over by the fire, four of the boys cautiously sat Mercedes up and tugged her over to a pillar, so that her back was supported. They'd gagged her and tied her wrists together. One of the boys raised a hand, and Pagan almost cried out as he slapped Mercedes, once, hard, across the face.

"I'm not sure she's going to..." He put a hand under her chin and peered closer at her.

It was hard to see exactly what happened, but it looked like Mercedes snapped her forehead into the boy's face. He reeled back, clutching his nose, screaming, and Mercedes was on her feet. Pagan put one hand to her throat as she saw that M's ankles were bound, too.

"Don't let them kill her," she said to Vogel. "No matter what!"

He hefted his gun and sited at the boys, but they had already piled on her, all of the remaining eight of them.

"Go!" Vogel urged Pagan in a low voice.

Crouched low, Pagan scuttled through the doorway and down the steps, padding as quietly as she could in her sneakers. She kept her head down until she paused, ten steps down, and looked up.

"Can't you keep one girl still?" Dieter was shouting in frustration.

While the boy Mercedes had head-butted crawled over to sit against the base of a statue, Wolfgang had gotten another rope. Together, the eight boys tied Mercedes to the pillar in a seated position. Her nose was bleeding, and her eyes glinted in the candlelight. She was very much alive.

"One more move like that," Wolfgang said to her in Spanish, "and we'll just kill you both now!"

Mercedes's head turned to the altar, as if seeing Naomi there for the first time. Her shoulders slumped, and she leaned her head back against the pillar, as if exhausted.

Dieter's hands dropped from behind his back. The line of his shoulders was tense with excitement. "I think it's time."

One of the boys handed a padded glove to Dieter. He lifted his right hand and placed the glove over it with great ceremony as Wolfgang lifted the glowing brand over his head and walked toward him. Now that she was closer, Pagan could see the brand more clearly. It was a burning swastika, wide as the mouth of a teacup.

Of course. These were exactly the sort of lump-heads who thought using that tired symbol of hatred and oppression had some kind of sacred significance. They wanted to strike fear, to call upon the spirits of those who had first used the crooked cross to terrorize the world.

But they were just a shabby clutch of moronic boys in a damp crypt aping ghosts. It would have been pathetic if two girls' lives didn't hang in the balance.

More feeble was them treating torture like it was the lighting of the Olympic torch. But the posturing conveniently captured the attention of the other young men, and she was able to get all the way down the steps and right up to the foot of the altar, where the bulk of it hid her from everyone.

Shoulders against the cold stone, Pagan hefted the knife and looked toward the entrance. Alaric Vogel was halfway down the steps, pistol in hand, walking as if he didn't care whether anyone saw him. What was he waiting for?

Shadows were moving. Pagan peered around the altar and saw Dieter's feet and the tip of the swastika brand swinging in her direction. "Are you ready for your purification?" he asked, stopping near Naomi's head.

Oh, God, was he going to brand her face? Pagan switched the knife to an overhand grip and eyed Dieter's leg, less than five feet away. She could stab his foot, maybe, or the beefy part of his thigh.

Naomi uttered a muffled groan. Her dress rustled against the stone above as she struggled. Dieter's free hand was on her. Pagan couldn't see where.

Pagan raised the knife, gathering her legs under her to lunge. She looked back one more time for Vogel, but he wasn't on the steps. Where…?

There he was. He'd moved to take cover behind the crumbling statue of a saint. He saw her looking at him, smiled and mouthed a word: *Bereit?*

Ready? He was asking *her* if she was ready?

Jawohl! she mouthed back at him. *Go!*

"Hold still, bitch," Dieter said. "Or it will be worse for you."

"Halt! Or I will be forced to shoot!"

Vogel's voice rang out as he stepped from behind the statue, his pistol leveled at Dieter.

Dieter's feet swiveled around. The tip of the brand was still glowing. He hadn't pressed it to Naomi's flesh yet.

"What are you doing here?" Dieter yelled, rather predictably. "Who are you?"

"You will back up toward the far side of the vault," Vogel said. "All of you."

"Get out of here!" another boy shouted, and the others began yelling things like, "We'll kill you, too!" and ruder things. Their footsteps shuffled forward and back, voices bouncing off the rock.

Dieter hadn't moved back. Pagan crawled around to the side of the altar opposite him, grabbed the first rope she saw and began sawing at it with the knife.

Crack! Vogel fired a shot at Dieter's feet. Chunks of the stone floor flew up, and Dieter recoiled, arms up to ward off the shrapnel, dropping the brand.

"Back up, or it'll be your head," Vogel said.

"Jew lover," Dieter spat. He didn't back up farther. What a stubborn meathead. "Race traitor. If you come any closer, we'll kill them both."

Damn it, Pagan couldn't see Mercedes from here. But she heard the scuffing of feet, and one of the boys whispering urgently, "Get your knife! To her throat, stupid!"

The rope Pagan was cutting parted quickly. Vogel's knife was scary sharp. Pagan resisted the urge to reveal herself to see Mercedes and started on the second one. Two more to go after that.

"Stupid little boys," Vogel said. "Hitler himself would

have laughed at you. Branding girls. What's next—cutting the whiskers off mice?"

The knife cut right through the second rope. Pagan heard Naomi's feet kick now that they were free. She started cutting the third rope, and poked her head up over the top of the altar to get the girl's attention.

"Lie still if you can," she said, very low. "We'll get you out of here."

Naomi lifted her head, eyes wide, and saw Pagan. Her lips around the gag were bloody. Her bra had been pulled down to expose one breast. Seeing that, Pagan had to steady herself. That must be where Dieter was going to put the brand. She still couldn't see Mercedes on the other side of the altar.

Focus! She spared a moment to put one finger to her lips, nodding at Naomi, then resumed cutting. The strands of the third rope, which was slung across the girl's waist and looped around her wrists, were giving way.

"Every Jew we brand or kill is one less to poison the earth," Dieter was saying. "They'll see our work and know fear."

Vogel laugh derisively. "Tell that to Adolf Eichmann. Or your father."

"One more step, and they'll cut the *indio* girl's throat." Dieter's footsteps scraped closer.

Mercedes!

No, focus. The third rope gave way, and Naomi pulled the rope off her bloody wrists first, then pulled her bra up and started to wiggle her way out from under the last rope as Pagan started cutting it.

"Get away from her, all of you," Vogel said to the boys

near Mercedes. "Or I'll start shooting. I've got enough bullets for you all."

"Stay!" Dieter ordered. "Cut her throat if he…"

Vogel fired his gun, and a boy screamed.

Pagan kept sawing, and prayed Vogel was a good shot. *That wasn't Mercedes. That wasn't M screaming at all.*

"And that was just your shoulder I was aiming for," Vogel said. "Imagine if I'd wanted that bullet in your head. Now move back, all of you!"

Feet were scuffling again. Voices muttered in German. "Help him."

"I told you we should have gotten guns."

Pagan could only hope that meant the boys were obeying Vogel. Would this goddamn last rope never part?

"She's getting free!" Dieter said. He must have seen Naomi wiggling.

"Stop!" Vogel ordered. "Or I'll kill you where you stand."

"You can't kill us all before we reach you," Dieter shouted.

"Maybe." Vogel didn't sound impressed. "But as a clever girl I know once said, 'I'll just kill you first. Let's see which one of your friends wants you dead.'"

Pagan couldn't believe it. Vogel was quoting what she'd said to him when she'd pointed his own gun at him back in Berlin. The man had a twisted sense of humor.

This last rope was actually two ropes wound together. That's why it was taking longer to cut. Naomi couldn't seem to get out from under it, but she did pull the gag from her mouth.

"Who is that there?" Dieter said. "Behind the altar? Who is that?"

Pagan stood up. It gave her a better angle for cutting, anyway. "Just me, Dieter."

She could see Mercedes now, and a clump of boys, supporting their two wounded members, clustered thirty feet away from her, staring at her as if she was a corpse popping out of one of the crypts.

Dieter's whole body arrested in midmove when he saw her, as if he'd been struck by lightning. "Pagan Jones?" he said.

"Hello," she said, and shot a glance at Vogel. "Carry on."

While her attention was on Vogel, Dieter surged toward her. He was faster than she thought possible.

She caught the movement in the corner of her eye, and turned to lift the knife. He didn't seem to care. His face was a grimace of anger and hate. His large hands reached for her throat.

One stab wasn't going to stop him. She raised the knife and slashed. He ducked and got one hand on her knife arm, forcing it down, the other reaching for her neck. He was going to choke the life from her. Beside them both, on the altar, Naomi was kicking and yelling, unable to get free. Somewhere behind them, Mercedes was standing up, pulling free of the rope that tied her to the pillar.

Pagan twisted her wrist against Dieter's grip and kicked his thigh, missing the more tender area she'd been aiming for. Again. Damn it, she didn't want to die at the hands of this jackass.

Something cracked loudly behind her. Dieter's right eye was gone. A red hole had taken its place, and something redder spewed out the back of his head.

Naomi Schusterman screamed.

Dieter fell over backward, his face frozen in its mask of hate.

Poor Emma.

Pagan looked back at Alaric Vogel.

"You're welcome," he said in English, his pistol still smoking.

"Get him!" Wolfgang yelled over by the fire, and all nine young men, wounded and otherwise, surged forward.

Alaric Vogel calmly began firing, and Wolfgang went down, clutching his side. Another boy fell, and the others spread out, taking cover. So much for not killing anyone.

There wasn't time to feel bad about it. Pagan tugged Naomi's leg free of the last rope. "Run!" she said.

But Naomi was already up and off the altar. Pagan ran, head low, around the altar to avoid the charging boys, over to Mercedes, who was hopping toward her. She'd worked the gag off from around her mouth, and said, "My feet!"

Pagan resisted the urge to throw her arms around her friend and fell to her feet, sawing at the ropes around them.

More shots echoed through the vaulted chamber. Pagan didn't bother to count. Mercedes's feet were free. Pagan steadied her, hand under her elbow, and they ran for the stairs.

The shooting had stopped. Pagan pushed Mercedes in front of her up the last few steps and took a moment to look back for Alaric Vogel.

He was calmly shoving another magazine of bullets into his gun as three of Dieter's gang left their hiding places and ran for him.

He shot one down before a second one tackled him.

"Keep going!" Pagan shouted to Mercedes, putting the knife in one of her bound hands, and ran back down the stairs.

The third boy had piled onto Vogel, as well, trying to take his gun away. Pagan sprinted for the glowing brand, lying where Dieter had dropped it. Dieter's padded glove lay a few feet away.

She slipped on the glove and grabbed the end of the brand. She could see two other boys skulking in the shadows, not brave or stupid enough to emerge.

Vogel had kicked one boy between the legs and was wrestling with the other. She couldn't see the gun, but she recognized Vogel's gray trench-coated back as he rolled. She danced a few steps to the side, waiting. As they rolled again, she raised the brand and, using it like a club, whacked the other boy on the back of his head.

He made a guttural sound, and his grip went slack. Smoke rose from his hair, where the brand had touched.

Vogel pushed him aside and got to his feet, still holding his gun.

"Time to go," Pagan said, and, dropping the brand, she bolted for the stairs again, not looking back.

There were people in the tunnel. The headlights were shining in her face. The voices were speaking in English, and relief washed over her so strongly her knees turned to jelly.

She squinted into the light, putting up a hand to her forehead to see. "Mercedes? Where's Mercedes?"

"Pagan." A man's voice, tinged with a Scots accent. "We've got them both. They're all right."

She stopped and smiled weakly at the lean silhouette jogging toward her. "Sorry," she said. "I've been coloring outside the lines again."

VIBORITA

Little viper. A back and forth slithering motion with the leg.

Devin was angry with her, although he said nothing. She could tell from the way he curtly waved off the driver as they exited the car and in the tone of his voice as he spoke into the phone to make sure Mercedes was okay.

Mercedes hadn't been happy with her, either. She'd accepted Pagan's hug before the cops put her in a car and took her to the hospital, and she'd nodded when Pagan sobbed, "I'm sorry, it's all my fault," but she hadn't said a word.

Not that Pagan blamed her. Mercedes had wanted to leave her violent old life far behind. Instead, Pagan had dragged her into something even worse.

At least she wasn't injured. The boys hadn't molested her or beaten her beyond a few blows. Devin thought they'd spiked her breakfast with a powerful sleeping drug, then broken into the suite, expecting to find Pagan, and found Mercedes instead. After they'd released Mercedes from the hospital, she told Pagan she needed to be alone and went into her room in their suite and shut the door.

Pagan didn't blame her one bit. Still, she wished M would talk to her.

Now it was Devin who wasn't talking to her. Or anything.

"I'm sorry," she said as Devin hung up. They were in his suite. "I really am."

"I'm not angry with you," he said, pacing by the bed, where she was sitting, kicking her feet.

"Like hell you're not," she said, drumming her fingers. She was jittery. She wanted him to hurry up and forgive her, touch her, make her forget about the events of the night for a little while. "Should I go to my room?"

"I'm not angry at you for saving Mercedes and Naomi," he continued, as if she hadn't spoken. "That was brave, and calling upon Alaric Vogel to help you was dangerous but brilliant."

"I still can't believe he helped me," she said. Compliments were nice, but she didn't want to talk about what happened. "I wonder how he got away without you finding him. Maybe there are other tunnels in or out of that sunken church."

"He'll be an excellent agent for the Stasi," Devin said. "Assuming they don't find out he risked himself to help you tonight and execute him."

"They won't," she said. He wouldn't look her in the eye. "If you're not angry with me, then why aren't you over here right now, taking my clothes off?"

"I'm not angry with you." He stopped and lifted his gaze to hers. "I'm furious."

"You said you weren't!"

He sighed. "You've become far too used to acting on your own. That's not how a good agent works. This is the second bloody day in a row you ran off like that, Pagan. You're part of the team. And you should have waited until you had your team to support you."

"That would've been too late!" She fell back on the bed, her feet dangling off the edge. "Naomi would've been branded or worse, and Mercedes would be dead by then. Do we have to talk about this now?"

"Dieter's death and the injuries to the other boys will be officially blamed on a rival gang, but that could lead to more reprisals against the Israelis."

"The Israelis will figure out I was involved," she said. "Naomi will tell them."

He waved a hand dismissively. "The Israelis probably already know all about you working for us. If the CIA hasn't told them already, they'll figure it out for themselves."

"What about Emma?" Pagan's heart ached for that girl right now. "Now that Dieter's dead, what's going to happen to her?"

"She's sixteen, so she might be allowed to act as her own guardian. Otherwise, I think she still has cousins in Germany."

"She's all alone in the world now." Pagan stopped kicking her feet. She knew how that was.

"Stop trying to distract me." Devin stalked over to the edge of the bed to stare down at her. "Ten men, Pagan. You went up against ten men, alone."

It did seem stupid when he put it like that, and if you didn't know the outcome.

She looked up at him frowning down at her. His tie had come loose from his jacket and dangled over her. "I didn't mean to. Can we stop going over all the bad things that could've happened? Because they didn't."

"Even though you had Vogel's help, Dieter nearly got to you," he said. "There's a fine line between bravery and stupidity."

She reached up and grabbed his tie. "You get angry when you're worried," she said. "It's cute."

His expression didn't relax, but he didn't pull away. "I may have to recommend we give you no more missions," he said. "You're too unpredictable."

She shrugged and tugged on the tie, pulling him toward her. "Very well." It was something her mother often said, in a very final tone. Pagan gave it a lilt at the end and a smile.

He didn't fight her, but put his hands down on the bed on either side of her head to keep from falling into her. "I mean it. I'm officially telling them you're unreliable. I won't be coming to you for help again."

"Fair enough," she said, releasing the tie and raising herself up on her elbows, so that their faces were only an inch apart. "Any chance you'll be coming to me for something else?"

That made his lips twist as he tried not to smile. She pushed herself up and kissed his neck.

"Miss Jones," he said, his voice huskier. "Are you trying to seduce me?"

She tugged his tie loose and kissed up his throat to his mouth. His lips opened beneath hers, one of his arms curled around her back and he rolled down onto the bed, pulling her on top of him.

"I'm still angry," he said as she sat up and pulled his tie loose.

"Uh-huh." She unbuttoned his shirt so she could run her fingers over his warm skin.

He lifted both hands and ripped her shirt open. The buttons went flying.

She gasped, jolted with desire. He sat up beneath her and kissed her with a ferocity that turned her bones to putty. Her bra was off. Her bare breasts brushed against his chest and she reached down to unbuckle his belt.

An image of Naomi Schusterman, the front of her dress ripped, tied to the altar, flashed into her mind.

She shrank from it. *Not now, not now.*

"What is it?" Devin said, concerned. His touch became gentle. "Are you all right?"

She climbed off him, trying not to breathe too quickly. Why did it feel like the walls were closing in?

"I'm sorry," she said. "I saw Naomi again for a second, on the altar. Dieter was going to put a brand on her, right here." She covered her breasts with her hands. "I'm sorry."

He got to his feet and put a hand to her cheek. "Shh, now, don't be sorry, *mo gràdh*," he said, his voice so Scottish, so soothing. He tenderly took her in his arms and pulled her close. "I'm sorry. I should have realized."

She pressed herself into him. "I didn't want to think about it. I don't ever want to think about it."

"It only just happened," he said. "It must have been awful, but try to remember that Naomi Schusterman is home safe with her family now. Mercedes is flying home tomorrow and you're safe, too."

"I didn't stop to think about it at the time," she said. "So why would I think about it now? This doesn't mean I don't want to be with you."

"I know," he said. "It's not required, you know."

"But we might not have a lot of days left before I have to go back," she said. "And I don't know when I'll see you again, so I wanted to be with you as much as possible."

"You are with me now," he said. "It's okay to need some love and care, Pagan. It's a grievous world and sometimes we must grieve."

He led her over to the bed and she got in with him under the covers, snuggling in close. "Can we stay here forever?" she asked.

"Let's pretend we can," he said. "You've seen enough ugliness for one lifetime. Try to be more of a spoiled movie star after this, will you?"

She chortled. "It's a challenge, but I'll see what I can do."

In the morning, Devin got off a call with someone that was probably Reggie Pope, and slammed the receiver down. "It's confirmed. That minger Von Albrecht is taking the deal from the CIA to go back to working on our nuclear program, under special guard, once he's feeling better." He looked at Pagan. "Sorry."

"It's not your fault," she said. Her heart had started hammering inside her, hard. So much for trust in her own government, in anything, really. What a fool she'd been to ever get involved in any of this. "But it's horseshit, as Bennie Wexler would say."

"I'm pure scunnert with them myself," he said, and when she shot him a puzzled look, added, "I'm fed up with them.

Pope says they're not going to give you your mother's file. Even after all you've done."

"Damn it." It wasn't a surprise, really. Anger stirred, but she'd worn out her rage with overuse. So the CIA had strung her along, used her and now wouldn't give her what she wanted. Why should they? If they were capable of coddling a man like Von Albrecht, they were capable of anything.

"Are you all right?" he asked, jacket in hand, coming over to the side of the bed to touch her face.

"I don't know," she said, and she didn't. She felt oddly blank inside. "That's all I wanted—to know why Mama killed herself. But maybe I'm getting used to not getting what I want." She took his hand. "Well, I was lucky enough to get you, wasn't I?"

He leaned down to kiss her hand before putting on his jacket. "I wish I didn't have to go in and watch Von Albrecht today of all days," he said. "Right now I'd like to punch Reggie Pope in the throat and sic Rocket on Von Albrecht all over again."

But he wouldn't. He was a good soldier, Devin. He'd do his duty.

And Rocket was safe in her suite with Mercedes. The concierge was arranging for her to take the dog back with her to Los Angeles on a flight this afternoon.

"Try not to poison Von Albrecht accidentally," Pagan said, forcing herself to smile up at him as Devin came in for a goodbye kiss. "Or push him off any cliffs."

As he left, Pagan's heart was still pumping as if she'd been dancing with Fred Astaire. It kept thumping away as she went back to her own suite.

Mercedes was packing her suitcase, Rocket curled up on the foot of her bed.

"Did you let him sleep on the bed with you last night?" Pagan asked, sitting next to the dog to pet his healing head while his tail thumped on the bedspread.

"Did Devin let you sleep in the bed with him last night?" Mercedes countered. She hadn't met Pagan's eye yet. She really hadn't said much of anything.

In spite of her concern over her friend, Pagan couldn't help remembering how it had been in that bed with Devin last night.

They'd made up for lost time in the middle of the night with the sweetest, sleepiest lovemaking she could've imagined. She'd told him that she was off the movie, and he'd shyly asked if she wouldn't mind staying a few more days so he could see her. She'd joyfully agreed.

So she should have been glowing with happiness as she made everything okay with Mercedes once again.

Instead, this strange thumping rhythm kept pounding in her head, invading her chest. All she could think about was Mercedes, tied to a pillar. Naomi, bruised and bound. Dieter's fault, yes. But he was Von Albrecht's creation. He was the one who had tortured animals and people, planned to kill millions and created a monster like Dieter. And the worst he would suffer was to be forced back to work in the US, maybe with a guard by his side. It was eating at her, sucking the life and color from everything else in the world.

Mercedes stopped shoving her stockings into a lingerie bag and looked at her at last. "What's wrong?"

"My head is pounding," Pagan said. "I'm so worried about

you, and how you are. And ever since Devin told me about Von Albrecht not being punished for anything this morning, I can't stop thinking about it."

"You probably need a nap and some peace and quiet after all this craziness. I know I do."

"Maybe." Pagan conjured up a half smile. "I don't blame you for hating me right now, M. But please don't move out before I get back, or anything like that."

Mercedes sat down heavily on the other side of Rocket and put a hand on his back next to Pagan's. "I don't hate you," she said. "I don't even blame you. I just want to get away from this place as fast as possible."

"Of course." Pagan felt a small weight lift. M didn't hate her guts. She could figure anything else out. "Thanks for taking Rocket."

"Thanks for finding him." Mercedes gave her a small, rare smile. "Remember how I said we needed a big dog back home?"

That's right, she had. Pagan patted Rocket again. "He's quite the guard dog, too. You should've seen him tear into Von Albrecht."

M nodded, her smile fading. "Let's hope he gets to lead a nice quiet life from now on."

"Yeah." Pagan did hope that, for Rocket, and for Mercedes. But she didn't feel that way herself right now. Right now she wanted to tear the lid off the world.

"I'm crazy restless for some reason," she said. "I need to get outside, move."

"You always did hate being boxed in," Mercedes said. "Go, walk. See you before I go to the airport?"

"I'm going there with you, silly," Pagan said. "I'll be back soon."

She grabbed her purse and left the suite, barely seeing the gilded hallway as she paced down it to the elevator. The pounding in her head didn't hurt, really. She didn't have a headache so much as a heart problem. Or maybe she was going crazy.

She had her head down, thinking hard. Behind her, someone followed, his footsteps moving in perfect rhythm with her own.

She stopped. So did he. She turned.

Alaric Vogel stood a few feet away. He wasn't wearing a trench coat, but he had on his faithful gray fedora and a natty gray suit that couldn't have been tailored in East Germany.

"How are you?" he asked. His eyes on her were serious, assessing.

"I'll live," she said. "And so will Naomi Schusterman and Mercedes, thanks to you."

He shrugged, but he seemed pleased. "I already said you're welcome."

"How did you get away?"

He smiled. "Easily. Thank you for helping me with that last stupid boy. I probably would have beaten him without you, but you made it a little easier hitting him like that."

Typical. "It's good to see your arrogance hasn't suffered."

His smile broadened. He took a step toward her. She could smell the trace of Winston cigarettes on his clothes. "I have a request, one you might like to fulfill."

"I bet you say that to all the girls," she said. She didn't like him getting closer to her, but she stood her ground instead of backing toward the elevator.

He stopped only two feet away and took out a cigarette. "I know you want to see Von Albrecht punished for his many crimes. Something your country is unlikely to do given his expertise in nuclear physics."

She didn't reach for the lighter, but watched as he pulled out his own. This one was plain silver, appropriate for a spy. "So?"

"So, if you found out where they're keeping him and told me, justice might be better served." He lit the cigarette and blew the smoke up over her head.

"You want me to give information to the Stasi?" It was laughable. "Have you met you? You're far worse than the CIA."

"So when you think about a Nazi war criminal being given a second chance to build better bombs, and you could stop it—your conscience doesn't bother you?" He cocked an eyebrow at her. "Not even a little?"

She stared at him. That's what it was, the insistent drumming going on inside her. It wasn't her heart, or a migraine, or insanity. It was her conscience, calling out to her.

"Giving him to you wouldn't be any better," she said automatically. "Your government would do the exact same thing as the CIA."

"If you tell me where they're keeping him," he said, easing closer to her. She could smell the smoke on his breath. "I promise you, I'll kill him myself."

She almost believed him. She looked him directly in the eye. "I never said I wanted him dead."

He smirked down at her. "But you do."

"Killing is wrong." Her heart was pounding harder than ever now. Could he be right? Would that be justice? "I asked you not to kill Dieter and his friends, remember?"

He shook his head at her, pityingly. "You deny it to yourself. But you can't see the look on your own face. You know that Von Albrecht has done the worst things a human being is capable of. He's a tumor, and he must be removed."

Pagan said nothing, staring at him, trying to steady her battling thoughts.

"That ship he was taken from was headed for Germany," Vogel said. "Whatever he had planned, it was intended for my country. Let my country punish him for it. It's only proper."

There was a rightness to what he said. But when Pagan thought of East Germany, all she could see was the head of the Stasi punching her friend Thomas, torturing Thomas, taking Thomas's mother and sister into custody while he put up a wall to keep his own people prisoner. The East Germans weren't exactly a portrait in integrity.

But there might be someone else out there she could trust to see justice done, based on past experience. Maybe. In this case at least.

"I've met the head of the Stasi," she said. "And your leader Walter Ulbricht. They're not much better than Von Albrecht. Sorry. I won't be your traitor."

She started to push past him. She needed peace and quiet so she could think. But he slammed both hands into the wall on either side of her head, stopping her cold.

"You owe me," he said. His arms stayed there, blocking

her. He leaned in with a cold smile and exhaled smoke into her face.

It was a negotiating tactic. She didn't think he'd actually be violent with her. But he really wanted this. Thank the god of actors she had learned to cloak her fear with a paper-thin veneer of strength.

"Let me by," she said, edging her voice with steel. "Or I'll arrange to let your bosses know you risked your life and your mission to help me last night."

His hands on the wall beside her head tightened into fists. For a moment she thought he might strike her. But in the next moment he withdrew, backing down the hallway.

"You always have an answer," he said. "But I'll be there the day you don't."

He turned and was gone.

Pagan leaned against the gold-and-red wallpaper of that hallway and listened to the sledgehammer pounding of her scruples. She knew what she had to do. And she had Alaric Vogel to thank for that.

SALIDA

To exit, go out, but used in tango to start a dance, as in "go out onto the dance floor."

The ice-cream parlor was crowded, so it took Pagan several agonizing minutes of searching to find the empty table with the straw hat lying on top of it. It was a table in a quieter corner, far from the windows. At the table beside it sat a handsome older man with closely cropped receding white hair. He was reading the paper and dipping his spoon in and out of the chocolate sundae in front of him without eating any.

That had to be him. She took her second to last bite of dulce de leche and gave him the once-over.

He didn't look the way she expected him to, but then she was learning that spies rarely did. His short-sleeved linen shirt covered wide, strongly built shoulders and muscle-bound biceps that would have suited a much younger man. His hands were veiny but powerful. His face, lined with deep wrinkles from nose to mouth, was smoothly shaved and very tan. He looked like a local man out for a chocolate sundae, except that his deep-set brown eyes would dart up from his paper at regular intervals to circle the room. He'd probably seen her several times already.

He looked up again, and his gaze swept over her without stopping.

She'd made up her mind about this after running into Alaric Vogel yesterday. One phone call had been enough to set it in motion, and here he was, at the time and place she'd agreed to.

If she was going to do this, better to get it over with.

She walked over to the table with the straw hat on it, smiling at the old man with the chocolate sundae. "Hello. Is this table taken?"

"No." He took the hat and set it on his own table. "Please."

She set her purse down and sat so that she was facing him. She wanted to see his face as he spoke, to make sure she was doing the right thing.

"My name is Lev," he said. He didn't hold out his hand, but he seemed to want her to know it. "It is a great pleasure to meet you."

"I'm Pagan," she said. "But you already know that." His voice wasn't the one she'd spoken to on the phone. He must be someone they trusted greatly, then.

"Naomi Schusterman sends her regards," he said.

Oh, very clever, to start with that. She clasped her hands together to keep them from trembling and, using Lauren Bacall's trick, lowered her head to look up at him. The posture helped keep her head from shaking, too.

"How is she?" she asked, and took the last bite of her ice cream.

"She will recover, unmarked, thanks to you." He put his spoon down and looked at her from under bushy white eyebrows. "You have already done a great service by saving her. Thank you for that."

"You're welcome," she said, and thought of Alaric Vogel, saying, "You're welcome," to her after he'd shot Dieter through the eye. She hadn't had a nightmare about that yet. Something to look forward to.

"I hope you will think I have done you another service today," she said.

"Why are you here?" he asked.

She frowned. "You know why. The people at the embassy I spoke to must have told you."

"Yes," he said patiently. "But why?"

That really was the question. She couldn't answer him straight off. Her voice might crack.

"If your people find out, you could be tried for treason," he said. They were speaking English, but his voice held a faint accent that could've been German, or Austrian like Bennie Wexler's. He must have emigrated after the war. "So you must have a good reason."

She found her voice. "It isn't that you're better than us," she said. "Or worse. But this one time, I think you're more likely to dispense justice. That's why I'm here."

"Justice." He mulled that over, looking down at his melted sundae, and nodded, almost reluctantly. "You may be right. But just this one time?"

"One time," she said. "I won't come to you again, with anything, ever. I don't want anything in return, and I don't want anyone coming to me to ask for more."

"Very well," he said, and the way he said it made her catch

her breath. That phrase had been one that her mother said frequently, in exactly that final tone.

How could it be that an agent of the Israeli Mossad, one of the most notorious secret service agencies in the world, reminded her of her Nazi-collaborating mother?

She had a sudden desire to tell Lev about it. But that was crazy. He'd take it as an insult.

"I want you to promise me something first," she said. "I don't know you, but I ask you to swear on whatever you hold sacred that no one else will be hurt by what I tell you here today. No one but him."

His eyes never left her as a smile flickered over his face. It wasn't a smirk or a condescending smile, but one that was almost fond, admiring. As if he liked that she'd asked him that. It was strangely reassuring.

"When a man voweth a vow unto the Lord, or sweareth an oath to bind his soul with a bond, he shall not break his word. He shall do according to all that proceedeth out of his mouth," he said. "Numbers, 30:2."

"That's probably from the Bible," she said, feeling a little stupid. "But it's not a promise."

He broke into a full smile, looked down at his sundae again, as if to keep from laughing, and nodded. When he looked up, his face was serious again.

"I promise you, on the lives of my grandchildren, that on this mission I will do all I can to prevent any harm coming to anyone other than the man we speak of," he said. "That is all I can promise—that I will do my best. But you shouldn't worry. We will watch for now, wait until they move him and choose the right time."

That was more information than she could have hoped for. And although she could never be sure, she believed him. Maybe it was because she wanted to believe him. But there was something about his face, about the firm, kind look in his eye, that she trusted.

In this at least. She would probably never trust anyone completely again. Under Lev's linen shirt and the aging, muscular chest no doubt lurked a heart of steel.

"The address is 35 Avenida Garibaldi," she said. She could envision Devin, mouthing the address over and over to memorize it. "In Tigre. He should be there for another day or two, but I can't be sure."

"We'll find the place quickly," he said. "You have technically betrayed your country. Can you live with that?"

"It sounds so serious when you put it that way," she said lightly, but the intensity of his gaze sobered her. "They'll never know it was me," she said. "Unless you tell them. And it's for the greater good. Von Albrecht can't be allowed to get away with his crimes."

"As your mother did with hers?"

Heat suffused her face. She nearly got up and walked away. But she needed to know more, so she shoved down her anger, put her temper aside as she had all her life and asked, "Does everyone on earth know? If they do I should probably cancel the ad I was taking out in the *New York Times* to announce it."

"The child cannot atone for the mother's sins," he said.

"I have my own sins to atone for," she said. "Including this one. But thanks."

As Von Albrecht had said, she wasn't her mother, after all.

Mama had believed in her cause so much that she'd broken laws, endangered her family and helped a war criminal or two. But thanks to Von Albrecht and the CIA, Pagan would never believe in any government or cause that way again.

She was risking everything now to follow her own path. Maybe the name her mother had chosen for her had been the right one, after all.

Lev was studying her, as if memorizing her face. "I have left you something, in the briefcase by your feet."

She glanced under the table. There was indeed a slim brown leather briefcase there.

He was standing up, wiping his mouth with a napkin as if he'd been eating, though he hadn't taken a bite. He threw the napkin down and walked around the end of her table. He paused by her side and put one strong hand on her shoulder. It was heavy but gentle, and strangely calming.

"Be careful," he said. "You're being followed."

So much for calming.

He looked down and smiled. "I hope we meet again. In different circumstances."

She opened her mouth, unsure how to reply, but he was already striding away.

She sat there for a few moments, staring at his melted ice cream. Then she reached under the table, pulled out the briefcase and popped it open.

It contained a single file, less than half an inch thick. The name on the label read Jones, Eva Murnau.

Under that were some characters she couldn't read that looked like Hebrew. Probably Mama's name in that language. The file was stamped Copy in red.

The persistent hammering of her heart had stopped, but now it took up a strange skittering beat. The sound of nerves. There was only one way to be rid of this kind of anxiety—read the file.

She looked around. No one seemed to be paying the least attention. She opened the file.

The description of Mama was spot on: five foot five, light brown hair dyed blond, brown eyes, slim build. They'd left out "strong willed," but the rest of the file seemed to confirm that. She skimmed the beginning of it, which laid out Mama's birth in a hospital in Berlin to Ursula Murnau, until she got to the words after "Father:" They'd been blacked out.

Were the blacked-out words the name of Emil Murnau, the man her grandmother claimed to have married? The Israelis must have discovered that he couldn't possibly be the right man, as Pagan had.

She kept skimming. Mama's work for the Nazis started before the war. She'd used her presidency at the local German-American Partnership Council to help elect local candidates that were more favorable to Hitler's Germany. By 1942, the FBI had given her the code name Mata Hari, and had labeled her a "fifth columnist."

From what Pagan knew, that was basically another word for traitor. Pagan herself could be labeled a traitor for what she did today. Was she in any position to judge Mama harshly?

Pagan's birth—and Ava's—barely merited a mention. Poor Daddy. Arthur Jones was labeled "Probable dupe. No sign of disloyalty to the United States."

Except that it was Daddy who had kept the letters from Von Albrecht and broken the code embedded in them. That wasn't in the file. Daddy had uncovered evidence that his wife was a Nazi sympathizer when Pagan was eight, but he'd loved his wife and children too much to do anything other than kick Von Albrecht out of the house. They called him a dupe. Another word for it might be loving father.

How strange it was to read the bare facts of the life of someone you loved. There was more to Mama than promoting Nazi Germany, and more to Daddy than being Mama's doormat. Mama had been her daughters' fiercest protector. Daddy had made sure to tell Pagan and Ava that he loved them every day.

Maybe spy agencies didn't think that mattered. But it did.

After the war, Mama's activities picked up. She became more politically active and three German men's names were listed as visitors to the Jones household in the late 1940s and early '50s. Von Albrecht was the last. They all had notations to see their file, with a blacked-out number beside their names.

The other names meant nothing to Pagan, but they had to be the fellow Nazis Von Albrecht had mentioned. Pagan had no memory of these men, but from the dates, it looked like they'd stayed with the family briefly when she was only three and four years old.

At last, she reached the fatal date—her mother's death, November 15, 1958. Two weeks after Pagan's twelfth birthday. The words on the page were brutal in their bald simplicity.

Found by husband in family garage hanging by the neck, dead. Coroner ruled time of death approximately 4:30 p.m.

Such a brutal way to take a life, particularly your own.

No note found.

The type jumped up half a line here, as if someone had added it in via typewriter later, and Pagan's breath stopped as she read it.

(Blacked out name) indicates CIA gave orders to "make an example" of Jones two days before her death.

Wait, wait, wait. Did this mean what she thought it meant? Pagan put the file down and rested her face in her hands, pressing her fingers against her closed eyelids. This Israeli file was saying that an informer had heard the CIA give orders to make an example of Mama.

Two days before she died.

Pagan picked up the file again. There was another typed note after that.

No autopsy performed. Coroner ruled suicide: death by strangulation. No explanation given for second set of ligature marks. Possible that Jones attempted to hang herself once and stopped before completion, then attempted a second time and succeeded. Or possible foul play.

Possible foul play. Days after the CIA gave orders she be made an example.

A second set of ligature marks. Had she been strangled

first by someone else and then hanged to make it look like a suicide?

No wonder the CIA didn't want to give Eva Jones's file to Pagan. They'd murdered her.

It all came into focus with a horrible, gut-wrenching click. The unease gnawing at her ever since Devin told her the CIA wouldn't be bringing Von Albrecht to trial, her impulse to give his location to the Mossad… It wasn't only the East German government that was horrible, or its Stasi. It wasn't only the Communists and Nazis who had secret agencies working outside the law, doing horrible things in the name of patriotism. The United States had killed a mother of two and sheltered a war criminal. Any government, maybe any large institution, was capable of horrible things, justifying anything and everything in the name of their security.

But Mama had been a true believer in the worst of the worst—the Nazis. She'd died because she believed.

Pagan wasn't much better. She'd believed working for the CIA was the right thing, the good thing. She'd gone out of her way to help them because she wanted to feel like she was making a difference.

And Devin. His need to make up for his past had trapped him in their net, too.

God, she wanted a drink. She made herself look away from the menu over the counter of the ice-cream parlor. They probably didn't sell alcohol, but it was better not to entertain the option.

She dipped her head down, fighting the self-disgust threatening to smother her like an itchy wool blanket.

This life she had chosen, so like her mother's, led to death.

But she could get out from under it, and so could Devin. Maybe if she showed him this file and talked to him rationally she could save him from this cynical life of lies.

She had to move, to get out into the fresh air, feel space around her. Pagan shoved the file back in the briefcase and made her way blindly toward the exit.

As she opened the door to the ice cream parlor, a familiar profile caught her eye.

Alaric Vogel was sitting in a dark corner, eating a cookie.

It was an almost ridiculous sight. Normally she would have thrown out a funny remark—something about how he could use some sweetening. But not today. If Vogel had someone following Lev, Pagan could only wish the East Germans luck. Let them deal with the Mossad.

She didn't nod or indicate she'd seen him. She pushed through the door and down the sidewalk, heading for a taxi stand. She needed to get back to the hotel room, to reread the file.

The taxi stand was right around the corner. She came around it and looked up to see Devin Black waiting for her. His face was dangerously blank.

"What have you been doing?" His voice was silky smooth.

Warning bells went off in her head at the sound of his voice. He knew very well what she'd been doing. Lev had said she was being followed. Turns out it was both Alaric Vogel and Devin.

"Are you checking up me?" she said.

"Are you secretly meeting with agents of foreign governments?" he said, imitating her indignant tone.

Trust had never been their strong suit.

"I need to talk to you," she said.

"And this?" He snatched the briefcase out of her hand. "What's in here?"

She didn't bother to grab for it. He was far too strong, too dexterous to outmaneuver that way, and he needed to see the truth.

"It was a gift," she said. "You should read it."

Devin moved in close, his eyes like the ocean before a hurricane. "Who was that man? *What have you done?*"

"What had to be done," she said. "It's for the best, you'll see."

He stared at her thunderously as the car pulled up to the curb with Carlos driving. Devin walked over and jerked open the door. "Get in."

His anger was understandable. He thought she'd betrayed him. But he'd understand once they talked.

The short ride back to the hotel took place in complete and ominous silence as Devin opened the briefcase and read the file. Devin probably didn't want to discuss it in front of Carlos. But as soon as they entered his suite, he threw the file down on the desk with a smack.

"That is a Mossad file. How long have you been working for them?"

All the blood drained from her face. It hadn't occurred to her he'd think she'd been a double agent all along. "I don't work for them," she said quietly. "I never have. I didn't ask for the file. They gave it to me. Did you read it?"

He took a deep breath as if trying to remain calm. "Yes. I read it."

She was having trouble staying steady herself. It was difficult to say the next words. "Then you know the CIA killed my mother."

"No," he said, looking at her very directly. "I don't know that. I only know that's what the Mossad wants you to think."

Heat flashed through her. "A second set of ligature marks, Devin. No autopsy. No note. The CIA knew she was a traitor and wanted to make an example of her."

"An example—to whom? Everyone thinks it was a suicide. It probably was a suicide! This whole file could be a lie, Pagan. At the very least it's been doctored."

"But what if it isn't?" She got up and walked slowly over to stand within a foot of him. She wanted to take his hands, but they were on his hips, clenched in fists. "We can't work for people like this anymore, Devin. It's time to get out."

He frowned at her. "You're already out, remember?"

"But you…" She put a hand up to his cheek. "You can't work for people who would do this—for murderers, for people willing to overlook war crimes…"

He flinched and took a step back. Her heart shrank as he did it. "What makes you think I can't?"

She stared at him, trying to see past the flat mask that had become his face. "Because it's wrong. We may not be as bad as the Nazis, but our governments are doing unspeakable things. You've got to get out before it's too late."

"They'd never let me go," he said. "Even if I wanted to."

She couldn't quite believe what she was hearing. "You want to keep working for them? After all this?"

"The fact that the US and United Kingdom have their secret services do questionable things isn't news to me, Pagan. Governments have the right to defend themselves." He moved in close to her, his face near hers, trying to persuade her. "It doesn't matter what you believe. They're going to keep doing it. Whether you like it or not. Whether I work for them or not."

She nodded, swallowing hard. "But I don't have to be a part of it. And neither do you."

He stepped away from her again, as if her nearness was unbearable. "And if I told you I wanted to keep working for them?"

She was speechless. Inside her, a safe warm place was breaking apart like the set on a movie shoot that was over. She'd spent many happy hours there, but the walls were hollow, the furniture fake. One swing of the sledgehammer, and it all came crashing down.

Devin paced away from her, his posture and voice crisp. All business. "Why would you meet with an Israeli agent in the first place?" As he said the words, his eyes widened with a realization. "You told them where we're keeping Von Albrecht, didn't you?"

"I…" She'd thought she could persuade him that, too, was for the best. But that possibility was fading fast. "Yes."

His face had gone slightly gray. "You overheard me say the address. You've used me to get your revenge!"

He was taking this all wrong. She said, "No, no—don't you see? It wasn't revenge. It was justice!"

"I never should have let you overhear the address." He rubbed a distracted hand through his hair, his eyes casting about as if he was lost. "But I trusted you."

"I'm sorry," she said. "But the CIA will never know it was me, or that I learned it from you. Not if you don't tell them."

Ignoring her, he strode over to the phone, and gave the operator a number. "I need Pope," he said into the phone. "It's Black. Seven-seven-four-four-three-two-three."

He was going to warn Von Albrecht's keepers. She moved over to his side and put a hand on his arm. "Don't, please don't."

Devin shrugged her hand off. She recoiled. He'd never pushed her away like that before.

"Pope, there's been a leak. Unfriendlies may know your location." Devin would not, could not, look at her. "Either they've gotten better at tracking me, or I got worse at losing them. I didn't see them on my way there today, but as I left, I noticed a tail. Maybe the East Germans. They know to follow me because of Pagan Jones." He paused. "Yes. I'll see you later."

He'd fudged the truth, covering for her and himself. But still, he'd warned them. The CIA would get Von Albrecht to a different location as soon as possible.

Lev had said his people would move quickly. She'd have to hope it was quick enough. If the Mossad agents got to 35 Avenida Garibaldi soon, they might be able to follow wherever the CIA took Von Albrecht next.

But there wasn't anything more she could do about it. Forces were at work now that she couldn't control. Forces she had unleashed.

She moved closer to Devin, trying to get him to look at her. "You said yourself that as a spy you're forced to do things that aren't much better than what you did as a thief. You and I wanted redemption for our pasts, but the CIA and MI6 can't redeem us because they're beyond redemption themselves. Only we can save ourselves. That's why I went to the Mossad. That's why we have to leave."

One hand still on the phone, Devin turned slowly to look at her. "You speak to me of redemption? You who lied to me and took my trust…" He stopped, struggling with something—anger, betrayal, sadness. "And still I covered for you. If I hadn't… My God, what were you thinking?"

"Justice," she said. "For Von Albrecht's victims. That's what I was thinking. That's it. That's all."

"If the CIA ever finds out what you've done, you could land in jail. For the rest of your life. Was it worth that risk to yourself, to me, to what we have?"

"There's no risk if you don't tell them about it," she said. "And we can't let him get away with it, Devin. We can't let Von Albrecht off the hook."

"We?" he said in a tone that reminded her of Alaric Vogel. "You did this, not I. Who are you to decide whether or not he gets away?"

Wrath edged out pain. How could he so quickly forget the evil Von Albrecht had done? "Don't play that card with me, Devin Black. I'm a human being with a conscience. That's all anyone needs to understand what justice is in this case. If Von Albrecht doesn't pay for what he's done, then all of this, everything that's happened—it's all been for nothing."

Her anger seemed to cool him down. "It's not for nothing. You said it yourself. We stopped a bomb from going off in Berlin."

"Yes, we did that. Hooray." The words came fast and short. "But what about Emma? She's devastated. The death of her brother and those other boys, the deaths of those animals, of all the innocent people Von Albrecht tortured and murdered during the war. If we let him live a nice quiet life, what's the point of all of that? What's the point of anything?" She circled around him, as if trying to find a weakness in his armor. But there was none. "If we don't draw the line somewhere, the meaning of right and wrong disappears, and we all descend into hell. How is it you can't see that?"

"Because life is complicated!" His hands were open, palms up, almost pleading with her. "You used to value all life. You didn't want anyone to die. You know the Mossad won't kidnap Von Albrecht and put him on trial as they did with Eichmann. The US is their ally, and they won't embarrass us like that. No. They'll try to track him if we don't get him out of there fast enough. Then they'll wait for their moment. They'll kill him, quietly and in such a way that the CIA never suspects them. You've sentenced a man to death today."

"Good," she said, and she meant it. "I should have killed Von Albrecht when I had the chance. If I'd shot him at the docks, you would have shrugged and walked away. But I didn't pull the trigger because I thought you and your agencies would do the right thing. I thought making myself their instrument was enough. But they were too deeply flawed. I had to become my own instrument instead."

"My God." Devin's voice was low, almost a whisper. "I've turned you into a killer."

"It isn't you." She felt a thousand years old all of a sudden. Looking back on the Pagan Jones who had agreed to go on this adventure was like peering through the wrong end of a telescope. "I was so eager to please. I thought working for them would make me different than Mama. Instead, it began to turn me into her. I won't let that happen."

"There's a difference between working for the Nazis and working for the CIA, and you know it," he said.

"Yes," she said curtly. "But the CIA killed my mother."

His eyes on her were reddened, distant. "That file is not proof. You can't trust the Mossad, either."

"Maybe not," she said. "Maybe the CIA killed Mama or maybe she killed herself. Maybe it was the Mossad or maybe it was little green men from Mars. But the Israelis won't give Von Albrecht a cushy job in a bomb factory. So I gave him to them. I had to. I couldn't live with myself otherwise."

"Well, so long as you can live with yourself, what does treason matter?" he said with vicious sarcasm. "You betrayed our trust, my trust!"

"And I trusted you. But governments and their creatures can't be trusted to do something simply because it's right."

"Government creature?" he said slowly, his voice low and deadly. "Is that what you think of me?"

She looked him in the eye without flinching. It was killing her to say this to him, to feel this about him. "You work for the agency that may have killed my mother, that's happy to work hand in glove with a man like Von Albrecht. What else should I call you?"

"So not only do you betray my trust, but you think I'm as bad as a Nazi war criminal." He was looking at her as if he'd never seen her before. "You know me better than that!"

"Do I?" she asked. "I came here today hoping to save you from living your life like this."

"Give me, at least, the courtesy of finding my own redemption." His voice was flat. All the life in it had been drained away. "You think you alone know what justice is. *This* is how the world works. Governments do shady deals to gain an advantage. Not every criminal is punished. Justice is not always done. But the world goes on."

Some part of her wanted to recant everything she'd said, to tell him he was right, to go back to how things were so they could be happy together again. But she'd crossed a line somewhere. There was no going back.

She said, "If we don't punish people for torture and murder, what's to stop more people from doing it? What's to stop *us* from doing it?"

"You're one girl! You can't regulate the world's governments!" He was almost shouting, but he looked so troubled, so lost.

"No." She wished there was something she could do to stop everything from coming apart. But she could see it in his eyes. Too late, too late. "But I could do this one thing, this one time. And I did it. It's done."

His face hardened. He'd come to the decision. "And we're done."

Although she was braced for it, she didn't quite understand at first. She gaped at him like a child.

He walked toward her. His voice was steady and certain, his tone final. "There is no way I can trust you now."

Someone had cleaved through her chest to scoop out her heart and leave her hollow.

But he was right. It didn't come as a surprise so much as a long-dreaded agony that she must begin to endure.

She forced herself to her feet and walked to the door.

Shoulders back, head high. Mama had been right to drill that into her, even if she'd been wrong about so much else.

"Very well." She used her mother's tone, her mother's phrase, as Lev had earlier. She would take the good of what she'd learned from Mama and reject the bad. That's why she'd done what she did with Von Albrecht. She was no longer her mother's daughter, and no longer the eager-to-please starlet turned spy.

Who she was, she couldn't be sure. But it would be real, and true.

"I'm not sorry," she said. "I love you too much to pretend otherwise."

He dropped both hands to his sides, his jaw clenched. Those damned blue eyes, which had looked on her once with so much love, were now so far away.

"Goodbye," he said.

CORTE

A break in movement or the final bow of the dance.

The letter had no return address, but the postmark was from Albuquerque, New Mexico. Someone had written Pagan's name and address in a firm, angular hand across the front.

Inside there was a newspaper clipping, and a note.

The clipping came from a paper called the *Los Alamos Monitor*, and the headline was small.

Scientist Dies in Car Accident.

A car accident, of course.

The article went on to state that a physicist named Rudolph Beck, who worked at Los Alamos National Laboratory, had died when his car hit a telephone poll head-on late at night. No one else was hurt. A coroner's autopsy would decide if he'd been drunk, fell asleep or committed suicide.

There was no photo.

The note that came with the clipping was in the same handwriting, and it was brief. It contained no greeting and no signature.

I thought you should know: he's dead. At least no one else got hurt.

I never told anyone, and I never will, but I know this happened because of you. And I'm sorry. I blame myself for pulling you into this world. It's my fault, and I wanted you to know that.

I hope you find a good life.

She put the letter and the newspaper clipping carefully back in their envelope. Her fingertips brushed over the handwriting on the front, over the black jagged lines of her name.

She flicked the lighter to life, the lighter she'd stolen from Alaric Vogel, and put the flame to a corner of the envelope. The fire licked up the paper, curling and blackening, until it burned clean away.

★ ★ ★ ★ ★

ACKNOWLEDGMENTS

My father became ill and passed away while I was writing and rewriting *City of Spies*, and I could not have continued to get through life, let alone write a book, without love and kindness from many people. A big hug and shout-out to my editor, T.S. Ferguson, Natashya Wilson and everyone at Harlequin TEEN for their help and support during the creation of this book.

Many thanks, as well, to my amazing agent, Tamar Rydzynski, who sometimes seems to know what I'm thinking before I do, and to my fabulous beta readers (and writers of great books themselves) Elisa Nader and Jen Klein.

I got mountains of support from my marvelous mother, Jackie Berry, and my Berry cousins—Kate, Chrystie, Eileen, Paul and Dave. And my eternal love and gratitude to amazing friends John Mark Godocik, Brian Pope, Wendy Viellenave, Kathleen and Tay Bass, Joe and Sharon Salas, Diane Stengle, Maria de la Torre, Valerie Ahern, Michael Musa, Matthew Matzkin, Bari Halle, Peter Shultz, Jennifer Frankl, Katherine Hand, Alden Zecha, Matt Chapman, Geoff and Emma Chapman, Roger Alt, Chris Campbell, Cathy Kliegel, Lisa Moore, Cheri Waterhouse, Cathleen Alexander, Pilar Alessandra, Pat Francis, Maritza Suarez, Ruth Atkinson, and Pam and Scott Paterra. I'll always be grateful to you all.

Big thanks as well to my very understanding fellow YA Series Insiders—Martina Boone, Kimberley Griffiths Little, Tracy Clark, Lori Goldstein, Claudia Gray, S.E. Green, Kim Liggett and Nikki Kelly.

During my father's illness, his friends became like family, and they stepped up in ways I still cannot quite believe. There are, literally, dozens of them, maybe hundreds. Too many to list here. But I do want to send special love and thanks to the members of Team Berry—you know who you are—who made Dad's life and death as graceful and full of love as he was himself.